WINGS OF CREATION

BRENDA COOPER

A TOM DOHERTY ASSOCIATES BOOK
NEW YORK

TOR®

WINGS OF CREATION

Copyright © 2009 by Brenda Cooper

A Tor Book
Published by Tom Doherty Associates, LLC
175 Fifth Avenue
New York, NY 10010

www.tor-forge.com

Tor® is a registered trademark of Tom Doherty Associates, LLC.

Library of Congress Cataloging-in-Publication Data

Cooper, Brenda, 1960–
    Wings of creation / Brenda Cooper. — 1st ed.
      p. cm.
    "A Tom Doherty Associates book."
    ISBN 978-0-7653-2095-7
  I. Title.
PS3603.O5825W56 2009
813'.6—dc22

2009031653

First Edition: November 2009

Printed in the United States of America

0 9 8 7 6 5 4 3 2 1

To Mary Cooper

ACKNOWLEDGMENTS

Thanks to all the readers in the Pacific Northwest who saw fit to grant the Endeavour Award to the first book in this series, *The Silver Ship and the Sea*. It means a lot to win an award from readers.

My agent, Eleanor Wood, is supportive and insightful, and I appreciate her very much.

Thanks to Tom Doherty, Bob Gleason, and the support staff from Tor. Without you, this book wouldn't have become real.

My friend Linda read through the whole draft and made excellent comments. Her sons, A.J. and Nick, both said nice things, too!

Thanks to my writing friends. The locals—John Pitts, Jay Lake, Patrick Swenson—and the Redmond Writers, who are most commonly Louise Marley, Melissa Shaw, and Cat Rambo. Thanks to my fellow researchers in the Big Books reading group, and to everyone from the Oregon Writers Network.

My partner, Toni, and her daughter, Katie, are infinitely patient and supportive. Last book, I had two dogs to thank. This time I have three. (Although I'm not sure the puppy deserves thanks—she hasn't been patient at all. But then, she's a border collie.)

My parents and my son and his family are wonderful. My futurist mentor, Glen Hiemstra, says nice things about my writing and gives me interesting ideas to think about.

There are many other people who have offered support and help of one kind or another and, although there are too many to thank individually, I am grateful for each of them. I am truly lucky in the people I work and play with.

WINGS OF
CREATION

PROLOG

A CONTINUATION OF THE STORY OF CHELO LEE, DATED SEPTEMBER 17, YEAR 222, FREMONT STANDARD, AS BROUGHT TO THE ACADEMY OF NEW WORLD HISTORIANS. . . .

War leaves fear and loss worse than bitterlace in the hearts of every-one associated with it. There are no winners. Only scars, and for the lucky, the time to heal them. We were not lucky.

The first tale I told you detailed how I separated from my brother, Joseph, and three of the other six people that made up my heart. The second tells of the events before an even bigger sundering, after Joseph came back. He saved my life, and the life of my world, the colony planet Fremont. He won the second war fought on her soil. Not single-handedly, but he made the difference.

Joseph almost died. My children almost died. Some parts of me died.

So now I'll tell you about war, since my life is built on its bones. Then I'll tell you about the actual sundering, since you asked how I felt when we left Fremont for the Five Worlds. But since it's an old memory, I'm going to creep up on it so I can tell it fresh.

I was born during the first war of my life. That happened on Fremont, a planet big enough and empty enough and challenging enough that everyone involved could have lived there in peace. That war cost me my parents and many who might have been my friends, all gone, fleeing or killed by the first settlers, who refused to give up their claim. And who could blame them? They were, after all, on Fremont first. They went there to escape people like my parents. They lived through paw-cats and yellow snakes and earthquakes and meteors rather than face a world of shifting genetics.

At the end of the war, my parents' people had to leave seven of us behind: six children and an injured adult. The colony raised us, but made us pay for being different.

So you see, even before the Star Mercenaries came, I knew the sharp pain of war. We were beginning to lose our scars when my own father caused the second war. He sent mercenaries from Islas to kill everyone on Fremont. I cannot feel guilty for that, since he and I were separated when I was six. I didn't even see him, or know he lived, until the day he died. But I feel tainted anyway. How could I not? You see, my decisions helped further the war he started. I chose the first deaths. I helped until the day the Star Mercenaries fled my brother's strength, leaving Fremont free. That's a story I've already told, and it hurts to think about it.

So on to the sundering.

I remember how my body felt trapped. I lay strapped to an unfamiliar chair aboard the space ship *Creator*, watching the only home I'd ever known grow small in a viewscreen that hung above my head. Already the people I loved were too far away to see; their absence a sharp twintree fruit thorn thrust deep into my heart.

Akashi, Sasha, Mayah, Sky. The hot breath of my riding animal, the hebra named Stripes. The dead: Nava and Stile and Eric and a few hundred more. They might as well all be dead now, at least to me. I had no illusions I would see any of them again.

Fremont was warm, wet, and wild. The space ship, *Creator*, was cold, dry, and followed my brother's commands like a well-trained house-dog. Far more metal than life filled the hull.

Kayleen and her mother, Paloma, watched over the two children. For the takeoff, they occupied our new, tiny home—a section of sleeping compartments that shared a common room, which included four ugly benches that could each be turned into something full of restraints and support that Joseph called acceleration chairs.

Liam and I lay strapped into similar chairs in a different set of rooms, unblinking eyes fastened to the last sight we would ever have of home. We were close enough that I felt his warmth as we watched the single city, Artistos, grow so small that the view included the cliffs and the Grass Plains and the Lace River and the High Road and then even the volcano Blaze. The force of flight kept me from turning my head, so surely Liam didn't see that a tear fell unbidden down my cheek. Even though the people of Fremont had hated us, how could they live without us to help them? Who would stop the paw-cats and tend the electronics?

My own family had cast me out. I could never know how their tales ended, and they could not know how mine ended.

My eyes stuck to the viewscreen until Fremont was only a speck around a sun and the thrust had fallen off enough for Liam and I to look at each other. He was beautiful, with honey-colored hair that fell around his broad shoulders, and his face, in profile now, showing his high cheekbones. "Is it safe?" I asked.

"To get up? I guess."

My brother, the pilot, had told us we could move around when we were no longer forced down by acceleration. Joseph had warned me, so I didn't stumble when I felt too light. I clutched Liam for balance, and he pulled near too easily, as if I were drawing a child to my chest. A reminder a ship is not a planet. At least he still smelled like himself, and still, faintly, of the Grass Plains and of hebra. For that smell, I clutched him to me, breathing deeply while I massaged the stiff muscles in the small of his back. He leaned down and kissed me, and then we stared at each other for a long time, as if breaking away would be the final movement away from home.

But of course, we eventually slid from each other's arms. There were no words for our loss. It was as great as the gulf between us and home, widening into forever.

Thirst and hunger drove us to the nearby galley for bread and goat's milk cheese and water. After, I returned to the viewing room and Liam went to check on the others. By the time I sat back down and focused on the screen, we must have turned or gone farther than I thought, and I couldn't find Fremont in the vast starfield. Just darkness and points of light that were whole suns.

So many stars. It made Fremont so small. Me so small.

Joseph had warned me of the vastness of space and how *Creator* would be a small speck of dust traveling between grains of sand on a beach of stars.

I had been made to find the positive, to see opportunity in difficulty, to lead through hope. And what better place to feel the hope of worlds than the incredible beauty of space? I had expected to live and die on a single grain of sand. And now, now I was going off to a new future in a faraway place.

This is the loss and awe that frames this part of our story, writ large: leaving everything we knew behind, and moving through the vastness of space with our tiny, fragile family. We didn't yet know we flew toward beings more beautiful and complicated than I'd ever imagined, and so my worries were diffuse. Under the awe that filled my very bones, I knew there would be humans in space and, thus, there would be war.

I swallowed and saluted the viewscreen, then got up and went to find my family. Among humans, there would also be love. This moment was good for love.

1

JOSEPH: THE SHIP'S NURSERY

Space is full of stark beauty and darkness, and largely empty. But there are still surprises in it. The day our plans changed started with only the small chaos of children and a dog.

I leaned against the warm wall of the simulated sun in the nursery, hearing Chelo, my beloved sister, my best support in the whole world, laugh as she watched her son. Two modified maintenance bots trailed after one-and-a-half-year-old Jherrel as he toddled from Chelo's arms toward me. The bots looked like a cross between dogs and spiders, scuttling on four feet and holding two up, ready to save Jherrel from any emergency, including himself. It amazed me that he hadn't figured out how to wreck the whole ship yet. If he were older, he might have.

Certainly, the nursery floors and walls showed evidence of the reasons we kept the two children mostly contained; the walls were scratched and even, occasionally, slightly dented. The room smelled like bot-grease and the sweet sweat of children. "Un-cle Jo-seph!" Jherrel exclaimed at me, his mouth twisted in a huge grin. He always came to me right away when I entered the room, as if I were his favorite toy or perhaps his pet dog.

Speaking of dogs, Sasha, the black-and-white stray I'd taken from Fremont, stood by my feet. Her ribs no longer showed and her coat had grown glossy. She bent her forelegs and head down in a play bow and wagged her tail at Jherrel.

Across the long silver floor, Jherrel's slightly bigger half-sister, Caro, actually rode one of her keeper bots, while her mother, Kayleen, held her hands, balancing her. Kayleen's smile was as wide as Jherrel's, the one blue eye not covered by a stray fall of her dark hair twinkling a welcome even though she'd known I was coming. I'd spoken to her via the data nets as I neared the nursery, a warm sharing of our silent language.

Caro noticed me and squealed, but then Caro squealed a lot. Verbal, like her mom. Kayleen stood up and Caro got a little ahead of her. She lifted a foot up onto the robot's rounded back, maybe trying to stand. Her foot slipped and she fell backward onto the floor with a screech.

Sasha raced for the robot, snapping at its front legs as it tried to turn around and help Caro. Kayleen came between the dog and the robot, holding Sasha off so the mechanical minder could help Caro up.

I burst out laughing, and Kayleen and Chelo both glared at me with their most severe mom faces.

I put my hands behind my back and squatted down so I'd be closer to the children's height, marveling yet again that Chelo and Kayleen and Liam could possibly be parents. Yes, they were older than me by the three years or so of cold sleep I'd spent on this same journey when I went to Silver's Home, but they seemed as fresh and innocent as wild field flowers in the spring.

Jherrel waited patiently for Caro to make her way over to us before looking at me expectantly. I pulled my hands in front of me and opened them, palms flat, so the two tiny aircars I'd carved of cured lace-leaf wood lay on them. The cars were baby-fist–sized, and styled after the cars they'd see when we got to Silver's Home. The children snatched them up, toddling around and pretending to fly the toys through the nursery. The robots clattered and whirred after the children. Caro came back to me, burbling engine noises while she flew hers beside my knee.

I laughed and caught Caro's eye. "Really, they're quieter than that."

She ignored me, following Jherrel toward the far corner. Kayleen grinned as she watched her daughter go, completely intent on the noise of flying. "Thanks. It always fascinates them to have new toys."

"I like making them things. It's not like there's much to piloting way out here."

Chelo grimaced. "I know."

"It felt good to create something with my hands." Sasha uncurled and stood, sniffing my hand for a pet. I knelt and gave her one. I'd bathed her yesterday, so she smelled of shampoo more than dog-breath. She was the closest thing I had to a child of my own, and kept me from feeling too hungry for Chelo's attention. Long ago, my sister had been as inseparable from me as my dog was now.

Chelo gave me a hug, her voice wistful. "If only they could have open space to run in."

She needed it, too, but there was no point in saying that. A space ship has no fields or plains in it, no High Road, and even though it is surrounded by stars, it has no sky. We made do with the wall I stood against. It gave them a dawn, midday, dusk, and night. Liam had demanded it, saying his kids would never acclimate to real time if all they knew was the no-time of space flight. In reality, I think he needed a clock as much as Caro and Jherrel.

By now, we were all stir-crazy.

The children were too young for cold sleep, so Chelo, Liam, and Kayleen chose to stay awake for the whole trip. They all swore they wouldn't miss a moment of the kids' growing up, but I thought they didn't want to be separated from each other. How different might our lives have been if our parents had taken us when they fled Fremont? But *Creator* was outfitted for a waking crew, and perhaps our parents had not had this choice.

At eleven months out, we were almost halfway home. I was the only pilot, and Marcus had warned me not to trust the small ship's defenses to autopilot. Alicia refused cold sleep, and I wanted her near me, so I gave in. She'd teased me, saying that she was afraid Kayleen and I wouldn't be able to resist each other since we had so much in common. Silly girl. I loved Alicia with all my heart, needed her, spent my daydreams on her. Of course there were special ties between Kayleen and I that came of being the only Wind Readers on Fremont; capable of plucking data from the air itself. But those were bonds of friendship, even if Alicia did not believe it.

Besides, Kayleen and Chelo and Liam loved each other. How could they not have? They were the only ones like themselves on a whole planet. Their bonds were as strong as mine with Alicia, and Kayleen often looked soft and sweet when she gazed at Liam.

Friend or not, it was time for Kayleen's lesson. There was so much I had learned while I was away from her, and which she needed to know. The other seven people on the ship lay inert in cold sleep. When I'd protested to Jenna she had just smiled at me, and very softly said, "You are the pilot, and you are responsible. Consider it an extension of our agreement on Fremont."

Meaning, I supposed, that I had led the attack on the Star Mercenaries. Meaning that Jenna trusted me, at least on this leg of our flight—the part where we flew through nothing for almost two years.

I did notice Jenna had programmed herself to wake three months before we got to Silver's Home. Meantime, that left me to deal with lessons for everyone, and most important, for Kayleen, the only possible backup pilot we had. I crooked a finger at her. "Ready?"

You are a mean man, she spoke silently to me across the data streams.

I know, I answered the same way.

She sighed and glanced at Chelo. "Can you handle them both?"

"Sure. Liam will be along any minute."

Kayleen followed me up to the command room. At any other time in her life, Kayleen chattered. But on the daily trip to lessons, she was almost always silent. I took a seat at the table, letting her choose where to be. There were only four chairs, and she selected the one closest to me, on my right.

"You can do it," I whispered, and took her hand, letting it lie calmly on mine, a resting of the two together rather than a grip. If she was ever going to fly the ship, she had to learn to track multisourced data.

She dropped her head, not even bothering with preambles anymore.

I was already there, waiting for her, linked well enough to the streams of ship's data that I simply breathed information. Kayleen caught up to me, suffering as I drilled her on ship speed and gravity, on water supplies and nearby stars. *Creator* was fast—just under lightspeed—so our place in the starscape changed regularly. Marcus had taught me that even though *Creator* did the daily course charts, a real pilot would know these things. If nothing else, it kept me linked to the physical world.

Pilots went crazy even more often than other Wind Readers. Kayleen knew.

"Are you ready?" I asked her.

Agreement. Something I felt as much as saw.

We matched our breath. I led, slowing her, slowing us both. She did this part easily now. It made me think of Marcus, who had taught me to match breath with him. Much like I was teaching Kayleen now.

She and I folded our virtual selves nearly inside of each other, and plunged into the ship's library. I began to bombard her with questions.

"What's an affinity group?"

She twisted her hands absently in her hair, a habit from early childhood that she'd never lost, and which she did now even while in a near-trance. "A family of economic and other interest."

"What is the Port Authority?"

"A power that hates you." That came from her conscious self, not the data. I waited for her to get it right. "Regulator of space travel and thus commerce for Silver's Home."

"What are the Makers?"

Her answers came fast. She hated this. I knew because the way we saw each other, raw and unfiltered, inside the data meant we were, in some ways, naked to each other. At least her fists weren't clenched today. "A term loosely applied to Wind Readers who create new living things. Also means the affinity group that created the Silver Eyes, the island chain that you left from."

And where we were returning to. "What is Lopali?"

"Home of the fliers."

"What are the fliers?"

"Humans who can fly."

"What are the swimmers?"

"Humans who live under the sea. There are not many of them."

"How many?"

A long silence fell. Some of the other questions she'd answered before, but every day I asked some new ones, probed deeper. She'd have to figure out how to find this number. So much time passed that I worried she'd become lost. Eventually, she said, "When *Creator* left, there were fifty-two, but three were starting the de-sculpting and won't count."

Very good. I had the strength to open my eyes and watch her, even though she was so disconnected from her body that if she felt her heart beat, she'd probably drop most of the data threads she held now. The cadence of her answers and the breaks between words made clues, but it was even easier to see the autonomic responses as emotions flitted across her face. The small muscles in her jaw and neck tightened, relaxed, tightened, even as her answers remained perfect. But I couldn't make this easy for her, I owed her better than that. "Where is Caro right now?"

I wanted to scream triumph when she didn't skip a beat. "In the nursery with Liam." That meant she went up to ship's data from the library seamlessly. Harder than it sounded. And her hand hadn't even twitched.

"What is the condition of the carrots in the garden?"

Hesitation. "We can harvest a few more this evening."

Good. "What is the best school for Wind Readers on Silver's Home?"

She'd need to go back into the library. I waited.

She didn't quite make it, her hand pulling away from mine, her presence gone from the nets. I caught her as she jerked up and back, so her head nestled against my arm, the long fall of her hair nearly brushing the ground. A light breeze from the air recirculation systems blew the loosest strands lightly, as if a true wind touched her, and her jaw quivered and tightened before she snapped her eyes open and sat up. "It's always so hard to be back." She lifted her hands and clenched and unclenched her fists, then stood and shook her oversized feet. "I forget I have a body at all."

At least she wasn't mad at me. Three days ago she'd emerged screaming that I was too hard on her. I wasn't. She had always been more fragile than I was. I had needed to hide for months on Silver's Home, adapting and learning, lest the flood of data leave me a trembling idiot. After Kayleen had trouble in a place as simple as Fremont, it was all the more important for me to drive her hard. I was being far kinder than the impartial data streams of a full economy. They would not care about her.

An alarm went off, and the data that I still breathed like air thrummed with warning so sharp my fingers jerked involuntarily and my spine stiffened.

Something man-made approached us.

2

JOSEPH: MESSAGES

Kayleen, too, heard *Creator's* message about an intruder. Her eyes widened and the little-girl-lost look fled as she focused in on the implications. "What's out here in the middle of nowhere?"

I shivered, but kept my voice calm. "Not an asteroid or space junk—*Creator* treats those differently. Besides, you're right, we aren't near anything." I triggered the *all hands to command* bell, praying everyone remembered the high sound from the drills in the days after we left.

Alicia came first. She walked straight toward me and planted a proprietary kiss on my forehead before she waved at Kayleen. She might have been a twin of Kayleen's, except her eyes were a shocking violet and she always appeared more sure of herself. She took the seat on the other side of me, scooting it closer so she could put a hand on my knee. "What is it?"

"*Creator* sees something."

She glanced at the empty walls. "Any ideas?"

"No."

"Do you know what it looks like?" she asked, her voice cool and calm. The salty-sweat smell of her told me she must have been working out when I called. "Or where it's from?" Because I knew her base nature as our risk-taker, I understood how excited she really was, even though she only showed it with a flicker in her eyes and, every once in a while, a little lick of her tongue. She was probably hoping for something dangerous.

"*Creator* promised to send pictures."

She glanced at the still-empty wall. "Soon, I hope. What do you know?"

Chelo and Liam joined us, full of noise and questions, toys and blankets. The toddlers swarmed around their feet, still clutching the aircars. As if *Creator* had been waiting for all hands, the walls around the square room lit with pictures.

A metal cylinder hung in the air. Man-made. Beautiful, but it made me shiver. It was impossible to tell the size from the picture. "How far away is it?" I asked.

Creator answered in my head. "Ten kilometers."

Wow. Close, in space. Too close, really. Something was really wrong, and finally it slipped into my thick head. It should have been past us and gone. I closed my eyes and focused down on the data feeds. The object tracked us, matching our speed. That was the only possible explanation for it not being far behind us by now. I could get the size, too—about as big as a real version of the aircars Jherrel and Caro still clutched to them. Tiny for this far out. I told the group what I'd learned.

"So where did it come from if it's that small?" Liam asked.

Alicia looked over her shoulder, checking all the wall-screens. "Is there another ship around?"

"No." I wished Jenna or Dianne or one of the other, older, people was awake. But there was no time to thaw anyone.

This was mine. Mine and *Creator*'s.

My breath came fast in my chest, and I clenched Alicia's hand so hard she leaned over and whispered, "Relax. Trust yourself. You're the best."

I waited for *Creator* to identify the object. We were only one year into an almost two-year trip, so it wasn't something random from one of the Five Worlds. Inter-system space is too vast for random encounters. "It's looking for us."

"Correction," Alicia said. "It's found us." Her nails raked my thigh and Caro squealed and pointed as it grew bigger in the screens. Surely a trick of the cameras. It looked new, barely blemished by flight. "The Port Authority?" Alicia asked. "Could they find us?"

"Maybe. But why? I'm going to them, after all." I thought about other options. "The *Dawnforce* isn't much faster than *Creator*. The mercenaries can't have gotten home yet." Besides, *Creator* was alert, not alarmed. Not that it had feelings; but it had responses. We weren't being ordered to strap down and the weapons systems weren't doing more than warming up.

Chelo tucked Caro under her arm and grabbed Jherrel with her free hand and took them both into the adjoining galley, murmuring something about snacks.

Liam tensed. "Could the mercenaries have sent a message?"

I glanced at Kayleen. "You were in their nets more than I was."

"They spent a long time between attacks waiting for answers from home." She closed her eyes and furrowed her brow. "No, it can't be them. Not unless it's been waiting for us since before they left Fremont."

"*Creator?*" I asked, signaling I wanted a verbal exchange for the benefit of the others. "Is it communicating with you?"

"It's silent," the ship answered, its voice silky and genderless.

"Can you tell where it's from?"

"My owner."

Marcus! Worry turned to excitement.

Alicia's hand relaxed on my leg, but she didn't take her eyes from the picture floating in front of us. "So send it our identification."

"I have been."

Maybe it wanted me. "Is there any kind of data link?"

"Not an open one."

A puzzle. Marcus's own ship didn't have access to his probe? Did he need to know it was me somehow?

Jherrel, escaped from the galley, flew his aircar into my knee, and then stopped and grinned at me. I waved him away and his little face fell so hard I picked him up and looked him in the eye. "I have to figure something out. And I think I have to be quiet to do it. Can you and Caro and your dad," I glanced at Liam and waited for his nod, "go and draw that ship so we have a record of it?"

Even though he was only a little over a year old, Jherrel nodded seriously. "Yes, Uncle." Smart kid.

Liam scooped them both, and I leaned over and kissed Alicia on the cheek. "Can you help him?"

Alicia tensed, still staring at the wall. "If it was meant to hurt us, it would have by now."

She drummed her fingers on my knee.

"Please?"

She raised an eyebrow, "Well, Liam is rather cute."

Damn her for making nothing easy. Unless it was a joke, and I could never tell with her. She didn't like being cooped up in a tin can with no easy risks to take, no long runs, no cliffs to climb. I put my hand over hers and whispered, "I love you. I'd keep you here if I could." We tried to keep one adult per kid.

Alicia smiled and, as if she'd never fought the idea at all, she hopped up and balanced Caro on her fabulous hip and grinned at me, and then at Liam. She flipped on the mod she shared with Induan that made her basically reflect her surroundings, and it looked like the empty air was bouncing Caro up and down, only a periodic slight smear of shifting color giving away Alicia's physical presence. "Call us when you know something," she said as Caro left the room.

"I will," I said to the air.

Chelo came over and stood behind me, massaging my shoulders, establishing the closeness we'd used ever since we were little. I had no words to tell her how steadying her presence was, how the feel of her fingers and her familiar scent helped center me.

I stared at the image of the cylinder. There was no way to get to it physically. Not at this speed. Besides, to find us and match us like this, it had to be all engine and navigation and communications gear. It didn't take much to maintain any speed you reached in space, but getting speed took lots of energy. This ship was too small to have the tools to return. What message was worth this expense?

Another thought struck me, bringing with it a fear for Marcus. This had to have been sent shortly after we left. It took us two years to get to Fremont, we spent about two weeks there, and then almost another year getting this far back. It would have taken the little ship, or probe or whatever, over a year to get here and get aligned in our direction. A year and a half maybe—the sling out, the turn, the thrusting acceleration necessary. So he'd have sent it no more than a year and a half after we left, and probably sooner than that. I could see its likely trajectory in my head. And the timing—it had reached us before we burned the fuel to start slowing down.

What did that mean was happening at home? Had the rumored war started?

Worrying wouldn't make answers.

"Kayleen, can you watch over me, stay linked to *Creator* in case I'm . . . gone? Tell the others what's happening?"

"What do you mean, in case you're gone? Surely you won't go far enough I can't reach you. Besides, I can't fly *Creator* yet. I don't know when I'll be good enough to fly. Should I use the PA system or call them if something happens?"

If I hadn't felt that way myself, I'd have laughed at her nervous rambling. I put up a hand to forestall her usual thousand questions. "Just trust yourself."

There was a moment of silence, and I wondered what Chelo thought. She'd never been in space before. I touched her hand with mine, noticing that she trembled slightly. "It will be all right. Marcus is a friend."

"Go," she whispered.

I shifted in the chair, looking for a position where I didn't feel the edges of it. Eyes closed, I clenched and opened my hands, stretched my ankles. What kept me from just knowing what to do?

I talked myself through it. *Open. Be the data. Be the maker. Be my blood, the gift of my genetics and the nano that swims in me.* To fly the ship I didn't need to be it, just to feel it in me. The last time I'd let myself be as open as I was trying for this time, I lost control. I could say it was in the heat of battle, except I was on a ridge far away from the skimmer and people inside when I threw them screaming in the sea. Their dying voices still echoed in my head. They hadn't been trying to harm me. Not that moment. They were innocent. And dead.

Chelo felt my tension, my distance, and worked my shoulders harder. "Focus," she demanded, her voice just louder than a whisper. "You can do it."

Don't think about losing control. Know you can keep it. Fall deeper. Start someplace safe. Creator thrummed through me and in me, and me in it. Data in my blood and bones, until my awareness of the bones and ligaments and veins and cells that made me live began to fade into streams of information. Kayleen rode the same data, higher than me, not so absorbed in it. I felt her register my presence, wish me well. It helped.

I let myself fill the ship, take the feeds from the cameras and sensors outside. I worked my way into the communication stream from *Creator*. At this speed, small packets. I tried sending my name.

Nothing.

Marcus's name.

Nothing.

My father's. Maybe Marcus was expecting him to be piloting instead of dead.

Nothing.

I curled back about and watched *Creator* ping the ship, which responded to every question with its speed and location.

There had to be another thread. "Send it our speed and location," I told *Creator*.

This time it responded, but only with an opening . . . machine talk for the way Alicia could ask me a question with her eyes.

If Marcus were me, what would he do?

And then I got it. I sent it a challenge. Marcus constantly teased me for being too naïve. "Who are you and why are you in our space? Prove yourself!"

A burst of data leapt across the void, flooding the *Creator*, captured by its sensors.

"Let it in?" *Creator* queried.

Who else would have known where to find us? "Yes."

The data flowed into the *Creator*. My instincts had better be right.

After I made sure *Creator* accepted the data from the strange little message ship, I slid back up into the slower, normal world. Chelo had one hand and Kayleen the other, my hands cold in their warm ones. Their eyes held questions, but they waited, letting me adjust. *Creator* still hummed inside me in all the usual ways, status and speed, atmosphere and temperature, all the little facts that keep a fragile cylinder safe inside emptiness. "Water," I whispered, rewarded as Chelo slipped into the galley.

Kayleen's hand trembled slightly. "What did you see?" I asked her. "What data came in?"

"It was too fast to read. Not meant for me anyway."

That made sense. Marcus had never met her, hardly knew she existed.

Chelo came back in with water and I drank, feeling the water fill empty places deep inside me. "*Creator?* What did we get in? Is the message urgent?"

"Yes."

Dumb question. I sounded the *all hands* bell again, and waited for the room to fill up before shifting us to the galley, which had a makeshift playpen for the kids across the back. I filled everyone in quickly while Kayleen served up col she flavored with redberries so that it smelled like Fremont.

Finally, everyone sat looking at me with expectant faces. "Okay, *Creator,* what's the message?"

Even the children quieted as the screen showed Marcus seated in his garden. I recognized the light-link butterflies caught like prisms in the purple flowers behind his head. The video was just a frozen image at first, giving me long enough to drink in the sight of him. My savior, my teacher, the man who bankrolled my trip to save my sister. As always, he looked like power. Sunlight poured down on his brown hair, touching the ends with red almost as deep as fire, a contrast to his green eyes.

If only I could reach through the air and touch him.

"He looks so young," Chelo said. "Like he's our age."

The slight condescending tone in Alicia's voice made me squirm as she said, "They all do."

I sipped my col, hungry for a rush of clarity from the stimulant. Colors sharpened. The video sprang to life, the butterflies and small birds moving, and Marcus's face still showing no hint of a smile. "Joseph . . . or David, whichever of you gets this message"—Alicia squeezed my hand at the mention of my dead father's name—"do not return to Silver's Home. Joseph has been declared 'wanted' by the Port Authority and the Planetary Police. If you're seeing this message, I'm uploading a new destination. You must have trusted this ship but, Joseph, don't be so naïve."

He paused and smiled. Damn the man to hell. "I love you, too," I whispered almost silently, although Alicia, Chelo, and Kayleen all gave me quick, odd looks.

The video Marcus continued. "I trust we found you before you slowed. If so, do nothing—the new coordinates will be in Creator's nav subsystem. If not, work with Creator to get as close as you can with your remaining fuel, and we'll figure it out from there."

His smile faded again. "Don't try to communicate with me. I'll reach you." He looked directly into the camera. "Trust me. I'll find you. I found you now, didn't I?"

And that was it.

I shivered. Alicia looked both angry and excited. "He must be sending us to one of the other Five Worlds," she whispered.

"I want to go home," I said. There were things I wanted to do on Silver's Home. Swimmers mods. Go back to Pilo Island. Meet the other people in our affinity group. That's what Marcus had been preparing me for—to take my place there.

Alicia had apparently been thinking, too. "Lopali. Maybe we can go to Lopali. Where the fliers live."

But as always, it was Chelo who saw the real truth and spoke it. "That means we have no home."

ALICIA: INVISIBILITY

I was better at being invisible than any of them thought. Even Joseph, who knew me best. At the moment, he didn't see me on the floor across the room from him and Kayleen. They sat side by side, holding hands, lost in the other world of data where he sometimes became as invisible as me, even though I could still see his body. He'd grown as tall as Liam. Even with the slightly slack-faced look he wore when the data fields took him, he still glowed with energy, like there was more of him than anyone else. The muscles in his hands and calves twitched from time to time, as if he could leap up from whatever far place he'd gone to and chase me around the ship. We'd done that just this morning, me leaving my invisibility mod on low-res so it'd change too slowly from time to time and give him clues. I'd been grateful when he caught me in a maintenance tunnel with only the silent bots to see what we did after that.

We didn't get much time together anymore. He was always worrying about something. So I watched him when I could. It let me feel like we were still close.

Kayleen, beside him, looked like me with her eyes shut. Hers are blue and mine are a violet that screams bioengineering even though she's actually more altered, since she can Read the Wind like Joseph. I can't. Her feet are bigger. We're both a head shorter than him, slender and strong, and beside him, right now, her dark curly hair fell in a mess down her shoulders, the edges licking her breasts.

They'd been down deep in the data for so long that one foot had gone to sleep. I twisted it gently, feeling the pins and needles of blood rushing into cramped veins. It was important not to make a sound; me being invisible didn't make them deaf. If Joseph woke and caught me, he'd think I was jealous of her, but I wasn't really. Not much, anyway. Being invisible had taught me how much she loved Liam, and Chelo, the little family they'd made.

I worked my foot back alive before Kayleen twitched and moaned, burying her face in his shoulder for a moment. He whispered to her. "Shhhh . . . you did well."

"I crashed."

He pulled her close to him and held her. "You'll get it. You have to relax more. It's not possible to keep it all in the front of your brain; you have to let go and trust your subconscious enough to let it handle the hard parts."

She had a frustrated edge to her voice. "I can't. I get all tangled up."

They had been flying a simulated version of *Creator*. I don't know how many times they'd tried since I didn't watch him work with her every day, but she always crashed. He had trouble teaching her things that came like breathing to him. But he stayed patient. "You'll get it. If you ever have to fly a real ship, you'll do fine."

The look on her face suggested she didn't believe him. Neither of them much liked these lessons. Sometimes I had to tease Joseph for hours afterward to get him laughing. Kayleen tried hard, but Reading the Wind so deep scared her. I knew; I'd been an invisible fly on the wall by accident once, when she cried in Chelo's arms and wished all her powers away.

A gentle warning beeped in my ear for the second time. I only had a few minutes before the mod failed for lack of power and needed me to move and charge it. I tried to stop everything but breathing to make it last.

Joseph pulled Kayleen up and held her to him, and though they didn't say anything I'd have bet they were talking anyway. I wanted that; to be so close to him I could talk inside his head and hear him inside mine. At one point, he looked right at the bit of wall I leaned against, and I wondered what I often wondered: Did he always know where I was in spite of my invisibility? Did the data that made me invisible to the eye betray me to him and Kayleen?

He looked away quickly.

They went through the door before my mod gave out, and I breathed a great sigh of relief and let the mod turn off, leaning back against the wall for a few long breaths before I stood and slipped through the door, rewarded with an empty corridor. Still, I walked for a bit, stepping quietly, turning and turning. I knew *Creator* like no one but Joseph did, and maybe Kayleen. Down near the back, there were holds half-full of stuff from home. I worked my way along two outer corridors, the slow movement enough to give some charge to the magic that transformed my skin to a mirror. As I went back and back, I grew lighter, approaching the half-gravity of the cargo area. Enough to hold everything in place, not much more.

I undogged the hatch of my favorite hold: the biggest one. Inside, the walls were lined with boxes and crates full of art made by the roving scientists called roamers. The art didn't matter—nothing from Fremont did. I was glad to be rid of the place. What mattered was the space.

Most of *Creator* was corridors and small rooms or packed cargo holds. Or the shared workout room, where anyone might be.

I stood in the middle and bowed to the openness, fully visible. A ritual: me showing off for myself. Then I leapt, the lightness making me feel like I could fly. I leapt and leapt again, each jump taking me a little higher, and then I leapt into the wall and pushed off, the thrust of my legs giving me more height, enough to reach a pile of boxes strong enough to land on. I crouched, for just a moment. Like a butterfly might. I went again, going up and down and across, extending my arms and find the far wall. I had to push hard enough each time—even in half gravity it was possible to fall. I made it all the way to the ceiling, barely breathing hard, and came back down the same way.

I imagined people watching me. Joseph clapping. The children. I imagined people liking my strength and my power instead of chastising me for it. I didn't want a real audience. But I wanted this one, the one in my head. It made me jump faster.

I did the whole routine two more times, still visible, Alicia the flying girl.

Then I turned on my mod, now more fully charged, and did the cargo dance again, up and up and up, pushing and extending and almost falling. Alicia the invisible girl.

At the top, I had to be extremely careful not to fall.

I loved that feeling.

CHELO: THE SISTER WORTH A WAR

D ocking with a space station is nothing like leaving a planet. Liam and Kayleen and I sat with the kids in the cramped space of our room, playing word games with the children, when Joseph stopped by, followed by his shadow, the dog he'd named after my friend Sasha. He greeted the children and kissed me on the forehead. "We're getting near the station. You should sit down in case we need to do anything, but I'm pretty sure we won't be flying her in—it should be automatic."

Kayleen, beside me, tensed. Fear flashed across her face. I took her hand and squeezed hard, telling her to be strong.

"Do we need to strap in?" Liam asked, and I shuddered at the idea, remembering how confined the takeoff had felt.

"No—but sit down and hold onto the children. Can I leave you Sasha?"

"Of course." After Joseph, I was Sasha's second favorite, and she quickly curled around my feet, her tail thumping.

Kayleen left with him, so I sat with Jherrel in my arms, and Liam beside me, and Paloma, Kayleen's adoptive mother, beside Liam. Caro leaned back against Liam, laughing, the way she always laughed in his arms. A daddy's girl, so at home with him it made me hate my father's death yet again. In front of us, a vid screen pretended to be a window and showed us Marcus's secret destination: Jillian May Station.

I wanted sky above my head and the ability to ride across open plains, grass tickling the bottoms of my feet and the air smelling of grass-flowers and mice, of the Lace River and rich dirt. I wanted my son, Jherrel, strapped behind me, and Liam and Caro and Kayleen alongside and nothing else. Joseph, of course, but he would hate such a life. I didn't care if I never saw this, or any other, starship again. But, of course, that would be too much to hope for.

The space station we were approaching clearly had no open spaces. The secret destination Joseph's mysterious Marcus had sent us to actually looked like a pile of space ships left in the void, sort of like hebras left piles of poop on the plains, or paw-cats piles of bones by a trail. Ugly, yet organic.

A few days ago, when *Creator* had finally admitted our destination to Joseph, we'd learned Jillian May served as a transport stop and cargo hub for the Five Worlds, and would have ships coming and going regularly. Paloma had paced nervously and then blurted out a question. "Won't whoever is looking for Joseph be watching?"

Jenna replied, "There are more space ships in the Five Worlds than stars in Fremont's sky."

Joseph smiled. "I trust Marcus."

I didn't know this man who had earned my brother's loyalty, but I did understand Paloma's worry.

As we neared the station, *Creator* shrank. The pile of space ships resolved further to look like a silver pole festooned with charms. Then the charms turned to ships and the pole was clearly taller than any of the volcanoes on Islandia. Almost every ship here was larger than our guild halls, some by a factor of hundreds, and almost all bigger than *Creator*. How was my little family supposed to maneuver in a place so vast? I squeezed Liam's hand. "What if we get there, and one of us makes a wrong turn, and we never find each other again?"

Liam placed an arm around me, pulling me in close, smelling like worry and love. "You are supposed to be the positive one."

"I know." And so I let a small prayer touch my lips. *Let me keep this man by my side always.* "To hold us all together, I have to worry."

As we slid between two huge ships, Jherrel squirmed on my lap and burbled. "Big ship! Big ship," and I saw the ghost of Joseph in him, and clutched him to me. He was too young to leave now, but like Joseph, he'd far surpass me some day. And he would leave. Parents should not have to think about that before their babies are too big to carry.

I held Jherrel close and snuggled closer to Liam and Paloma. Caro climbed on top of us, queen of her hill of people. *Creator* rocked once, gently, and then stopped. The screen went dark.

A few moments later, Joseph came and stood next to me, his eyes shiny and excited.

"How will you find Marcus?" I asked him.

His grin widened. "He already found me." He practically bounced as he stood there. "He's coming. You're going to love him, Sis. You will."

I hoped so.

"Are you ready?"

"Sure," Liam said.

"Be careful—it's just over half the gravity you're used to."

We followed Joseph down a corridor and then up an elevator, and then through a round coupling with a thin walkway between us and Jillian May. Being lighter made me feel as if I'd drunk too much beer, even though there'd been none on *Creator*.

At the far end a slender man waited. He looked taller than he had on the video. I expected Joseph to race to him, but my brother hung back beside me and watched Jenna approach Marcus like a moth drawn to a candle. She stood on tiptoes and Marcus lifted her and kissed her deeply and almost reverently.

And for a long time.

Jenna, who didn't trust anyone when she was the wild woman of Fremont.

I blinked, watching the fall of her hair and the way his arm curled around her and how they seemed to fit together, and it made me want to gather Kayleen and Liam to me. Kayleen looked as open-mouthed as I did, and then leaned into Joseph. "Why didn't you tell me?"

A small smile touched the corners of his mouth. "It's her story to tell."

Kayleen frowned. "She never tells us anything."

Then Marcus was dishing out hugs to Jenna's sister, Tiala, and Dianne. Both women seemed to hold onto him a long time, and Dianne held on so long I wondered what the rules were here. On Fremont, Liam and I and Kayleen were the only group of three I knew of, and even then we'd have never have become a family if we hadn't been alone in the wilds for a year with no expectation of rescue. I couldn't quite decide whether to be fascinated or repelled.

Alicia and Induan approached him next, fully visible with no sign of their strange ability. Rather, they were solid and sure of themselves, dark Alicia and blond Induan. He shook hands with them, gave them short but warm hugs, straightening quickly to look at the rest of us. When his eyes met Joseph's, his face looked as if a sun had bloomed near it, but he stayed where he was, a one-man greeting line. You'd think we were attending a party instead of a space rescue.

Dark-haired and smooth-moving Ming came up next, standing silently in front of Marcus while he regarded her in equal silence. The other women stopped and watched, too, and Joseph visibly tensed. I knew a little of Ming's story, how she'd worked for the Port Authority and yet helped Jenna and Joseph and the others escape from custody when they first got there, and then, in the end, run away from the Port Authority and joined Joseph's crew by stowing away. She was a bodyguard and a dancer, and somehow made it look normal to be both. Once, she had been Marcus's student.

They were silent so long I thought neither of them was going to move.

Marcus broke first, his eyes and facial features softening visibly even though I was twenty feet away from him. His arms opened until she stepped forward and filled them. It wasn't a long hug, about what he gave Alicia and Induan, but even from a distance it looked like tension ran off of them both, as if they became lighter by touching. The moment passed. Ming danced away, literally light on her feet.

Our turn.

He came over to us, and he looked at me instead of Joseph. He searched my eyes, my face, my whole body, and then looked back and forth between me and Joseph. In my arms, Jherrel stilled as well, regarding Marcus as silently as I did. Liam stepped close to me and put his free arm around my shoulder. Marcus's eyes were the most amazing color I had ever seen, bright green with flecks of gold and silver, and they seemed to be drinking in my very soul. His voice sounded soft and sure. "Chelo Lee. The sister worth a war."

I waited for him to explain.

I didn't realize I was holding my breath until he smiled, and I smiled back, and Jherrel reached toward him and Marcus took him from my arms and held him, smiling like all people smile at toddlers, but also seeming to look for something more. The moment to ask about his comment was gone. But I'd remember.

Marcus glanced at Sasha, at Joseph, and then at the dog again. Joseph looked uncertain, and starved, and I realized then how much he needed this man. A quirky smile touched Marcus's lips, but then he handed me back my child and held my brother. Joseph's face relaxed, and for a moment he looked younger than I'd seen him since he came back to Fremont for me. The two of them could have been a father and son. It showed in both of their faces, trust and regard, a bond so close it made me nervous even though it felt good to see Joseph happy.

Feet scraping on metal reminded me we weren't entirely alone. Strangers dressed all in gray clothes with black pockets began unloading our cargo.

I didn't have time to get lost on the station.

In no more than twenty minutes we were climbing into yet another starship—this one at least five times bigger than *Creator*. It was also rougher: the floor and some walls were scratched and dented. Layers of yellow and green paint peeled from high-impact corners.

The extra room would be good for the kids. At two and a half and two and a quarter, they had become racers and leapers, and both now needed two modified maintenance bots to keep them even a little safe. Luckily, the bots from *Creator* had stuck at the children's heels the way Sasha stuck to Joseph.

Gray-suited people roamed the halls carrying things, but other people looked regularly dressed. We turned and climbed up or down enough times that I felt lost before Marcus finally stopped in a big room full of cushioned chairs with straps. I grimaced as I recognized acceleration couches. "Are we leaving?" Liam asked.

Marcus nodded. "Welcome aboard. This is the *Migrator*, a cargo ship which will be departing in about an hour. Clearly you got one of my messages, since you arrived here."

One of? He'd sent more? And we were leaving so soon?

"Things have . . ." he paused, and looked very serious ". . . gotten worse. Silver's Home has banned Joseph, Jenna, and me. If they find us, they'll at least lock us up. Maybe kill us."

He stopped, looking around to see how we took the news. I tried not to look as scared as I felt. Alicia looked disappointed, and Joseph, next to her, had an angry set to his jaw. Jherrel and Caro didn't care, and started a game with Sasha, running between people. Marcus frowned at them, and they stopped for a moment, then went right back to running and giggling. I'd had my children threatened once. Now they might be threatened again. Or maybe I should just say they were still threatened. Who was our enemy, and why?

"So where are we going?" Jenna asked.

Marcus shook his head. "I'll tell you along the way."

Jenna looked bemused at Marcus's refusal rather than angry, blowing through my expectations yet again. "Is there war yet?"

He shook his head. "Almost." He and Dianne shared a glance. "But I think it started on Fremont, and it will grow from here. Some people are still trying for a diplomatic answer, but Islas has a large fleet at the ready, and Joy Heaven has aligned with her. Paradise is with Silver's Home."

He didn't say with "us." But surely he wasn't aligned with Islas, whose mercenaries had almost killed us on Fremont.

"And Lopali?" Tiala asked.

"Remains neutral. We need to change that."

Alicia had told me about Lopali, where people who could barely walk flew gracefully in the air. Only a certain gravity and atmosphere allowed human flight, and Lopali had that.

Dianne asked, "So how many of us are for peace?"

Marcus looked disappointed, although the list he read sounded long to me. "The builder's guilds and the Family, of course, and the universities and most of the groups that work on the climates. The swimmers. Two or three of the religions."

He must have seen that we didn't really understand what he meant, so he added, "On Silver's Home, there are affinity groups for almost everything that needs to be done. Those who deal with money and trade and make space ships and weapons are mostly willing to fight, and they're the primary funders of the Port Authority, which thrives on the idea of war. And Islas personally offends our way of life, which is enough for some people." But not for him. The way he said it, I could tell he didn't think much of intolerance, and I liked him for that. He stood. "There's more to tell you, but for now, we have to go. Joseph will stay with you."

So Joseph wouldn't pilot the *Migrator*. His face looked calm as he watched Marcus walk away, but I could tell by the set of his shoulders that he felt worried. I dodged a flying Jherrel on my way to Joseph's side. I put a hand on his shoulder. "So who, exactly, wants to kill you?"

He shook his head. "I'm not sure if Marcus even knows. People with power and money on Silver's Home. You can't understand without being there. It's so different from Fremont."

I hated that. And I hated specific threats from faceless people. "Are you okay?"

"As long as you're around, I'm okay."

Deep inside I knew how true the words were, how much love and need drove us both around each other, like a planet and a sun. "I love you, brother."

His answer was to hold me close, so we stood side by side, facing our future.

Three days after we left Jillian May Station, I used one of Marcus's mandated exercise walks to explore the ship. I'd tried singing to cheer myself up, but my voice sounded hollow and bouncy in tight spaces. So I switched to amusing myself by trying to walk quietly. Around a corner, movement startled me. Bryan. He'd come back to Fremont on *Creator*, but we'd been in the thick of a battle. We'd left, and there had always been people around before Bryan was frozen. So I hadn't really seen him alone since before we left for Little Lace Lake years ago.

He'd been designed as a strongman and a fighter; wide and tall and well-built. His dark brown hair fell just above his eyes in front and barely curled to the nape of his thick neck on the back. All of his scars seemed to have been erased, except, of course, the ones inside him. He looked both pleased and wary to have come up on me. Had he been avoiding me on purpose? I'd sent him away. But it had been the only way to save his life.

My voice sounded as stilted and unsure as I felt. "Bryan? How are you?"

"I'm . . . I'm okay."

He was lying. "I'm glad to see you."

"Really?"

I would have gone to find him on purpose eventually. Really, I would have. He'd always been wary and full of deep anger, and he'd always been a rock of support for me. When I was a girl, I'd expected to grow up and marry him. "Walk with me? There's a wider corridor I just came through, and at the end there's a little galley."

"I'm not hungry, but I'll walk with you."

We walked, both going the way he had been going. In the old days, I'd have held his hand or leaned into him, and we might have laughed. "You know my story, from Fremont. Joseph told me how he worked with Marcus, but I don't really know how Silver's Home was for you and Alicia."

"There were a lot more people like me there." His voice sounded natural, but he didn't look at me.

Surely there was more to the story than that. We made the turn into the wider corridor, and something different about the acoustics meant our footsteps echoed, slightly out of sync with our actual movements. "So it wasn't like Fremont, where we were freaks."

"Joseph was still a freak. But I was less of one."

"Less of one?"

"Than almost anybody." He flicked his hands just so and the knife edges of his fingernail implants exploded from the tips of his fingers like claws. He held them out in front of him.

I'd seen them, of course. But this time I stopped and took his palm gently, turning it so the light shone on the built-in weapons. I reached a finger toward them.

"Don't touch," he warned, and I drew back, a bit too late. A single bead of blood showed on the tip of the third finger of my right hand.

He flicked the nails back in, and took my hand in his, licking the drop of blood from the pad of my finger. My breath caught in my throat and I pulled my hand away and looked down.

He started walking.

I followed, and for a long time there was only the off-beat echo of our steps—his sure and heavy, mine light and almost a jog. We passed the galley I'd thought to stop in and kept going, curling up a long vertical corridor using the handholds as steps, and coming out on a level of the ship I hadn't seen yet. "Have you been here before?" I asked.

"I walk a lot."

Oh. Maybe he was lonely. Although I saw him with Ming often, the two of them a funny contrast of bulk and grace. "Do you miss Fremont?"

He didn't answer until we'd walked about half the length of the ship. "I miss us all being together. Now you and Kayleen and Liam have each other, and Joseph has Alicia."

And he felt left out. "We love you. We're all family."

He turned around and looked at me, his brown eyes ashy and his face white, as if tears or anger lay at bay right underneath his skin. "Easy for you to say."

"We came back for you."

"And I came back for you."

And he couldn't have known how it would be, that I would be with Liam and Kayleen and have kids. What had he expected? Why hadn't I ever asked myself? Worse, what could I do now? I reached toward him, wanting to give him a hug.

He shook his head. "Don't."

We separated at the next corridor, and I stopped and watched him walk away, his rolling gait even, his head resolutely turned away from me until he got to the far end of the corridor, and before the turn, he glanced back as if checking to see if I was there or not.

I smiled at him, and he smiled back, and then went around the corner.

I walked for an hour, hoping I would find him again, and hoping I wouldn't.

Instead of Bryan, I found Marcus, alone in a small room, staring at a viewscreen wall that showed the stars we flew through in real time, as if it were a window. I'd already learned that ships are not houses and windows are weaknesses in space. Every view to the outside is through cameras. The room looked as well-used as the rest of *Migrator*, with six metal chairs bolted to the floor and tattered orange cushions tied to the seats and backs of the chairs. Small tables had been stuck onto each chair like awkward afterthoughts.

Marcus turned as I came in, and once more I was struck by the humor in his incredible eyes. He seemed happy to see me, and secretly bemused as well. "Hello, Chelo. Would you like a glass of col?"

I hadn't learned to like the stimulant even after two years of opportunities, but it wouldn't hurt to be polite, so I nodded and took a chair.

He left me to watch stars for a few moments, and when he returned he held a cup of steaming liquid out like an offering. "This is the way I like it best."

It smelled different than I'd been served so far, richer. This version was a deep brown, like djuri hide. The taste was spicy and very smooth. He waited for my reaction.

"It's good."

"It's dark chocolate. A taste from far back in our human past, and cultivated anew on Silver's Home. I was hoping you'd like it."

"I do." I liked that it had history, too. As usual, even a few sips clarified my vision and gave me balance. Subtle things, as if I were growing younger and the world becoming brighter.

He relaxed, leaning back and letting his long legs dangle in front of him. His movements were fluid, like Ming the dancer's. Almost feline. "So, did you come to find me?"

"Yes." The question that had been filling my head since I first met him didn't want out yet. "I . . . I wanted to meet Joseph's mentor. He thinks a lot of you."

"And you aren't sure what to think?"

"Not yet."

He hesitated a moment, sipping his own drink and letting me sip mine. Even though his whole being radiated power, he felt comfortable to be with. When he did speak, it was softly. "I first met your brother as a—presence. He was flying the *New Making* in, and he was so strong and so cocky and so—utterly alien it amazed me." He grinned again. "Oh—he was naïve and rough, and he still is, but strong. It was like meeting myself, only you never get to see yourself as a young adult. That's all eighty years behind me now."

I swallowed at the reminder of his age.

"And later, when I tried to figure out how Joseph could be so strong and yet not go stark-raving crazy, the best answer seemed to be where he came from. If he'd been raised here," he waved a hand at the screen, as if here meant all the stars in the sky, "he'd have been identified early on and isolated and taught by the best. But there—he had you and the other kids, and Jenna, and no other Wind Reader to tell him he might go crazy. And you all were in a dangerous place, so every one of you had to be smart and focused all the time."

I bristled at that. "So did the colonists. All of us. Together."

"Joseph told me you loved them."

"I miss them." I looked away from him, needing to keep control. "But I missed Joseph more. I hear I've got you to thank for him coming to get me."

"It was nothing."

Not true. Joseph and Jenna had told me what it cost to outfit a ship, and the goods from *Creator's* hold wouldn't pay off even part of our debt to Marcus. "Why did you do it?"

"Because I wanted to meet the girl who could keep someone of Joseph's strength sane for so long. It will be good to study how you were both made, but the strength of people is more than genetics. I wanted to meet you."

"Jenna told me once we were designed to support each other. More than just me and Joseph, but all of us."

He nodded as if he already knew that.

The question that had been burning in me had cooled enough to rise to my lips. "So why did you call me the woman who was worth a war?"

"The sister worth a war?"

"Yeah, that."

He took another long moment to finish his drink, setting the empty cup on the tacked-on table and staring at the stars for a bit. "Your father started the little battle on Fremont."

"Little battle!" Tell that to the dead. My fists clenched.

He held up a hand. "Shhh . . . it *was* a little battle. You'll see." And now he was the one looking angry. "Your father started the fight because they killed you all. That's what he thought—that Fremont's people killed his children and so he had a revenge right to kill them."

"No one has a revenge right to anything."

He looked pleased. "I know. But then Joseph was hell-bent to get back and save you. I helped him because otherwise he would have gone crazy. He needs you to keep going, and if you'd been killed, Joseph would have been useless. And he needed to be away—a lot of people have had interest in him. He's . . . more than any of us. Even more than me."

I hated Marcus's tone. He expected a lot from Joseph. I'd hoped being in a place where everyone was genetically engineered would mean people would treat us—well, like themselves instead of like freaks. And what did this mean for Kayleen? Already Marcus had started spending time with her at Joseph's insistence, and she seemed calmer, though still fragile. Sometimes at night I'd wake and find her staring open-eyed at the ceiling, unresponsive to her name, lost in data or craziness or dreams. I'd try to bring her back by stroking her cheek or kissing her lips gently, and she would moan off time to my actions, staying lost to me.

If only I knew how to help Kayleen as well as I knew how to help Joseph.

I refocused on Marcus as he started talking again. "So even though the real reasons were more complex, and your father was driven by revenge and I was driven by love for Joseph, the buzz across the whole system is that your father sent the Star Mercenaries on your behalf, and I sent Joseph on your behalf, and so you see, the battle on Fremont, the first shot in this war, was fought over you."

"But . . . I hate war." My voice rose and the blood pounded in my veins, hot and protesting. "I want people to just stop fighting. It doesn't make any sense to kill each other."

"Truth doesn't have anything to do with rumor. Myth often places beautiful women in the middle of war. You're going down in history as the woman who started this war."

5

CHELO: THE FIFTH WORLD

I t took six months and two more rushed transfers from ship to ship
before our feet touched a planet. It was midmorning when the *Harbinger*, the ship we now rode, turned lazily in the sky, surprising my
stomach, and sank tail down to land on a shimmery flat surface on
Lopali. *Harbinger* was a squat round cargo ship with a ramp wide
enough to send small ships through. I'd never landed, of course—we'd
left Fremont and gone through three docking and releasing maneu-
vers.

Only now did I really feel in my bones that we were somewhere.
Below us a small planet hung in space barely more blue than green,
its five continents rounded like very big islands. Each pole had a
round ice cap. As I watched Lopali grow in the viewscreen, I stroked
the uneven surface of the belt the original Sasha, the girl from Fremont, had hand-knotted for me. She'd put a prayer for safety in every
knot, and as I touched the belt, I remembered how earnest her face
had been when she told me about her work. I'd worn it in the battle
for Fremont, and I had been safe.

Lopali bulked bigger than Fremont by a factor of at least two,
maybe more. As we made a full orbit above it, the dark side glowed
with strings of lights over the land, so many I couldn't imagine a
person for each light, much less many people for each light, which is
what Alicia promised I'd find. We landed on the edge of a small
spaceport. Green fields stretched in neat squares toward a forest.

I closed my eyes, hoping for a place I wanted to be, a home, or at least a warm, friendly town.

I didn't care how small the big ship and the big planet and the wide ramp made me feel. As soon as Marcus gave us the all-clear, I rushed down the ramp with Jherrel and Caro beside me. There were no people nearby—just the empty landing place and the empty field, and not far off, the forest. I squinted at it, looking for trees similar to twintrees or lace-leaves or even the tall and spiky pongaberry trees. These trees had wide branches and great tufts of leaves near the ends of the branches. It made me feel like a roamer again, like I should pull out a pad and pencils and make scientific drawings and notes. Maybe soon. In the meantime, nothing looked threatening. Best of all, there was ground under me and sky above me.

It had been two and a half years since I had felt either.

I started dancing.

At first, the children looked at me as if I'd lost my mind, but they got caught up in the kicking and swaying and twisting as soon as Liam joined us, the four of us stepping in time, jumping, breathless. Dancing joy, dancing the smells of dirt and trees, of flowers and sky and wind. While Lopali didn't smell like Fremont, it also didn't smell like grease and metal and sweat the way a space ship did. It smelled almost like heaven.

We'd been in so many versions of gravity across all the ships and years that it took a few moments for me to realize how light I felt here, and how much our dancing was like flying. Liam took one child in each arm and began turning circles with them both held close to his chest, all three of them laughing and smiling. Paloma came down and stood at the foot of the ramp, staring. She looked younger than she had when we left Fremont, but still older by decades than any of us. She smiled, and lifted a foot, then another, taking Caro from Liam and putting her on the ground and holding her hand. Liam did the same with Jherrel, so the four of them were a line, two tall and two short people bounding in low gravity so the children jumped twice their height.

Alicia came and stood beside me, her mouth open and an expression of pure delight on her face. "I never thought I'd get here," she whispered.

"To a planet again?"

"No. Here. To the fliers." She scanned the sky, turning her head this way and that. She stood on tiptoe, bouncing, laughing. She turned on her mod and flickered once and nearly disappeared, becoming the color of the ground, and then Induan turned hers off and appeared and I shook my head, bemused. What had gotten into Alicia about this place?

Induan had an impish look on her face. She walked toward the forest, and as soon as she'd gone even a few feet I could tell the trees were farther away than they had looked. I had been good with scale and distance at home, but here everything seemed a bit off.

Induan raised her arms above her head.

The trees began to rise. Or some of the great bunches of leaves rose from the branches. They spread out in the air, becoming wings, spiraling up with powerful slow beats, like the great blaze fliers from home. As they rose one by one, all of the leaves became fliers. Behind them, a circle of empty perches gave lie to the idea that we were surrounded by forest. As they came closer, I could see that they were much larger than the birds at home, and at least as graceful. Light poured onto them and illuminated bright colors and flashing sparkles as the evening sun caught their wings. Greens and golds, whites, even a pale lavender. Two had wings so black they'd have become lost in a night sky.

And then they were above us, at least twenty of them, silent and so very beautiful.

I had never seen such grace.

Human bodies hung suspended between the great wings, each one thin and long. They wore tight-fitting clothes that left their legs and arms free. Their shoulders seemed to be two sets: forward shoulders that hunched more than ours and that attached to long arms, and a second set of shoulders, or perhaps a very different back, mounded up behind their slender necks and attached to the great wings. Wide torsos tapered to slim waists and hips, and long slender legs. Everything about the shape of their bodies looked designed to hold their wings. Some wore colored shoes to match the tight-fitting clothes, and a few had tied strings with beads or shells or bits of metal on them to the toes, so they glittered behind and below them.

They kept some distance, so it was impossible to see their facial expressions or what their wings were made of.

Invisible, Alicia clutched my arm so tight her nails dug furrows in the soft skin of my inner arm. I pulled away. She flickered into herself, openmouthed and staring. Transfixed. Paloma had gathered Caro into her arms, and they pointed up together. Liam and Jherrel stood hand in hand, openmouthed.

Induan dropped her arms and came and stood by Alicia.

The others walked quickly down the ramp, Marcus in the lead, Kayleen beside him. Then Ming, Tiala, and Jenna. I didn't see Joseph, Bryan, or Dianne. Everyone else was soon at our side. Marcus's eyes narrowed in worry. He watched the fliers carefully, his gaze flicking from one to the other, bouncing on his toes. It felt like I was standing beside a paw-cat, the feline strength of the man again clear and dangerous.

As if Marcus's arrival triggered a change, a flier with silver, white, and gold wings spiraled down closer to the ground. The others flew up and hung off a little ways, beating their wings slowly, almost hovering.

As the single flier neared us, tiny round breasts gave her gender away. This close, her wings more closely resembled bird's wings than I had thought, complete with bones in the front and feathers hanging from them. Amid the feathers, various decorations streamed in the wind. Beads and metal glinted in the flier's hair, which was a mass of braids held back from her face by a strip of black leather that contrasted with her golden hair.

The flier threw back her head and gave a great hard beat with her wings, sending warm air in a strong puff that momentarily lifted the loose edges of my hair. She landed with a hop, and her wings tilted a bit forward, her shoulders slumping to take the weight of them in this new position. She moved toward us, nearly as awkward on the ground as she had been graceful in the air. The other fliers stayed in the same slightly stilted formation.

"Hello Matriana," Marcus said, leaning in and giving her a gentle hug, as careful of her wings as if they were glass instead of feathers.

Matriana wore a long thin sheath strapped to one side. She had a water flask and a few other items I couldn't identify strapped to the other. I hadn't noticed them as she flew, so perhaps they had been situated on her back then. She reached into the long sheath and withdrew a shimmering silver feather with a gold tip. It matched her wings.

She handed the feather to Marcus, who took it gingerly by the quill, raised it to his forehead, and only then slid it into a similar sheath belted to his leg. It seemed to be made to hold the feather. Clearly, he had been expecting the gift, for he simply said, "Thank you."

She looked around, as if checking on each of us. Her eyes lingered longest on Liam, comparing his features to the children's. Her gaze flicked back to Marcus. "Where is this strong Joseph?"

"He is on the ship. I will be glad to introduce you."

She narrowed her eyes and glanced at the *Harbinger*, as if counting the painful steps between here and there. I had the sense she was used to giving orders, and held back, wanting something. When she nodded her head, the gesture implied quiet power, like Hunter wielded on Fremont. "I will meet Joseph and the rest of your group in town this evening. We will offer a feast."

"Our quarters?" Marcus asked.

"The gold guest house has been unlocked for you."

"Thank you."

And with that she turned, crouched low, and with a single powerful wingbeat, she launched herself into the air. As soon as she joined the other fliers, they turned and flew together in a formation that reminded me of wild birds flocking across the Grass Plains.

Although my feet didn't want to dance anymore, my shoulders itched to understand the weight and heft of wings.

6

JOSEPH: SETTLING

I watched on a viewscreen as the fliers rose up in a burst of power and color and left our party standing on the ground, staring up at them. The angle of the cameras made them seem small and insignificant against the vastness of the remade moon. I couldn't see well enough to make out their expressions, but Chelo bounced Caro on her hips, and Kayleen and Paloma had their heads bent near each other in conversation. Ming walked beside Marcus, looking up, though the fliers were almost invisible now.

It was tough to make out much of Lopali from the spaceport. We were surrounded by cargo ships here, but Dianne had already mentioned that other spaceports catered more to human passengers. Beyond the sterile garden of ships, the careful shapes of fields cut up the land, and beyond that, trees, and here and there the sparkling blue of streams. The largest road headed east, which must be toward the city.

Dianne and Bryan sat on either side of me. Dianne stared at the screen as if she daren't miss any nuance, and Bryan sat as still, except that he flicked his nails in and out almost absentmindedly. I watched them, not wanting him to slice my flesh by accident. A strategist, a strongman, and a maker. Marcus hadn't said it, but surely if he trusted the fliers completely, he wouldn't have left us three behind.

As soon as they returned, Marcus drew us all together into a meeting. We were passengers rather than pilots on the *Harbinger*, so there were no gleaming meeting rooms full of viewscreen walls available to us. The *Harbinger* was sparse and utilitarian, but it did have a single big oval room designed for gaming and working out, and we gathered in the mismatched and comfortable chairs there, surrounded by video screens and weights and machines. The edges of the room hosted an indoor running track and, on the walls, a pull-gym for low-gravity workouts.

We settled, the children sticking close to Chelo and Paloma, Liam sitting beside Kayleen, an arm across her shoulder, whispering in her ear. At my side, Alicia kicked her feet and twisted her hands in her lap.

Marcus sat on a black bench, his legs splayed out on either side of it. "We've about a half hour before we need to leave. Questions?"

"What was the feather about?" Chelo asked.

"Flier's feathers can be very valuable. We could buy passage home for all of us on a comfortable ship with the one Matriana gave me, because it's a pinion feather—one of the long ones at the end of the wings. Those molt once every few years at most. They've got a reputation for bringing luck."

Paloma looked intrigued. "Do they?"

I thought Marcus was going to burst out laughing, but he just said, "It's not been proven. The longest flier feathers are a valuable trade good everywhere, including Islas."

He hadn't said no about the luck. Interesting.

Alicia started pacing the edges of the group, holding her arms in, watching Marcus primarily, but also everyone else who knew about Lopali: Jenna and Tiala, Ming and Dianne.

Ming lifted a beautiful, shapely arm and waited for Marcus to nod before asking, "What did she want us to have luck in?"

He smiled. "Give a prize to the dancer. She wants us to help her people have babies."

I knew what he meant, but Chelo looked puzzled. "What?"

Marcus answered her. "We know how to make fliers . . . the Wingmakers from Silver's Home designed them for Lopali. Years ago. A subset of the Wingmakers, the Moon Men, made Lopali. Fliers can only have babies when the Wingmakers make them. Every year a ship comes with babies, only it's never as many as are wanted. It's not even close."

"Why can't the fliers have, or at least make, their own children?" Paloma asked.

Marcus stood up and walked around as he answered her. "They're sterile, so they can't have children. The processes that make them are owned, and secret. The fliers have beauty, and power, and by now a history. Lopali is almost five hundred standard years old—that's almost as old as the civilization on Islas, and older than Joy Heaven or Paradise. The fliers have been living here for almost four hundred years. The Moon Men are long gone now. Those that could, turned into fliers or died trying. That's what they hired the Wingmakers for—they were something else then, too, and took the name after they failed here."

"After they failed?" Alicia asked. "It looks like they succeeded to me."

Marcus stopped in front of her. "If they'd succeeded, the fliers would be able to have babies, and humans everywhere could fly if they wanted to."

"Wow," she said. "That would be great."

"But they failed, and yet they became rich because they failed. Generations ago, they gave up even trying to succeed anymore. They charge the fliers a lot to give them children, which are really just new, young, fliers. There is no real genetic link to the parents." Marcus's tone was tinged with scorn. Once, I had stood by Jenna when she lectured Alicia and Bryan and me about how unfair the fliers had it.

The look on Paloma's face said she might get sick, and Chelo looked green. Alicia was curious; Bryan showed no emotion at all, which meant he was still thinking about it, and given the situation, probably seething inside. Whoever designed us made us so injustice drove us nuts.

As Marcus told the tale, I watched Chelo's face. When he said, "Over half of flier children die before they reach puberty," her mouth thinned into a small line, and she narrowed her eyes and then raised her hand. He waved her hand down. "Some live, and stay in town. You'll see them." He grimaced. "It is unfair. But fliers are prized for their beauty and grace, and Lopali is a spiritual haven. People come here to meditate, to fly, and to learn to balance joy and sorrow like the fliers. For that, a high price has been accepted. Death of the fliers' children, and early death as well—the oldest fliers are only a few hundred years old." He sounded proud. "Finally, the fliers want to change their situation, stop being at everyone else's mercy."

I suspected he had something to do with their new attitude.

"They can't keep killing children!" Chelo hugged the two children overtightly to her chest.

"Shhhh . . . I agree with you. That's why we're here. They want Joseph to help them create their own children."

Huh?

"It will be a test for Joseph." He caught my eye and grinned at me, then added, "I'll help."

"You'd better." What did I know about creating fliers? The last day Marcus had talked about my ability to create the way he could, he was teasing me about almost killing simple plants.

Alicia stopped pacing and stood near me again, facing Marcus. "Why Joseph? Why not you? He has no experience in genetics."

Actually, I had a little.

"It's got to be hard!" she said.

Marcus laughed. "I just told you I'd help. There are two reasons. Joseph is stronger than me, and he can hold more data than I can. And you're right, this will be . . . a challenge. Kayleen will also help. So will the fliers' own geneticists here."

Alicia looked even less happy.

Jenna's voice sounded biting. "Silver's Home likes their power over Lopali."

"You mean the Wingmakers," Tiala clarified.

"It is the same thing," Dianne broke in, uncharacteristically animated. "The Wingmakers have too much power and are allied with those who make ships and gain from war. Which is why Lopali stays neutral. They won't side with Silver's Home while they're enslaved by your people. We've agreed to set them free."

"Not my people," Tiala retorted, giving Dianne a sharp look.

Liam frowned. "What's to keep them from going to Islas if we free them?"

Dianne said, "Fliers hate control. Islas is the essence of control, and the fliers shouldn't join them. But you're right. No outcome is certain. Maybe they'll stay neutral."

"I wouldn't blame them," Alicia asserted.

"Is that bad?" Chelo asked.

"We need their fleet," Marcus said, resuming his pacing. "Islas is more war-ready than Silver's Home, and Lopali has agile ships."

Chelo still looked puzzled. "Do we have permission from Silver's Home? To do this?"

Marcus's laugh suggested that time would run backward first. "Neither the Planetary Police nor the Port Authority owns the fliers' genetics. And yes, powerful people want to stop us. That's where the bounty came from. But we're doing the right thing."

Chelo sighed. "Sometimes that's all you can do."

I noticed he hadn't named our enemies.

"Agreed." Marcus stood, and motioned for Alicia to sit down. She did, as close as she could, leaning back into me, warm but still quivery with excitement.

Marcus cleared his throat. "We'll leave for town soon. Take everything you brought with you." He grinned. "And be sure to have easy access to your best clothes. We'll be going to a formal event, and while we'll look shabby beside the fliers, we should look our best." He clapped his hands and everyone scattered to get their gear.

Alicia went with me. She and I shared a cabin. We'd both already packed, so I pulled her down next to me on the single bed, breathing in the sweet salty scent of her. She reached a hand up and stroked my face, tracing the outline of my nose and jaw and forehead. "Can you imagine flying?"

A risk-taker's heaven—flight on a new planet. "I guess—sure. I'd like to try it. But I already fly ships—so I guess I feel like I know how to fly."

"Silly. With wings of your own. Can you imagine being so beautiful?"

I shook my head. "Maybe with the wings they've made for people. But I've heard over and over that humans who try to become fliers as adults die. A lot of them, anyway. It changes everything about you." And suddenly I knew that was really what she meant, that she wanted to sprout wings and be free. A shock of fear for her made my hands shake. "Don't do it. I couldn't bear to watch you die."

"But imagine me with wings."

She was more beautiful than any of the fliers. "You have everything I need." I touched her face and then her breast and belly. "You're perfect."

She rolled over to face me. "If you can truly help the fliers have children, then you can help me fly."

I swallowed. "I can't even do the first thing. And I won't risk losing you trying the second." Maybe no one would help her. I certainly wouldn't. Could I keep her from trying? Might as well force the wind not to blow. "Promise me you won't try to make me do this, and you won't try it on your own. Settle for flying with the kind of wings you can take off afterward."

She said nothing.

"I love you. I even love the way you take risks. But this is too big. Promise?"

She pursed her lips. "I'll promise until we understand what all the options are. But I won't promise anything to anyone forever."

"Thank you." I brought her to me and kissed her. Maybe she'd like fake wings well enough. Maybe she'd find something else to want more. Maybe the wind would stop forever.

At least, when she kissed me back she was greedy for my touch. She might want to fly, but she still wanted me, too. She tasted of chocolate col and ship's air and salt, and she fit perfectly in my arms.

I'd seen Chelo's dance through the viewscreen, and after I walked out from the ship into a sky for the first time in years, I understood it. Lopali smelled of rain and life and death and rebirth. It smelled like the windborn scents of fecund flowers and the sweat of a real climate. Even though it didn't smell like Fremont, it smelled like home.

Belongings in hand, we stood at the edge of the road, waiting with a few of the crew from the *Harbinger*. A big, slow-wheeled vehicle stopped and picked us up, filling to cramped once you counted us and the crew and all the stuff. The cargo carrier was simple; wheels and a flat surface, the whole thing made of shiny ship's silver, and thus unscratched. Rows of seats looked out in all directions, and a tarp covered them all, shading us from the sun. In the middle, a raised cage held our stuff, the boxes and duffels rattling together and the wheels bumping along. Whatever propelled us was, however, as silent as a starship.

We drove slowly through a patchwork of fields: grains, vegetables, and some fallow, but all neat and tidy. Every once in a while, another wheeled cargo carrier of some kind passed us, and once we passed a small cart. Occasionally, a group of fliers passed by overhead, paying no attention to the ground. Chelo leaned over near me and said, "That's why no skimmers. So they don't hit any fliers."

She was probably right. A scattering of low- to medium-sized buildings grew in size, and we turned onto a road that circled them. Twice, the vehicle stopped and people clambered off, walking toward the center of the circle. The third time we stopped, Marcus gestured us all off. "We're here. Follow me."

The one common thing about ship's quarters is they're small. My body had been cramped into tiny beds forever. As much as I love ships and flying, I felt happy as Marcus led us unerringly to a tall house with big windows and long balconies. Inside, half the building was open air with high ceilings. The walls cupped at least four stories of stepped rooms and hallways and living spaces, like blocks stacked artfully inside a much bigger room. The wide stairs had low handrails. Most floors and doors and window-work looked like wood, with some smoother substance painted on the walls. The gold guest house wasn't gold, except for the roof. Inside, the ceilings were sky blue, the walls off-white, and the floors brown and tan, all of the colors muted and restful.

Alicia stopped right behind me in the doorway, blocking Dianne and Ming so they frowned at her. She looked reverent. "It was designed for fliers."

Easy to see she was right. "But the furniture will fit regular people." For example, the kitchen table, which was in front of us, had normal chairs that made no provision for sweeping wings.

Alicia took a deep breath. "It smells good. Like garden and fresh air and wood."

"Go on." Ming's voice was edged with irritation. "Don't block the door all day."

"Oh, sorry." Alicia sounded as distracted as Ming sounded driven.

I took her by the arm. "Come on, let's choose a room."

"I want a window."

"Fine." And so we ended up with the top room, which would take the longest to get to and from, and be the most awkward for taking Sasha out in the middle of the night. It had a floor-to-ceiling window, twice as tall as we stood. Maybe Alicia would feel more like a bird here. The bedroom had a door that closed, but the sitting room beside it was so open a flier could probably just land in it.

When we got behind the closed door, I nuzzled the back of Alicia's neck, but she just made a little mock-moan and started unpacking. So I settled for watching her get dressed in midnight blue leggings with a silver shirt I'd never seen before. It appeared to be shot through with multicolored threads, and I realized they were data receivers like the physical data threads I'd needed earlier in my life. The material felt soft and pliable under my fingers, but strong, so it would take a knife blade to rip.

"I got it while you were with Marcus." A slight sadness crept over her face. "The threads are just decorative. They'd work at home, but not here."

"It looks good on you."

I picked my blue captain's coat, even though it was a little worse for wear. It would be nice to complement each other.

An hour later, Marcus led us, now clean and well-dressed, into the late afternoon brightness. We headed through wide streets toward a park in the center of town. Or maybe it *was* the town. We passed dwellings fit for regular humans or fliers on the way in, and approached a grassy area that had clearly been designed for fliers. Trees like the ones at the edge of the field near the spaceport ringed the area, for defense or privacy or maybe even convenience, since fliers sat on them here and there, deep in conversation. I touched a copper-brown trunk as we passed in under an archway, and found it hard, and oddly warm. Engineered living thing or simply made thing? I couldn't tell. Because Marcus had asked me to, I kept myself too tightly shielded to read its data signature.

Through the archway, perches and sculptures designed for fliers to rest on lay scattered about. Even though their bodies were our size, or at most a head or two taller, the fliers took up far more space, needing room above and below for their wings to rest, and at the side to spread them. If this was their home, it was big and open and roomy, but not very private.

Marcus hadn't exaggerated their finery. As he led us, weaving toward the center of the gathering place, Alicia and I gaped at the jewels and glittering robes all around us. Green and gold ribbons. Blue ribbons. About half had long hair braided with more ribbon and beads and various charms, and the other half had short hair, probably in both cases to keep it from covering their eyes when they flew. Up close, their wings were even more varied in color and shape than they had appeared when in the air, some nearly translucent and others thick and dark, almost oily looking.

Apparently the people who designed them experimented regularly. The thought made me stiff with anger, but I hid it as well as I could. Beauty and freedom were not the same thing.

The air smelled like water and nuts and the thick perfume of flowers, which grew or stood in vases in every direction. The fliers seemed obsessed with flowers.

Caro raced up to a man with iridescent green wings, and he shook them softly, so that a small feather fell out, just the size of a child's fingers. He smiled as Caro picked it up and clutched it to her chest. It was thin and fine, fluffy, and certainly nothing like the long pinion Matriana had so reverently handed to Marcus. But all the same, maybe it would bring Caro luck.

Although a few fliers sat silently, probably linked into data given the vaguely vacant looks on their faces, most were engaged in animated conversations. When we came close, their melodic voices fell and slowed, and they watched us with curious eyes and hopeful faces. I remembered the fliers I'd seen walking free on Silver's Home. People had flowed around them as if they were rocks, with no real acknowledgement of the stiff-gaited beings with the beautiful faces wearing sour, pained expressions. Seeing those unfortunate beings had in no way prepared me for Lopali.

Here, in this place they were meant for, the fliers looked more like the joyful statue we'd seen in the memory garden near the spaceport at Li, the day I first met my father. Alicia clutched my hand as we walked, but said little. Her eyes were wide, and I hoped she didn't already regret her promise. The fliers were so beautiful I understood her desire, but so alien that the idea of transforming from the pale beings we were into fliers seemed unimaginable.

If it was supposed to be a feast, I didn't see anyone eating.

The long string of us, led by Marcus, began to climb up a hill so steep there were occasional steps, five or ten risers at a time, between the flatter parts. The population of fliers was greater here and, if possible, even better decorated. And of course, since this was a genemod world, almost all of them looked young. I glimpsed one flier with gray hair and droopy pale blue wings, but generally we might have been surrounded by a flock of teens.

There were no children except for ours. There were plenty of wingless humans and surely they had children, but apparently they did not have them with them. Although none of the fliers was quite as obvious as the one who'd dropped the feather for Caro, heads followed the children's movements.

The last set of steps stopped at a large flat expanse with circles of evenly placed perches, almost all occupied. Below the perches lay row upon row of tables piled high with trays of food: steaming hot dishes, bowls of vegetables and meats, soups, nuts, plates of bread, and sparkling colored drinks. The brightest green and gold grapes I'd ever seen, practically glowing with juice. Even though most of the tables were tall, with what amounted to raised walkways for the convenience of fliers, there was one at our height, decorated with sprays of blue, violet, and yellow flowers between the dishes.

Here and there, humans stood near the tables, obviously waiting for something.

Or for us.

As soon as we got close, Matriana and a male flier landed on low perches in front of us, wings cocked up a bit to keep the tips from trailing on the ground. She pointed to her fellow flier, who was dark-haired and light-eyed, with skin the color of cream. His wings were pale orange with striking maroon tips. He stood taller than Matriana, taller than any of us, and he reminded me of Marcus—he was comfortable in his skin, and powerful, and he knew it. "This is Daniel."

Marcus nodded formally. "Pleased to meet you."

Daniel spoke equally formally, "Welcome, Marcus."

He looked at me next. "And this is Joseph." A statement of fact, not a question.

I nodded, struggling to return his gaze as calmly as I could. "Pleased to meet you."

"And who is Chelo?" Daniel asked.

Chelo stepped forward. "Me." She cocked her head at the flier but stood her ground, and I would bet I was the only one in our group who could tell by her stance and voice that she was nervous. Her response was unusually bold. "Why do you want to know? What am I to you?"

Matriana smiled, and her eyes softened. "If you hadn't been left behind, and your brother hadn't rescued you from your father's war, you all wouldn't be here today. It is not often an unknown young woman causes such big events. It is a bit of fairy tale, yes?"

Chelo stiffened and gave the majestic flier an even and slightly disapproving look. "If it is a legend, it is a sad one. Many people died."

"We all have pain." Matriana turned to Marcus. "And who else have you brought to Lopali?"

As soon as every single person in our party had been painstakingly introduced, and sorted as from Fremont or from Silver's Home, at least by introduction, Matriana gestured toward the low table. We took plates and filled them, following Marcus past the tables to a ring of mixed seats, short for humans and tall for fliers, with single or double steps they could walk up so they sat with their wing tips above the ground.

Other humans, built like the fliers but wingless, joined us at the table.

The human seats were benches fit for three or four at a time, and Marcus gestured for me and Kayleen to sit beside him, for Chelo and

Liam and the children to take another bench, and from there Alicia and Induan joined Jenna and Tiala. Dianne and Paloma sat together on their own bench, heads together, talking in low tones. I puzzled over Marcus's last choice, pairing Bryan and Ming. Bryan had been fascinated with Ming on the way to Fremont, in the *Creator*, when we first woke her after her stowaway job. We hadn't trusted her then, and he'd volunteered to watch her anytime. Now, they sat closer to each other than they needed to, heads bent in quiet conversation. He did seem to be watching her, but it wasn't exactly with suspicion. Other memories surfaced. This wasn't new; I'd been distracted. Maybe it wasn't good. I needed to ask Chelo about it.

Wingless humans stood in a quiet ring around us.

After years of ship's food, the variety of smells and textures felt overwhelming. The grapes were as good as their bright, translucent skin promised and the breads melted in my mouth. While we ate, the tall benches around us remained eerily empty. Fliers began to fill them only after the waiting wingless whisked our empty plates away and filled our hands with glasses full of cool amber liquid that smelled of honey. The arriving fliers were given glasses, too.

Marcus whispered into my ear, since I was still shielded and couldn't talk silently to him. "This is the Convening Council of Lopali. The primary decision makers. They've come from all over the planet."

I looked closely at them. Most appeared friendly. One woman waved. A few looked simply appraising, like we were a curiosity. One or two seemed bored.

A tall blond flier who chose a seat beside Bryan and Ming glared in our direction, her lips a fine, pursed line and her brows drawn together. Because the flier's eyes were wide-set it was hard to tell if she was specifically looking at us, or if her malevolent gaze was meant for Matriana, who sat close to Marcus. Either way, it made me shiver. I tried to memorize her distinguishing features: long blond braids, blue eyes that matched great round blue circles on her wings, which were otherwise a pale purplish blue. I would recognize her if I saw her again.

When all of the perches were full, Matriana held up her glass, and the other fliers held up their glasses. I started to raise mine but Marcus hissed, "Watch me."

His hand was down.

Matriana's voice was amplified by something I couldn't see, maybe even loud enough to be heard across all the space between here and the ring of perch trees. "We welcome strangers into our midst tonight. Most importantly, we welcome Joseph, Chelo, and Kayleen from Silver's Home, who are renegade and cast away, and have landed on our shores after a long flight."

The fliers answered her back, each softly but together a thicket of voices. "Welcome."

All the fliers sipped.

Matriana continued. "We dream that these three will help us take away the pain in our heart. We dream they will help us fill our emptiness."

The actual pain that tinged her voice, the yearning, made me want to help her more than anything.

The answering chorus sounded bittersweet and hopeful. "May they remove our pain."

Kayleen grasped my hand. I noticed Marcus had raised his glass, so we all did, Kayleen and I still holding hands and using our free ones for the toast. Across the circle from us, Bryan and Ming were in the same pose. Marcus's voice was as amplified as Matriana's as he spoke. "In the name of peace, we hope our skills will help make you whole."

He leaned down and whispered in my ear, and Ming whispered in Bryan's, and Chelo and Liam simply followed along. "In the name of peace."

Chelo smiled broadly. It was a good toast for her.

Matriana's voice rang out again. "Once we are free, we will fight in the name of peace."

"Once we are free."

"We will win peace for us all."

"Once we are free."

"In the name of peace."

We drank. The liquid was thick and sweet, but not alcoholic, missing even the sweet clarity of col.

Of all the fliers in the circle around us, only the blonde with the blue eyes and blue-eyed feathers looked sour. But one sour face made a difference, and I could almost feel an exhalation of relief when she pushed up off her perch and made a great showy circle above our heads before flying off, her light wings visible like mist for a long time until the dusk sky folded her up inside of it, and we all finally looked back at each other.

Music sprouted from somewhere over near the tables—drums and wind instruments and a deep hum that seemed to set the inside of my bones vibrating. Small talk started to rush across the circle, and it finally began to feel like a party.

ALICIA: THE AFTER PARTY

Induan and I sat side by side on the bench in the circle of fliers. We were both visible, but who would see us in the midst of so much beauty? She slapped me lightly on the arm. "Alicia. Close your mouth or a bug will land in it."

I did, but I couldn't stop watching. The last few fliers who had participated directly in the ceremony rose smoothly from their perches, wings rustling the cooling air. A man with blue wings landed on the grass near us, leaning forward so as to keep the tips of his wings off the ground. A slender pink-winged woman landed on a stone, standing comfortably, talking to a few of the people with no wings. She belonged in a painting or an animation instead of in the real world, and I wanted to touch her to see if she was real. Three others flew away entirely, fast. After all of the perches were clear, I stood and stretched, finally, belatedly, looking for Joseph. I saw his back as he and Marcus walked away, lost in conversation.

He should have looked for me first. At least to say he had to ignore me for a while longer. There should have been infinite time to be together on space ships, but there hadn't been. Not once Marcus found us. Some of the joy I'd taken in seeing the fliers leaked out as he walked away.

"Shake it off," Induan said. "He has duties. You and me, we're closer to nobody. That means we're free to explore."

"Yeah." It'd be nice if she were wrong once in a while. Not that it hurt to have her on my side. She'd told me to dress even more outrageously than Marcus had suggested, and she'd done the same. She wore white leggings and a white lacy blouse with long, belled sleeves, everything so stark her white skin looked almost normal. She and her outfit took on a bit of a glow in the fading light. We'd both belted on boosters for our invisibility mods, to help them work with our clothes.

She did not seem as beauty-bit as I felt, so I asked her, "Aren't they the prettiest people?" I remembered how awkward the first real fliers I saw looked, waddling through the full gravity of Silver's Home, pain lining their faces. "I mean here, where they belong."

Induan's laugh came out kind. "You've got Space Ship Shock."

"Huh?"

"You know. When you've been locked up in a big tin can for years and you finally get onto a planet and everything looks big and beautiful?"

But it was. "Did you feel like that when you got to Fremont?"

"Until I realized everything had sharp edges."

It was my turn to laugh. "That should have taken five minutes."

"Two."

I looked around. The ground was rolling grass, nano-bot–trimmed like in the parks on Silver's Home. Purple and yellow flowers held their petals open to catch the last rays of sun, and beside them, a line of white flowers had already closed for the night. Hills rolled away in all directions. We were high enough up to see the humped bellies of the closest ones, all dotted with people and fliers and gardens. "I don't see edges here. The fliers are beautiful."

Induan smiled faintly, then nodded, both unconvincing. "Fliers make strange allies. They're unpredictable in interworld politics."

I shrugged. "Can you blame them? They can't even walk on some of the worlds."

"Don't underestimate them."

Oh no. They must be powerful. But more than power, they had grace. Calm. The first one I'd seen had been a statue, and no dead thing had ever exuded so much calm and peace coupled with action and movement. And here? Live? They were more beautiful than the artist had made the statue. I wanted to be one.

We snacked on a few of the richly scented grapes that exploded sugar into our mouths. No one bothered us, although from time to time I caught a flier or a wingless looking at us out of the corner of their eye, or offering a small smile. It felt weird to be watched. "Let's take a walk. See what they're like in the wild."

She understood my unspoken meaning.

We found a bathroom and slipped in. We waited for two normal-looking women, and a tall slender man who looked like he should have wings, to leave before we turned our mods on. I liked switching on in bathrooms; the nano had to think about how to re-flect the wall behind us into the mirrors. It took enough time that for the space of a breath or two I looked infinite.

Outside, we climbed invisibly, and cautiously, down the hill. In-duan led me through groups of fliers and around flower beds, both of us careful how we set our feet. I didn't want to get caught. The fli-ers might feel spied on, and Marcus would be mad for sure.

As full dark fell, globe-shaped lights brightened. In a few cases, groups of fliers sat on rock formations, some filled with crystalline structures like the geodes we used to bring back to trade with the townies on Fremont, except twenty or thirty times as big. Some crys-tals were artificially lit from within, as if fires burned inside the faceted stones.

A few fliers wore swirls of tiny ribbons braided in their hair or woven into necklaces, lit at the ends so the fliers who wore them glowed. I didn't dare talk since we didn't know how good the flier's hearing might be. Instead, it seemed like we glided silently through a fairyland of wonders, Induan and I holding hands so we didn't lose each other.

Farther away from the central hill, there were fewer and fewer wingless. The few we did see all moved with purpose, bringing plates and bowls of seeds and breads and grapes to knots of fliers lost in conversation.

Induan pulled me to a low mound of rounded rocks. "Watch the regular humans," she whispered into my ear. "Tell me what you see. Quietly."

Twice in the ship, we'd been caught talking while invisible. I leaned my head into hers. We could talk quieter if we touched skulls. "That one's tall, like he was meant to be a flier but no one put wings on him. The woman over there must be an original human. She's no bigger than me."

"What are they doing?"

"Well . . . they're waiting on the fliers." I'd noticed that already. "They don't look unhappy. I mean, look, they're all smiling. I'd wait on the fliers to be near them."

"You're addled. Do you think the fliers are better than you?"

She wanted me to say no, but I couldn't get the word out. "Maybe."

Her hair tickled my cheek as she shook her head. When she'd stilled again, she said, "The Wingmakers designed them to make you feel inferior. They're taller and prettier and they can do something all humans want to do; fly by themselves. They also made them martyrs, and slaves. Since they can't have their own babies, the guild controls both an income flow and their culture. The Wingmakers created a being no one would ever kill, so they could watch it grow. They even made Lopali first, designing it for the fliers while the fliers were cartoons on a drawing board."

She almost sounded like she admired that, and yet disapproved. But then, it was probably a good strategy, and Induan liked a good chess move. "Isn't that what they want Joseph and Marcus to change?" I asked.

"If no one kills them first. If they can do it. Marcus is good, and so's your boyfriend, but the fliers guild isn't exactly bad."

I hadn't thought of Joseph maybe getting killed for this. Induan tugged on my hand, the angle telling me she'd stood. She started us walking toward a small crowd of fliers. Always the strategist, she'd said something shocking, and now she was making sure I couldn't respond right away.

She led me around the crowd, and stopped with us standing between a flower bed and a rock, which probably meant no one would step into us by accident. I didn't say anything, just stopped and listened.

A few of the fliers' voices were raised. We weren't terribly close, but I caught a few words here and there. I heard Joseph's name. Every once in a while, whole sentences would emerge clearly from the conversation. "Meddling . . ." cut off by "Daniel's out of his mind. He can't commit . . ." and then someone else saying, ". . . can't fight."

Induan's hand tightened on mine.

"There's almost enough of us," a white-winged flier said.

"Patience," said another one, and then too many people were talking at once again. I wanted to go closer. I stepped over the flowers, but Induan pulled me back so hard I almost fell.

I couldn't ask her what she was doing. We needed to know what the argument was about. I tried again, tugging her gently in the direction of the group.

She pulled on me so hard my shoulder hurt.

We were both strong. But she was better—she locked my arm behind me and walked me a few meters away before hissing, "Quiet. Let's go."

I started to answer her but she slid a hand over my mouth. "Save the risks for another time. We can't get caught tonight."

On the way back to our own people, I kept my eye out for a feather to give Joseph. Maybe he was going to need the luck.

CHELO: MADE THINGS

After the heavy feast, I tossed and turned so much I was afraid the children would wake. The ceiling felt far above my head and dark. When I did graze the top of sleep, my half-dreaming self imagined fliers inside the guest house, battering to get out, feathers falling all around me, the images so real I sneezed and startled myself awake again.

Even lying awake, my imagination replayed what I knew about the fliers over and over. Their beauty, the sadness in their ask-and-answer formal ceremony. The way giant wings made all of their movements foreign, their very balance occurring around different fulcrums. Theoretically, they were like us. But I did not believe that for a moment. Surely there was a point when genetic engineering made a different race entirely, and the fliers were there.

I gave up before dawn and untangled myself from the pile on the bed, lifting Liam's hand from my shoulder and sliding Jherrel's small arm from around my waist. As I fumbled for my shoes, I made a mental note to ask for small beds for the kids. There appeared to be plenty of everything in this town. In fact, since leaving Fremont I'd seen richness beyond dreams everywhere, even on the least well-kept of the ships. I was beginning to understand both why people from the Five Worlds found the settlers on Fremont hard to sympathize with, and why the original humans at home mistrusted the rich and almost unnatural people from other planets.

And of course, we six were both.

Maybe that kept me up. The idea that this foreign place could become home.

I succeeded in getting out of the door to our quarters without waking anyone else, and crept slowly down the wide, steep stairs toward the kitchen. I wanted to go outside, but I didn't understand the rules we might be under.

This wasn't home yet, not if I couldn't just open the door and walk outside. I almost did it anyway, but that would be a trick of Alicia's. A soft scrape of spoon against cup suggested someone sitting in the dark kitchen. Maybe Jenna—she often woke early on the various ships, and we'd shared col and quiet many mornings.

Instead of Jenna, the reserved Islan, Dianne, sat so quietly in the kitchen that I didn't notice her until I reached the table. She smiled at me, and silently got up and poured me a cup of col. A pile of red, blue, and purple fruits I'd seen at the feast last night adorned the middle of the table. I took a red one with smooth, taut skin. I expected it to taste a bit like redberry from home, but instead it reminded me I was in a completely alien place.

Thin and tall, Dianne moved awkwardly, without Ming's or even Jenna's grace. She brought the cup to me and sat down. As we breakfasted in silence, I watched her angular face, which gave away very little of what she was thinking. She'd never really talked to me, not outside of groups, and she was usually quiet. But I'd seen her take charge well a few times, and when she did talk, she usually said something intelligent.

The sky was just beginning to lighten when we finished. People would be up soon.

Dianne caught my attention with a raised finger. "I'm going out," she whispered. "Will you come?"

"Sure." I took both our cups to the sink. She held the door open, closing it quietly after we both passed through. The graying of the light in the window had been a bit of a tease; it was dark enough that I could barely see my feet. Even though I had been the tallest woman on Fremont, I had to take three steps to Dianne's two. We walked quickly in spite of the near dark, and in a few minutes I wasn't cold anymore. "Have you been here before?"

She nodded. "Once. And of course, to the Autocracy where I was born, and once, on vacation with my parents, to Joy Heaven." She glanced at me, "And to Fremont." She knew this was the only place I'd been except home. "Do you get homesick?" she asked.

Why did it matter? We'd never go back. "I won't be once I know where we belong."

"I'm seventy-seven, and I still don't know where I belong."

After a while, I asked, "Why are Islas and Silver's Home fighting?"

We paused briefly at a fork, where she chose the path toward the city, clearly intent on some particular destination. "Pride." She fell silent for a few steps before she went on. "Islas believes that Silver's Home is experimenting too loosely with genetics, playing God too much. They want rules around the choices that are made, and to be able to veto some things. The Islan government believes they are supposed to chart Islas's destiny, and that what Silver's Home does interferes with their control. They dislike it when people like Marcus or your brother do things they say are God's prerogative."

"God?"

"A power no one can see or touch or taste, but that some people believe in with all their hearts." Her voice was slightly bitter, but she had been born and raised on Islas, and left it for Silver's Home. She took a sip of water. "Not many people really believe in God these days, that's not the real issue. It's a question of how much we should alter the created world. Since God's existence can't be disproved, he or she is a convenient tool for powerful people to use to pretend they are subject to something even more powerful."

"What has Joseph done that this power might do?"

"Nothing yet. But once he helps the fliers, Islas may declare him an enemy."

So she thought he and Marcus could do this thing. "But don't the fliers deserve help?"

"Of course they do. They're slaves. They're beloved and reviled, controlled and yet sought out. Silver's Home sees them as the product of its creative output, Islas as abominations. If they become able to bear their own children, then they'll be able to take charge of their own destiny. They'll be a race of their own instead of manufactured things." She paused and we walked a bit more, the soft earth almost silent under our feet. "If they find the strength to claim freedom."

I remembered my strange dreams of fliers battering the walls of our house, trying to get out. "They already seem so different I don't think they're human. What does it really change?"

We stepped over a little stream that ran straight and true in its banks, sliding through rocks covered with mosses that the rising light showed as bright green and a deep, nearly purple, blue. "For one, it will challenge the Court of the Five Worlds."

"What's that?"

"There are rules and laws that govern commerce between the worlds. Some define who has what rights, and as long as the fliers are human, they have our rights. If they aren't human, Islas will try to give them fewer rights. And there aren't any fliers on the Court to speak for them. Silver's Home does now, but they might not if we succeed."

So neither side would help them? That was why they were neutral? I chewed on my lower lip. All of the powers in the Five Worlds seemed so delicately balanced. "Why don't they have a voice?"

"There aren't enough of them. There are only a few hundred thousand fliers on all the worlds, so despite their visibility, it's a small contingent compared to either of the big planets. Lopali has a seat, but it's held by a human who doesn't like them."

Well, of all people, my family and I understood how you could be more capable but have less rights than the people around you. Fremont had tried to enslave us. "The world isn't fair."

The first morning birds began to sing. Dianne seemed to be listening for a moment, and then she said, "The fliers are as much a symbol as you are."

There it was again. "So—why does everyone talk about me like they know my story?"

Dianne stopped me with a firm hand on my shoulder. Her gaze made me feel small and young and vulnerable. "Because you're a story. The Five Worlds are an information economy—new stories fill up a whole planet in moments, and spread across us all in months. Joseph was a story before you. Islas is using your story, and frankly so are we. The Port Authority, who helped start the stories about Joseph, are trying to suppress them now, which is like fueling a fire, since everyone hates the Authority except the Authority itself."

I swallowed hard, watching the rising light make shadows on her face, and struggling to think about what she said and not just get angry. "You're using my story? Our story? Why?"

"Well, you don't understand our worlds yet, even though you came from here. So you can't be trusted to know how to spin your stories. For now, you must leave that to us." Her face and voice softened a little. "So think about how you hated it when the Star Mercenaries killed the people on Fremont. I could see your heart in your face—you loved those people. Even the ones who didn't love you."

"I don't want anyone killed, anywhere."

"Well, I left Islas even though I loved it, because I thought too freely for them. You left Artistos on Fremont because you were persecuted and told to mind the leaders. You went to another island; I went to another planet."

"That wasn't exactly how it happened!" I protested.

"But that's the story. And that's the heart of it, right?"

Not really. But good enough for her. How could I possibly communicate the way the West Band of roamers loved us while the East Band didn't, or how some would spit on us but some would help us? So I just said, "Sure."

"It's the same for me. I couldn't bear to live on Islas anymore, couldn't bear the control. I had to leave. I love Silver's Home. It's full of brave and clever people, even if some of them have too much power. I don't want anyone to die in either place. So you see? I'm just like you."

I'd reserve judgment about that for the moment. In fact, I was pretty angry, although I bit my tongue. The idea of my family's stories being spread throughout the Five Worlds made my skin crawly. We were being used in a way I didn't understand and across places I had never been. My life had been fed to strangers.

We walked over halfway to the forest of perch-trees before I felt like I had enough control to respond. "I'd like to see how these stories are told. I want to read them."

"Your brother can find them for you." Dianne took a few long steps to get into the lead, and then turned to the right before reaching the perch-trees. I followed, still unsure of her. Joseph was not, but as far as I could tell he was willing to trust her because Marcus did, and I wasn't yet sure I trusted Marcus.

The path we followed looked like it might circle the whole town. From time to time, other paths, some dirt, branched away.

The sun, the whole orb now above the horizon, began to splay near-horizontal beams through the trees. It touched her eyes, then mine, so I held up a hand to shade them. Last night, as we walked into town and then to the feast, Lopali had seemed wild. This morning, it didn't feel wild. Sure, I noted grass and trees and rocks, bushes and butterflies, dirt and, once, a thin stream. Flowers grew. Everything was big and wavy, the stalks thinner, but that was easy enough to figure—the lower gravity changed the way the plants shaped themselves. We'd seen that in the ship's gardens. But something else about the landscape bothered me, even though I couldn't tell what it was, like a name on the tip of a tongue. "How long has Lopali been settled? Is everything here native?"

I couldn't see her face since she was in front of me, but it sounded like she was laughing quietly. "Nothing is native. This was a dead rock five hundred years ago."

I blinked, looking more carefully. No thorns. No trip-vine had struggled to entangle my feet, nor insect bitten me. "It's all a garden?"

"That's one way to think of it."

So complex. "Did it come from somewhere? The ideas or the plants or something? How does anyone get a whole ecosystem right?"

"They don't always."

"What about Silver's Home? Is it made everywhere?"

"Mostly." She stopped for a moment, looking around, and I imagined she was trying to see it all new, the way I saw it. She shook her head. "Silver's Home had a natural ecosystem that man could live on with help, and so did Islas. But they've been remade. Silver's Home gets redesigned all the time. Islas changes slowly and with great deliberation, and even has some places on it that haven't ever been changed. Lopali and Paradise were built from moons, and then set into the best possible planetary orbits around their suns, and Joy Heaven was manufactured from nothing."

Wow. As I looked around me, every flower and stone and bird looked and sounded perfect. By now, I'd decided the perch-trees weren't natural, but I had thought everything else was. When Dianne paused for a moment, I bent down and plucked a fist-sized blue flower and crushed its stem. It bled light green water onto my fingers. The petals bruised if I squeezed them. I brought the flower up near my nose, inhaling a faint, sweet scent.

Dianne raised an eyebrow.

"It's as real as I am," I said.

"Of course it is." She appeared to be looking for something specific near the ground. Finally, beside three small stone sculptures of leaves, she turned down a thin dirt path. It wound through trees and ended at a wooden door to a smallish house that looked old. "Seeyan?" she called. "Are you here?"

The door opened almost immediately and a tall chestnut-haired beauty threw herself into Dianne's arms. "You did come back."

Dianne's return hug was more reserved than Seeyan's, but for just a second I thought I spotted a tear in Dianne's eye. But then she blinked and turned away for a short moment, and the next sight she let me have of her face showed her usual control. She disentangled herself from the other woman's arms, and I got my first good look at Seeyan. She had the broad shoulders and wide-set eyes of a flier, but no wings. Her eyes were a deep brown, with reddish glints that matched her hair. Unlike everyone at the feast last night, she was dressed simply, in a loose flowing dress of pale green. She gave me a little bow, and said, "Pleased to meet you, Chelo. I'm Seeyan."

I tensed for a second, then held out my hand. It wasn't her fault she'd heard of me. "Pleased to meet you."

"Would you come in?" she asked.

Dianne glanced at me, her eyes encouraging me to accept Seeyan's invitation. Why not? If the children needed anything, Kayleen or Liam could manage for a bit. "I'd be happy to."

Inside, the house was small, essentially three rooms: a bathroom, a large kitchen, and a single room that seemed to serve as bedroom and living room and study all at once. Plants and leaves hung from the ceiling in the kitchen in small bunches, drying, but still filling the air with pale, savory scents. Paloma would have a hundred questions for her, and I immediately made a note to myself to try and bring her here. This small place looked and felt more like home than anywhere I'd been on Lopali so far, and maybe it would help Paloma feel less lost. Was that why Dianne had brought me here? Because it was like home?

Seeyan offered to make us tea. When we nodded, she looked pleased, and clipped bits of the hanging herbs and placed them in mesh bags. The bags went into cups shaped like flowers, and she poured water into the cups with a ritualistic grace.

Even though I'd have sworn she poured in cold water, the cup was warm to the touch when Seeyan handed it to me, and then moments later it was so hot I set it down on the table.

As soon as we were all seated, Dianne looked at Seeyan. "Can you please tell Chelo your story, like you told it to me?"

Seeyan looked out of the window, then down at the table for a moment, then back at Dianne. "Will it help?"

"Perhaps. Chelo will be helping her brother."

"I will." Seeyan dropped her gaze to her slender hands and took a deep breath. Dianne leaned back, looking relaxed, watching us both. Seeyan started talking, her voice soft and her words slow in coming. "The first thing I remember is waking up inside a big space with tall walls and a high ceiling and a floor painted green. A woman held up a mirror, and I could see myself. I was a little girl, and I had wings on my back."

She stopped and smiled at me, watching for a reaction. "Go on," I said. "I'd like to hear."

"My wings were a soft yellow, with brown on the ends and a red stripe. Even to this day, I haven't seen any adult fliers like me. After a while, there was also a little boy with the same wings, and they called us brother and sister." She sipped her tea, gazing through me as if I weren't even there. One side of her mouth quirked up. "His name was Will, and he and I learned to open our wings and fan them and to jump up and start flying together. We learned this in a big cage on a ship. I didn't know it was a ship then, or that there were fifty other flier children on board.

"Will and my teacher, Siona, were the only people I ever saw. And since I didn't like Siona, Will was my only friend. We talked to each other almost all the time, and we shared the same locked-up bedroom, and since that was all we knew it didn't seem strange at all." She looked at me, as if shy for a reaction.

I smiled, hoping it would encourage her.

Dianne gave her a go-on gesture, hurrying her back into her story.

Seeyan's words came faster. "Eventually, Will and I could both jump up inside the ship and fly around, almost to the ceiling. Siona was pleased. One day, she took us into a different cage—a big open cylinder with dirt on the bottom and some trees. She told us it was a park, and invited us to fly.

"We flew."

She smiled wistfully.

"The park was a beautiful flyspace, with more open air than we'd ever seen. I soared and banked and turned, and I loved the wind against my wings. It was hard—and my wings and back hurt after each flight. For six weeks we went there every day and flew, just me and Will. And after every flight, Siona rubbed ointment into our long wing bones. She tugged and twisted our wings and shoulders, hurting us, all the time whispering she was helping us fly.

"Will had more trouble than I did. His body was heavier than mine, and his wings were the same size, so he sank when I glided, and he couldn't follow me all the way to the top. Siona saw this, and she promised he would get stronger as he got older, and we'd both be able to fly as high as we wanted."

She paused and sipped her tea, and her gaze fastened somewhere through the window. She took three deep breaths before she started again. "They started changing the conditions on us, making us heavier. I didn't know it then, but we had started flying in almost no gravity. They began adding and adding, with the idea that we would be strong enough to fly here by the time the transport ship arrived.

"But we were only halfway when Will fell out of the sky one day. He just fell." She swallowed and licked her lips. "One of his wings broke." She pointed to a picture on the wall of a flier with widespread wings, and touched a place halfway along one broad wing. "I could still hear him screaming as he went down, and worse, his silence when he landed."

She fell quiet and I imagined her hearing her brother's screams again.

"I never saw him again. I asked, and I cried, but Siona would never answer me."

I wanted to strangle Siona. Maybe I'd get to meet her some day.

"After that, I was afraid to fly. Siona was gentle with me at first, but I kept seeing Will fall. I knew that if I flew, I'd die, too. I thought maybe if I fell and my wings were cut off, I'd find Will."

"Did you?" I asked.

She shook her head. "Of course not. I know the statistics now. There were fifty of us on that ship. Every one of us cost the families who wanted us over two years of work. Flier families chose us before we were born, even helped choose traits like hair color and eye color and the tint of our wings. Of the fifty that were made, twenty are fliers now, seven are like me, and twenty-three died."

I'd heard about the death rate; Seeyan's story made it real.

"Will and I had been meant to be brother and sister to a family that lives in Oshai, near the spaceport. I see them sometimes, and I want to cry every time I do."

"So Will died?" I asked her, imagining Joseph dead.

She nodded and got up to get more water for her tea. In spite of how I could see that telling her story affected her by the look in her eyes and hear it in the cadence of her voice, there was an ethereal grace to her movements.

"So what do you do now?"

She smiled. "What they tell me to. I'm a Keeper. That means I get to live here, and watch over the land between me and the next Keeper's plotline. It's about as far as I can walk for two hours in every direction except the town."

"What do you watch for?"

She frowned. "Death. Imbalances. Unwanted evolution. A plant that grows too fast, or too slow, too high or too wide. Keepers also manage the aesthetics of plant and stone—what is placed next to what." Again, she looked out the window. "I'm not a very important Keeper yet and this is only a small plot meant for people like me, and not for spiritual growth, except in the way that all things are for truth. It's a garden of the town, not a garden of the soul."

I wondered what a garden of the soul looked like.

"If I become accomplished, I might get to work in the gardens we make for visitors."

"Do you like being a Keeper?"

She shrugged. "All fliers live with few choices. It would be easier if I could also fly."

"Well, I can't fly either, so you're no more failed than me."

"It's different."

"How old are you?"

Dianne interrupted me. "It's a rude question."

"No," Seeyan said, "I'll answer. I'm only twenty-five. People like me, well, we only live to be thirty or forty. Our bodies were meant for wings."

Twenty minutes later, Dianne and I were on our way back. I understood why she brought me to Seeyan. How could I help but want Joseph to succeed now? Not that it would actually help Seeyan. But she was a pseudo-slave the way we had been once, except she was enslaved for lack of abilities, while we'd been in trouble for having too many.

"I like her," I told Dianne. "But why won't she live longer?"

"Fliers have a faster metabolism than most people. Even with the nanotechnology and drugs that they need to stay healthy, they don't live as long as the rest of us can."

The implication soured my stomach. "So they don't give their own failed children the tools for a long life?"

"No." The set of her jaw told me she approved of the situation as much as I did.

But I did like Seeyan, particularly her grace and fluidity. "Can I go back there sometime? I can find my way."

"If we have enough time here."

"Why wouldn't we have time?"

"The Port Authority is looking for us. The Star Mercenaries may look for us. Someday, we'll be found."

"And then what?"

"Then we go someplace else."

I want my children to grow up under a sky.

The sun warmed everything now, the colors of full morning golder than back home. Even though everything around me had been manufactured and placed, I looked for small senses of the wild, and found them. We passed through copses of trees, bright wildflower meadows, each with a stream, and back into trees. Sometimes blue flowers stuck up from fields of red, or one plant waved above my head while the others like it grew to my elbows.

Far above, fliers flashed by and, closer to the ground, a flock of small bright songbirds with blue heads and green wings flickered from tree to tree.

In front of me, Dianne gasped and stopped, her back rigid. I stopped, too.

Just ahead of us both, a flier blocked the path. I didn't recall seeing him at the feast, but we had seen hundreds. His wings were an iridescent, shining black, his eyes as dark. He wore plain black boots over his long feet instead of the usual jeweled creations. His hair was short and simple, too, and his only jewelry was a band of blue leather around his neck, with a small, single pale blue feather hanging from it. His luck?

He stepped forward and spoke over Dianne's shoulder, addressing me. "Chelo. It's not safe to wander the side roads here with the riff-raff."

Dianne tensed, but said nothing.

He didn't like Dianne because she was Islan? "Dianne is my friend. She left Islas."

His lips thinned, and puzzlement covered his face before disappearing back into the haughty look. He hadn't meant Dianne at all, but Seeyan. After a moment he nodded. "Well enough said. But out here, not everyone is friendly to us, which means they are no friend of yours. You are," he hesitated for a fraction of a second, "encouraged to stay in the gold guest house, in the area around it, in the city center, and wherever your brother goes."

"Encouraged" was not exactly a rule. I chewed on my upper lip for a moment. He stood taller than even Dianne, but would be no match for me on the ground. I would never have to match him in the air. So which choice? Stand down, and set him up as a keeper of mine, or risk angering someone of rank? I usually liked the middle, but there wasn't a clear one. Dianne drew in a breath and I spoke before she could speak. "Thank you for your kind consideration. I have enjoyed my morning walk, and I find Lopali to be very beautiful."

His body language did not relax.

"You know my name. I don't have that advantage."

He hesitated, and then said, "I'm glad you find it to your liking here. Just remember that a pretty façade can hide dangers. Not everyone wants you to fix what you came here to fix. I am speaking for your safety."

He lifted his wings, and just before he crouched and drew them down to take off, he said, "I am a protector."

Protecting us from? The wind of his wings in my face was warm.

We stood and watched him go. Dianne put a hand on my shoulder. "Well done."

"Thank you." I had been bred to be a diplomat, and I wasn't exactly sure I'd done the best possible thing, but I hadn't given all of my own power away. Maybe the middle didn't really work, and being strong worked better.

I hadn't expected to need strength so quickly.

JOSEPH: WAKING ON A WORLD

For the first time in years, the light of a sun poured in on my closed eyelids and drew a promise of heat across my skin. Alicia sat on the edge of the bed in her underwear and a thin shirt, her face bright with joy as she gazed out the window. When she saw my eyes open, she leaned over and kissed me, squeezing my hand before jumping up to stand at the windowsill. "Come look, honey. It's the most beautiful place in the world." She paused. "That makes no sense. Every place is the world to itself. It is the most beautiful place in the universe."

I joined her, close enough to smell sleep on her skin. Outside the window, fliers danced in the air, flocking in groups of three or five or even twenty. Some seemed to have places to go, and others to fly for joy. The ground was splashed everywhere with the bright colors of flowers, like the Grass Plains three days after the first spring rain. I heard birds, and here and there, butterflies moved almost in precision.

It was beautiful, in the way Marcus's garden on Silver's Home was beautiful, except the scale was entirely different. In spite of the harmony of the view, it made my skin crawl. I couldn't really get at why, but the words that came out of my mouth were, "Jenna was more interesting before her eye and her arm were fixed."

Alicia turned and gave me a funny look. "What do you mean by that?"

"I don't know. I guess Lopali looks too pretty, like a painting instead of a real thing." I pointed down at the grass below the window, where small mammals grazed in a herd of about ten. "Look—those animals aren't afraid of anything. They're not even watching for predators."

"So it's a safe place."

"Maybe."

"I think you just want to find something wrong."

I shook my head. "Maybe I just dreamed badly. Let's eat."

Alicia went with me to take Sasha out. The dog pranced about with her tail waving in the air. She looked better than she had all trip. So maybe I shouldn't feel so out of sorts. Maybe it was because I remained shielded per Marcus's instructions, and I missed the chaotic fullness of data. Or maybe I was feeling the pettier results of having become used to the role of ship's captain until we ran back into Marcus, who still saw me as student. Whatever the reason, I chafed.

Alicia must have felt my mood. She paced, then took my hand and led me to a tree, leaning me back against it and delivering a thoroughly improper kiss that echoed in my belly. Then she cocked her head and smiled. "Relax. I know you'd rather be on a ship, but this is better. There's a lot to see here. We can start today."

I didn't want to ruin that moment by reminding her that my day had been planned. I turned her around, so her back nestled against my chest, and rubbed her shoulders and nuzzled her hair, wallowing in the smell and feel of her, skin and girl and excitement.

By the time hunger drove us back inside, Jenna, Marcus, and Tiala sat at the table, laughing and joking with each other. Marcus cocked an eyebrow at me, a half grin on his face. "Sleeping in on the first day of work?"

It wasn't the first day of work. He'd had me in private classes on biology and chemistry and nano and genetics and politics since the day he found us at Jillian May. "The fliers' unborn won't mind giving me an hour of sleep, all the better to think about their problems with." I poured a cup of col from the pitcher on the table, and made a face when I tasted it. One of Marcus's favorites, bitter and a little like licorice root. "You'd have woken me up if you needed me."

"We're leaving soon."

Alicia looked over at Marcus. "Can I go? I can help him."

He gave her an appraising look. She wasn't his favorite influence on me, but I'd thought he'd come to terms with her some on the way here. His voice gave nothing away as he said, "No, I need Kayleen and Chelo."

She looked like she wanted to give him a few choice words before she seemed to notice the pleased look on his face and the silly, "got you" grin of his. Then she just cocked her head at him, waiting.

He nodded and said, "You have a surprise coming any moment."

"Huh?"

As if on cue, a flier glided up near the house and back-winged perfectly, coming quite close to the window. I admired his wings, so black they looked purple, and the way he moved like a precision machine. A flash of dark eyes and pale face, a glimpse of white teeth in a smile, and then he lifted himself up and disappeared from view.

Marcus pushed a button and a section of the roof slid open. The flier came through the hole in the ceiling, slowly and elegantly, and stopped close to the kitchen table. A light sweat ringed his lips and eyes, and his breathing sounded faster than ours but not labored. He looked—mischievous—as if flying in here gave him a guilty pleasure. A risk-taker like Alicia? Did the fliers have such a thing?

Marcus grinned. "Alicia, meet your flying instructor, Tsawo."

Alicia stood and held out a hand, her face and body so infused with excitement it made me want to take her back upstairs and lock her in—maybe both to keep her safe and because she was looking at this Tsawo with as much pleasure as she ever looked at me. But then, everything about my emotions seemed off today, so I probably saw things that weren't there.

Tsawo's first words to her didn't help me out any, though. "You are very beautiful. I have never seen eyes that color."

Alicia blushed. I winced, waited for her to blather something about his wings, but she just said, "Thank you," and then looked at Marcus and me. "Can Induan come?"

Marcus shook his head. "Dianne needs her."

Alicia pursed her lips in brief disappointment, but when she looked back at Tsawo it was gone. I had a sudden vision of her with her invisibility mod on, so that a set of wings flew by themselves, and had to cover a smile. Maybe Tsawo was in for more than he bargained for.

"What do I need?" she asked.

"Just tie your hair back and be comfortable."

She nearly floated up the stairs.

"How will you teach her?" I asked.

"We have wings designed for regular humans. Within a day or two, we can teach her to use them, and then she'll be able to fly by herself."

I hadn't seen any of these. Not last night, and not out of the window this morning. You'd think that at least the failed fliers we'd seen at the feast would use them. "What do they look like? Are they safe?" *Since you don't need them, will you be a good teacher, and keep her safe?*

"They don't look like our wings, of course. They attach to your arms and legs, and across and up and down your back. Don't worry, it's almost pleasant." He grinned. "People come to Lopali from all the worlds. Mostly, they come to fly. Our atmosphere makes this possible. For example, for humans to fly on Silver's Home takes equipment that is nearly as large as a person, and bulky, or it takes engines. Here, you don't need either."

Liam and Kayleen appeared with the children, each carrying one. "Who let in all the cold air?" Kayleen asked, eyeing the open ceiling.

"It's time to get up anyway," Marcus said.

Kayleen noticed Tsawo. She gasped briefly and stood still, holding onto Jherrel. They both stared, wide-eyed, before Jherrel smiled.

Caro, cupped in Liam's arms, leaned in toward Tsawo. "Pretty. Can I have wings like that? Will you teach me to fly?"

Tsawo gave her an odd look, and took a step back. "I don't think we have wings your size." Didn't they have normal babies here? Kayleen put Jherrel down. He'd lost his baby fat and his head was above my knees. He took a few steps forward and then stopped, eyeing the flier suspiciously. Tsawo looked equally wary, but both were saved from the other as Alicia reappeared, her heavy black hair tamed into a single thick braid and secured with a violet ribbon that matched her eyes. She started toward the door, but I stopped her and gave her a kiss, whispering, "Good luck. Be careful."

She nodded, and returned my kiss absently. Then she stopped and gave Marcus a grateful look. "Thank you."

He looked pleased that she'd stopped to acknowledge him, but by then all of her attention had returned to the flier.

Tsawo gave her simple directions to someplace called Fliers' Field.

She took off through the door and he rose out of the open ceiling without saying anything else to us. After he left, Marcus closed the roof.

I looked around for Sasha, and found her wedged into a corner with her head hunched between her shoulders and the ruff along her back sticking up. Even after I called her, it took her a few tries to get up the courage to come to me. I leaned down and whispered in her ear, "You didn't like him either, did you?"

"She'll get used to the fliers," Marcus said. "They're just new to her."

"Are you sure it was a good idea to send Alicia off with one?" I asked him.

"She needs a constructive way to stay out of your hair. It's a skill she needs and wants, and one we'll probably be able to use. It would be good for us to have a few competent fliers. You and Chelo will get flying lessons a little later."

"Can I have a flying lesson, too?" Caro asked.

Marcus shook his head. "When you're bigger."

Caro gave him her most serious look. "But I want to be big now."

He gave her back an equally imposing face. "Of course you do. You can keep growing all day, but it will take more than that."

Caro stamped her long feet and glared at Marcus. He looked over at Liam. "You'll have to watch the children. I need Kayleen, Chelo, and Joseph."

Liam groaned. I may have gone from captain to student, but he'd gone from being the heir to the leader of a band of roving scientists to a babysitter. I'd have to talk to Marcus later about how to best use everyone. Surely Liam's skills as a roamer would help us. Alicia's, too, for that matter. There must be things that needed observing.

Like Tsawo.

10

ALICIA: FLYING LESSONS

Following Tsawo's hurried directions, I threaded through the dawn-dark trees that surrounded the guest houses until I found a wide, flat path. A shadow fell across it: Tsawo showing me where to go. He flew so his shadow led me. At first it was slow, but when I caught his shadow he sped up, and when I caught it again he sped up again. Eventually I ran all-out, almost floating across the ground with the long strides possible on this light world, his wing shadow just too far ahead for me to catch. The morning air, still damp with dew, cooled my skin as blood thrummed through my body and my strides lengthened.

A flier! A flier with me! And to run without a circle of metal around me, without anyone but Tsawo watching. Maybe Induan was right and I had Space Ship Shock. Whatever it was, I felt fully, gloriously alive for the first time since Induan and I saved the babies from the mercenaries.

What would Tsawo be like? He was sexy and wild and winged. That excited me, too. Perhaps that's what I liked—powerful men. Like Joseph. Like Tsawo. I nearly stumbled. Best not to get confused. I added speed, and for a moment I outran the flier's shadow, and then he caught me and started slowing down, so my own strides shrank to keep me near his shadow.

The grass beside the path shortened and changed color, as if I'd just run into a park. I noticed three long low buildings to the right of me, and a wider road that ended beside the buildings. Small humped hills scattered across the shorter grass, and here and there round circles had been made with bright green grass. Thin strips of red and yellow flowers created straight lines on the field. Designed to be seen from the air!

Tsawo put on a burst of energy and changed direction above me, turning me off the path and onto the ground, putting the sun forty-five degrees to my back. Then he came down, his shadow and feet joining as he landed a few meters in front of me, laughing with exertion. The look on his face suggested he knew how polished his landing was, and how it awed me to see him put down so smoothly. I was breathing too hard from the run to say anything, but I gave him a thumbs-up, figuring that was pretty universal.

He grinned, gasping, too, although not as noisily as me. "You're fast!"

I used the back of my hand to wipe sweat from my forehead. "Could you have flown faster?"

"Only for a while." He laughed, and I heard a hint of jealousy in his voice.

"You'd like to run like me, wouldn't you?"

"Who wouldn't? Welcome to Fliers' Field. We'll see if you can fly as well as you can run."

"I want to fly like you do."

He raised an eyebrow, studying me, not responding.

"Really. I want to have wings. I want to know about the mod."

Now he shook his head. "You are clearly made to run like I am made to fly. As well switch a cloud with a river."

"A river is water, and so is a cloud."

"Perhaps, but the river is too heavy to fly without evaporating first." Now there was laughter in his voice—not cruel, but not companionable either. Perhaps he thought I was a child.

"I am willing to try."

He started toward one of the long low buildings, gesturing for me to follow. "Most who try what you're asking evaporate, and never become clouds. I wasn't hired to change your form, but just to teach you to fly."

I decided to wait and ask him later, after I proved I could fly with fake wings. He opened the door. Inside, row on row of olive and off-white and brown contraptions hung on pegs. He pointed at them. "Your wings await."

Oh. "There aren't any pretty ones?"

"You can make something better after you pass some tests. We want to spot students from a distance."

"Will it take long?"

"It usually takes years. But maybe if you fly as fast as you run, it won't be so bad."

I would. I'd fly really well. But I'd imagined looking like the fliers, graceful and kissed by sky. Everything about these wings looked awkward.

"How come there's no one else here?" I asked.

"There will be. We're early."

Here and there, fliers touched the sky with color, but no one appeared to be heading our way. "Are you going to teach other people, too?"

"Right now?"

I nodded.

"No. Just you." A puzzled look crossed his face. "Why?"

My cheeks heated and I looked away. "I'm just curious. I'm still trying to learn what Lopali is like."

He started walking down the row of hanging dead wings, his own ebony wings making them into a mockery. He walked less awkwardly than most fliers, but even for him, the ground wasn't comfortable. About halfway down he plucked a set from the wall and gestured me close. "Hold out your arm."

I did, and the wing he held up was twice as tall as my arm, and slightly longer. "These'll do." He plopped them into my arms. I tensed, expecting weight. As big as the wings were, they were as light as my shoes. "What are they made of?"

"Carbon cloth, coated with temperature-regulating nano."

At least they were probably more elegant in design than looks.

He grabbed a different rig from lower on the wall below the hook he'd plucked the wings from, and started back toward the door. I flipped the lightweight wings up so they rested on my shoulder and followed him, noting that from behind he really looked like nothing more than a pair of wings with a set of long feet below them. He even waddled a little.

That didn't stop me from noticing his chest muscles and his long, strong fingers as he fit the wings carefully to my arms. He smelled of air. He smelled of sweat and the oil on his feathers and something musky, like sex but not quite that. Maybe it was just the difference between man smell and flier smell.

I didn't want to feel so swayed by his nearness.

I loved Joseph. I had loved Joseph since I was five.

But there had been only Joseph and Liam and Bryan, and Bryan and Chelo had been inseparable as children. They should be together today; I saw it in Bryan's eyes. He loved her, still and desperately. Kayleen had always had a crush on Liam. Since, back then, I only saw Joseph twice a year, I had loved a boy in my own caravan, thought maybe he loved me, but he died. Varay, of the dancing brown eyes and the fast hands and easy laugh. After him, there was just Joseph. Joseph who I loved and who was maybe going to save this world.

And now there were hundreds of thousands of men with power and grace and beauty, if only a few had as much as my Joseph.

I forced my focus back to helping Tsawo put the wings on me. Once all the parts were buckled and tightened and fitted to my shoulders and back and arms, and my fingers curled around the grips on the ends, and my legs fastened into fluttering thick-and-light material, I felt like a chicken trussed for dinner. There was nothing light and airy about the wings. Nothing beautiful, nothing comfortable. My shoulder blades itched with dried sweat from my run and there was no way I'd be scratching the itch until I got all of this stuff off.

I trotted a few steps and raised my wings.

Behind me, Tsawo laughed. "Not yet."

But I wanted to fly.

"Remember, if you fall out of the air, the ground is hard."

Duh.

"Follow me." He sounded like Liam talking to Caro. *Be patient. Do what I want*. Well, I wasn't a three-year-old, and he was my teacher, and so I followed him. Four steps in, I tripped over my own toes and almost fell, pinwheeling my arms to stay up.

He smiled. "Come on. It'll be all right."

"Can you help me?" I asked.

"You've got to learn to walk before you can fly."

I listened for warmth in his patient voice. I'd heard it when he admired my running, but now his words sounded rote. Like words he used with students every day. Now that I was all dressed up in awkwardness, I was probably less attractive.

I needed to peel my stupid self away from thinking about how Tsawo affected me. I was here, where I wanted to be. I was on Lopali, with a beautiful flier, learning to fly even before Joseph or Kayleen or Chelo, who were learning how to save the world.

I waddled forward, keeping my head up, determined not to fall before I reached wherever it was Tsawo was taking me.

More sweat poured off my face than when I ran to Fliers' Field. A lighter sheen beaded Tsawo's angular face and his feathers glittered in the noonday sun. Two other students with another teacher had come, flown off, returned, and left, all while I stood in the sun being corrected, and corrected, and corrected. "Okay," he barked, sounding like Jenna or Marcus forcing us to exercise on the ships, "Last ground exercise. Bend."

I bent my knees so deep they screamed, holding the ever-heavier wings out to the side.

"Thrust." I stood up, pulling the wings down gently, feeling a touch of lift at the top of my stand. This time, I managed to stop the downbeat before the wing tips brushed the grass.

"Very good. Bend."

I thought he said one more. I bent.

"Thrust.

Bend.

"Thrust."

And then silence for three breaths while I stood there, thighs and butt clenched for strength, knees slightly bent for balance.

"Very good."

I spoke through teeth clenched with the effort of standing just right. "Can I fly now?"

"No. Your wings aren't part of you yet." He glanced up. "Besides, it's too hot. Your first flight should be a morning."

Which morning? But I held my tongue, since I knew anything I said now would result in a third lecture about how flying could get you killed. I had thought I did well, but the look on his face suggested maybe I didn't. I didn't ask. "Can you fly in the heat?"

He glanced up. "Almost no one flies this time of day. We fly in the morning. In the middle of the day the sun bakes our crops and flowers and the Keepers work and we sleep, and then later on we fly again if we want to."

The sky was empty of fliers.

"So now you sleep," he said.

I didn't want to sleep. But I didn't think he was going to give me a choice. "So do I go home?" I didn't relish the trip in this heat, and I didn't want to be done with Tsawo yet, even though I should.

"No. There are rooms here. I'll put you in one."

And him in another. I could hear that. I was a chore to him. "And then?"

"Then Marcus asked me to show you the general layout of the town."

He didn't sound thrilled about it. He sounded patient, like he'd sounded all morning. Hopefully the rooms had some way to clean up so I could get the salt and sweat off my face and neck before we went anywhere public. If I couldn't fly in them, I wanted the wings off. I slid a hand out of the wing-tip grip and reached it toward the other arm. One wing hit the other, and all my careful balance fled as I struggled to stay upright at all.

"Do you remember how I said you should get them off?"

I held them in front of me, and slid just my wrists free, using my right hand to unbuckle the left forearm fastening, and the left, awkwardly, to get the right fastening loose. Now I could bend both arms at the elbows and free my biceps. Except the wings slammed together again and this time I fell on my butt.

11

JOSEPH: THE SCHOOL OF HEAVEN'S FLIGHT

A full hour after Alicia left with the dark-winged flier, Marcus led me, Chelo, and Kayleen out of the house and back into the city. Fewer fliers graced the air than we'd seen out our window, and nearly everyone aloft seemed bent on specific tasks. I watched for Alicia, or for anyone in a harness and fake wings, but saw neither. But then, surely it would take more than a day to learn how to fly.

As we passed the boundary that marked the common space of the city, I noticed the name of the town on a wooden arch—SoBright. I almost groaned inwardly—it went with the too-pretty everything else and the lack of anything that looked like predators. An amazing number of the fliers seemed to have nothing to do. They sat about silently, apparently lost in data. I took a few extra steps to catch up to Marcus. "Don't they work?"

He laughed. "They are working. Think of this as a great church—part of what the fliers do is internal, and some between and among each other. Besides, they do most of their work in the first few hours of dawn—that's when they patrol for things to fix in the wilds, and practice long flights. Even here, on a planet designed to support human flight, people can't fly all day. It's too hard."

"So the silent ones are working with data?" Kayleen asked.

"You'll understand more after you're not shielded."

"When is that?" I asked.

"After you understand Lopali on the physical level."

He wouldn't bend. Besides, Kayleen was new here, and new to

these kinds of data streams, and fragile. But not patient. "When will that be?" she pressed.

"As soon as you learn enough. Data flows are a language themselves, and reflect culture."

Kayleen grinned up at him. "Like the difference between Islas and Fremont."

"Exactly."

We walked all the way through SoBright and left it again on the far side, continuing down a street full of buildings sized for fliers. Unlike the guest house, which felt like a regular place when the roof was closed, and had walls and windows on every side, these were open—just roofs over benches and tables.

Marcus clearly knew where he was going. Ten or twelve airy buildings that only vaguely matched each other in style sprawled across a large and immaculately gardened campus. Benches and perches had been fit artfully into nooks and crannies, making outdoor study space that was full of fliers and wingless, some sitting alone and others in groups. A warm breeze carried the soft voices of people lost in conversation.

Shadows blocked the sun for a breath, just before Matriana and Daniel landed in front of us. After greetings were exchanged, Marcus asked, "Is Chance here yet?"

"In just a few moments." She turned her gaze to me. "Are you ready?"

"Yes." Sure. For whatever. Why did Marcus always like to surprise me? I glanced at him. "We're ready."

Kayleen cleared her throat. "Ready for what? Is this a school? Are your geneticists here?"

Chelo grabbed her hand and squeezed it, stopping the flow of words.

Daniel smiled. "Ready to start learning, and yes, this is the biggest university on Lopali, the School of Heaven's Flight, and yes, our geneticists are here."

Kayleen grinned.

Chelo pointed up into the sky, and I got my first glimpse of a flying regular human. The wings were smaller than a flier's, and more rigid, and clearly made rather than grown. The sun glittered on slen-

der sparkly stripes of bright white across a gray-blue just duller than
the color of the sky. They stretched from just past the human's fingers
on each side, and swept back to tuck in near the hips. The legs had a
second set of small winglike protrusions that looked like they might
be used as much for stability as steering. It eventually became clear
the wings carried a smallish and slender man. The whole contrap-
tion creaked, the wings flapping audibly and squeaking on the downbeat as he came within a few meters or so of us. He slowed, then,
with a little hop, stopped on a patch of green grass in front of us.

Marcus headed straight toward him, so I followed, curious.

He looked young and healthy, like everyone else here, except his
hair was a silver-gray that offset bright blue eyes and a wide, friendly
smile. "Good to see you! I hear you've brought us a protégé"—he
glanced at me—"and I'm betting this is him."

I nodded and stuck my hand out, then realized he didn't have a
free hand. "I'm Joseph."

"And I'm Dr. Chance." He started peeling off the wings and handed
one to me and one to Marcus. They were much more elegantly made
up close than they'd seemed from a distance, with clever spars and a
soft fabric. "Or just Chance."

The single wing I held weighed no more than a few ounces, and
balanced easily a little off-center on a single finger. "You're the gene-
ticist?"

"You were expecting a flier? No. I mean, yes I am, and I'm from
Silver's Home, too. I couldn't stand the death rate, so I came here to
help when Marcus asked."

We started back toward the others, who appeared to be entangled
in one of Kayleen's grand convoluted conversations. "So why do you
need us?" I asked him.

His cheeks reddened. "Well, I'm no maker, for one. Not even a
basic Wind Reader. And I didn't have access to all the secrets. But I
know a few things, and between us all, we'll puzzle it out."

Matriana laughed softly at something Chelo said, and then she and
Daniel swept back up into the air. Marcus led the rest of us to a long
room where Dr. Chance clipped all the parts of his flying gear together and stuck them on a hook next to three other pairs. We entered what must be one of the fliers' classrooms. Partway across the

floor, a rope ladder dangled from a lattice platform. Marcus held the rope for us so it wouldn't sway too much as we climbed.

The platform was only about twice as high as I was tall. Matriana and Daniel had flown in through the wide-open wall and they sat comfortably on two of many tall benches that surrounded a single square table. At their invitation, we scrambled up, and even with each of us taking a bench, the table was less than half full. While I felt like the table was the right height for my hands, my feet dangled over empty space, as if I were a child sitting in a grown-up's spot.

Chance got right down to business, plugging a data button into a clever reader built right into the table. Images shimmered to life, duplicated for each of us. A slightly see-through three-dimensional flier hung in the air in front of us, wings spread. "What do you see?" he asked.

I glanced at the very real fliers sitting across from us. "The wings are bigger than the body. They might be heavier."

He nodded. "Wings and body usually weigh about the same. What else do you see?"

"The muscles are different. Longer and more . . . I don't know? Streamlined."

"Like a bird's would be," Chelo mentioned. "Look at the hands and feet. The feet are long like Kayleen's. The fingers and toes aren't claws, but they're thinner than ours."

"Their bones must be light," Kayleen added.

The pictures changed to show a cutaway of the flier's bones, including the wing bones. The structural components of the body seemed to be in the usual places, but finer and longer, the bones hollow. "Because the bones are so much thinner, and the muscles designed not to bulk, fliers seldom walk far. They aren't designed to carry their own weight for long."

"So that's why the fliers I saw on Silver's Home seemed to be in pain?"

Chance shook his head. "Those are different yet again. Much stronger people were made for Lopali. If Matriana tried to walk on Silver's Home in normal gravity, she would crumple."

Chelo spoke up, her voice tightly controlled. "So someone decides before the flier child is born if it will live here or not?"

Matriana answered her. "A flier designed for Silver's Home can live here. But we cannot live there and walk the normal streets. We would be confined forever to the domed cities."

Kayleen followed one of her typical tangents. "But if you could decide yourself, for your own babies, what would you choose? Would you make any at all for Silver's Home, or would you make them all for here?"

Matriana and Daniel looked puzzled. He answered. "We'd live here. This is our home."

"How are flier babies born now?" I asked

Daniel frowned. "Normal women bear them. They get paid to do it. Then the babies are changed across the next few months."

Chance picked up the answer. "Nanotechnology thins the bones, teaches the muscles to grow longer, and changes the shoulders, essentially adding a shelf for the wings. It's structural engineering that's as much nanotechnology as genetics, although it does change the underlying biology. But not like Wind Reading, which can be passed from parent to child. The mod for fliers is very painful." A bitter anger boiled lightly under his words, and showed in his eyes. "The infant fliers-to-be are drugged so they forget the pain of growing wings. Many die."

Kayleen grimaced. "So why do it at all? If it kills so easily, why make fliers? And worse, why let kids try it? They haven't chosen."

Chance nodded, his face softening, but his words were matter-of-fact. "The death rate for infants is far lower than adults."

She shivered. "It seems . . . wrong."

"It is wrong," Chelo snapped.

The table fell silent. Chance's fingers did a short dance over the data-button reader, and in front of us, the fliers flew. They morphed from the simplistic holograms we had been looking at to the beautiful beings that had taken our breath away, from sketch to real video, to men and women riding on air, smiles filling their faces. After we'd all watched for a few moments, Matriana echoed Alicia's words from this morning, "Because to be us is the most beautiful thing in the universe."

"Except that most of your babies die."

True sadness swept across her eyes for a moment, as pure as the joy on the faces of the tiny video fliers doing loops above the table in front of us. She grit her teeth, her pretty smile forced. "That's why we're trying to change things. We want to have children who are already partway there—made that way, in utero. We could never birth wings, but maybe we can get a head start, slow down the mortality rate."

But they would still do it. I understood the confusion and disgust in Chelo's eyes.

"Can you?" I had to be blunt. "Do you have the right body parts?"

Matriana sighed. This close, her skin had a papery-thin quality that glowed health and strength, contrasting deeply to the sadness in her eyes. "We're sterile. Perhaps our children or our children's children will not be barren."

Chance leaned forward like he wanted to add something, and I saw what looked like a physical effort to hold his tongue.

This might take months or years. We didn't have months or years, not with the war.

Chelo's lips thinned, and she stiffened, maybe at the coldness of Matriana's statement.

Daniel must have seen it, since he took her hand. "We're used to suffering. If we suffer now, we may be able to change enough of ourselves that we can have babies able to fly here."

Chelo stared back at him.

"If we accept the pain of changing ourselves, then we'll be free of the tyranny of the guild who makes us. We will make ourselves. That will be better."

Chelo pulled her hand back. "So why don't all the fliers want this fixed?"

It was Matriana's moment to look cloudy. "Who have you been talking to?"

"Dianne and I met a flier on the way back from a walk this morning." She looked pale at the memory. "A man with wings black as night and a small feather hanging on a choker around his neck. He wouldn't give me his name. He said we should be careful and not go far from home. I couldn't tell if he was warning me about him, or about Dianne—since she's from Islas—or about Seeyan, a Keeper we met, or something else, but I'm very clear that he was delivering a warning."

Matriana's eyes darkened. "Tsawo."

The flier who had taken Alicia off this morning. Surely Marcus had vetted him. She would be okay. Still, I felt chilled. I hadn't liked him, and neither had Sasha. "Tell me about Tsawo," I said.

Daniel started. "He's young, and drunk on the idea of change. Unlike us," he waved a hand at himself and Matriana, "he thinks Lopali can function on its own. But even if we do manage to free ourselves of the Wingmakers, we won't be free of the need for trade. There will be seekers coming here, and we will go out. Many of our young get influenced by people at the edges of society. He'll calm down in time."

Matriana shook her head. "If we're lucky." She looked at Marcus. "Surely you understand that not everyone who comes here wishes us well. Wingmakers and Islans and others all want a piece of what we have, but they don't understand what it takes to get it. They try to buy their own souls. Or the souls of our young."

Daniel answered her, "They've all grown out of it so far. Give him time."

Matriana glanced at Chance. "He's young and wants power. He's probably been influenced badly. Many humans here are rich—they get that way because we need so much." A slight bitterness edged her voice. "Some like to pretend they can influence us with money or baubles or promises. Some like to tell our young that things must remain the same, that without our pain we could not be so beautiful and strong, so spiritual." She glanced at Daniel, who took her hand and let her go on. "A convenient myth, and attractive to young people, who like to suffer."

Daniel said, "Others give them treats from Silver's Home. Like special mods, or promises of babies, or even just piles of credits, which we don't need. We have wealth in common, but some people think they need it for themselves."

Matriana interrupted again. "The humans want to make us small, like them. They think they can tempt us with pretties."

So she didn't see fliers as humans? I tried to recall Tsawo's clothes in my head. He hadn't been overly decorated. Less than usual. After meeting him, I felt certain he wasn't driven by greed.

Something else was bothering me. "Does he have a reason to keep us from succeeding?"

Chelo asked, "Is it the Court?"

Matriana and Marcus both looked surprised. Daniel asked, "What have you heard?"

Chelo shook her head. "Just that the Court of the Five Worlds may not be friendly to you."

I made a mental note to ask her where she was doing her research.

Daniel put a hand on her forearm, his long fingers wrapping all the way around the slender part above her wrist. "That is another fear that has few grounds. Some say if we change, then the rights we have today will be gone."

That would set Chelo off. It was what the Town Council had tried to do to us years ago.

Daniel continued. "It's just propaganda. It means nothing." He shook his head, as if fussing at a three-year-old's failure to pick up its toys. "Tsawo will come out of this."

Marcus sat back and asked the most important question. "Tsawo is teaching one of ours to fly. Is she safe?"

Chance said, "Yes. He's a little full of himself, but he won't hurt anyone."

Maybe he wouldn't have to hurt anyone. Alicia could be easily misled. I addressed Matriana. "Do you know what Tsawo wants in particular?"

She shook her head. "I heard he doesn't want a war."

"Neither do we!" Chelo blurted out.

"He says we have to stay neutral—that Islas and Silver's Home will balance each other to peace if we don't join either of them."

"Is that true?" Chelo asked.

Marcus and Daniel both frowned, and Matriana said, "It's much more complex than that."

"It doesn't matter," Daniel said. "Tsawo won't decide the course of this war."

Marcus glanced at Chelo and me, and I swallowed hard. *Neither would we!*

Daniel repeated himself. "He won't hurt anyone."

Matriana shook her head, clearly not quite agreeing. I wondered if they were a couple or just coleaders. They sounded like they'd been married for decades.

I glanced at Marcus. "I want to go find her."

Marcus took a deep breath and sat up straight. "We have work to do. Tsawo's not supposed to bring her back until the end of the day. I asked him to start teaching her to fly, and to show her around town. He might even bring her by here."

For the hundredth time, I wished Alicia were a Wind Reader so I could just reach out and talk to her. Except Marcus hadn't really forbidden the two of us to talk, he'd just told us to shield. Kayleen was on my right, so I squeezed her hand, and opened a bit, calling to her. *What do you think? I want to find her!*

Through the crack that let me speak to Kayleen I heard bells and the rise and fall of breezes and the music of waterfalls. Kayleen was beside me, floating in the dip and sway, her energy and mine running close, breathing together. I looked absently for tools to help me find Alicia. Nothing. Instead, I heard the universe breathing. I didn't want that—I wanted something to grab onto, something to follow logically. Something I understood, but anything concrete seemed far away, wrapped in gauze. Bells rang inside me, and a low drumbeat matched my heart. I began to distinguish the voices of other instruments: a flute, a harp—

Clap!

My eyes flicked open to find Marcus about to bring his hands together again just in front of my face. "Mmmmmm . . . okay. Okay. Sorry." I glanced at Kayleen, who had slumped over her arms on the table with a beatific smile on her face. Marcus clapped again, near her ear, and she smiled wider. I tried to tug her into a sitting position, but with no purchase for my feet I didn't have enough leverage. She felt as if all the muscles in her body had simply slacked. "Kayleen!" I called sharply, and then again, "Kayleen!"

Nothing.

I shook her shoulder and Chelo, on her other side, shook her, too, also calling her name.

She coughed and blinked. As she opened her eyes she looked like someone who had nearly drowned, as if part of her was still far away in some other place.

"Shield!" Marcus demanded, his face sour. "Move. Climb up and down the ladder. Put yourselves all the way back into the physical."

He didn't let us stop until we'd each gone up and down eight times, swaying, working at it, with no one to hold the rope ladder anchored like he had held it for us on the way up.

When I finally settled back down on the oversized bench, Chelo's smile was tense with worry, and I sensed a brother/sister row coming if we ever figured out how to be alone again.

Marcus looked over at us, and I realized he'd gone from mad to trying hard not to laugh. But he apparently didn't want to talk about it. He raised an eyebrow and then spoke to Chance. "Go ahead. There's more to show them."

Matriana interrupted. "We'll be going. But we'll check in on you every day." She and Daniel stood on the two far corners of the platform, bent their knees sharply, and then sprang up in unison. Clearly they'd practiced this, as their powerful wing beats synchronized exactly until they were up and out through the wide-open wall, heading toward SoBright.

We spent three hours learning the finer details of flier anatomy and history. The light had faded into the orange-gold of early dusk when Chance suddenly stood up. "Gotta get home before dark. Bye! You can demonstrate what you learned tomorrow!" He popped the data button out, stuck it in his pocket, and scrambled down the ladder, leaving us all gaping a bit. Marcus whispered, "Watch," and in two or three minutes he was winging away from us, the odd thin material of his wings reflecting the dusky light like red-gold fire.

Finally, I could go find Alicia.

I kept trying to hurry. Marcus stopped along the way to chat with fliers, who all wanted introductions to us. After ten introductions I stopped even bothering to try and remember names, although in a few cases the wing-patterns of various fliers looked so unique or so bright I thought I'd remember those, at least. Twice, black wings caught my eye, but one pair belonged to a woman with long black hair and another to a redheaded man with a rich laugh that carried across the lawn.

We passed through the arching entrance on the side near our lodgings. Kayleen immediately filled the silence, slowing me down again. "So what was that interlude about? What's so different about their data? It grabbed me, like right away. I felt like I was floating down a river, like it took *me* and put me to sleep. It was like taking a drug or something."

Marcus smiled down at her. "Great analogy. Now you know why I've been having you shield."

My worry for Alicia set my teeth on edge. "But I can't stay shielded and figure out how to help the fliers make babies all at once!"

"Of course not. I'll teach you how to navigate this soon." He grinned again, apparently amused by our misadventure. "It would be easier if you understood more about the fliers. But you really need to promise me you'll stay shielded until I tell you not to."

"Okay." As fun as being told to walk around blindfolded.

Kayleen nodded.

Marcus glanced at Chelo. "We'll need you once Joseph gets started on his work. You can come tomorrow and keep learning, or you can go with some of the others."

"Like maybe with Alicia and Tsawo," I suggested.

She gave me an odd look. "I might like to stick with Dianne, and maybe Jenna and Tiala."

"Maybe. Let me check with Jenna when I get home."

"Can we take the kids? Give Liam a break? You'll need Kayleen."

"Go with Alicia and Tsawo," I said again.

Chelo glared at me. "You're not my big brother, you know."

Marcus laughed. "You can decide in the morning."

"I'm starved!" Kayleen proclaimed.

"Well, we're almost home, and I'm sure someone saved us some dinner."

"Race you!" I called to Chelo, and she grinned and immediately took off. I'd never loved running as much as she did, but this time I beat her home.

I rushed through the door to find Jenna and Tiala working side by side in the kitchen. Except for an underlying wariness in Jenna, the sisters looked like twins. Tiala chopped vegetables neatly as Jenna peeled them and handed them to her.

"Have you seen Alicia?" I asked.

Jenna shook her head.

I glanced out. The windows were darkening squares, the first stars beginning to fade into being. I ground my teeth.

We left an empty place for her at dinner, which made her absence conspicuous. As we were finishing, Kayleen voiced my fears for me. "Could she have been hurt? Did Tsawo kidnap her? Is she coming back?"

Jenna looked exasperated. "Normally I'd tell you that if you'd asked one question at a time, I could answer them, but in this case, 'I don't know' works."

"How did you find Tsawo?" I asked Marcus.

He tapped his fingers on the table. "He came to me, and offered."

"Offered what?"

"To teach you to fly." He glanced at my sister. "I think he was hoping for Chelo, but I need her with me, and Chance will teach us."

"So Alicia's not as important?"

He laughed. "No. Alicia's not as diplomatic." He swallowed. "Let's wait a little longer before we worry. I'm not sensing anything dangerous in the webs."

So? He didn't know her as well as I did—she could be off doing something really stupid. "When will you teach us to use these webs?"

"Now?"

Kayleen glanced at me. "Can you work now? Aren't you worried?"

I was her teacher, which meant I had to set a good example. "Let me take Sasha out first."

Marcus nodded. "Okay."

Outside, the sky was bright with stars and the flashing lights of ships. None seemed to be headed toward the spaceport near SoBright. There was a much larger city a few hours flight away, Oshai. The bright lights of a passenger ship fell gracefully toward it.

Sasha gave a low growl, and crouched.

I looked around, but didn't see or smell anything wrong. "Maybe it's nothing, girl." She snuggled close to me, whining low and baring her lip to show her teeth. Then, with the mercurial nature of dogs, her tail started going fast, and she gave out a happy little yip as a slender silhouette rounded the corner on the path to our door.

Sasha ran to Alicia.

"Shhhh." Alicia knelt down and Sasha turned her nose up for a greeting. "Gee, you make it hard to sneak home."

"Why would you sneak home?" I asked.

Alicia turned slightly guilty eyes on me. "I didn't mean to be so late." Her words were stilted. "Did you figure out how to save the fliers from themselves?" she asked.

Why would she put it that way? "Not yet. I think you should tell me about your day. Did you learn to fly? Where's Tsawo?"

"He was flying above me most of the way home. And no, I can't fly yet. But every part of me is sore from trying. Maybe tomorrow."

"How is he? It turns out that he's a bit of a rebel."

She stiffened.

"And maybe you should find a new teacher. It might . . . make problems for you to keep working with him."

It was hard to see her features in the dark, but she sounded almost angry. "I had a great day today. The best I've had in a year or two."

Her words stung. "Of course you did. It's the first day you haven't been stuck in a space ship since we left Fremont. I bet we all had the best day we've had in a long time."

"Well, good. So we're both happy." She stood up and walked into the house.

The only problem was, I didn't believe her. She hadn't even said hello, or kissed me, or anything. Or I her.

Somewhere above and behind me, I heard a sharp exhalation of breath and the downbeat of powerful wings. When I looked up, I didn't see Tsawo, for surely that was who had been listening, but a thick black branch quivered against the backdrop of stars.

CHELO: WHAT SEEYAN KEPT

The next day I woke early. A gentle rain had fallen most of the night, so the soaked path damped my footsteps and the air smelled even fresher than usual. It wasn't yet full light as I approached See-yan's house, although sunshine brightened the roof. I hesitated, suddenly nervous. Maybe being away from people for so long had made me shy. Hopefully she meant her invitation. Just as I lifted my hand to knock, the door swung open and I let out a relived sigh to see Seeyan's warm smile. "I was hoping it was you I heard."

"Wow, I thought I was quiet."

"Oh—well, flier's ears are better than most people's, and those didn't break when my wings broke."

My ears were enhanced, too, but apparently not as much as hers. I still wasn't used to a world full of *altered* like us. She sounded upbeat, and I decided to match her mood. "I was hoping for tea, and then I thought maybe you'd show me the area you're keeping? I'd love to learn." I pulled out a gift I'd asked Joseph to carve for me. I handed her the palm-sized wooden animal. "These are from our home world, Fremont. They're called hebras."

She held it up, turning it all directions. "What a long neck! How big are they?"

I stood on tiptoe and held my hand out way above my head. "Their shoulders are about here when they're full grown."

Her eyes widened. "Wow."

"We rode them." That was the moment I realized I hadn't seen any riding animals here, or for that manner, any animals bigger than Sasha. Something to do with the low gravity, or with the choices people made about what to create for Lopali? It was probably the choices.

She ran her fingers across the smoothly carved and polished surface. Joseph had made it last night while we were getting a lecture on flier etiquette, his fingers moving through familiar patterns as he listened to Marcus and Dianne lecture us. "It's well carved," she said.

"My brother did it."

"Joseph the Maker?"

So we were both legends. I could hear it in her voice. She invited me in for tea, and made us two cups with the magic self-heating water again.

"How does it do that?"

She grinned. "Fliers are good with materials nano. The cup's got chips that sense the water and release energy, warming, whenever fresh water is poured into them."

"Wow."

"We have to be light, so we need pure, light materials. Every tiny bit of weight slows a flier down, or limits their range. Some fliers are so obsessed with weight purity they don't even grow their hair long." She handed me a mortar and pestle so light I could balance them on my little finger, yet strong enough to use to crush herbs. "See?"

"Amazing." Like the silver ship skin.

She handed me more: a fork, a tool for peeling fruit, a glass. Everything flawless. Utilitarian, too—a contrast to the way the fliers decorated themselves.

While we drank our tea, I shared stories about Fremont with her. At one point, I talked about my anger when Nava treated us like slaves. My voice rose as I told her how Nava made Kayleen stay in town.

She held up a hand. "You need to stop and breathe."

"What?"

She looked serious. "I hear anger. It's in your voice, even though you are talking about something you can't change. There's no point in anger about the past."

"How do you stop anger?" I felt perplexed. "I mean, I do get mad at injustice. I hate it. People killing each other and thinking they're better than each other. People that talk behind other people's backs. When people with power are clearly unfair."

Her laughter was high and genuine. "Listen to you. You're angry now. At abstractions."

"Well. And I'm angry at how you've been treated. That's why Marcus brought us here. To fix it."

She sat back in her chair and took the last sip of her tea. "Is it? Or did Marcus bring you here to help change us for his own purposes? Dianne told me he wants to keep Silver's Home out of the war. Have you ever been there?"

"No." I was pretty sure she knew the answer to that. Her tone didn't sound confrontational, just curious. "But I don't think you're being treated fairly."

"Are you angry because our children die and your people control us, or at how my people treat me, by leaving us separate if we fail as fliers?"

"I . . . at all of it." She still called the fliers her people after they abandoned her?

"Are you finished with your tea?"

"Sure." I took the last quarter of the liquid in one warm sip and set my cup down in her small sink.

"Follow me." She flowed out of the door, her movements almost as smooth as Ming's. "You asked to see the area I'm tending."

We went farther down the trail I'd followed on my way here. She left the beaten path at a grove of wide trees adorned with sweet, hanging purple flowers the size of my palm. As she stepped from root to root, she left no footprints. I followed her lead, and she occasionally reached a hand out to help me since my feet were smaller and lacked her long, gripping toes, which curled over round things even in her shoes. The root-path took a long time to traverse, and while we were on it, she didn't say anything. I felt compelled to be quiet, too. She stopped at the edge of the trees and waited for me to come up beside her. A soft breeze lifted the wild edges of her chestnut hair and dried the sweat from my forehead.

In front of us lay one of the nearly perfect meadows that I'd noticed between the copses of trees on the way home with Dianne. Only more perfect. The meadow had a song. The stream meandered like the wild ones from back home on Fremont, moving fast or slow over rocks so that it played notes I could have found on my flute. The colors were as perfectly random and soothing as the sounds, a wave of oranges and yellows over a multitude of greens.

How did they grow meadows and gardens with no weeds? Had they just never imported them here? I might have been looking at an idea, or an icon, as much as a real thing.

"Do you like it?" she whispered.

"Who wouldn't? It's like a painting."

Her grin was wide and genuine. She led me to a bench in the middle of the meadow. The bench cupped me comfortably, and was just the right height to rest my head against the back. We sat side by side with our legs crossed at the ankles. "I made the bench and finished the meadow."

"Wow." Fremont was as pretty, but its beauty masked thorns and predators. "Is this what the gardens are like in the city?"

"Oh no, those are much grander. They also have a stronger effect on people—we like to be sure the seekers don't bring anger into our world."

"Seekers?"

"People who come to find themselves in the beauty and calm here. Sometimes it's for a few days or a few weeks—but the real seekers stay until they change."

"Change?"

"Become so different that even their families don't recognize them. One part of that is that they lose their anger." She sounded mysterious. "But that's only a part."

I licked my lips, unsure how to respond. I really didn't want to change much. Finally I said, "It's hard to imagine any place more beautiful than this."

"You can come here when you're angry, or sad, and the meadow will help take away any feeling you no longer want."

And sure enough, in that moment, I felt no anger at all.

Strangely, I missed it.

I found time alone with Joseph early the next evening. He and Sasha were outside and partway around the side of the house. Sasha trembled at his feet, watching the small grass-eating animals that the dusky light had emboldened into coming quite close to the house. They were about the size of jumping prickles back home, but without any apparent protections, and would be two to three bites for the dog. When I came up beside him, Sasha shifted to make room. Her eyes never left the small creatures.

Joseph's arm snaked around my waist and I voiced my thoughts. "Tough for her. I bet she's the only dog on this whole planet."

"Maybe I should let her eat them. This place is too placid."

He had that right. "I'll show you the place I told you about last night—the one Seeyan took me to. I think I understand what they're buying with this. Since they have everything they want, they're free to be peaceful. It's what I always thought I wanted."

"But not now?" he said.

"Still." Maybe. I didn't know. "I'm not sure this is a peace I trust. It's too engineered. Seeyan seems happy in spite of everything. And that's how I think it should be—maybe because, like Jenna said, they made me to be positive. But positive and happy aren't the same." I glanced down at Sasha. "I never thought I'd miss paw-cats and demon dogs."

"There're places on Silver's Home with predators. They probably have paw-cats by now." He grinned. "I'll take you sometime if you want."

"Great." He knew that wasn't what I meant at all.

He pointed out a ship taking off from the spaceport we'd landed at, the graceful arc of its trajectory making a quarter-circle in the sky before it flamed through the atmosphere in a brief hot flash. After it was gone, he turned back to me. "On Fremont, it was our war. We were fighting for our peace. This isn't our peace. It's someone else's."

I couldn't have put it better. "Dianne told me to ask you about the stories they're telling about us."

"That who's telling?"

"Your enemies in the Port Authority, for one. But us, too. Dianne for sure. I think Jenna and Tiala, too, and maybe even Marcus. That's why so many people know our stories. They're using us for something."

He knelt down to pet Sasha. It was his way to disappear from his own presence from time to time. The fading light painted his hair a lighter shade than usual while it shadowed his face. I dug my fingers into his shoulders, trying to loosen the tension in them. All his life, his body had held onto his worries.

When he stood back up, he said, "I'll look into it more. I'm sure there's a good reason."

Code for he'd talk to Marcus. "Marcus might not always be right."

"I trust him."

"Didn't we used to say, never trust an adult?"

"We're adults."

"Not compared to these people."

He sighed. "I know."

"Keep in mind, little brother, that we could be in over our heads. Maybe we don't want to help stop this war. We don't understand it yet. Maybe it's not our job."

"Got any other plans?"

"Maybe we should make some."

One of the small gray animals raced just in front of us. It was too much for Sasha. In one bound, she broke its neck. Her teeth crunched on the small bones.

"Well, someone's happy," I said.

Joseph laughed. "We're alive. We're happy enough. Aren't we?"

"Sure."

We waited until Sasha had completely consumed her dinner before we went in. Although we didn't say a word to each other, neither of us said anything to anyone else about Sasha's hunting either.

13

ALICIA: WHAT ARE PROTECTORS?

Tsawo knelt down, canted his wings back, and took three steps. On the fourth step, he threw himself at the sky and drew his wings down. He rose, three quick beats, four, five, and then he slowed into an almost eerie hover that drew a sweat out on his nearly perfect brow.

My turn.

I sighed. A light breeze filled Fliers' Field with the thick honey-sweet smell of the flowers that lined it. Even though my shoulders screamed from the past ten attempts, I swallowed, took in a big breath, and checked my balance. I lifted my wings. I jumped into the first high, long step of my run, took the second. The wings felt heavy dragging against the air. Third step, fourth step. I drew my wings down as fast as I could. Fifth step, sixth, into the air. My wings rose and fell again, and again. I scrunched my eyes closed, counted wing beats. Four, five.

My abs hurt. My shoulders hurt.

"Good!" Tsawo's voice floated down from above. "Let go. Don't feel the pain."

How did he know what I was thinking? Six. A little off. I listed right. Seven. I tried to correct, twisted to the left instead of the right.

"Hold! Take your time."

My breath was too fast and I was too big to fly. I sank in the air, my feet almost dragging the ground. Eight, nine. Okay. That was better. Ten. Higher. I twisted right again, and sank fast. I lowered my legs. With a disgusted backwing, I let myself down, hard enough to jar my knees. I'd landed on one of the red lines of flowers, breaking stems.

Tsawo landed right in front of me, the expression on his face as frustrated as I felt. To my disgust, a tear gathered in my right eye and insisted on falling down my cheek. I didn't cry in front of people. I just didn't. I felt another one gathering in the other eye, and lifted my wings up to hide my face, fumbling with the straps. At least I'd learned to free myself without falling down.

By the time I finished and held my wings in my arms, my eyes were dry.

To his credit, Tsawo didn't mention the tears.

It wasn't like me to cry. Lopali wasn't what I'd expected. Hell, I didn't know what I'd expected. To fly. I wanted to fly so badly I could taste it. I couldn't bring myself to say anything until I'd taken the gear back and hung it up on its peg for the day. One more lesson day gone, and I'd gotten—what?—six feet off the ground? Maybe ten.

I stopped in the bathroom and washed my hands and face and brushed my hair, making sure I was in control before I went out to meet Tsawo. There was an hour before our afternoon nap, when I'd lie down and stare at the ceiling for an hour and he, presumably, slept. Fliers had unique weaknesses. I could run without a nap afterward, but they seemed to need to sleep to rebuild for the night. Once he'd skipped the nap and been slower than usual and his eyes had been red.

I'd learned that this time between lessons and downtime was often good for talking to him. He was, after all, supposed to teach me some of Lopali's culture.

He was gracious when I caught up to him standing at the edge of the field, looking up at a group of human fliers like me, only better. They could keep up with their instructor. "You improved today."

Not really. Not nearly good enough. "I still think it would be easier to fly with wings like yours."

"You're obsessed."

I hadn't made any headway on this topic since the first time I'd broached it to him. And I still had my promise to Joseph, who was just as confusing and irritating as ever.

Although this was only the fourth day of lessons, Tsawo and I had a bit of a routine now. We couldn't, of course, take a walk, or a long run. He couldn't do that any more than I could fly. So we sat on two rocks, side by side, him on the taller of them so he sat above me, his wings falling just behind my back. Up close, his feathers were a thousand faceted colors of black when the sun lit them, so pretty it was hard to drag my eyes from them. He'd taken to letting me start the conversation, so I asked him, "So what do fliers do when they aren't flying?"

"Sleep."

"Very funny. I mean for fun."

He grinned. "Well . . . we meditate."

"I said for fun."

"Some of us are artists. There's an art building over at the university. Want to go there after our nap?"

It was a serious request. He spent the afternoons teaching me about SoBright. "Maybe. But I don't see . . . I don't see . . . play. What do you do for fun?"

He stood up and stretched, adjusted his wings, and then he sat back down. "When Marcus first asked me to teach you, I was willing to bet that you were supposed to act like a diplomat. I thought this was a job for you."

I laughed and shook my head. "They don't want me near them. They're all doing important work." I probably shouldn't talk like this. But I was way past frustrated with Marcus for always shunting me off, and Joseph for letting him. "See, we were all made for something, the way you're made to fly. Chelo's our leader, Joseph's our creator, our pilot, and a bunch of other things. He can do almost anything. On a space ship, he's in charge of us. Kayleen is like . . . she can do part of what Joseph does. I guess she's his backup. Liam is like Chelo, only he's a scientist, too. He came from a roamer band."

Tsawo had turned his face toward me and seemed to be listening really closely.

So I continued. "Bryan is our strongman. Our protector."

He raised an eyebrow. "Tell me what a protector is for you."

It went like this a lot. He was supposed to be teaching me about fliers, but he often asked me questions. Last time, it was all about

Joseph's abilities. "If I answer you, will you answer a question for me?"

He sighed. "Maybe."

"Why not?"

"All right." He sounded wary.

"Thanks." I didn't want to push him, so I gave him as complete an answer as I knew how to. "Well, Bryan looks out for us. He's always watchful. He's a worrier. Like, my opposite. I'm a risk-taker, so sometimes I don't think as hard as I should about something. Bryan often watches a situation and thinks about it. Sometimes he just does stuff. When he knows what to do. He also makes us work and stay strong. Even when we were little kids, way back on Fremont, he'd do that." I smiled at the memory. "I used to look forward to coming to town twice a year so I could finally see people like me. I only saw him a few times a year then, but he always watched for me. Once he and Liam helped me escape after someone locked me up."

He blinked at me. "People locked you up? Why?"

"They didn't like me. I was different. They didn't like me the most, but Bryan used to get beat up, too. Only Liam really had it easy." I left it there, not wanting to go into our whole history. Tsawo wasn't exactly a stranger, but some of it still seemed pretty personal.

He looked across the field. Even though we were far away from where I'd fallen, I could see the short, ugly break in the flowers where I'd stepped on them. They'd be fixed tonight; a Keeper would come through and clean up all the lines, cutting away the dead flowers. Not just the ones that I stepped on, the flowers that were through blooming and the leaves that had gone brown at the edges, too.

We were silent together for a few moments. I'd learned he liked that. Silence.

After a while he asked, "As protector, does Bryan make the decisions for you?"

I shook my head. "He thinks too slow. And he gets mad too easy. That's why Chelo and Liam mostly run things, except here it's really Marcus."

He must have heard the bitterness in my voice since the next thing he said was, "And you don't like that?"

"Sometimes Chelo hesitates. And Marcus doesn't like me."

He didn't answer that. Maybe he couldn't; Marcus had hired him. "I'm telling you all about us. What about you? If you don't have any fun, what do you do?" I remembered the first feast, when Induan and I were invisible. "What do fliers fight about?"

He held up a hand. "That's three questions. I promised I'd answer one question." He tried to look serious, but one side of his mouth quirked up. "So think about the question you want to ask."

Okay. The rock was getting hard, so I stood up and walked around, pacing in front of him. What did fliers fight about? But I wasn't sure he'd give me a complete answer. But would he answer anything? I really wanted to know if he had a girlfriend, but he was always so careful to keep his distance I was willing to bet it wouldn't matter even if he didn't. What did we need to know?

I stood in front of him, pondering, making a bit of a show of it. At first he didn't look like he liked the way I was playing with him, but after a few minutes he lost his ability to keep a straight face, and burst out laughing.

"See? Fliers can have fun."

"There's not much time for that. And it's nap time. What's your question?"

"Chelo told me that you told her you're a protector. What did you mean by that?"

By the way he sighed, I could tell he was hoping for a different question. But I knew he'd answer. I stood as quietly as I could, waiting. Fliers valued quiet and patience. I had to count to ten over and over in my head to keep looking patient.

"All right. This is going to take some education. It's a longer answer than you bargained for. Are you sure you don't want to change your question?"

"I'm sure."

"All right. Well, at least sit back down."

I did. On the grass, at his feet. The sun was almost directly overhead, so his shadow and my shadow pooled around us, barely touching.

"Tell me what you understand about how fliers fit into the Five Worlds, so I know where to start."

"Well, you're the only humans that can fly. People come from all over to learn from you. Marcus thinks whatever side of the war you come down on will win." I hesitated. "I saw the first flier. A statue of her. The artist made her very beautiful."

He didn't react to that. He just asked another question. "What's our relationship with Silver's Home?"

"They made you. You need them to make more of you."

"All right. You get the basics. So here is the rest. A lot of people love us, and many people want to be us. That's because they want the peace we've made here. They . . . romanticize our lives. But they don't understand our lives at all. They don't know the hard choices, or how many strings others try to pull on us. We do have some freedom, but it's very hard to keep." He stood up and stretched his wings again. "They want things from us. Feathers. Peace. Songs and ceremonies. A place to come to get away from their own lives. They never get to stay here—we send them all back."

"Really? All?"

"Almost all."

"But you let some try to become fliers."

"You're obsessed."

He was right. "So what do fliers need to be protected from?"

"From giving away so much of ourselves that there's nothing left." He watched me carefully.

"We all worked hard to help the people on Fremont. We were stronger and braver and smarter and faster. Jenna—Jenna used to have one eye and one arm, and she was the best hunter of Fremont. But they tried to kill her."

His answering smile was soft. "So then you understand that we need to be protected from others. But why do you think we need to be protected from ourselves?"

"So you don't kill them all?"

He nodded.

14

CHELO: CARO AND THE WIND

After five days here, we'd starting finding patterns. At the moment, Kayleen snored quietly beside me. Something in the way the data flows worked here was soothing to her, and she'd actually started sleeping through the night again, and looked happy. Maybe too happy, and maybe that wasn't a better problem. She didn't feel like herself.

Caro and Jherrel stirred in their small bed against the wall, and I looked forward to them waking. Even with all the mysteries on Lopali, I loved being bound to a ball of life instead of held inside a metal shell. The children liked it, too, except that they pined for the little robots, which had followed them around on the ships.

Alicia's voice carried from downstairs as she said good-bye to Ming and Bryan, who were up early with Liam, getting ready for a trip to Oshai. The door closed, undoubtedly after letting Alicia and Induan out into the wild to be our invisible spies. I worried about her, but I worried more and more about us as time passed here.

Kayleen rolled over and blinked sleepy eyes at me. "Good morning."

"Yes." The door above us opened and closed as Joseph left his room.

"Ah . . ." Kayleen whispered. "I predicted immediate emergence. The two who used to be never separated always get up at different times now. How long do you think it will be before they want separate rooms?"

I shook my head. "I hope forever. There was a time I wished they weren't together, but not anymore."

"Why not? She's a distraction for him. There's not just six of us for you to save now, sweetheart. There's millions, and maybe we'd be all right if she faded into them. She might be happier."

I hoped she meant millions of people like us, and not millions for me to save. I put a finger over her lips. "We six. We have to stay together."

She stared up at the ceiling. "I know you think that."

I sighed. "Besides, if he loses her, it will break his heart."

"I know."

"We'll figure it out. We're family."

As if to prove my point, Caro leapt up on top of us, giggling wildly. "I didn't even hear you," I teased her, although I had.

"Get up!" Her hair had grown into long dark curls as wild as Kayleen's and her eyes had settled into Kayleen's blue. Her long toes dug into my side. "Famished."

I grinned at her. "It's not always a good thing for kids to learn more words."

"Yes it is," Caro stated.

As I predicted, Paloma and Seeyan immediately took to each other. Paloma took a deep breath the moment she walked inside the door, her eyes sweeping across the tied bunches of drying pastel-colored herbs. Seeyan had a full head of height on Paloma, and she frowned down at Paloma's gray hair, reaching a hand out to touch it curiously, and then running fingers across the spiderweb of wrinkles at the edges of Paloma's eyes. "Why do they let you get old?"

Paloma smiled gently. "Where we came from," she made a gesture that included me and her, "people die of old age. At home, they don't like the ways you stay young." She shrugged. "I'm old. Almost everyone on almost every ship has offered me some way to fix it, but it's just me and I don't see any reason to fix it yet. Maybe I will when my bones start to hurt."

Seeyan still looked confused. "You're lucky it's your choice, although I don't understand it."

It was Paloma's turn to look confused. Nevertheless, exactly as I'd expected, she pointed to the herbs hanging from the ceiling above the sink. "Can you tell me about those?"

Seeyan started a detailed description, and they became immediately lost in conversation. I took Jherrel and Caro, walking away from the town. I didn't want the kids trampling Seeyan's carefully kept places, but I needed to find them someplace to run. Marcus warned us to run and lift weights daily so we didn't become soft in the slight gravity. Luckily the kids were enamored of being able to jump so high and happy to go outside.

Following Seeyan's direction, we found a path directly behind Seeyan's house. A small forest gave way to grassy ground, which in turn led to a large perch-tree fence and, eventually, to croplands. The fields were well-tended, but naggingly wrong. The warm soft winds and steady sunshine had convinced my body it was late spring or early summer. Even though most of the food here didn't match what we grew on Fremont, I had been close enough to farming in my childhood chores to notice these fields randomly changing from newly planted to just harvested. No seasons?

The ring of perch-trees that surrounded the spaceport sprouted beyond the fields like a fence.

"See ships?" Jherrel asked.

I eyed the distance. Just what I'd wanted. "It will be a long walk."

He nodded, with all the seriousness a three-year-old can muster. "Okay."

His barely older sister observed, "We can't walk across the crops."

"There's a road." He pointed and, sure enough, there was at least a visible space between rows of crops. "We can run."

"If you get tired, I'm not carrying you."

"We won't get tired," they said in unison. And they wouldn't, unless they wanted attention. Our genetics had bred true physically. They ran fast and climbed well—Jherrel the faster runner, and Caro, with outsize feet like Kayleen's, the better climber.

I followed them, the pace easy for me even though their little cheeks reddened. Halfway across I called a halt for breath. I pretended to pant as hard as they did. "Sure you want to go all the way?"

"Follow the fliers," Jherrel said, pointing up.

"I like the purple one," Caro proclaimed. "And the yellow one."

Sure enough, a set of seven fliers flew straight and fast overhead, directly toward the spaceport. I squinted, pretty sure that one was the blonde with the pale purple wings who had been so happy to get away on the feast day.

"Race you!" Jherrel called my attention back closer to the ground.

I let him beat me to the perch-trees by two strides, and Caro caught up with us before we'd got our breath back. "Let's look together," I suggested.

Jherrel took off, running toward the one opening in the thick line of perch-trees that we could see from here. I grabbed Caro up and took off, racing after him. With Caro's weight in my arms it was tough to catch up. Even with short legs he was a good sprinter, and had time to catch his breath. So we ended up getting to the opening all together. It turned out to be a wide road meant to carry cargo between the spaceport and SoBright. We stopped just at the line of perch-trees, both breathing hard this time, just as a warning bell went up and a stern voice demanded, "Clear the area."

Fliers rose from whatever they were doing and fluttered into the air, and I finally understood the perch-trees' purpose here. It was far enough away that the fliers who worked the spaceport—or others, like Matriana when we came in—could safely watch ships arrive and depart. So we had come at a perfect time. Jherrel would like this: he loved ships as much as his uncle Joseph.

After forty or so fliers found perches all the way around the spaceport, the bells rang again. Two more fliers popped out from behind a ship and headed for the trees. A safety bell? A last-minute notice?

After the two fliers landed gracefully, I glanced back at the spaceport. Was something coming down or going up? There was no movement, and I couldn't see anything in the sky. In front of us, the flat, hard surface looked like a game board of dark- and light-colored squares, and every few squares, a ship rested. "How many ships do you count?" I asked the children.

Caro was fastest. "Eleven."

"Is one going to go up or come down?"

She grinned. "Go up." She pointed to one close to us. "That one. The fat one. *The Ind . . . tegreetor's Dream.*"

"*Integrator's Dream?*"

She nodded, smiling.

There were no engines or lights on it, and it didn't look any different than the other ships. How did she know its name? I couldn't see it from here. Only one ship here looked like *New Making* or *Creator*, sleek and fast and meant for interplanetary travel. Everything else, including the one Caro pointed to, was squatter and fatter, designed to go between here and the space stations that blinked overhead at night like slowly shooting stars.

"Where is it going?" Jherrel asked.

Caro answered him. "Up. It's empty except for two people. It's going up to the space station to get some men."

What? I remembered Joseph sitting in the park on Fremont, telling me the demon dogs were coming, when he couldn't possibly see them. I knelt down beside her, and brushed unruly curls from her forehead. "What else do you know?"

"About what? That ship's the only one that's talking. And the man that told all the fliers to get up." She looked over at me. "Cover your ears, Mommy Chelo."

I did, pantomiming Jherrel to do the same.

He slammed his fists hard against his ears, his face screwed up in concentration. Even so, his eyes stayed on the ships.

Nothing happened.

Just as I was beginning to wonder if Caro was right after all, the ship she'd pointed to gave a great low rumble, and rose into the sky, starting out ponderously slow, almost hovering, and then picking up speed and flashing away from us.

If I'd had more than tea, I'd have thrown it up. Caro was a Wind Reader. Powerful. Capable. In significant danger of going stark-raving mad in her teenage years, and never free of the possibility. Like Kayleen and Joseph. She'd be able to talk to others like her in the quiet of a world of data, and maybe she could fly starships. I could only hope she was steady, like Joseph, and not plagued by her skills like Kayleen. "Jherrel?"

"What?"

"Did you know which ship was going to take off?"

"No."

Good. I didn't really want him to be as different from me as Jo-seph and Kayleen sometimes felt—as I saw them feel. Kayleen, at least, was likely to be killed or driven crazy one day. I was often afraid for her. I clutched Caro in close to me, murmuring, "Good job, honey. We'll tell Dad and Mommy Kayleen when we get home, okay?"

"Tell them what?"

"That you heard the ship talk."

She pondered the idea. "Okay."

I turned to Jherrel. "Was it fun to watch?"

He nodded. "Yes. Can we go again soon? I miss the ships. I want to learn to fly."

Which he might not get to do, if he wasn't a Wind Reader. "Don't you like this better?"

"The sky is too big."

I cringed. "You'll get used to it. Ready to run back to Grandma Paloma?"

He shook his head. "My legs are tired now."

"You promised I wouldn't have to carry you."

"You carried Caro."

He was too smart for his own good, and he'd gotten heavy, too.

Paloma and I returned with the kids by late afternoon. Paloma stopped from time to time, snipping flowers and herbs, telling us the names. By the time we got home, she'd filled two bags Seeyan had given her and carried an extra clipping in each hand. "Maybe I can talk Seeyan into introductions to the other Keepers. I want to interview them, and see how all of this is used. Seeyan said some were designed for beauty and healing powers."

"I thought you'd like Seeyan and her herbs."

"Maybe I can make more of my salves."

"We'd like that." At home, Paloma had been the town apothe-cary.

"I hear there's great gardens in Oshai. We'll have to ask Liam about it when he gets back tomorrow."

Hopefully the guest house would start smelling like Paloma's old place soon.

I settled the kids down for a nap with Sasha, and then went downstairs and made a cup of col while Paloma made notes about her collection, including detailed drawings. Jenna looked over her shoulder. "I suppose you want me to find a way for you to hang those in the window."

Paloma nodded placidly.

Jenna sighed. "All right. Let me think."

I took three long sips of col before I let out my secret. "Caro is a Wind Reader."

Jenna came over to my side. "How do you know?"

"She spotted which ship was about to leave the spaceport before it started its engines."

"And there was no other clue?" Jenna asked.

"Not that I saw." I thought back. "She said it was going up to get some men. I suppose you could check on that."

Jenna frowned. "Did you see the name of the ship?"

"Caro told me. Something really weird. '*The Integrator's Dream*'?"

"Well that ought to be unique. Dianne and I will look it up."

"I'm sure she was Reading the Wind," I said. "I practically raised Joseph."

"I know," Jenna said.

"About time she told you," Paloma said dryly, and picked up a delicate flower, holding it up to the light and turning it slowly, so it shone a translucent bright blue.

15

ALICIA: A RUN ABOUT TOWN

Joseph rolled over, flopping an arm out and pinning me to the bed with it. He mumbled, "The blood vessels in the lungs are twice as effective as ours. Biology is helped with flexible carbon bones in the chest so a flier can . . ." His face turned down, muffling whatever the flier could do.

I needed that biology. A full week of Tsawo's flying lessons had left my shoulders heavy and thick, and layered tender bruises on my bottom. I'd even barked my shins on a rock trying to land. Flying was beginning to give back some of what it cost me, but there was no freedom in it. Not yet. The middle of my back ached. Joseph's heavy arm felt stifling across my sore chest, and I lifted it and rolled away. He'd been so busy since we landed I almost never saw him, and half the time, even when we were in the same room, he didn't notice me. I wanted it to be better between us, but I needed him to tell me he loved me, and instead he spent all of his time with Marcus and Kayleen, and sometimes Chelo. And now that Caro was a Wind Reader, with her, too.

Morning was painting gray into the black sky, and already the earliest fliers were up. It still enthralled me to see them; at dawn they seemed to fly for joy and fun.

Marcus's voice called up the steps. "Jo-seph. Morning. Jo-seph."

I turned back to Joseph, watching the shadows on his face. He didn't stir. His jaw had a strong angle that I loved, and his hair had grown long enough to fall unruly around his ears. He smelled of dreams and sweat. I inched closer to him, hoping he'd feel me there and move toward me.

He didn't move at all, except his eyelids fluttering with dreams. A soft grunt escaped his lips.

"Jo-seph." Marcus had come closer up the stairs. "Jo-seph."

"Mmmmmphhhh." Joseph rolled away from me and sat up, rubbing the sticky hair from his forehead. "Coming."

I lay, listening, as he readied himself; the slide of pants up his naked legs and the even softer fall of a shirt across his shoulders. Water running and the mildly astringent scent of Paloma's homemade toothpaste.

The door opened and closed behind him. He called a cheery good morning down to Marcus. I wanted to cry and pound the pillows, or maybe scream out angrily. Maybe it would have been better, after all, to go back to Silver's Home. Of course, he'd been separated from me there, too. Ships and genetics mattered more than me, and worse, he wouldn't even let me help. Why put a risk-taker near your careful projects?

I waited until he left with Chelo and Kayleen and Marcus, heading back to the university. Downstairs, I found Liam getting the kids ready to go on a butterfly hunt, and Dianne deep in conversation with Tiala and Jenna. As usual, Bryan sat off to the side, watching. I sometimes wondered if he wished he'd chosen invisibility like me and Induan. He'd had the chance, but picked fighting fingernails instead. Just like a guy, pick something that was really only useful as a surprise once. Bryan gestured me to the chair next to him. I poured some col and sat down beside him. "Morning. Where's Ming?"

"It's you and me today. She's out with Dianne already."

I raised an eyebrow. I'd not been out without a minder or Tsawo since we got here. "And they've asked us to . . . ?"

"Stay here. Check the news. Jenna has some chores for us. After we run."

Ah. Almost a day off. We could run, and then go somewhere, and then come back. They'd never know. They'd be gone. Dianne and Jenna drove everyone but me as hard as Marcus drove Joseph. I glanced at Jenna. I'd been good for so long that she ought to trust me again. But she didn't. "No one else is running with us?"

Bryan shook his head.

"Let's go."

He pushed a plate of flatbreads and orange fruit at me. I shook my head and lifted my col. "I'll eat . . . later." In town. That could be an excuse, too. I drained the col and took my cup over to the sink. Jenna stopped a moment. "Bryan filled you in?"

I nodded.

"When you get back, I want you two to do an analysis of the shipping patterns I downloaded last night. Start with intercity travel: tourists and goods. I'm looking for baseline patterns, and once you get those, for aberrations."

"Induan would be good at that."

"She'll be with me. Paloma's already out gathering herbs, but she can help you when she gets back."

"What are you doing?"

"There's a tour group in town. We're looking them over and meeting with some of the guides. The tour is people from Paradise and Islas and Silver's Home all together."

That made me laugh. "All the warring factions in one place? Studying interplanetary communication?" I often didn't get what they were looking for. As far as I could tell, they didn't either—stray bits that would somehow come together. But they brought Induan to watch invisibly.

Never me.

Jenna put a hand on her hip and gave me a stern look. "Don't be flip. They've been all over, and I want to learn more about the various cities without having to visit every one of them. Matriana's brokering an invite." At least she had the grace to look slightly uncomfortable. None of us six would be there.

Well, it gave me some freedom. "We're heading out."

"If you wait for Induan to get ready, we'll go with you."

"I wouldn't want to throw you off schedule." Besides, Induan was like me; she could already be in the room and none of us would know. I tried to set off the slightly bitter edge in my tone with a smile. It would be nice to be naïve like Chelo and not see how we were being excluded. But I wasn't like Chelo, and even though I loved her for worrying about us all, she hated conflict. Too hesitant.

Besides, being alone with Bryan would be a nice break.

And so, five minutes later we'd changed to running gear and grabbed water. We stood side by side, leaning into one of the smooth-trunked trees. Paloma had told me it was called a water-cup tree for the big green flowers it dripped at the ends of its branches. The flowers caught rainwater every night and drank it throughout the day. Birds and insects drank it, too.

Stretching reminded me of every bit of soreness that had come from flying, and I cried out twice. The first time Bryan laughed at me, and I laughed back, but the second time he came over to me and cupped my shoulder in his huge hand. "Are you okay?"

He'd saved me once, a long time ago, and we'd both been to Silver's Home together. I didn't even bother to try and fool him. "Flying hurts. I feel left out. I hate it that Joseph and Chelo and everybody else are excited about keeping people we don't know from getting into a fight we don't know much about."

He pulled me close to him, his hold brotherly and warm. "We know some things."

"Do you trust anything they tell us?"

He nodded. "I trust Jenna. And I trust Joseph and Kayleen to smell lies. They can go places we can't."

How come no one had the common sense to question everything? I needed to change the subject. "Catch me?"

Of course, he had to let go of me first. But he did. It was already later than we usually started out, the day warming like every day did at this time. I led, choosing to run away from Fliers' Field. Starting was slower, here. At first, we raced under sun-dappled leaves, passing flowers and butterflies, and bees that I suspected wouldn't sting. Then we were in the open, the sun pouring down on us, sweating, racing. I had gotten the hang of speed in lower gravity. Longer strides and managing the bounce helped. Bryan's extra weight actually gave him an advantage here, and he caught me twice before my stamina let me burst ahead of him, five meters, ten, twenty. I kept it there, teasing him for a bit. After thirty minutes of drawing him after me, I stopped under a small copse of trees, panting in the shade.

He stood beside me, both of us looking out. We'd come close

enough to the spaceport to see it in the distance. He had a broad smile on his face. "Good." Pant. "Practice."

He used to say that to us when I raced him on Fremont during Trading Days. Years and lifetimes ago. When we were ten and eleven and twelve. "Always. We must always stay strong."

He laughed. "Ming practices her dancing every day. She fights and dances all at once, and sometimes she even does it with her nails out."

"Is that why you like her? She chose the same mod as you?"

He blushed. "She has more than that."

I bet she did. "Like what?"

He blushed. Sweet and tender and awkward. And silent.

"Why do you like her so much?" I pushed him.

He stared off at the spaceport. His breath was almost normal now, but his face still red. It took him a little while to answer. "Same reason you love Joseph. She's the first person that ever loved me all for myself."

He might be a strongman by design, but they hadn't left out his heart or his brains. I took a long pull from the flask of water on my belt, and he did the same, the two of us comfortable with each other. Happy even.

We were too far away from the spaceport to see details as we watched an ungainly box of a cargo ship land in its own heat shimmer.

"Want to go to town?"

"Let's run around to the university."

"It's a long way." But who would complain at us running too far? "Sure, let's go."

We made it to the School of Heaven's Flight and Ridiculous Names before the sun was full up. The one time I'd been here before, it had been eerily quiet, but today fliers went in and out of buildings in small clouds of color. Wingless also walked along the paths in groups, chattering. For the first time, I saw a whole string of people in the ugly wings going by just above me. They flew so easily I winced. Maybe Tsawo was right and it would take years before I had beautiful wings.

By now my stomach and my backbone were chatting with each

other about how stupid I'd been to refuse Bryan's suggestion of food, so the first thing we did was trot slowly through the streets trying to find some.

Bryan smelled it first. Fresh bread. We followed our noses to a busy loft with food laid out on a long table. Winged and wingless crowded the space, and holo projections of various types spun and danced in the air above their tables.

Bryan watched in silence, his eyes narrowed, trying to understand the system. He never jumped right in. I waited, letting him find his bearings. Others watched us back, and it dawned on me that I'd seen few strongmen like Bryan here. But trust him to be practical. "It's not free," he said.

Meaning we'd get caught out since a credit transaction would go back to the guest house. "Maybe they'll miss it. The others probably eat here, too."

He looked dubious, but surely his stomach was empty, too. It took more energy to run his body this far than mine. "My stomach doesn't care if we get caught."

"You never care if we get caught."

"Do you?"

Of course he did, but he laughed and flexed a bicep. "What are they going to do? Beat me up?"

More like keep us from coming out alone together. Besides, it was eat or hobble back, or maybe not get back at all. No one had altered us enough to eat the air.

I felt deliciously guilty as I ordered col, fruit, and protein bread, and refilled our water bottles. We found a table near the edge of the room. The food was good, but being in the chaos of a busy place was better. After we'd settled, we appeared to blend more than we had standing in the doorway. Snippets of conversation flowed around us.

A pair of fliers passing: "The two-tone ceremony is tomorrow."

"Who's playing?"

A shrug. "I'll see when I get there."

Another set going the other way: "Are you sky-dancing tomorrow?"

"No. Henrie is convinced I'll fall."

"Will you?"

A laugh. "Not if I don't get to fly in the first place."

Two wingless women, laughing: "The tall man came from Paradise. That's why he's so handsome."

A giggle in response. "Will you ask him out?"

And faintly, as they faded into the crowd. "Tonight?"

I silently wished her luck and kept listening. Bryan seemed to join me in the endeavor. Our ears were good anyway, and being almost ignored like this, I felt better than I had since we left Silver's Home. More normal. The daily chatter of a world, which wasn't centered all on us.

Two flier men flanked a woman, talking loudly since they had to walk a little distance from each other to protect their wingspreads: "Matriana says they'll know soon."

"Know what?"

A female answered. "If the Maker can make us better."

I perked up my ears and kept my head down. The first flier defended us. "Joseph Lee and his sister already saved one world."

The woman's voice was more scornful this time. "Does that mean he can save this one?"

"Nothing can save us."

And then they were gone. Bryan had heard them, too. He gave me a sardonic smile, and stood up. We cleared our table and left, subdued.

Outside, we stopped to look up and down the wide street. Bushes, flowers, and an occasional small stand of perch-trees lined the road. He put an arm across my shoulder. "Joseph will figure it out."

"What happens if he doesn't?"

A rustle of wings above our heads drew my attention. The palest lavender wings went by, dotted with great blue circles: the blond female flier we'd seen at the ceremony the day we got here, the only one there who seemed unhappy and almost mean. I whispered in Bryan's ear, "Do you recognize her?"

"Yes."

I hadn't been able to catch the expression on her face, or even to tell for sure that she had noticed us.

I looked over my shoulder once on the way back. She was there. She must have thought her wings blended into the sky more than they did. Or she didn't care. I took a few extra steps to catch up to Bryan. "Don't look now, but blue wings is following us."

"I'm not surprised. I saw her before."

"At the feast the first night? She was the only one who looked angry."

"No. I saw her after, once when I was out running with Ming."

"So she's following us."

"Yes. I think so."

I didn't like it one little bit. Why follow us?

16

JOSEPH: THE MEN ON THE SHIP

On the evening of our tenth day on Lopali, we were all in one place. Even Alicia was home, although she sat across the room from me. She appeared completely lost in a conversation with Chelo, Induan, and Kayleen about Caro's new skills. Liam had brought us each back colorful shirts meant for the tourists. I wore the one he'd brought me, a bright blue like my captain's coat from New Making, with black edging and buttons. He wore a paler blue tunic decorated with moons and stars. He'd chosen fire red with suns for Chelo, and a pale green tunic with images of feathers laid across it in a multitude of colors for Kayleen. Alicia's shirt was gold on gold, and glittered as light from the windows struck it when she moved. Induan, now a rare sight since she'd been conscripted by Dianne for household planning and security, wore a shirt much like Alicia's, except that it was white on white, washing her pale features even paler, as if a ghost woman sat in the room with us. The four of them looked like a blooming garden.

I wanted to go run my fingers through Alicia's dark hair and feel her slender shoulders under my hands so badly it hurt. Apparently now that she was leaving and arriving home at about the same time as everyone else, the idea that Tsawo could be trouble seemed to have gotten lost. I felt it; the distance between us at night was the longest half a meter I'd ever felt. I'd apologized twice even though I didn't know what I was apologizing for, but she'd only softened far enough to be polite. I had asked Marcus about Tsawo a few times, but he clearly took it as jealousy.

Sometimes Alicia even slept with her mod on, so unless she was moving, all I could see of her was a shape in the covers, as if my girlfriend had become a wraith.

Jenna cleared her throat, pulling my attention away from Alicia. She stood at the top of the stairs looking down at us. I hadn't seen that feral look on her face since she'd stopped being hunted, after we left Fremont the first time. Even her body stance was more the old Jenna, the paw-cat hunter and killer of ten-foot-long yellow snakes.

Marcus came down the steps behind Jenna, one hand on her shoulder, protective. They'd been in their room for an hour or so and, where in that hour she'd become the warrior, he'd become sad. They watched while we slowly stopped, until all of us—even the kids—looked up at the two of them.

Marcus spoke first, his face statue-still and his eyes angry. "Islas has declared war on Silver's Home, and both fleets are heading toward each other." Why such a production? We'd expected that. He continued, "The Port Authority has upped the fee they'll pay for anyone who finds Chelo, Joseph, Jenna, or me. We have to be even more watchful, and may have to move into hiding soon."

As high-profile as we'd already become? Chelo looked at Caro and Sherrel with worry and clutched Liam's hand. It wasn't fair she couldn't have a quiet home and raise her kids, that no place in the world had ever been safe for her.

Marcus clapped his hands before the room could erupt in conversation. "We're going to redouble our efforts to fly well—in case we need the skill. Not only will that help us blend in, but it will help us escape if we need to."

Jenna nodded and spoke very quietly. "The battle is a distant threat; it will be many months before the fleets get close enough to each other to fight. Consider it background news."

Now she had my attention.

"When Caro told Chelo the ship she saw taking off was going to get some men, Dianne and I decided to verify that as a way to check how accurate Caro is." She paused for a second to let that sink in, and I felt a touch of pride, just like I had when Chelo first told me about

Caro. I wanted to spend more time with her. When, I didn't know, but when I was a kid, I had been so lost. . . .

Jenna continued, her voice low, which only served to emphasize her words. "The two men it went to get are from Silver's Home. We don't know for sure, but it's a strong possibility they're bounty hunters."

And the prices on our heads had just gone up. Although Jenna hadn't said, they must have come in on an interstellar starship and been dropped off at one of the orbiting stations. "When will they come back?"

Marcus's face was deadpan. "Well, if we'd asked the three-year-old that question, we might know." Then, he broke into a grin. "Otherwise, well, there's no recorded flight plan back. We'll watch for it. But the fact that we're watching may alert these people to come down on a different ship. We should assume they know the tricks we know."

Chelo's stricken face made me mad.

Marcus continued. "That's all for tonight. Tomorrow morning, we'll head for Fliers' Field as a group."

The room erupted in too many conversations to keep track of, so I took Sasha out, figuring she might like some peace and quiet.

After a while Marcus came out and stood with me, throwing sticks for Sasha, letting the moment just be. Then he put a hand on my shoulder. "Training."

Kayleen and Marcus and I spent the next two hours curled into three of the comfy chairs in the tiny sitting room in Marcus and Jenna's quarters. We had been practicing reading each other or, to put it into Marcus's words, learning the human genome. But tonight, we didn't sit and read each other's nanomed data streams. Instead, we drilled into the Lopali data fields and learned key phrases to more easily find the common nets: finances and goods and services exchanges and, to some extent, the data that cared for the world. Lopali was much simpler than Silver's Home since there were no microclimates and no guilds of Makers changing things regularly. Lopali, instead, changed slowly and gracefully.

Between worlds, on beaten-up cargo ships, there had been sensual data flows meant to comfort lonely spacers which were easier to break free of than the measured, beautiful song of Lopali. Marcus kept exhorting, "Look for patterns. Break through the low-level patterns and search for higher ones."

Kayleen saw it first. Marcus sent us out for a long swim across the surface of the data. "Don't look at any details." Usually we were trying to isolate threads. "Let yourselves relax and just sense what's out there for you. Sip as deeply as you can."

That meant fading far enough down into the data that the air on our skin or the fact that we had fingers and toes and bellies, that we even breathed, all if it became nothing. We let our bodies go to the autonomic processes and nearly became the flows of data that moved through us.

"Soft focus," Marcus urged, in with us, the three of our virtual selves staying still as data danced through us. "Like a dream," he said.

I tried to balance on that place between focus and not-focus, to keep my thoughts from wandering to Alicia or Tsawo, but often when I jerked back I'd pick up details I didn't want. Crop yields. Temperature. Tourist and seeker schedules. Other times I just kind of melted into the seductive rhythm of the flows, listening to the music.

Kayleen gasped and pulled up. It's tough to explain how it feels to be deep in data, but I noticed her disappearance as a hole beside me, a cooling wind made of the absence of her energy. I surfaced, too, Marcus ahead of us both, already alert.

Kayleen's eyes were smiling as hard as her face and lips. "Did you see it? The mandala?"

I shook my head.

"The whole thing," she said. "Every city, every road and street between them, every garden and house. The whole thing is designed to resonate."

"Huh?"

Marcus looked pleased with her.

She brushed the hair out of her face, twisting it. "You've studied religions, right?"

Marcus had made me. I nodded.

Kayleen and Paloma had explored faiths for weeks on one of the ships, driving us crazy with their enthusiasm at dinner every night.

Kayleen had that same look on her face right now. "Well, it's like the Golden Numbers laid out on the beating heart of the cosmos into a mandala or a sand painting—into a sacred organization. It's designed to keep people calm. This data design is part of why Lopali has the reputation it has: for luck and for spirit."

"You saw that quickly," Marcus said. "I'm proud of you."

"But you knew it was there?" she asked.

He nodded. "Some of our work may disrupt that harmony." He hesitated, then grinned. "Politely, of course."

Kayleen stiffened. "No. It's so pretty! I've never seen anything like it."

"There is nothing else like it." Marcus stood up and swallowed. "It's effective. Haven't you all felt it since we got here?"

"Not really." I mean, Alicia and I weren't exactly overrun with harmony.

As if he knew what I meant, Marcus said, "But you're not fighting, are you?"

"No."

"Or loving?"

Who was he to point that out? Still, no wonder Lopali was neutral—it was pretty hard to imagine getting all riled up about anything here. "Marcus?" I asked. "Did the people of Lopali design the data flows this way, or did their creators? Who made the religion?"

"Why don't you research that and let me know the answer?"

"Now?" Kayleen asked. "I'm exhausted, and when I'm tired I can't stay free of this place. It gets in me and keeps me, and I think it's changing me."

Marcus smiled at her, and I knew what he was going to say before he said it. "Yes, now. You must learn to ride this data. Otherwise, you'll be tired and chased and in danger some day, and you'll sit down to rest, and you'll sleep in it and dream of enlightenment while your enemies catch you."

"Remember all the ways the mercenaries killed on Fremont." I took her hand and whispered, "I'll help you."

She smiled, grateful, but Marcus interrupted. "She has to be strong enough on her own. Go on. Get a good night's sleep. We'll be in Fliers' Field at dawn tomorrow."

I leaned down and gave Kayleen a kiss on the top of her head, and she took my hand for a long moment. My palm felt her warmth all the way downstairs.

Alicia was already in bed, her hair tumbled beautifully over her face and one hand covering her eyes. I reached over and touched her hair, and whispered, "Good night." She didn't respond at all, even though I sensed she was awake.

I was often stupid enough to push her. "I missed you today. Sleep well."

"You could choose to spend time with me instead of her."

"Marcus was training us."

"I'll never be a Wind Reader." Bitterness edged her words.

"So? I don't care." I reached a hand for her, tentatively, afraid she might bite it.

"It would be like asking a flier to love someone with no wings." Her hand was still over her face, but I saw a tear catch on the tip of her little finger and fall to the bedclothes. Funny, how a Wind Reader and a starship captain can find a tear so frightening. I should have grabbed her and held her, and never let her go. I wanted to, but instead I just whispered, "Good night," and "I love you," and hoped she heard me. I pulled the covers up over my head and tried to sleep.

The next morning, Marcus and Jenna woke us all early, feeding us col and making snacks and water for our day at Fliers' Field. The hill where the fliers' feast welcomed us is the center of the wheel of SoBright, surrounded by the park where we'd had the feast. Then, in concentric circles, there's the city with homes for fliers and humans, a row of forest where the Keepers also live, and then cropland. If you put them on a compass, the guest houses would be north; the university south, by the road out to Oshai; the spaceport to the west; and Fliers' Field is in the east. A beaten path flowed almost directly from the guest houses to Fliers' Field.

Dew slicked the short grass, and the first flights out of SoBright were just spiraling up above the city as we arrived. Since Marcus no longer made us shield, each flier who rose into the sky changed and adjusted my sense of the day's data, reinforcing the idea of the living mandala of Lopali's data. Now that Kayleen had pointed it out, the subtle shifts that matched the fliers' routines to the layers of data designed for meditation were clearer to me, and it was easier to avoid traps for my consciousness.

Real fliers, of course, had no need for Fliers' Field. It was meant to teach humans. Although Liam had described a large, gardened Fliers' Field outside of Oshai, this one was fairly small. We had all been here a few times, learning to don and doff wings and getting accustomed to the weight and balance of them.

This morning, Chance had beaten us here. He walked over and started organizing us into groups. When he came to Alicia, he smiled, and said, "Alicia? You've had a few lessons, right?"

"Yes." The look on her face was guarded at best.

"You can teach." He sent her toward Induan, Ming, and Bryan. "Can you help Ming get fitted? I'll be along to help you with Bryan in a few minutes."

Alicia had kept her back to me all morning, and I expected a visible relaxation when she realized she wouldn't be working directly with me. Instead, she seemed stiffer.

A tall chestnut-haired woman walked into view, and Caro and Jherrel ran to her. This must be the mysterious Seeyan of the herbs and meadows. She was quite beautiful, and very poised, almost ethereal. Her height and the shape of her shoulders gave her away as a failed flier, and once, when she turned her back and bent down to pick Caro up, I saw the stumps where her wings had been cut away from her.

She represented all I wanted to fix here. Before I could talk to her, Marcus called me over to fit my wings. They extended past my arms, so the widespread tips nearly brushed the grass, and connected down my side to just above my knees, so they were more like butterfly wings than bird wings. "These are so long," Marcus teased, "because you've been eating entirely too well." He grinned. I knew I was thin, but well-muscled. We'd been living in ships at full Earth gravity, and had much more muscle than humans on Lopali, or even from Silver's Home, which was about ninety percent of full gravity. Marcus had warned us away from treatments to adjust to Lopali gravity, since we might need strength when we left. Flying, he said, would keep us strong. He'd even winked and continued, "Besides, if you're heavy enough to make it hard, flying will be a great work-out."

The thought made me glance over toward Bryan, who had been designed for strength. He was heavy. Chance and Alicia together were fitting him with a completely different device, one with a motor to help. Every time he flapped his wings there was a bit of an assist, and he could even hold his arms still and move forward, al-though slowly.

Marcus tugged on the straps holding the smaller wings, which started partway up my calves and ended in lightweight soft boots that would theoretically allow my feet to help steer. I felt clumsy and awkward. Unlike a starship, this wasn't data, and being a Wind Reader gave me no advantage.

We broke up into small groups and fanned across the large field, moving away from the long low building that housed the wings and rest rooms and classrooms. Matriana, recognizable by her bright sil-ver and white-gold wings, flew down and joined the group with Alicia, Induan, Bryan, Chance, and Ming.

A man with deep violet and silver-barred wings joined Jenna, Tiala, Paloma, and Dianne.

There hadn't been so many people at our past lessons, so clearly the news of moving battle fleets had somehow goaded the fliers, too. A black-winged flier circled above us, dipping down.

Tsawo.

He dove into a graceful landing near Matriana and Alicia, and I grit-ted my teeth and nearly overbalanced, so I had to fling my wings back-ward to keep upright. I swallowed, slightly embarrassed. Marcus leaned down and whispered in my ear. "You cannot choose your teachers."

I stared at him. "You knew he was coming? And you didn't tell me?"

"You were asleep before I stopped working with Kayleen last night."

"You could have told me this morning."

"And that would have helped you how?"

I took in a deep breath and let it out slowly, trying to find my bal-ance. A trick Marcus himself had taught me years ago. "Okay. Do you know anything I don't? Do you have any reason to trust him?"

"We'll know more about whether or not to trust him if we can see him."

I hated it when Marcus was right. Like almost always. I still couldn't take my eyes off of Tsawo, so I watched him snap up away from the ground and fly toward us. I braced myself as he landed, expecting a cold shoulder or a mean look or something. But he simply smiled at all of us, me included. I felt wildness in him, and distrust, like Alicia had in her, although in Tsawo it felt like a coiled cat waiting for the right moment to strike; and perhaps, still and always evaluating. Alicia was more like a loner demon dog, circling whatever she wanted until she pounced.

Looking over at her, I suddenly regretted not wrestling her back into my arms somehow the night before. When we were children, Alicia had it the worst of all of us, and I forgot sometimes. And now I was looking at a man I was pretty sure she liked as much as me, and he was handsome and winged. His voice and manner were calm and competent as he led us a little distance out to where mounds of earth rose up like upside-down coffins.

We spent nearly forever balancing, belly down, each on top of the raised grassy rectangle. Tsawo called out right, left, up, and down, up hard, and down hard, and we made the requested shift with our booted feet or our full sets of wings. After that, when we were already tired, he made us raise our wings up over our arched backs and tilt our heads to prepare for landing. Even though the wings were no more than a few grams of weight, after an hour of exercise they seemed far heavier. He corrected each of us on our landing technique, and when it was his turn to correct me, he seemed to spend extra time on my balance. I couldn't tell if I was more awkward than the rest, or if he simply wanted me to feel that way.

We stripped our wings and ate fruit and bread and nuts, which seemed to be the most staple food here in spite of the meats we'd eaten at the feast. It made sense for fliers to eat like birds—constantly and lightly.

Tsawo sat on the outside of the circle. The new flier with the purple wings introduced himself as Miro. Matriana sat beside Chelo, talking about the babies, who couldn't fly by themselves until they understood the mortal danger of mistakes in the air. Alicia sat beside

Chelo. From time to time she looked at me or at Tsawo or at Matriana; her glances furtive and confused. She caught me watching her gaze at Tsawo once, and her cheeks turned bright red.

Marcus stood up. "Enough of a break. More work."

Tsawo frowned and went over and talked to Marcus. I couldn't hear much of the conversation, but at the end Marcus said, "They have to," and Tsawo looked over at us and nodded, looking unhappy.

After that, we drilled takeoffs, and by dint of necessity, landings. The real fliers, of course, couldn't demonstrate exactly what we needed to know. So Chance did it. Takeoff for Chance was simple—a few steps and a lift of his wings, and then a hop and a downbeat and he was gone. But I, at least, was heavier and more awkward, if stronger. The first time I actually got off the ground it was because I did a series of three of the best low-gravity leaps I could manage, and then pulled my wings down so hard my shoulders screamed. I got three whole strokes of my wings before I fell out of the air and skidded on my knees. But Chance smiled anyway, although I swear his jaw was tight and he had to force the "good" he offered me through clenched teeth.

He left, leaving me with Tsawo, and I failed twice to even get off the ground. Tsawo was patient, although cool and distant, as if he did this a lot and I was no more or less special than any other student. Which should be right. But his demeanor irritated me anyway. Beet red and determined, I made it up the third time I tried and got twenty searingly painful wing beats in before landing a little sideways so the last half-meter of my wing—the part from my fingers out—crumpled backward and ripped.

Tsawo frowned. "You're too tired to fly."

Chance came over to examine the break, and pronounced, "Well, you're out of it for the day. I'll fix it tonight."

So much for impressing Alicia with my grace and gifted flying ability. I'd take a space ship over wings any day. It was beginning to look like I had a list of nearly insurmountable problems. Flying at all. Learning skills in weeks that had taken Marcus years to develop. Keeping Alicia interested in me. Saving the Five Worlds by fixing the fliers' reproductive life. There were more after that, but as a current list it was enough.

If the way-too-perfect metronome of data here on Lopali would just gain a few interesting twists, I might even solve one or two of my problems. But right now, I didn't have an original idea for any of them. Data dipping here felt like thinking through molasses.

The one bright spot was now I could watch Alicia fly. I settled onto the grass and looked up. I found her, high overhead, swooping with her arms extended. She looked natural, as much a part of the air as Chance, anyway.

Except . . . it wasn't Alicia.

From a distance, Alicia and Kayleen looked similar, and Kayleen had been the one in a green shirt this morning. So where was Alicia?

I finally found her only five or six meters above the ground. She wobbled in the air. Her wing beats were erratic, and after a long, tortuous flight that was hard to watch, she landed hard enough to need a few little jumps, her face a storm and her cheeks red with exertion or embarrassment or both. When she noticed me watching her, she turned away.

We arrived home after dark, tired and sore and hungry. Tiala, with an annoyingly cheerful grin, made us a great big mash of vegetables and bread for dinner. I was too tired to taste the food, and the others looked the same. Even Alicia. She ate with her head down and her hair draping across her face, hiding most of her expression. I wanted to offer her comfort, but her quick sharp movements were a sign she wasn't ready for it.

That night, she lay beside me with her mod on once again, like a ghost in the bed. At first, I couldn't tell if she had her face or her back to me, except once when it flickered for just a second and she lay there watching me with tears streaking sideways down her cheek. I moved closer to her, and she shifted, turning, the solid weight of her real in spite of the fact that I couldn't actually see her. I pulled her close to me, but she stiffened and got up out of bed. I called after her, "Alicia." Then, "Alicia, please. I love you."

The mod was nearly perfect in the dark and, without an answer from her to give away her location, she could have been anywhere in the room.

17

JOSEPH: A MOTHER AND CHILD

I sat in the dark kitchen. The strong mixed-up smells of Paloma's herbs filled the air all around me, so it almost smelled like her house back home. Except for Sasha's soft breathing by my feet, no sound interrupted my thoughts. Even the morning birds still slept. I tried to focus on Lopali. We'd already been here almost three weeks, and so much about it bothered me. I felt like I'd been given a quarter of the pieces of a puzzle. On Silver's Home, or *Creator*, or any ship in between, I'd be able to swim the silent fog of data long enough to find the other pieces. Here, the bliss of the surface data swept me along in its current, barely letting me see ghostly shapes below. Not being able to grasp them was driving me crazy.

Flying lessons had continued every other day, leaving our exhausted muscles a day between to heal, and giving Marcus, Jenna, and Dianne all time in the off-days from flying to force us through long sweaty calisthenics sessions and grueling study. *The Integrator's Dream* had not yet returned to the spaceport, but to listen to the urgency that laced Jenna's and Marcus's voices, it could come any moment, and it might hold an army instead of two men.

Alicia and I made no worthwhile progress on the ground. On flying-lesson days, we were simply too tired. The other days, I went to the university and Alicia helped Dianne plow through reams of local news.

The air became better to us than the ground.

By the fourth day of flying, our natural ability levels had shown up. Tiala flew gracious circles around most of us. Jenna was fast, and almost predatory; a butterfly with fangs and claws. Chelo, Dianne, and Paloma were steady, measured fliers. Liam was strong and no nonsense and, like a watcher, hovered above whoever else was up. Ming brought her dancer's grace to the air. Bryan barreled straight on behind her like a cargo tank, but looked deadly nonetheless. If any of us were unsure they were a couple, the way they stuck together in the air swept doubts away. Of all of them, Liam and Jenna were the ones I'd count on to fly the farthest and be in the most control.

Kayleen surprised us. She was the first of us to master staying in the air for long, the first to relax and let go, to fly as an autonomous act like walking. In the air, she had Ming's grace and Jenna's focus, Liam's stamina, and her own playful games. She had, best and scariest of all, no fear. It seemed as if flying let her rise above her demons.

Watching her brought beads of sweat to my forehead.

Unfortunately, so did flying. I could do it—far be it from me to let anything at all actually stop me and, when it looked like it might, Chelo encouraged me to the point of embarrassment, which finally got me up long enough to circle Fliers' Field completely, even if I did land shaking.

Alicia, with twice the wing time that I had, flew slightly better. Which made her the next-to-worst flier of the lot of us. I had expected Alicia to be an incredible flier, and Kayleen hesitant. But while Kayleen rode data with a dogged roughness heavy with her fears of insanity, she rode the winds of the air with so much grace I often stopped just to watch when she was up. For Alicia's sake, I desperately wished that their skills were reversed.

I spent as much time as I could find watching native fliers. The controlled weather provided many sparkling clear mornings to watch them dip and sway, race, and fly on focused missions. Even though we'd spent days studying flier anatomy and flier culture, I didn't yet really understand what Marcus thought we should be doing. I kept hoping for a flash of inspiration as the graceful winged bodies flew above me.

Dawn turned the sky gray, then pale blue. Thinking wasn't helping. I paced, Sasha's head twisting back and forth with each turn I made across the wide floor. I knelt by her and patted her head. "I've got to figure this out." She returned my worried stare with her own unquestioning acceptance. Even though Alicia still kept her distance, at least I had Sasha for steady love.

I climbed the steps to Marcus and Jenna's room and knocked softly on the door. "Marcus?"

"Joseph? Come in."

Of course he knew it was me. He probably already knew what was bothering me. I pushed the door open and found him and Jenna, both already up and dressed. "Marcus, can we talk before we go over to the university?"

"What do you need to know?"

A lot of things. I'd start with a question Chelo and I had puzzled over. "In the big picture, we're trying to undo harm the Wingmakers did to the fliers, so that the fliers will take Silver's Home's side in the upcoming war. But the Wingmakers are from Silver's Home."

He picked up a brush and ran it through his hair. "Silver's Home has a lot of factions."

"Yes. And this will hurt one of the richer ones. What will that do to the war?"

Jenna answered me this time. "We hope that will help stop it."

"Do you know?"

She came over and stood by me. "There are some things you can never know. We all have to be patient, Joseph. You have a part to play. Worry about that."

"No. I mean, sure. But it would help to have some context." I looked across her shoulder to Marcus.

He gazed at me for a long time, as if contemplating something. His eyes held all of the love and respect they always had for me, and worry as well. "I'll tell you what I can, when I can. I need you to trust me on that. But information shared is no longer secret."

That stung. "I can keep a secret!"

Marcus came over and stood beside Jenna, near me. He spoke softly. "Words can be recorded. I helped build the data streams on Silver's Home, and I was able to make them secure. You know that."

I recalled times he'd built a shield around us both and shared data with just me. We'd done no such thing here or on any of the ships in between. I swallowed back my disappointment, and found dismay behind it. Where could we really talk, ever? Were we in as much danger as his answers implied?

Maybe I needed to draw him pictures. "Can we at least go talk about the fliers? What we're going to do?"

He smiled. "I'll go for a walk with you."

"Can we take Sasha?"

"Of course."

The shock of the cool morning air made me shiver. We headed toward the fields and crops outside of town. When we emerged from the last line of concentric circles of perch-trees, the sun made us both blink. A few minutes later, we stood warming at a crossroads in the middle of four fields. "We're going to start today."

"Start?"

"On the fliers. You know how we've been developing the computer model? We're going to study someone real today."

"Cool." In truth, his words made me nervous.

"I'll be the conduit. There won't be any actual changes today, but when there are, I'll do the work, and you'll boost my energy. Kayleen and Chelo will support you."

"So, I'm the bigger battery?" I suggested, surprised to hear an edge in my voice.

He laughed, breaking the seriousness out of the moment. He stopped and leaned down and picked up a short, heavy stick. He waved it in front of Sasha's nose. She crouched, her body still and her eyes following his movements as if nothing else in the universe existed. Even her tail might have been a sculpture. Without taking his eyes off the dog, he asked, "What do you think we'll be doing?"

"We know the fliers have the right body parts, but they're sterile. Have they always been sterile?"

"They were made that way." He kept swinging the stick through the air above Sasha's nose, watching her watch him. "And their genetics, and the nanoprograms that make them fliers, are owned by the Wingmakers."

"So how does that change? If we change the genetics is it then their property?"

He grimaced. "Power is more than business law. If they can

reproduce, they'll be empowered enough that it won't matter. No sentient being itself is patented or owned, just their DNA signature and any biomechanics associated with making them. In fact, there's precedent. Two species of dog and a bird have been declared semi-sentient, which is enough to get them free of slavery even if it doesn't give them our rights." He threw the stick in a great even arch, so it landed far ahead of us on the same straight path we were walking between fields. Sasha exploded after it, a blur of black-and-white fur.

"But the fliers are sentient now, right? I mean, legally? Not semi-sentient."

"They have so much support from so many factions—followers, almost—that we're pretty sure they can't go backward. They aren't politically naïve."

"You didn't answer me."

Sasha brought him back the stick and he threw it again, not quite as far this time. "Darn. I believe they're human. So they can't be semi-sentient. The Wingmakers tell us they're human, too, and they can't help it if they can't make them able to reproduce. There is bad precedent. The Court has found creations that can't reproduce aren't sentient, or even semi-sentient. No one had brought the case about the fliers."

I didn't blame them. The morning flights were starting to rise from SoBright, far enough away they looked like butterflies as much as winged people. "What about Tsawo and the other younger fliers?" Alicia had told me some of the older fliers called Tsawo and his com-patriots the Rebel Flight. "He seems polite enough helping us fly, but he still spends a lot of time with Alicia. I'd hate to see her get in trouble."

He offered me a sympathetic look, clearly hearing the subtext in my question. "When I ask, the most common answer is that they're just young. Some of the older fliers claim they remember being like that."

Sasha had been sitting at his feet, waiting for him to toss the stick. She turned her head, whined once, and darted into the taller grass on the side of the path.

Something screamed.

She came out with one of the small rabbitlike grazers hanging dead in her jaws, sat down in the middle of the path, and began consuming it.

Marcus stopped talking and looked at her, his expression partly horrified and partly bemused.

"Breakfast," I said.

"Does she do that every day?" he asked.

"She can't live on nuts and golden grapes."

He shook his head. "No, I suppose not."

We watched Sasha until she'd finished everything but the skin, which she picked up in her mouth. She trotted off and started digging a hole.

"Smart dog," he said.

"Yeah. So do you believe the Rebel Flight is harmless?"

He nodded. "That's not what they call themselves. Tsawo is on our side."

"How do you know?"

"You'll see."

As soon as Sasha came back, we threaded our way through some trees and found a thin path that wound around a bigger grove. Ever since Kayleen's discovery of the link between the seductive nature of the data fields and the physical world here, I felt the link in my body. When we neared places of calm, I felt calm. When we got near running water or faced down a cool wind, I had more energy. "What about the men on the ship?"

He shook his head. "Escapes are being prepared."

I expected to go to the university again, but Marcus led us to Fliers' Field. When we streamed up into the air and headed south, I was the worst flier by far. Marcus and Chelo stayed with me, flying under their normal speed, encouraging. Kayleen stalled by doing beautiful full loops and twists in the air. About the time the strain was truly telling on my shoulders, Matriana, Daniel, and Chance joined us.

I felt even slower.

We turned east, and Chelo looked over at me, and called out over the air, "Joseph! Want to rest?"

I did. But I wasn't about to be a reason for the whole group to stop.

I tried to remember everything Tsawo and Chelo and Kayleen had told me. Relax into the air. Let your wings be a natural appendage. Turn slowly; no fast movements. Ever (although Kayleen moved fast). Don't stiffen your arms. None of it really helped.

We flew about ten times the height of a man over the ground, which was plenty high enough. I didn't have a fear of falling, but exhaustion could make me land. I tried to watch, and feel, the ground. Out here, far outside the concentric circles of SoBright, a long thin path meandered below us. It was hard-packed and free of vegetation, and lined with round rocks. Every so often, sets of benches sat off to the side, sometimes full of either people or fliers or, rarely, both. Geometrically shaped fields stepped away from the path on the right, and the left was the sort of meadow/forest/meadow configuration that made one of the outer rings of SoBright a carpet of green punctuated with darker and lighter greens and, from time to time, a spray of color. My aching arms, and now back, kept fighting for my attention. The real fliers were way above us, untroubled by the idea they might fall down.

We passed over two Keeper's houses, and then a great sprawling house with an open roof, maybe three times the size of the huge guest house we were in. For the first time ever, I got to land in the wild instead of on the big, fat targets at Fliers' Field. I landed too fast and needed to run, and then almost fell. I really did need to figure out what I was doing wrong: Kayleen and Marcus were barely winded and Chelo had a thin sheen of sweat across her upper lip and her brow. Chance might as well have been out for a stroll around the block. I dripped sweat and had trouble standing up.

We hung our wings up in a neatly painted wooden storage building with orange and blue walls, and yellow flowers blooming in ordered rows outside. The windowsills were deep gold.

Chance led us toward the main house. A wingless Keeper greeted him by name as we crossed a lawn. Inside, we walked purposefully through a spacious, airy home until we ended up deep inside the structure. The large rectangular room Chance led us to had clearly been designed from the beginning to act as a laboratory. The tones in the room were blues and silvers. It had almost no scent; just the underlying smell of being clean. One wall was refrigeration and heating units, beakers, jars of spices and other substances, and tattered and yellowed pieces of paper tacked to the wall. Benches and tables at various heights littered the main floor between perches placed so that if they were occupied, the flier would see whatever was being done on the table.

I leaned over to Marcus and whispered, "Is this associated with the university?"

"No. It's privately funded." The look on his face suggested that that was all I would learn, and I wondered if he had funded it. His resources seemed infinite and mysterious, and he hated questions about them.

Three women watched the relative chaos of our entry: a human, a flier, and a tall girl who was probably a failed flier. The human was a woman Chance's age, and he went to her as soon as he entered the room. Chance's usually serious face softened, and he turned with pride. "This is Mari, my wife."

Mari smiled broadly at me. "You must be Joseph. Welcome." She turned to Marcus. "Thanks so much for bringing them."

"I hope it helps." Marcus gave her a brief embrace.

Awkwardly, I added, "Me, too."

We introduced our group, and then Mari turned to the other pair, who stood quite close together. She gestured to the flier. "This is Angeline." Her bright white hair had been streaked with a blue so pale it nearly faded to white. Her wings matched her hair, the white a shimmery, shell-like shade. Angeline's wide-set blue eyes looked sad, an unusual emotion to see displayed so prominently on a flier's face. Mari pointed to the taller, younger girl. "And this is her daughter, Paula."

Paula's body was lithe as a typical flier's, with obvious wing stubs like Seeyan's. She had Angeline's wide eyes and high cheekbones.

"A genetic daughter?" Marcus asked.

Mari might have been Sasha with a bone. "Yes. Our first success."

A strange wistfulness flickered across Angeline's sad face.

I remembered the stories of how flier children were carried by normal women, and asked Mari, "You bore her?"

"I did," Mari said. "But she is Angeline's natural daughter."

"And her father is?" I asked.

"That's the best part," Mari said. "Her father is also a flier. He is not here."

They didn't offer the name. I filed the question away for later.

Chance looked proud. "She's got flier genetics. They breed true. What you don't see, of course, is the work of the nanotechnology to build and structure her wings. We didn't even try that part. We didn't want to risk her life. But she's prepped for it—if we had put her through it, the process would have been less painful, and less likely to be lethal, than the one in use now. She lives here, with us, so we can keep studying her, and Angeline comes as often as she can."

Chelo had indignantly relayed how Seeyan's prospective family had abandoned her when she failed, and so I wasn't surprised to hear her speak to Angeline. "Good for you."

Angeline smiled back. "Thank you. It's nothing to what you've sacrificed."

Chelo took a step back, looking confused. Because she had become an icon of the worlds, or because Angeline seemed to think it was sacrifice to stay in touch with her wingless child? Maybe both.

Introductions completed, an awkward silence filled the room. I glanced at Marcus. "What's next?"

"We go to work. Paula is the only fully flier-born child who's an adult. She has the genetics, and we've given her the kind of nanotech you have—tools of blood and bone that you can read."

I swallowed and glanced at Paula, who looked amazingly calm. I wouldn't want to be studied by strangers. "You don't mind?" I asked her.

She took my hand and Marcus's. "I've been told it won't hurt." She paused. "I want to help my people. I want to . . . to have a baby that can fly some day."

Okay. Wow. "How old are you?"

She laughed. "I'm twenty. Our program started twenty-five years ago." I glanced at Marcus, intending to ask him later if he'd been involved that long. Paula continued. "We thought we'd have to wait longer, but when Marcus told us about you, he said you might help us solve the problem sooner."

Cool. More pressure. And from a really pretty girl, at that. I smiled and said, "I'll do my best." I mean, what else could I say?

"Let's start," Marcus said, saving me from any more awkward conversation.

Chelo and Marcus must have conspired. Across the room, I saw a couch almost like the one I'd used back on Fremont. My long-dead stepfather had designed it for me when I was still a boy. An oval, with stiff sides and a soft middle that gave with my weight. It felt perfect to curl up in, halfway, the way a baby would curl inside its mother. I climbed in and out a few times, experimenting. Before I climbed in to start working, I took Chelo's face in my hand, and leaned down. "Thank you, little sister."

She grinned and slapped my shoulder.

Marcus laughed. "We'll call it the Joseph Chair."

In front of the Joseph Chair, Paula lay on her belly, her hair falling around a little handheld reader like a curtain. I'd have done the same if four strangers were going to stare at me—occupied myself. She focused so well she was almost completely still, and I hoped she knew she didn't have to be.

Marcus sat next to the chair. Chelo and Kayleen sat behind him, Chelo watching me grin as I curled into the Joseph Chair and let out a long sigh. It was one of those moments when it really seemed like there couldn't be a better sister, and maybe I really could do anything.

I smiled at Paula even though she didn't seem to be watching, and when she gave a tiny smile in return I felt better.

"Let's go," Marcus whispered softly.

I felt awkward, swimming through the data of a real live person who I didn't know like I knew Marcus or Kayleen. Marcus guided us through seeing the differences between normal human and flier biology. Chelo took notes, a familiar comfort to me, forcing Kayleen or me to actually articulate what we saw into clear enough sentences for Chelo to write them down. So much focus drained me, and when we stopped, Kayleen had bitten a bruise onto her lower lip.

Chance, Mari, and Angeline rejoined us as we prepared to leave the big building to don our wings. "How did it go?" Chance asked.

Paula smiled at him. "Boring."

"That's good," he said. "You wouldn't want them to be impatient."

Angeline folded Paula in her long, thin arms. "Thank you, sweetie."

"You're welcome."

As if that short exchange satisfied her, Angeline stepped a few meters away and threw herself upward; a pale white flower against a pale blue sky. She moved very, very fast. Paula's face seemed set tight against sadness, hard. "When will you see her again?" Chelo asked.

Paula stared at the point in the sky where Angeline had been. "Maybe next time I see you."

"Can we come early next time?" Kayleen asked. "I'd like to get to know you as a person, too."

Paula said, "I'd like that."

Marcus smiled, and spoke softly but firmly. "It'll be dark, soon. We don't want to spend the night here."

"Do people ever fly at night?" Kayleen asked. "I only see fliers up when it's light, and even you," she nodded to Chance, "always leave early. What happens if you fly at night? Is it hard to see? Do you carry lights?"

He laughed at her stream-of-consciousness questions. "Night is when we make the world rain. Sometimes you see a night flier inside of a town, more in a busy, bright place like Oshai than someplace sleepy like SoBright."

I didn't want to put my wings back on. I stretched my arms up, wincing at the sharp pain that shot down my arms from stiff shoulders. All the way down the path to the outbuilding, I rotated my shoulders, trying to loosen them up.

Before we put our wings on, Kayleen reached into a pouch at her waist. She gave me an evil grin. "Turn around and take off your shirt."

I complied, expecting to feel her hands on my stiff muscles. I'd never had a massage from Kayleen before. It felt like a guilty pleasure, especially if I imagined Alicia flying up on the scene. I did feel Kayleen's fingers, but even before she touched me with it, I recognized the smell of the thick silky substance that coated her fingers. "Paloma's salve!"

"Did she figure out how to make it here?" Chelo asked.

From behind me, Kayleen said, "I brought this from home. I just . . . I thought there might be a moment when we'd need it."

The salve warmed on my back, masking pain. "Thank you," I said. "My shoulders thank you, my back thanks you, my neck thanks you."

"And you might make it home now," she said.

"There is that."

We did make it home just as dusk began to dull the edges of our long shadows. By the time we put away our gear, we had to navigate home in almost true-dark.

Bright light poured out the windows and a silhouetted figure moved back and forth in front of the kitchen window talking with her hands—either Jenna or Tiala. We tumbled inside to catch Tiala in mid-sentence. "—we have a day at most."

Jenna looked to us. "We have to leave. At least, leave SoBright. *The Integrator's Dream* landed today."

"Here?" Marcus asked, crossing quickly to Jenna's side.

"No. Across Lopali. Near dusk. In Watersdeep."

Watersdeep was small, the size of SoBright. Just big enough for its own spaceport. It lay almost as far away from SoBright as you could get and still be on the same continent. The fastest civilian transport other than spaceflight was human-powered flight. So Jenna and Marcus looked more worried than they should. "Do we know there are bounty hunters on her?" I asked.

Jenna nodded. "Matriana has staff who can access anything. They had two men aboard. We could beat two. But we intercepted messages to five others. Two of them were in Oshai."

Oh.

Marcus put a hand on Jenna's shoulder. "Is everyone here?"

She nodded. "Family meeting?"

Marcus and Jenna explained three choices to us. Give up and leave, go somewhere else. Basically, the "get on a ship and run" choice. The second choice was to keep going, just do what we were doing, only do it from hiding, here. The third was do both—get in a ship, take some fliers with us, and go do the work somewhere else. Like, inside a flyspace dome or a flier ship.

This wasn't too tough a decision. When Marcus asked for our thoughts, Chelo sounded exactly like herself. "I don't want to get on a ship. So that leaves one option. Besides, we promised we'd help." It was the same stance she'd taken at home, and I really couldn't imagine her doing anything else. The fliers had almost become like the people of Fremont—in need of protection. It seemed to be built into her.

Kayleen simply said, "We should stay." She was getting better at holding her tongue in tough situations.

Liam argued both sides, kind of acting them out for our benefit, looking for all the world like his father, Akashi, leader of the West Band of scientists on Fremont. His little flock of four had become a band to him. He ultimately came down on the side of staying, but keeping options open and a clear escape path.

Bryan wanted to hunt down our pursuers. Marcus's eyes lit up at the idea, but I knew he'd never risk me or Chelo or Jenna that way. Although one glance at Jenna suggested that she liked Bryan's idea just fine. Ming, beside Bryan as always, might have even been the one who suggested it to him.

Alicia spoke as clearly as Kayleen had. "I don't want to run."

And when it was my turn, Paula's patient, steady gaze seemed to burn into me. "We keep helping."

Marcus looked around at us all, took a long slow sip of tea. He gave us a warm smile that suggested he was proud of us. In leader-like fashion, he spoke a single word. "Pack."

As I stuffed the last of my clothes into a duffel, I said, "I won't mind leaving this room." It was the only place Alicia and I had ever stayed together without making love.

Alicia's voice sounded small. "I liked watching the fliers from here."

I came up to her and placed an arm over her shoulder as casually as I could. She neither flinched nor moved toward me. "There will be fliers wherever we go," I whispered. "I suspect we won't be far, anyway."

"Oshai, I think."

So she knew our escape plans. "Is it pretty?" She'd been, once, but I hadn't had time for a field trip.

She chewed at her lip, contemplating, and then smiled. "I've never seen a place so busy and so pretty all at once. There's art everywhere. There're people from all over, too. Even Islas and Paradise."

Of course there would be. I hadn't thought about that. "Won't you . . . miss your lessons?"

I watched the pale white curve of her cheek as she looked out the window, toward Fliers' Field. Her lower lip began to tremble. Instinctively, I pulled her close, and she let me do it.

The silence between us felt softer than it had for a long time. Just our breath and the scent of Lopali on her skin: flowers and herbs and tea.

"You smell like Fremont," she said.

"Paloma's salve. My arms were so tired from flying I needed some to help me get home."

She turned into me, so my arm slid around her back, and her breasts brushed against my chest. I ran my fingers through her hair as she stood there, trembling like a spring leaf in a soft breeze. Her voice was nearly muffled by my aching shoulder. "I never thought I'd like the smell of Fremont again."

"Even though I don't expect I'll go back, I still miss it sometimes. It was easier there."

She looked up at me, the corners of her eyes damp and her chin still quivering a bit. "I thought . . . I thought I could . . . could fly here."

"Shhhh . . . you can."

"Like you. Slow. I want to really fly."

"You will. I'm sure you will. We all will." I had no idea if it was true or not, but it mattered to her. "In the meantime, fly with me and then you won't be the slowest."

That made her laugh, and she pulled away and started setting our fully packed duffels on the floor beside the bed. They would be carried—wherever we were going—by someone who wasn't flying. Beside them, we each had small belts with necessities in them. After she set everything down she looked at me and winked. "One more night here, and then we're into the unknown again."

In her comfort zone. The unknown. But I would go with her to the end of forever.

She reached up and took my face between her hands and delivered a grand, long kiss that traveled as heat down my spine.

Perhaps I needed to make sure there was always some uncertainty in our lives.

18

CHELO: THE KEEPERS OF THE GARDENS

SoBright, and the guest house, had begun to feel like a home, and I'd started routines for Jherrel and Caro. I hated packing. But not as much as I hated the idea of being separated from the kids. They must have sensed my mood since they picked up whatever I asked without complaint. Caro stopped with one of the wooden space ships Joseph had carved her held over her head, heading for the galaxy of the ceiling, and asked, "Mommy Chelo, why do we have to go with Daddy?"

I plucked the toy out of her hand and gathered her and Jherrel to me. "You aren't old enough to fly yet."

"I am, too!" Jherrel proclaimed. "I flew in the starships."

They had played in zero gravity a few times. Flying. "That was a place where you didn't weigh anything. Here, there aren't any wings just your size, and you're too big to be carried. Besides, your daddy would miss you."

Caro put her hands on her hips and with the complete seriousness only a three-year-old can muster, said, "Mommy, we should stay together. It's your job to watch us, too."

"I know." I struggled not to show them my angry guilt. My face and story were so well known that Jenna and Marcus had decided I should travel with Joseph. Kayleen, too, since she'd become such good help for him. I gave Caro and Jherrel each a special, deep hug and sang a summer song from home to give rhythm to our work. They picked up speed and sang along. It helped me a little bit, too.

Liam came in, brushing the hair from my neck softly and kissing the skin he'd exposed. "What can I do?"

"Give them a bath?" I kissed him on the cheek and excused myself, leaving him with a baffled look. Not that I wasn't baffled; I'd usually talk to him before I made big decisions. But I was afraid talking would diffuse my anger.

I found Jenna and Marcus in their room, crouched over a duffel bag. They looked up at me as I came in, both faces a touch guilty. I took a deep breath and planted my feet hard on the floor. "I'm not willing to be separated from the kids."

Marcus shook his head and stood up, pulling Jenna to her feet, too. "They can't fly."

"I know. So I can't either."

"What if Joseph needs you? Besides helping in the nets, having you around helps him fly."

"Kayleen can do that. It's not fair to take both their mothers!" I made my voice as firm as I could. "I'm not leaving them. I'm a mom, and maybe you don't know what that means to you, but I know what it means to me. I'm not asking you for permission. I'm telling you what I'm doing."

He glanced at Jenna, a pained look on his face. "I guess Jenna can go with you."

"For what? Protection?"

"Yes."

I tried not to sound as snarly as I felt. "I don't need protection. Liam and Kayleen and I hunted together, and made a house together, and met the mercenaries together and attacked them together. We can do this."

He raised an eyebrow, trying to lighten me up. "You're going to hunt fliers?" he teased. He used jokes to get us to do what he wanted. Not this time. This was about my kids.

"No. But we'll be fine."

Jenna glanced at him. "Chelo may be right. Maybe we should send Bryan and Ming and the stuff with them instead of having us split into three groups."

"They'll be recognizable," Marcus said.

"I'm recognizable anyway," I said. "You made sure I'm recognizable. You've told our story everywhere. Well, that's not my fault. I'm staying with my kids." So why was I standing here arguing with him? I'd already told him I wasn't waiting for his permission. This was like arguing with Nava all those years ago—when you grew up, the people you fought with just got stronger. "There's more safety in a bigger group."

Marcus objected. "That would let all of you get into trouble together."

Jenna started pacing the room, looking for items left behind. "So send Bryan with Chelo and Liam." She opened the drawers of the bedside table, peering into their empty darkness and closing them again. "Tiala and Ming can take the stuff in. Paloma can go with them. Seeyan can help the group with the kids."

"Seeyan?" I asked.

"How?" Marcus asked at the same time.

Jenna raised an eyebrow. "I know something you don't?"

She said it nice, kind of teasing, but he still looked taken aback for a second before he grinned. "Maybe."

Jenna returned his smile. "The Keepers know how to travel unseen. I mean, if you were basically slaves, and given the task of caring for everything, wouldn't you build in ways to get around?"

"How'd you figure that out?" he asked. "Do you know it for sure?"

I knew how Jenna had figured it out. "I bet she asked. The Keepers here are treated like we were on Fremont. They're invisible or worse until someone needs them for something, and then they have to do it." I could also tell I'd won. He wasn't going to tell me no.

Jenna knew it, too. She gave him a light kiss. "Seeyan told me, but I already knew. Someone's got to protect the kids, and Liam might not be enough." She cocked her head. "Caro and Jherrel are going to be important some day, you know."

"If they live." He turned and spoke to me. "You and Liam and Bryan and the kids, then."

"Thank you." How come I still couldn't decide if I really liked Marcus or not? Impulsively, I gave him a hug. His return embrace felt warm and comforting. He smelled like sweat and the outdoors. He felt . . . like protection and support all at once, and very physical. If I weren't way too in love with Liam and Kayleen, I might've turned my face up for a kiss. I did have the presence of mind to think about what energy to return, and decided on strength and reassurance. When we let go of each other, he looked a tiny bit surprised.

Fliers owned the skies here. Except for space ships, nothing that wasn't alive flew, and even the birds were small. No skimmers. We headed for Oshai in a bulky sun-powered transport with wheels instead of wings, closer to a wagon than a skimmer. It felt heavy, even in this light gravity. Three rows of seats fronted a cargo compartment that held our goods beneath a harvest of nuts destined for a processing depot. Seeyan drove from a seat in the front, Jherrel on her lap. Caro had fallen fast asleep in the back, her little head resting on Bryan's wide thigh and his great big hand cupping her shoulder against the rocking vehicle. His eyes were closed as if he dozed, but I could tell by the set of his jaw that he was quite alert.

At the last minute, Marcus had sent Alicia with us, "In case we needed invisible help." I had a sneaking suspicion he was trying to separate Alicia and Joseph yet again, and I felt bad for my brother over it. Either that, or it was because her flying was so abysmal, and that made me feel bad for her. I didn't mind having Alicia where I could watch her, but an invisible risk-taker was not a great idea.

Liam and I sat in the middle, looking out the windows as orchards and cropland gave way to town. Oshai had been laid out in circles like SoBright, but the first circles we passed were so big the paths almost looked straight.

Already, more traffic moved above and beside us than we'd ever seen in SoBright. Tourists traveled in faster versions of our transport and flew in groups with flier minders.

As we crossed the third big circular street, Bryan's eyes snapped open and he sat up straighter, dislodging Caro so she woke up and sat blinking in the afternoon sun. "I don't like this." He pointed up toward the busy sky. "There're too many people in the air. I don't know who's a friend and who to worry about. How do we know if we're safe?"

"Were we ever safe?" I asked him.

Liam grimaced.

A man with pale green made-wings and a brown pantsuit landed a bit ahead of us. He left his wings on and stood quietly, watching us approach. Seeyan stopped the vehicle and climbed down, and talked to him animatedly, her body language showing us he must be a friend. As soon as she turned back toward us, he flew off, low and fast.

When Seeyan climbed back in, she sounded pleased. "Now I know where to take you. You're very lucky." This was serious business to her, smuggling people around.

It made me wonder who and what else she smuggled.

A few minutes later we unloaded at a cargo depot and moved to a smaller vehicle that Seeyan also drove. I leaned over and whispered into Liam's ear. "This reminds me of our flight here. Transferring from place to place."

"Yes." He looked resigned. I felt for him. Of all of us, only Liam had known where he was going and what he would become, at least until Kayleen kidnapped the two of us. He'd never gone back to his position in the band; war, and then Joseph coming, had taken it out of reach. The last few days, and the trip to Oshai, had been good for him. Now we were all running again.

Jherrel, next to me, leaned his little forehead against the window and watched the busy city go by. Wherever we were, it clearly wasn't designed for fliers. Wingless of all types—some overly tall and long-limbed and a few strongmen like Bryan—made a colorful parade walking up and down the streets. Twice, we passed fliers on perches, talking to small groups gathered at their feet.

Caro sat on her daddy's lap, leaning back, entirely too quiet. She held a hand up over her eyes, her fist balled. We'd screwed up. Caro was with us, and both Wind Readers were with Marcus. Any way I looked at data here wasn't close to Caro's experience. Worse, most of it was an adult world she couldn't possibly understand.

I pulled her hand away from her eyes. She squinted more tightly. "Mommy . . . it hurts."

"Shield like Uncle Joseph taught you."

"I'm trying," she said.

Liam shook himself and reached down and folded her in a hug. "Does that help?"

She buried her head in his chest with one eye peeking out at me. "Yes, Daddy."

Now I worried about both of them.

Seeyan pointed toward a set of rolling grassy hills with perches, benches, and small gardens arranged in squares and circles and triangles. "Those are the Temple Hills. Most casual tourists end up there. It's kind of the first stop for people finding peace within themselves." She sounded almost in awe of the place. "You can barely tell from driving by, especially since a lot of them are away from the road, but some of the best gardens in Oshai are there."

"The gardens you want to work in?"

She turned her gaze away from the Temple Hills and back to the controls in front of her. "I will die long before I could become accepted to keep those gardens. I'm not . . . calm enough."

She could have fooled me. "I'd like to see the gardens."

"You will."

"Good." And I was looking forward to it. After a long silence, I added, "I appreciate what you're doing now."

"It's nothing." She pointed to the other side of the road. "See the flags up ahead?"

"Sure." Yellow, red, blue, and purple flags snapped in a light wind, surrounding small houses and open booths and wide walkways thronged with people. Metal and wood sculptures spilled out of the place with the most flags; surely the entrance. Above it all, fliers brightened the sky.

"That's the first of three summer fairs. There're so many people there you can get lost. Anybody could. So if you get in trouble of any kind here, and you want to hide, hide in the summer fair."

"What's at the fair?" Alicia asked.

Seeyan jumped, as if she'd forgotten Alicia was there. "Art, mostly. Some poetry and personal services and the like. You'd like it."

"That sounds like fun." I didn't know if she knew the five women were going there, so I didn't say anything. We traveled slowly enough that I could pick out details like a clothing booth and food stalls.

Seeyan continued. "If you need help, buy some bright blue clothes and find a tall man that tells tourists' fortunes and sells feathers. His name is Juss. Juss can reach me."

She looked so serious. "I hope it doesn't come to that," I whispered.

"Me, too. Can you tell it back to me?"

I obliged her, making sure that Liam and Bryan were paying attention. When I was done, I said, "Alicia?"

I still couldn't see her, but a small relieved breath escaped me as she answered, "Wear blue. Find Juss who sells feathers and fortunes."

As we came closer to the fair, it was easy to see a crowd mingling and talking, dressed in clothing from all of the other four worlds. Caro sat up straight and opened her eyes, looking much more like her usual curious self.

"How come there're not many human fliers here?" Bryan asked. "You know, like us?"

Seeyan laughed. "The skies here are too busy for students. You won't be able to fly here, either."

Alicia's voice floated forward from the backseat. "Could Chance?"

"Probably," Seeyan said. "You can ask him."

"Why don't you fly?" Jherrel asked her.

I grimaced at the intimacy of the question. Children's mouths said the strangest things. But Seeyan didn't miss a beat. "I had real wings once. I don't want to forget what that was like."

Caro stirred. "It's better here, Mommy."

"I'm glad." Maybe because we'd passed the fair, or because of the Temple Hills, which still rose and fell on our right?

The transport turned, heading even farther in toward the center of Oshai. We turned right again, down a smaller track between rolling hills. From the crest of a hill just past the turn, a flier with pastel purple wings and bright blue eyes on her wings pushed into the sky and flew away. The blonde from our greeting feast? Were we being watched?

Caro clambered across my lap and stuck her face next to Jherrel's, looking out the window. "I want to go outside, Mommy."

"I know."

We pulled up beside a long, low building, more like a line in the side of a hill with windows and doors in it and a walkway along the front. Earth mounded on top of it, and grass, and I could imagine picnickers on the far side not knowing they sat on a hollow hill. Were all of the Temple Hills fake like this?

Seeyan smiled as she slowed the vehicle. "Now you'll believe me. You'll meet some of the Keepers who tend the Temple Hills Gardens."

"Why are we going here?" Alicia asked from the back.

"You're pretending to be rich tourists. It's the only disguise that makes sense for the kids. The ultra-rich do what they want."

"Who's paying for it?" Bryan asked.

"The Keepers are donating rooms for you. Trade's down anyway, since the war is closer. You'll be taking the spots of a tourist family, since the ship they booked passage on went to war."

Liam glanced up at Seeyan, always interested in war news. "To fight?"

She shrugged. "I hear interplanetary ships are getting conscripted."

I had a lot more questions for her, including why the Keepers would help hide us, and why the government here didn't just outright refuse to give us up instead of hiding us. It made me uneasy that I couldn't quite tell who was supporting us and why.

Someone had been watching for us. A man—wingless and hairless—walked out of the closest door. He nearly glided to the side of the vehicle, and stood, hands in front of him, head slightly bowed, the very picture of patience. In a few moments, a younger-looking man and woman joined him just as silently. What training or mod made them move so elegantly?

After we all got out, the two latecomers unloaded the transport and carried our duffels and bags into the hill. I watched them go. Here we were. Wherever that was. Somehow I doubted it was going to be a new home, at least not for long.

19

JOSEPH: FLYING LONG

The rest of us stood under a grouping of three trees as Seeyan drove off with Chelo, Bryan, Liam, Alicia, and the kids. I couldn't see my sister or my sweetheart as Seeyan drove them away in a slow, overgrown version of our roamers' wagons, only made of metal and rubber with glass windows and powered by light and air. It creaked as they left us—as they left me. Kayleen stood so close I could smell the children's last hug on her, but we didn't touch. When they were out of sight, a soft moan escaped her lips, and I brought her into my arms, remembering that we were both losing all of our family except each other. "It will be okay," I whispered, not sure if I lied.

She gave me a hard squeeze and pushed away gently, walking over to the edge of the little meadow farthest from the road. She leaned against a tall evergreen tree with soft gray-green needles, she looked away from me.

A few moments later, Jenna kissed Marcus good-bye, and Tiala and Paloma hugged him good-bye, and then Paloma hugged me good-bye for good measure, looked up in my eyes and said, "Take care." They were the next to leave: Jenna, Tiala, Dianne, Ming, and Paloma. Induan had dubbed them the "Gang of Girls." I didn't know their ages, but I was willing to bet the youngest among them was over fifty years old. They walked away, none of them looking back at us even once.

The Gang of Girls had an elaborate plan. Unlike sleepy SoBright, Oshai had a lot more humans who weren't also Keepers. Since they needed to earn livings, the women had chosen jobs to ply at some kind of fair. Dianne had been preparing the way for them in the nets, building histories and professions. Not that it was too tough: everything in Oshai dealt with the tourists and seekers. Paloma had become, of course, a healer. Ming taught dance therapy. Jenna and Tiala had worked up a comical routine as good-gal/bad-gal physical trainers. Dianne swore she had developed an ability to lead people through guided meditations. Given her nonexistent sense of humor, I already felt a little sorry for her patients.

Of course, since I could barely fly at all, I ended up in the group scheduled to fly out of here.

The skies above us were clear, the air hot, and if we went up into them we would be the only fliers there. We had hours to kill. After a long walk, burdened with gear, we arrived at another meadow Seeyan had pointed out as belonging to a friendly Keeper. There, we waited the sun out in a shady spot halfway around the circle of So-Bright from the guest house we'd just abandoned. Induan showed off her planning and logistics skills. She pulled a bag out of her pocket with blue bands the color of Kayleen's eyes, blue buttons, blue shells, and silver beads. In moments, she had a third of Kayleen's hair in her hands, I had a third, and Marcus had a third. "Now," she grinned, "each of you make two braids so she has six when she's done, and decorate them while you're at it."

"Wow." Okay. Except I'd never braided a girl's hair and after two tries Induan reduced me to handing her silver and blue baubles to string onto blue ribbon as she spun Kayleen's unruly hair into a single, smooth braid. Marcus did all right, although Induan finished four braids in the time he did two.

Next, Induan pulled out a pair of scissors. She looked at me, the same evil grin quirking her mouth again. I shook my head until she pulled a long fake braid out of her other pocket. So maybe being the one to get my hair cut wasn't so bad after all; Marcus kept pawing at the extra hair that ran down his back, adjusting the fit and readjusting it.

We watched Induan fiddle with her wings. She seemed to enjoy being the center of attention. But hey, it made perfect sense for someone who liked to be watched to get an invisibility mod, right?

She'd figured out how to jury-rig her mod so she looked like a failed flier. Too bad she couldn't get all the way to looking like a flier. But at its core, her mod was meant to reflect her surroundings and make her invisible rather than to change her appearance, and it took some clever use of mirrors to get as much as she managed to out of it.

We were ready an hour before we could fly. Induan engaged Marcus in a berry-harvesting project, leaving me and Kayleen alone to watch our wings. She looked beautiful and exotic in her braids. Older. I felt . . . awkward. She must have felt the same way since she wouldn't meet my eyes.

"Can you still shield easily?" I asked her.

She nodded.

"Flying like you do must feel pretty good."

Her long fingers twisted one of her neat braids so loose strands poked out here and there. "I love it." She switched hands to worry another of Induan's masterpieces. "But I don't fly like you do. I mean, not ships. I'm always nervous there. They seem so big. Flying just me seems easier—I'm much smaller. Maybe after you've been flying for a while more you'll get the hang of letting go." Her hands fell to her lap and twisted. "The way you tell me with ship's data. Relax into it."

Like I wasn't already trying that. "You look better. I mean, back home, you were more . . . worried . . . than you seem now." I didn't want to use the word I meant: crazy.

I think she understood it, anyway, by her reply. "There's something soothing about the data here. So when I get lost, when I can't tell for sure what's me and what's the data, at least it feels like a safe place."

"You know it probably isn't."

She looked directly at me. Her brows were drawn together and her words trailed off, as if the whole thing puzzled her. "I know. But I'm not scared moment by moment anymore. I don't want to lose control, ever. You weren't there, but back home I thought I might kill some people once."

She hadn't killed anyone, but I had. I'd flown a skimmer full of people into the sea. I said, "I know," and left it at that. I mean, if I got crazed with power once, I could do it again, and I never wanted to.

Induan and Marcus returned and shared some small blue berries with us. By the time we finished, the sky had begun the long, slow fade into late afternoon. We donned our wings and gave each other thumbs-up signs.

It felt good to finally be moving, wings rising and falling through sultry air and the ground beginning to flow beneath me as I gained some sense of rhythm. I understood why Chelo chose her children over me, but I still felt her absence.

Matriana and Daniel met us just outside of town. We followed them, swinging north, away from Oshai. A circle? A ruse? I went with it for a while, but by the time SoBright disappeared over my shoulder I dipped my wings to signal for company. Kayleen responded, plummeting down from high above and slowing perfectly so she flew close. "What?" she mouthed.

"This is the wrong direction! We're not headed for Oshai."

"I'll ask." And she was gone, the ends of the long braids in her hair fluttering audibly against her wing-fabric. Except she didn't actually fly up to anyone—she just got far enough ahead of me to have some room in case she bobbled. In addition to flying better than me by an order of magnitude, she could fly without her shields. Marcus insisted I didn't have enough control yet, so I labored with no data feed to stabilize me. A short time later, Kayleen soared for a few breaths while I flapped hard to catch her. Even though I got pretty close, the wind thinned her voice. "We're going to Hidden Beach."

"Huh?"

"Marcus didn't tell any of us. He didn't want the others to know. In case they get caught."

Now I really wished Chelo was with us. And that the kids could fly. "Even Jenna?"

She shook her head so her braids swung back and forth.

"So are they going where we think they are?"

"I hope so."

Wow. Were we really in that much danger? Oshai was south, The Integrator's Dream was across the planet, a little northeast, and we were going northwest. We were going to end up far from each other.

I liked the idea even less as time wore on and my breath came louder and keeping up became harder. I tried to honor Kayleen's advice about letting go. It did help, a little, since I managed three or four wing beats without worrying or thinking hard about them. We intersected a major road and turned up it, now heading more directly north. With no access to data, I didn't have a map in my head, and no idea of how far we were from anything.

Two new fliers joined us, and Matriana and Daniel peeled away. I was so far below them I couldn't be sure, but one of them looked like Angeline. The other was dark, but I couldn't see his or her face well. The dark-winged flier had almost faded into the sky when we finally landed. My world had shrunk to the size of my aching lower back and shoulders, and my breath sounded like the breath of nearly spent prey, ragged and hard. As soon as I got enough control to look past the patch of grass between my feet, I let it register that it was, in fact, Angeline and Tsawo. They clearly knew each other, and for a moment, I wondered if Tsawo was Paula's mysterious father. Except he'd told Chelo to be careful, right? I mean, he wasn't happy about us being here, right?

I hated being clueless.

Kayleen's braids were all loose now, and one had come halfway unraveled. Maybe nothing could keep her neat.

We were someplace like Chance's house—not physically, but in character. A big house surrounded by neat fields, and trees, and Keeper's cabins. Colors were hard to make out in the fading light, but it seemed like a deep brown designed to blend into the native dirt. Inside, we found Chance, Mari, and Paula. "A friend's place," Chance explained as he helped us strip and stow our wings.

Marcus sighed with pleasure as he hung his fake braid from the edge of his wings. Induan faded to invisibility then winked back into full existence in her true colors as a pale-skinned blonde. Paula blinked at her and licked her lips, but just like we didn't ask about the friend who owned this place, Paula didn't ask Induan about her strange abilities.

Mari led us all to the kitchen and feasted us on salad and fruit and, best of all, great loaves of bread with butter and sweet jam. My eyelids felt like stones had been set on them, and with a full belly I caught myself swaying and grabbed the edge of the counter.

Marcus came up beside me and shook my sore shoulder hard. He clearly didn't quite get how I felt. "Come on. We've got work to do."

Paula blushed. "I'm not sure he's up to it."

"Mmm . . . sure I am."

Marcus handed me a cup of col. "Follow me."

This time there was no laboratory, but there was a grand library—a room full of perches and seats and desks and display walls, all the colors a muted blue darker than the banding on Angeline's wings, with accents in black and brilliant pink. At least it would be hard to fall asleep with the pink.

There was, of course, no Joseph Chair. And no Chelo. Kayleen rubbed some of Paloma's ointment on my shoulders, her fingers doing circles on my stiff muscles, grounding me enough that I fell into Paula's data streams in spite of Tsawo sitting quietly in the back of the room, watching me with a skeptical look on his face.

Marcus drilled me, this time more about what I would change. My answers felt slow and thick, but he made a lot of encouraging noises. The last thing I remember of that night is Paula's voice saying, "Let him stop and sleep."

I did, right there on the couch I'd been sitting on.

When I woke the next morning, my head was pillowed on a couch cushion and a red blanket had been tucked around me. My stomach had turned into a cave and my shoulders into stiff boards. Light stabbed in the high windows, and Marcus's voice boomed through the kitchen. "Five minutes!" And then, "Joseph! Time to go."

What? No breakfast? I stood up and made great big circles with my arms, groaning as the muscles popped. We might be built for strength and recovery, but even manufactured men had limits.

When I stumbled into the kitchen, Marcus shoved a full loaf of bread at me. He led me toward the little room off the side of the house where we'd stored our wings. "What?" I asked. "Why the hurry?"

"We think someone found us."

"From Silver's Home? The guys from the ship?" I stuffed a big bite of bread in my mouth.

"Maybe. Dianne sent me a coded message that means they've been found, but not caught yet."

Jenna was with them. Marcus would hate that. "They're in Oshai?"

He nodded. The others were already here, mostly in their wings, stretching. Kayleen gave me a wan smile.

"Is Chelo safe?"

Marcus reached for my wings. "As far as I know."

"Are we going to help Jenna and the others?"

He held out my wings, one at a time, and I slid them on, shoving another bite of bread into my mouth and thrusting the rest into my pocket. Impossible to get your hand to your mouth and fly all at once. I envied the true fliers, who had arms that didn't have to double as wings. I swallowed, and mumbled. "When did Dianne tell you?"

"Early this morning. But I wanted you to sleep as long as you could. You're tuckered."

That didn't mean I wanted to sleep through important things! "I need to know when any of us is in danger."

He raised an eyebrow. "We have to protect you, most of all."

I bit back the retort I wanted to make, and tried one wing and then the other, testing the way my palms and fingers gripped the end pieces. "We have to protect everyone. And sometimes I'm going to be the protector."

He laughed. "I know. But you're still an exhausted kid."

So did everybody over fifty think everybody under thirty was a kid? Not that I wanted the answer to that. We streamed up into the morning sky in a line, Angeline and Tsawo still with us. Tsawo took the rear, which meant he was close to me. After a while I decided that no matter what else he was, he taught well. He encouraged me. "A slightly longer stroke will give you more lift." It did. "Don't grip so hard with your fingers. Relax." That helped. "Get distance with strong, long strokes. Don't flutter."

I tried not to be too annoyed since I started flying better. And why hadn't Alicia learned better if he was her teacher? When he flew in front of me to give me advice, I still felt a drab beside his grace. The fake wings strapped to my aching appendages paled beside his brilliant ones. His face was pretty, too; angular, dark, with wide-set dark eyes.

We passed a few other groups of fliers, mostly true fliers, but in one case there were three humans under the clear tutelage of three winged ones. Eventually, Tsawo and Angeline peeled away, leaving the four of us alone.

Just as my arms began to threaten mutiny (which didn't take nearly as long as the day before), Kayleen asked for a rest. I was pretty sure she was asking for it for me, and I flashed her a grateful smile as soon as we landed in an empty field. We stripped off our wings and hid them under a tree, and sat down outside of it. Marcus and In-duan went off to find water.

It was a relief to be able to talk instead of yell, not to mention to be on the ground. I really hated flying this way. I dug the slightly squashed bread out of my pocket and handed her half.

She looked at it dubiously but took a small bite anyway, and then finished it. After she licked her lips, I asked her, "So did you learn anything else? Who is it that found the Gang of Girls? Did Marcus hear from Chelo?"

"Marcus won't say so, but I think that's worse."

Probably. I picked up a stone and threw it, sending pain ripping through my shoulder. "Do you have any more salve?"

She dug into her pocket.

"Ten minutes!" Marcus called out.

She grimaced. "I'll hurry." Her hands were warm, and just the smell of Paloma's mixture made me feel better.

"I'm worried," I said. "I don't like running. Maybe Bryan was right and we should have hunted the bounty hunters."

She let out a heavy sigh. "We have children. How could we risk the babies? But yes, I'm worried sick. Marcus told me to stay shielded this morning, too, so I think he's pretty sure we're being watched."

"So are we still going to Hidden Beach?" I liked the name, anyway.

"I don't know. I want my kids."

"Too bad they couldn't fly." Our lives were circles. We'd been chil-dren who couldn't thrive in cold sleep, so our parents left us on Fre-mont all those years ago. Kayleen and I helped each other get strapped back in. "But don't be scared. We've been separated before and we got back together."

"That frightened me, too." She glanced at Marcus, who paced, stopped and bounced on his toes, and paced again. "He's scared, I think. He never looks nervous."

I agreed, but I didn't want to say so. I pointed up at the cloudless sky, where two humans flew side by side, heading almost directly toward us. "Do you recognize them?"

She squinted. "I think it's Chance and Mari."

If so, Chance was flying with different wings. "I hope so."

Kayleen was right. They landed fast and Chance blurted out, "There're pictures of you going around on two of the nets. Can you fly low, and follow me? We're changing destinations."

My arms screamed so hard I barely made the turn. Chance flew so fast it hurt to try to keep up. No one else looked like they were having as much trouble as me, so I just kept going.

We flew over long fallow fields, two kinds of orchard, the stubble of prickly plants that had just been harvested, then a big square of pale green shoots too young to identify. Next, vineyards with ripening grapes hanging on tall trellises three times my height. The odd farming of a man-made moon with perpetual summer.

The vineyards went on and on, only occasionally punctuated with a shed, a road, or a house. Perhaps the vineyards, too, had Keepers. Like Seeyan. I wondered if there were more Keepers than fliers.

The day warmed. Sweat poured down my face with each wing beat. Flying itself was not too hard, but flying and flying and flying and flying some more was tough. I should have been out exercising with the others instead of studying with Marcus.

I started to fall behind, and Marcus and Kayleen both whipped around and yelled at me encouragingly, which made me wish for Alicia's invisibility mod. Embarrassment kept me up for a hundred more wing beats, the others getting farther away from me. Then I couldn't do it anymore. If I tried, I'd just fall out of the sky.

I leaned back just so and gave the powerful wing beat needed to change direction down. My timing was off enough that I landed running and hopping, and finally tumbled end-over-end along a thick path between the tall trellises.

I stood up, ruefully looking at one damaged wing. This was the second time I'd grounded myself; I couldn't recall anyone else missing landings so badly. My pants had a hole in the knee and my knuckles were bleeding. The ribbon of blue above my head and between the trellises was thin and empty. I half-closed my eyes and let the data flows overwhelm me. Potential harvest dates, planting years, soil pH, temperature. All of it twined together, smooth, soothing my hurt feelings.

I slid out of my useless wings and glanced up again. Surely Kayleen and Marcus and the others were looking for me. The grapes were ripening, some ready to pick. Unfortunately, they all hung above my head, and I couldn't pick any even now that I had my hands free. The sun painted them gold and delicious, tempting. Even an hour of flying made my belly scream hunger, and we'd been out all morning. In fact, it was so hot we shouldn't be flying.

The trellises were fairly far apart. There'd be room for takeoffs and landings. But they were tall enough to make seeing any distance tough.

I reached out for Kayleen and found her, the concern and worry in her energy like a knife blade cutting the serenity of the vineyard. *I'm okay,* I sent back to her. Then a picture, best as I could make it, of where I stood.

No, show me from above.

I tried to remember. I'd been so tired. Had I even been looking down? *I can't. But I think I'm near the end of the trellises. Not near enough to see the end.*

Can you fly up so we can see you?

I broke a wing.

I flinched as she cursed, even though she didn't form any specific words for it. Then silence, probably as she told the others. *We'll find you. Watch the sky.*

The vines on either side of me made a riot of deep and pale green, brilliant against the reddish black trellises. My feet crunched softly on the path. I tucked the long wings under my arm, amazed all over again at how light they were when I wasn't holding myself up with them. Maybe if I walked a little bit I'd find some ripe grapes low enough to pick.

Fifty steps later I spotted a bunch just over my head, and dropped my wings. Surely the trellis was no harder to climb than pongaberry trees back home.

It wasn't.

After three tries, I reached the grapes and spotted a better bunch just above. Once I had those in my mouth and had started down, the rustle of wings behind me drew my attention. Marcus stood a meter below me. I brushed a wide leaf aside to get a better view of him.

He used his most-mild speaking voice. "Did you think pasting yourself to the side of a trellis would make it easier to find you?"

"Uh . . . no." I shimmied down and offered him a grape. "I'm hungry."

"Maybe we should feed you more often. What happened?"

I looked down at the ground. "I just . . . my strength. I couldn't go anymore."

He grinned. "On second thought, maybe we need to feed you less. Maybe you're too heavy."

I looked him up and down. He was thinner than me, although not much. He still stood a head taller than me. "I'm no heavier than you are."

He shrugged. "So it's practice. I sent the others on so Chance can get the girls someplace safe. We're going to walk."

Great. Laying down and sleeping for six or seven hours would be better.

"Eat your grapes."

I did, sharing them with him, while he watched me, and maybe talked to Kayleen. Hard to tell. The grapes helped. I picked up my scattered wings and started walking. He followed. "It's about two-hours' walk. We should get where we're going before dark."

"Which is?"

He shook his head, a small glint in his eyes. He knew. He expected me to be pleased. "Did you hear any more from Dianne?" I asked.

"No."

"Should you go find them?"

"No."

"What if something happens to them?"

"Think of this as a battle in a war. We have to focus on our objective."

It took another hour for the end of the vineyard to even be visible. The sun was past midpoint, but still quite hot and insistent. It was nice to walk with him. We'd been together, just us two, for months right after I got to Silver's Home, but we hadn't had much time since then.

We stopped for one last handful of grapes before coming out from between the tall rows into the bright early afternoon. We followed a path through a fallow field. I felt exposed as vistas opened before us and on two sides. Four or five fields from the edge of the vinyard, trees marched neatly up low hills.

We were out of water. The hills looked closer than they were. Even the light wings were heavy by the time we reached the trees. Just as we came under the first cover, my wings were tugged backward out from under my arm. I turned to see them hanging in mid-air. "Induan!"

"Where the path forks, go right."

"I'll follow you."

Induan took Marcus's wings, too. Better yet, she had water. After we almost drained her flask, we followed the two pairs of wings bobbing through the air to the fork, right, then straight for a bit, left and along two switchbacks, and then back into a ravine. The rough dirt and grass we had been walking through gave way to colorful gardens. On our right, blue, green, and purple mosses lined the banks of a slow-moving stream filled with bright yellow fish. To our left, low-growing wildflowers had been planted in thick stripes, so we walked through purple, and blue, and yellow, and orange, then white flowers. Here and there, we passed stone benches. The morning would produce grand views down the ravine, but right now the sun made it nearly impossible to look directly behind us.

Our wings stopped at the mouth of a man-made cave. The ravine and the cave were situated so they'd have sun from midday through sunset. The mouth was over four times as tall as I was, shielded partially from view by slender trees, but surely it could be flown into. No wonder Marcus thought I'd be happy. We'd found our heritage in a cave in Fremont, used it as a secret place to tryst, and eventually hidden from mercenaries in it.

Surely this cave had its secrets, too.

20

CHELO: THE GARDENS

Seeyan's voice sounded reverent as she introduced us to the old man, who kept his eyes down and extended his hand to me. "This is Mohami," she said, "The Keeper of the Ways of the Fliers of Lopali."

When he took my hand, the strength of his grip surprised me. He didn't speak, but turned, and she said, "Follow him."

I gave her a hug, whispering, "Thanks."

"Thank you." And she was gone, with no further good-byes to anyone else, just a wave toward us all, as much a go-on gesture as a parting. Mohami was halfway to the door in the hill. I picked up Caro, Liam hoisted Jherrel onto his shoulders, and Bryan and Alicia flanked us. Mohami led us to a kitchen, where we were feasted in near silence, under the watchful eyes of the man and woman who had carried our packs in. Both had blond hair and warm, brown eyes and friendly smiles, and an eerie habit of silence.

The food was fresh and sweet: grapes and berries that filled the room with scent before we bit into them, and bread so soft it melted warm into our mouths. The children ate as if we hadn't fed them in a week. After we finished, our two silent Keepers led us down a long thick-walled hallway to a suite of rooms with a single bedroom lined with bunks, a small sitting room, and a bathroom. By this time, it was nearly dusk. "I don't see a light," Alicia said. "Is there a candle or something?"

I helped her rummage through drawers. All empty. A few simple signs pasted on the walls told where to find toilet paper and mentioned that morning services were at dawn and breakfast was an hour later. "So we just go to sleep when it gets dark?"

"Or bump into each other," Bryan said, sounding slightly amused.

Alicia frowned at him. "I thought Lopali would be like Silver's Home, where everybody has everything they want."

He grinned back, nonplussed. "Maybe they do. Maybe we should want less."

She grunted. "I want light."

Bryan laughed at her, softly. "I already like it better here than in that big open house."

It was my turn to frown at him. "At least we were all together there. I hate being separated."

"Yeah, but you're always worried about Joseph. He's a big boy." Bryan sat on one of the bottom bunks and played with his retractable nails, a habit I'd learned meant he felt tenser than he was letting on.

Last time I'd been separated from him and Joseph. Maybe we'd have time to become friends again. "It'll be all right," I said. "We'll find each other again. We always have."

Bryan looked at me intently, a little of his ever-present undertone of anger visible in his eyes. "The trick might be to stop letting anyone separate us."

"Yes," I answered.

Liam, who'd been playing on the floor with the kids, looked up and said, "We'll make the dark an adventure. A good night's sleep won't hurt us. Caro's all done in."

She was. She sat still, slumped, rubbing her eyes.

I sighed, worried. "Maybe they have a Wind Reader or two here. I'll ask in the morning."

He pulled me down for a kiss, and then farther down, so we sat cradling Caro. Her eyes were bright, as if she were fevered, although her forehead felt cool to the touch.

After we finally got everyone settled in, the room darkened so much the starlight barely made black-on-black shadows. The thickness of the hill above us, and around us, made me feel like we had been tucked into a dark, safe place. As I drifted off, the sound of so many of us breathing together in the same room comforted me.

My last waking thought was hoping that the children wouldn't need anything before first light.

I shouldn't have worried.

A drum sounded three times right outside the door, jarring my eyes open. The sky had become a starless gray, barely touched by night. I rolled over and put an arm over my eyes. Caro must have moved from the bed she shared with Jherrel to mine sometime in the night. She stirred next me. "Get up, Mommy. They're coming for us."

That was more efficient than the drums. I sat up and stroked her cheek. "Who?"

"The Keepers. It's okay. It's time to say hello to the morning." She hopped out of bed and went around the room, greeting everyone. She was usually cheerful in the morning, but this was over the top, even for her.

In no more than the time it took to get everyone dressed and shod, a knock sounded at the door.

The pair who had been with us last night waited expectantly outside in the hallway, dressed in long one-piece robes, and with clean, alert faces. I remembered the sign on the wall, and decided we were going to find out what morning services were.

"There you are," Caro told them, and then turned to the rest of us. "We should follow them."

Well, we would have figured that out, but Caro looked so serious it was all I could do not to burst out laughing. Our guides looked like they were having the same trouble, since both of them looked away for a few minutes. As soon as we were all ready, the girl leaned down to Caro and said, "Please tell everyone to be quiet. We will explain the services later, over breakfast. The other people you'll meet have all been here a week or more already, and are beginning to understand. You won't want to disturb them with noise."

Understand what?

Caro nodded, but then looked at Jherrel, who was standing beside me holding my hand. "He might not listen to me. Will you tell him?" She turned away and started down the line to carry out her task.

This time the girl couldn't manage not to laugh. Her laughter sounded unusually sweet and deep. She looked younger than me, but I reminded myself looks meant nothing here. "I'll tell him," I told her. "I'm his mother."

"Chelo."

"Yes." Apparently, I was never going to have to introduce myself here. "And you are?"

She hesitated. "Kala."

"Thank you." I looked down at Jherell. "Did you hear your sister?"

He nodded, shy at Kala's gaze.

Seriousness fell back across Kala's face like a veil. Caro loudly told every one of us to be silent and came back to stand at the head of the line with her chin up and her blue eyes locked on Kala's.

This time, there was no long walk down a hall, but instead a shorter traverse to the far side of the hill, the side we hadn't seen yet. As we emerged through the door, the land in front of us was still shrouded in the gray before dawn, but even so I felt like we walked into a field of art. The garden was a grand circle, half the size of the whole central area in SoBright. Even the dull predawn light hinted at a riot of colors in curving geometric shapes, much like the ordered chaos of the fractal math I'd learned on one of the ships between Fremont and here. The words organic and structured both leapt to mind.

So did a few lines of poetry, and a snatch of song or two.

Beside me, and visible, Alicia drew in a deep breath. Caro clapped a hand theatrically over her mouth as if to emphasize how hard it was to be silent, and brilliant curiosity lit Liam's eyes.

Was this the garden of the soul Seeyan had told me about the first day I met her?

Other groups emerged from doorways all around the circle of the garden. I watched carefully, hoping for some children for the kids to play with. I spotted a few smaller figures across the vast circle from us, but all of the people closest to us were adults. Maybe one in ten was a flier. Helpers or also tourists? Or students? I couldn't tell.

As much attention as we gave to being quiet, the other groups were more silent, some actually gliding like our Keepers and the old man who had greeted us when Seeyan dropped us off.

Early-morning cool enveloped garden and people. A stray wind puffed a strand of hair about my face.

We followed the example of the other nearby groups and spread out around the edge of the circle, holding hands, creating a continuous line of life enfolding the living mandala in front of us.

The last clasping hand seemed to be the signal. At least twenty fliers, who must have been hidden behind the rolling rises of the hills, leapt into the air as one. Only then did I notice that the hilltops were also ringed unevenly with watchers, winged and unwinged. So this was a big deal.

The fliers came together and spiraled up, fast and high, like an explosion out of the darkness. After flying myself, I could barely imagine the strength it took to rise so fast. They seemed so close together I half-expected them to hit each other and tumble, broken, from the sky. They might have been smoke rising from the fire of Lopali's soul.

Their precision made me forget to breathe.

Sunlight flashed and glowed in the highest flier's wings, and they were all high enough for the sun to bathe them, to flash on their jewels and illuminate the many, many colors of their many wings.

They came down again, synchronous, fast, plummeting toward the garden. Just as I wondered if I should grab the children and shelter them, two fliers dipped near the ground and back up, turning impossibly sharply with arched backs and an odd twist to their wings. The lot of them came back together in the center of the great garden, once more below the light of the sun, duller.

They rose again, slower this time, almost straight up, yet threading between each other. Surely a trick of the eye made them seem to be holding hands. This time the sun touched them lower in the sky. At the apex, when all of them were bright with morning, they darted away from each other all at once, flying until we could no longer see them.

I glanced at Alicia, expecting her gaze to be as rapt as mine. Instead, her brows were drawn together, and a bit of her old fury painted her mouth into a tight line and sealed her jaw taut.

I would think about her later. This was my first moment here, and I wanted a pure impression.

Around us, a chant started. Caro started right off in tune and in time, and we ended up following her as much as the more experienced Keepers and students who surrounded us. Her voice was clear and sure, and as innocent as the fliers had been beautiful.

"The beauty of flight."

"The pain of flight."

Voices spilled down the hills as well as from either side of us, a measured cadence. These were well-known and well-loved words.

"The light of flight."

"The joy of flight."

The old man who had greeted us the night before, the Keeper of the Ways of the Fliers of Lopali, rose from the bench in the center of the circle. Only then did I notice the strangeness of age here, where almost everyone looked young until they died. So much more about Mohami had been strange that his age had seemed unremarkable. Or perhaps it had just seemed to fit him.

He extended his hands up above his head, taking in the open circle of sky just in the moment it switched from gray to blue.

Voices spoke an answer to his gesture. "The joy of flight and the pain of life. The spiral of strength and love."

So many people speaking the same words all at once seemed to make them far more powerful than they should be. Peace and acceptance flowed through the group of people, as if it passed from hand to hand. I felt big with it, full of compassion and appreciation for the beauty that surrounded me here.

Hot tears spilled down my cheeks, startling me.

There were almost as many people here in this garden as in all of Artistos. They spoke in one voice.

I had never imagined such a moment.

Each and every one of them had an inner beauty. We were all perfect, all as perfect as the fliers, regardless of the pain we might have felt in our lives, the people or animals we might have hurt or killed, the wars we might have started.

The garden rang with one feeling, one voice, one peace, one magical note of song.

I didn't want to look at anyone, didn't want to break the powerful, personal spell. Liam's hand rose to my shoulder from behind me, and I knew he knew I was crying and that he didn't care, that he understood my tears.

We had grouped together, inexorably drawn to each other like the family we were. As if we connected to all of the other people around the circle, who simultaneously moved like we did, our feet began to tread the garden paths. At that moment, sunlight touched the tops of the hills farthest from us.

A circle of hundreds of people stepped together, drawing from the outside in, like a river flowing downhill. Tall and short, winged and not, from all of the five planets that otherwise prepared for war.

Caro led us, Jherrel behind her, then me and Liam, and Bryan and Alicia. Behind us all, and before the next group, Kala, head up, an amazed look on her face.

Our pace was slow. Not because of Caro's short legs, but because the beauty we passed needed to be admired. Each group traveled at close to the same speed, like a slow wave of humanity heading for the center. On either side, the flowers lining the path were miracles of creation, more beautiful and perfect than anything on Fremont. Each petal had the perfect shape, the perfect balance of wildness and sculpted design. Even though the sun had not yet kissed us or the garden around us (it was beginning to light the group across the circle from us), the colors were clear and crisp, almost as if I could see the very cells, the water the petals drank, the effect of air on a leaf.

The orderly, kept land around SoBright, too pretty just yesterday, had become pallid and unruly, and Fremont became a wildness beyond imagining. This perfection went beyond order to something more profound.

We approached the center of the circle, which was the only lawn in the garden, just large enough for all of us to gather, folded in rows. Sunlight spilled onto the grass as we moved into the middle, sunlight and us meeting, all of the people who had become the family in our circle meeting.

In the very middle, Mohami.

Caro went to him. He knelt and picked her up and held her above his head, his thin arms shaking, a smile pasted across his face.

One of my tears splashed onto my hand.

He set Caro down and came to me, his fingers under his chin while he looked into my eyes.

Then he knelt on the ground in front of me and my daughter. "We are blessed."

21

ALICIA: BEING KEPT

The withered old man knelt in front of Caro, his eyes shining. Chelo looked as beatific, almost lit from within. Sunshine poured down on the upturned and smiling faces of travelers from all of the five planets. Flowers filled the spaces people did not; tall stems netted with purple and violet, great yellow bells, bright blue stalks as high as a person. In keeping with this mad place, the flowers smelled stronger than the people, the scents mixing like honey in the air.

And we thought these soft people were going to join our side in a war?

More likely, Chelo's viewpoint would win. Everyone would sing songs and hold hands and watch the war, and then when it was over they'd kiss the victors without even bothering to check which side they were on.

Mohami offered Chelo his hand and she took it, putting her other hand in Caro's. Caro linked Liam in, and they all turned out, facing us in the four directions. Chelo looked toward us, her dark hair hanging on her shoulders, her olive skin sun touched, and her eyes full of tears. She clearly saw more than just me and Bryan. But maybe when you wanted a home so bad you prayed for it with every breath you took, it was easy enough to find one.

The crowd gently pressed Bryan and me forward, and we went, shuffling, having trouble breathing. I sidestepped to be in front of him, and tilted my head back and whispered, "Stop."

He did, whispering back. "Thank you."

The whole ceremony seemed overwrought and funny-sad. I stood in front of Bryan, his broad back serving as a wall that the slow stream of people parted around. They still moved forward all around us, many almost dancing in place, the group excitement worse than the day the roamers came into town. Three women passed us, looking joyful, sighing softly in the back of their throats as if they beheld a litter of new puppies instead of an old, bald man. A swarthy man in a gold shirt with black pants and gold sandals held his hands in front of him, folded, as if in prayer. A pair of tall lanky men held hands and walked solemnly forward, eyes shifting back and forth as if they were afraid they might miss something.

Above us, the sky was clear of fliers. Beside us, a flier with maroon wings striped in black and yellow brushed my arm and, absurdly, I looked to see if he had dropped a feather.

Bryan took a step back. Good. I followed. Slowly, ever so slowly, we two crept backward.

One step at a time.

I wanted the far edge of the crowd in the worst way.

The sky-dance of the fliers had enthralled me, but it hadn't painted me with love for everyone else nearby the way it seemed to have affected Chelo. Before the crowd closed entirely in front of us, I caught a glimpse of Chelo's face, laughing, her dark eyes sparkling as she said something to Mohami, the Keeper of the Ways of the Fliers of Lopali. I wondered if he'd studied at the School of Heaven's Flight and showered in The Stream of Heaven's Water and ate the Bread of the Enlightened and what the people called it when he went to the bathroom.

Once we finally moved far enough back for some fresh air and the crowd had lost its forward momentum, mumbled words I couldn't quite make out rose above the crowd for a moment, and then a great deep buzz started from among the people. It turned out to be a hum. A single syllable: "uu." Starting low and then rising, the syllable held through repeated breaths, in the end sounding like "you you you you" and then starting over.

All around us, people were clasping each other's hands.

A voice spoke behind us. "Hum. You'll like it."

I turned back to see our Keepers from this morning, Kala and the vacuous-eyed Samuel. His face was all sweetness, her voice encouraging. "Hum. Just do it. For some people, it takes a few days to feel the power of the ceremony of Morning Services."

Hopefully it would take me forever. But we were guests, and so I hummed and Bryan hummed behind me, and at least we two hummed together, even if there was no unison between us and the crowd. What we did was more like the uu of two people struggling not to laugh.

Thankfully, the grand all-together hum and holding of hands seemed to be the last requirement for the morning. People began to whisper to each other, and then to talk, and, finally, to walk back toward the barracks. I pointed at the tops of the green hills where the watchers had been, which were quickly emptying. "Let's go sit up there."

We made it up the first low part of the grade before Kala caught up with us. She called my name, and Bryan's, and we stopped and turned and looked down at her. "I just . . . wanted to see it from up above," I said to her.

That made her smile. "I'll go with you."

"What if I promise we'll come back?"

She only smiled again, and went past us, leading on up the hill. The ground below us that had seemed so crowded a few minutes ago was now almost empty. I spotted our family by finding Caro and Jherrel racing circles around Liam and Chelo, who walked side by side, intent on a conversation with Mohami. The mandala garden seemed even prettier from up here, but I'd come to mistrust all the beauty of Lopali.

On the other side of the hill's crest, more hills, just like we'd driven through. I watched Kala's back. She didn't have the misshapen figure of a failed flier, but rather looked like most women in the Five Worlds—well-formed and strong and pretty, with no gray hair or lines by her eyes. With Kala, I had the sense she was actually young.

Weren't they supposed to be keeping gardens instead of us?

I didn't want to ask if there was anyplace we could talk privately. I caught up to her. "Look, Kala, one of the things we need to do is exercise. Every day. We already missed yesterday. We need to run."

She looked like she had expected to hear something about the ceremony or a question about how we might save our souls, but to give her credit she parsed my words well enough after a few breaths. "There is a track."

"Can you tell us how to get there?"

"I'll take you there."

Of course. We weren't dressed in exercise clothes, but we had on good enough shoes. She was in a long robe; we could outrun her. Not to get away, not yet, but we could talk to each other and maybe we wouldn't even be overheard.

My plan worked, except for Bryan mumbling that he didn't want to work up a sweat in his good ceremonial shirt.

I decided to take that as sarcasm.

The oval track Kala led us to hummed with activity. A busy game that involved teams and balls threaded up and down the middle, the players calling and hooting back and forth to each other. The balls were large and heavy, and looked slick. A short wall separated the game from the track itself, where five other runners circled, two lazily, two together in a race, and the other running steadily with great long bounds.

I watched Kala to see what she would do, and she camped out on a low rise where she could watch the whole track. There, she folded her hands in her lap.

Bryan sprinted out ahead of me, the footing a soft foamy material that gave underfoot and had just enough roughness so that my feet didn't slip as I leapt into a slow run.

We went two full rounds in silence. A few more people joined us, probably also refugees from the ceremony. A woman from the game fell near us and bounced back up quickly. Bryan matched me step for step and spoke softly, his voice edged. "I need to get out of here."

Good. No kidding. "This whole planet creeps me out. But this is the worst spot yet. Besides, we're not exactly hidden standing around with hundreds of people every morning."

He must have understood my meaning. "You need to stay and watch over Chelo."

"She has Liam."

He waited until we'd turned halfway around the track before answering. "I don't want her hurt. You're strong enough to take care of her."

"So are you. You could stay and I can go."

He grunted. "We should have heard from the Gang of Girls by now."

I glanced across the track at silent Kala. "Neither one of us can stand this much longer, you know."

"Seeyan may hear something. She'll tell us if she does."

We sped up, passing the single runner. When we passed in front of Kala, it looked like her eyes were closed. "I bet if we just ran off the track, she'd follow us."

Bryan laughed. "So she's good. Want to try it?"

"Surely we'll hear from them soon."

"Ming was supposed to contact me yesterday."

I almost stumbled over my feet. "How?"

"We have a two-way she bought on one of the ships."

He wasn't carrying anything big. "Where?"

"In my jaw."

Good for him. Good for them both. "Nice. Sometimes I think we're all too compliant."

"You would think that way."

But he'd acted on it. He must be worried sick. "Maybe she just couldn't reach you. I mean, what if she's just out of range, or they're being watched too closely?"

"As a dance teacher?"

There was that.

22

JOSEPH: THE CAVE OF REAL POWER

Induan, still carrying our wings, seemed to disappear as she walked into the cave. I squinted after her. The cave made a door in a wall of rock. Here and there, yellow and light green grasses had found enough dirt in the cracks of the rocks to send up thin tendrils, and in three places, bright yellow flowers bloomed. Red and orange leaves on long stems hung across the mouth, like a high curtain. Behind them, just darkness. No Induan. No wings. No Kayleen.

Not even any sound.

Marcus grinned as he watched me stop and stare, and then take a few more steps. Induan had gone through, so I followed what looked like her footsteps, and walked into the blackness.

Light and sound startled me, and only Marcus's firm hand in the small of my back kept me going forward into it. When I looked behind me, the blackness was gone entirely. A ray of late sunshine speared into the cave, illuminating the darkness for quite a distance before bright artificial light took over. Our cave at home had felt big. This was . . . big enough to hold all of Artistos, and that was in this one chamber.

The walls had been made. The floor was flat, the walls a combination of squared-off and rounded, perhaps following the contours of natural veins of rock. "Wow."

"It was created long ago, fashioned inside the bones of the moon that was the seed for Lopali."

That sounded so Marcus. There were at least twenty or so people in view, maybe twice that many, mostly wingless humans like us. Buildings hugged the walls. Some of the main floor had been cleared with lines painted around it. Storage? Whatever, it was empty now. A shaft of light from above lit one corner, although I couldn't see the opening that let the light in.

I hadn't expected a small city.

Induan's light blond hair and Kayleen's unruly dark tresses drew my eye. They stood bent over something in a near corner of the cave. I started toward them.

A black-and-white streak emerged from between them and bounded toward me. Sasha. I whispered thanks to whoever had brought my dog to me.

I knelt down and let Sasha barrel into me, so tired that the strength of her enthusiastic leap knocked my feet from under me; I landed on my backside covered in black-and-white dog.

Laughing, Marcus helped me up. "It's grand, isn't it?"

"Yes. Yes, it is."

He grinned. I grinned back. "So why wasn't this always our destination? I mean even before SoBright?"

His cheeks actually reddened. "It's a secret."

"It looks safer than SoBright."

He gave me one of his steady you-don't-know-everything looks. "You needed to be seen."

I decided I'd regret answering that before I thought about it, and kept going toward the girls. Seeyan was seated on the far side of the small circle. That explained Sasha. I went right to her, and she held out her hand, putting her long slender fingers into my palm. She smiled. "Your sister is safe. And the others who came with me."

"Where?" They hadn't known when they left.

Seeyan shook her head. "They're near the center of Oshai, and well guarded."

"But I need to know where she is! What if she needs my help?"

Marcus had come up beside me. At least he looked contrite. "It's best . . . for security . . . if you don't know each other's hiding place."

I turned around on him, all the pain in my still-aching shoulders and the fatigue swimming through my body turning to a flash of anger. "I should never have let you separate us! We should never have agreed to this."

He shook his head gently. "I planned to keep her with us. It's the kids we couldn't have, and this was her choice."

I knew that. But separating me from Alicia was Marcus's choice. Ever since the first day he met us, on Silver's Home, he'd been mildly disapproving of Alicia. "What? No room for babies in this huge place?"

Kayleen, who had been watching quietly, spoke up. "Joseph. Relax. It's done now. We'll be together soon. I know we will."

"How do you know?" I snapped at her. "I don't know."

She gave me a hurt glance and walked off.

Maybe I should have followed her, but Seeyan's hands were still in mine. She squeezed lightly, her angled features giving her a wild look, her wide-set brown eyes intense. She seemed nervous. I remembered Chelo mentioning how weird it felt when everyone knew her. I bet I was learning the same feeling. She spoke earnestly, her voice quivering a bit at first. "It would have been hard to get the children here. There are no roads, and they're too heavy to carry. They *are* in a safe place, Joseph, I promise. They're very, very well protected."

"They'd better be," I snapped. I took a deep breath, surprised at how angry and worried I sounded. Chelo and Alicia were both strong, both adults. But I wasn't going to feel better until I saw them. I let out a long sigh and let go of Seeyan's hands, stepping back.

Disappointment crossed her face, and she rubbed her hands together in front of her.

"I am sorry," I said. "I'm very, very tired."

"Sit." She ushered me to a chair, and gestured to Induan, who reached into a large bag beside her. Seeyan poured me a tall glass of water from a carafe and then brought over a self-heating teacup. It smelled of Seeyan, and must have come from her house. I'd never seen one, but Chelo had told me about them. The glass of water disappeared first. The teacup was as magical as Chelo described. The tea itself tasted bitter but, as I drank it, I felt physically better, although still worried.

Marcus had disappeared somewhere else in the cave, maybe going after Kayleen. I wanted to go find them both, but even though I felt better, my tired legs really, really didn't want to move. So I sat with Induan and Seeyan. We shared a good view out of the cave from our seats, while the sun painted the sky with orange and pink and a purplish gold. The cave mouth acted like a picture frame, making the sunset seem like a vid wall from a ship. The brightening artificial light and the sounds of movement from behind us accentuated the effect. Sasha, curled beside me, made it all the more pleasant. When Seeyan got up and refilled my teacup, I looked up at her. "Thank you for bringing Sasha."

Her smile was tender, and she reached a hand out toward my face but then pulled back before touching me. "You're welcome."

"What is this place?" I asked her.

She folded down beside me, legs crossed. She wore thin yellow leggings and a green blouse that contrasted nicely with her auburn hair. "It's from before they made us. Before they finished Lopali. There are a few more of these. Most are just abandoned. Keepers inhabit at least five. And some, like this one, we lease to other people. It's a way to get credit so that we can do our own projects."

Did she mean ones the true fliers didn't know about? Although, there were a few fliers here. "Who do you lease this one to?"

A flustered look crossed her face and I sensed she wished I hadn't asked her. "A group of people like Marcus."

"Who work with fliers? People working on what I'm working on?" I pointed into the dusk outside. White and black wings moved toward us in near-perfect unison. Angeline and Tsawo. I looked for a set of made wings and found none. Paula wasn't with them.

"Do you know Paula?" I asked Seeyan.

She looked away. "I've met her. But Paula isn't one of us."

"Isn't a Keeper?" Because she wasn't a failure?

Seeyan shook her head. "Keepers who are the same age—and Paula and I are close—spend a lot of time in the same classes and building the same projects. But I've only met Paula a few times." She sounded proud of herself. "Paula doesn't have our training."

So Seeyan didn't like her? "Which means?"

Seeyan looked confused. "Well, if she were a Keeper she'd have a purpose in life."

I managed not to choke on the dregs of the tea. "I have a purpose in life."

Her eyes widened. "Of course you do. You're a maker."

Wow. "I was trying to say maybe Paula is okay. I've met her, and she's part of the work being done to help you all." After the words escaped, I realized I'd spoken too sharply.

Angeline and Tsawo landed, and turned to silhouettes as they looked back at the last of the sunset.

Seeyan sipped her tea in quiet, watching the two fliers. She'd been born by a mother she'd never met, taken to another planet, broken, rejected by a family that had bought her (bought her!) and then been given a simple job. No wonder she identified so with the job. Come to think of it, all of Lopali was pretty tied up around whether you were flier or a tourist or a seeker or a Keeper or another kind of human who lived here. "I'm sorry," I said. "I didn't mean to sound short with you. I'm just not very happy about being separate from Chelo, and there's still a lot I don't understand about this place. In case that's not enough, people are chasing me."

Her usual gentle smile came back. "Opposition is almost always an opportunity to learn."

"Sometimes." I could see why people would have taught her that. "Sometimes it's just an obstacle."

She picked up my teacup and took it away without answering me. She'd lost the smile again, but she still looked more contemplative than angry.

I went back to petting Sasha and watching for the first stars, which was a lot easier than understanding Seeyan.

I only got to find three stars before Marcus found me. He offered me a hand, which I took, and I let him pull me up. We stood side by side looking out into the darkness. His voice was soft. "I'm sorry."

"For?"

"That you're hunted. That you aren't all together. I've watched you and Chelo, and you're both stronger when you're together." He was apologizing, but I didn't hear regret in his voice.

"Kayleen's family is split up, too." Kayleen! "Where is Kayleen?" I should have gone after her a long time ago. She had to be even lonelier than me.

"Come on. I'll show you."

He led me toward the back of the cave, where a table had been set up with food for the taking. I looked around. "Where is she?"

"Grab a plate of food and come on."

I took bread and fruit, avoiding a pile of the same grapes I'd already gorged on. There was wine on the table. I reached for it.

Marcus put a hand out to stop me. "Drink water. You shouldn't be impaired."

I grunted, tempted to pour anyway. "Aren't we safe here? At least tonight."

"We still have work to do."

"All I want to do is find Kayleen, then eat, and have a glass of wine, and sleep."

He looked at me as if I were a small child, which made me feel like one. "I'm sorry. But I'm tired."

"Me, too. But the longer it takes us to stop this war, the more people will die."

I poured a glass of water, being deliberately slow. "And hiding in a cave on a planet full of bird people will stop this war? And aren't we only hiding from two people? How can they be such a threat?"

Marcus sounded exasperated. "I'll answer those backward. There are powerful people paying to have you killed. We can change that, but not immediately. And you and I are good, but we aren't the only strong Wind Readers in the Five Worlds. Why do you think I'm warning you off the nets when you aren't working?"

He didn't appear to want an answer so I took a bite of bread while he continued. "Lopali will make a difference in this war. We're almost even, but without them . . . we might not win. If we can help them, earn their trust and get them to our side, we'll have more power and a much, much better chance."

"If the people we're trying to get them to fight alongside don't kill us first."

"That's right." He picked up a grape and tossed it in the air, catching it easily. The next time he caught it in his mouth, completely breaking my anger. "Politics," he said after he finished the grape, "very seldom makes any sense." He plucked a slice of bread off the table and handed it to Sasha. She gobbled it up and stared at him for more. He picked out a few pieces of fruit.

"So if politics doesn't make any sense, how do you know when you're doing the right thing?"

"You trust yourself. Bring your plate. You need to see the war room." Huh?

We left the main room and walked down a wide hallway. Halfway down, Marcus waved his hand in front of a door, which opened for him. He stopped to let me pass, Sasha following at my heels.

Inside, I stopped and stared. The far wall was entirely video, a view of space like I'd had from *Creator*. Only it wasn't contiguous, it was chopped into squares, the edges visible primarily by the shifting of constellations and nebulae in the background. Here and there, ships appeared to fly in and out of the squares. As I looked closely, every square held a ship.

The ships looked like the bigger ones we'd seen at Li Spaceport back on Silver's Home, or at some of the space stations. Many had obvious weapons.

I counted. Ten squares up, eleven or twelve across. Over a hundred.

"That's what's at stake," Marcus said. "And as much as Silver's Home is often wrong, and as hard as I'm working to change the biggest wrongs, Islas is worse."

As if it were timed to his words, the view in front of us shifted to a widescreen picture of space with blinking yellow dots. "The Islan Fleet," he murmured. "To stop the war completely. To make all those ships turn around. That's what I want."

Lopali seemed really small compared to those fleets. "How many ships does Lopali have?"

He grunted. "Two hundred or so. That's the easiest way to stop this. The other two fleets are close in strength today, nearly a thousand ships each. But Islas's command is more unified." He glanced around and licked his lips. "The thing about Lopali's fleet is that they're very, very accurate. And agile. Small and fast. Also, the Islans look up to the fliers. They wouldn't want to shoot at them. They've been working as hard to make them to stay neutral as I am to get them to take a side."

"What's Silver's Home working for?"

He grimaced, and his voice sounded bitter. "It changes day to day. I've been working that angle since before your parents left for Fremont the first time. It's like swimming upstream; futile from the beginning. Maybe we'll get lucky, they won't be able to agree long enough to go to war."

I glanced up at the wall of ships, which still showed the Islan fleet. "Isn't that good?"

"Not if it makes us lose."

The wall changed to show a view of both fleets. Dots in the sky—individual ships couldn't be drawn at this scale. The Islan side looked more organized, even from this wide and far view. But I didn't know enough to know if that was better. "But the fleets aren't really that close to each other, right?"

"No. They're months away. It's just how we're displaying them. This wall is a simulation. The only real vid we have is our fleet." He was shifting back and forth on his feet, as if the sight of the powerful armies infused him with energy.

I'd forgotten the plate in my hand.

A blocky man with short dark hair and swarthy skin came up to me and Marcus. "Introduce us?"

"Of course. This is Joseph the infamous."

I looked. He was grinning. I managed not to drop the plate while I extended my other hand. "Pleased. And you are?"

"Stark."

Well, the name fit him. Everything was angles. His clothes were simple, and black, all the way down to his shoes. In a room this dark, he'd disappear if he wasn't looking at you or smiling.

Marcus elaborated. "Stark is an old friend. He's responsible for the security here, and for getting all of us information if anything changes."

I wondered briefly if he worked for Marcus or with him. No matter.

Stark smiled at me. "I hope I get to visit with you. In the meantime, it looks like you're planning on dinner. I'll leave you to it."

"Thanks. I'll see you soon." He walked away, fast, heading toward a tall man in the corner.

Marcus looked after him with a rather fond look on his face. "Don't mind Stark. He has a short attention span, but that's just because you're not broken right now. If you ever need anything, he'll be there for you."

Good enough. The room was pretty dim except for the wall, although I could see ten or twelve figures walking around, and in two places—far in the corners, away from the screens, smaller displays threw light onto the faces of watchers. I looked for Kayleen. Marcus took my elbow. "She's over here."

We walked to the back wall, which was lined with dark lumps in the dark room . . . the lumps turned out to be comfortable chairs, easy to sink into. Kayleen was the only inhabitant; her dark hair faded into the general darkness so only the contrasting whiteness of her face and arms showed. Her eyes were closed.

Marcus whispered, as if afraid he'd wake her, "Sit down and eat, then drop your shields." He walked off and left me with my plate on my lap, my friend nearly comatose by my side, and my eyes glued to the display wall.

Sasha stared at my plate until I gave her a bit of bread, then settled at my feet. I mentally thanked Seeyan again. My world was better when Sasha was around, my bit of home, my success story from the war (battle!) with the Star Mercenaries.

I barely tasted my food as I watched the ever-changing display in front of me. So many ships, and although real relative size was impossible to tell, all of them were bigger—by far—than anything I'd been in.

How many pilots did they take? How many crew? What were the weapons like? What would it be like to fight in a ship?

I'd rescued, and I'd fled, and I'd flown, but I'd never driven a ship that was itself a weapon. The closest we'd come was the Burning Void, back on Fremont, and I wasn't even there. Kayleen piloted her, and Liam and Chelo threw bombs out the door at the Star Mercenaries.

This was a different scale altogether.

Next to me, Kayleen breathed harder, making small moaning sounds. I needed to go down and see where she had gone, especially after I spoke so harshly to her. But I couldn't quite tear my eyes away from the screen.

This convergence of fleets was so much bigger than us. Changing flier genetics was nothing, and by the same token, couldn't be enough to change the trajectory of so many things already in motion. No matter what Marcus thought, how could we be any more than spectators?

At least Chelo wasn't here. She'd hate seeing this. It would frighten her and make her angry all at once.

But me? I wanted to fly them. I felt surprised at how much the powerful space ships spoke to my heart, my blood, my breath. This was not what Marcus had been teaching me; not how he'd want me to feel. That, I knew. Marcus had been more father to me than David Lee ever had been, had taught me more, pinned more of his hopes on me. He'd rescued me, and helped me rescue Chelo. He wanted to stop the war, not fly the ships. Chelo would feel the same. I should.

But to fly such a beast!

I set the plate down and lay back, opening to whatever data might be here.

Immediately I was wrapped in the familiar. This was like Silver's Home, like *Creator*, like the *New Making*. All of the sweet seductive slowness of Lopali was gone, and here information flooded my whole being, chaotic and confusing and welcome. I belonged here. It steadied me, feeling the threads, choosing some and rejecting others. I heard myself laugh—my *self* deep in the data hearing my physical laughter, and then I dove deeper, letting go of the physical, losing the sound of my laughter and leaving behind the flat pictures on the wall.

The room's data pulsed all around me, kept me from becoming lost out in the fleet, kept me from seeing too many details. Besides, I was here for Kayleen. I had an apology to make. I brushed her energy, sent her soothing thoughts. She felt thin and fluttery, virtually far away.

The room's data folded me, gave me structure, reminded me of where I was. At the same time, the data flowing into it—from space, of course—demanded attention. Trajectories. Weights and fuels and star systems and a thousand possible strategies, none of them decided. Some rejected, some gone because of one choice or another.

This was the data of impending war.

The details of hundreds of specifications and weapons, the hope and despair of possibilities. The ships' computers sending to this very room the calculations and recalculations they made over and over in preparation. The limited dreaming of ships' AIs.

So many choices meant the fleet, our fleet, had room still. Time could change the outcome.

In a way, the ships were like demon dogs. The captains and the AIs chattered across space and time, all of the conversation now hours old due to the lag between there and here, but urgent and awake and aware. Intense.

An incredible counterpoint to the calmness here, making both seem so outrageous they must be lies. Two truths so different they should not exist so close together.

I stayed close to Kayleen, kept one bit of awareness on her, while I followed other threads. Kayleen was easy to feel, familiar, even though I could tell we were far apart in the data streams. Being physically close probably helped. Knowing her helped. Still, the ships demanded attention, the raw purpose of this room as a place to watch the engines of war pulling me, almost the way Lopali data pulled me serene.

The ships' chatter rode the top of all the data, noisy and demanding; it took bandwidth to draw them on the wall. But there was more below. And Kayleen was below. I shrugged away the fascinating detail and dove, sensing when she and I were seeing the same thing. She felt curious and appalled, but she reached for me, sent me a greeting and pulled me into the part of the data threads or streams she inhabited.

Are you okay? I asked.

Mostly. These aren't the Lopali data streams. They scare me.

That's good. They're more likely to be real.

It's so fast. What if I get lost in here? What if I get lost?

I'm here. I'll help you if you need anything. I sent her peace and calm, a feeling of being present. I waited until she felt smoother. *What are you looking at? Show me. I'm here for you.*

I'm glad. Come see!

There were piles of data from all the planets' newsfeeds. I let her lead me, knowing I should come back and look and see the details. Metadata streamed past. Islans demonstrating against Silver's Home.

Riots on Silver's Home—some for, some against. People in both places being sent to war. Mothers and fathers crying at being split from their children, men and women angry or proud or scared when one part of a family left. Spaceports with remembrance stones around the edges.

Eventually, what Kayleen brought me to see: A newsfeed from Silver's Home had our pictures and unrecognizable descriptions of us. Joseph the big and brave, Joseph the powerful. Some truth: Joseph who could fling ships into the sea. I flinched. The Star Mercenaries stories, real, but realer than life. I had done that, but it had not been a starship, just a skimmer, and four people I killed in anger, but not by cold-blooded plotting. It almost threw me up and out, my heart pounding with anger.

If I could have clutched Kayleen's hand I would have. I stayed near her, following the threads she fed me, seeing stories about my sister having a real choice, and all by herself setting the starships in motion.

I had not been there but, from what she said, she might herself believe that. She should never see this story.

Marcus, angry and powerful instead of full of humor. The threads of bad stories branched to history rewritten, to the bounty on our heads, to rumors that we were here, on Lopali.

I'm not mentioned in the main stories, Kayleen sent.

Good.

She returned slightly miffed energy, a moment of laughter. *Good for her. Let me show you. The first ones are the official stories, repeated and repeated and repeated, like we should believe them because we hear them more than once. Some people on Silver's Home blaming us for the war, as if we wanted it or even knew the players. But there are other stories.*

She felt angry. There is no sound when you speak the way we spoke inside the world of data, but there is cadence and speed and choice of words. *Of course there are other stories.*

We showed each other.

Kayleen *was* rumored later. A few people said she was my sister. One said she was my sweetheart. No reports suggested she and my sister and Liam were a family. A few reports mentioned Bryan—as bodyguard or fighter. Ming was Ming the Traitor or Ming the Hero. Someone had even figured out Sasha's existence.

Chelo had asked me to find the stories Dianne had referenced, and I hadn't really done it. *Kayleen, which stories are ours?*

Ours?

From Marcus or Dianne?

I can't tell.

Which ones say we're good?

Oh!

Now that we looked together, our own story machine emerged slowly. Counter to the official one from Silver's Home. Sort of. Chelo the savior of the world, she and I the hands-down winners—solo—in the battle for Artistos. I didn't recognize how good I was at Reading the Wind. Try as I might, I couldn't track it back to us—couldn't prove Dianne or Tiala or Marcus originated anything. Marcus himself was featured as often as me—characterized as a rich, powerful, eccentric loner who'd gone beyond the law, and become the hero who would save the worlds.

The stories that I thought came from us didn't mention Alicia or Bryan, Kayleen or Liam. Just me and Chelo. Good. I didn't want any-one else compromised. The sheer volume of data made me angry, the number of people who must be working to add to the legends of us, good and bad. Back on Silver's Home, Marcus had called this *buzz*, but I no longer thought it arose spontaneously. Maybe sometimes. But we had been gone for years, and we should have been forgotten. Marcus and Dianne and the others were manipulating the stories. How much of that was to manipulate us, even though they almost never talked about it? The pressure was there, anyway.

How was I supposed to tell?

Beside me, Kayleen tugged. *I need a break.*

She'd been here longer than I had. I tucked away all I could re-member. My own exhaustion was beginning to slow my thinking down; even here, the physical melded to the world of data. It must be worse for Kayleen who had spent very little time this immersed. No single ship had this variety.

I could come back later. *Okay! Surface.*

She laughed at my wording, her laughter a little off, but reassuring anyway, and I heard it with my physical ears.

I blinked in the bright lights. One of my feet tingled from being held at an odd angle. I must have spent more time down than I'd thought.

Sasha immediately sensed my presence and popped her head up, nosing my hand until I petted her.

I looked around for Marcus but didn't see him. The vid wall still flashed pictures, but the room had at least partly emptied out. I only noticed a few people moving around.

Kayleen started whispering. "All those stories. That's so weird. I mean, I know there're some people who end up in stories, but it's never supposed to be you." Her voice shifted from thoughtful to a little angry. "I don't like how people are lying about you."

"People have lied about us all of our lives."

"This is on a different scale." She glared at the screen full of impending war, and swallowed. She didn't say anything for so long I began to worry, since Kayleen is never quiet. But then she looked back at me and said the characteristic, "I'm hungry."

"Let's take Sasha out, and then look for food."

As we went out the door, I realized Marcus had needed to open it and we might not get back in. A cool breeze blew down the hallway, illustrating how controlled the environment we'd been in had been. After the door closed behind us, I dipped into the data, sampling the surface threads, and found only the Lopali norm of everything in soft rhythm. Wow.

Doors within doors.

After we entered the night and felt the breeze outside, I looked behind me to see the blackness of an empty cave. There had been no attempt to hide the cave itself, but from outside, there might have been no one else for kilometers. Just me and Kayleen and the dog.

Sasha trotted off into the darkness, probably hungry. Stars hung above us in a brilliant tapestry, and here and there the brighter orbs of the other planets swinging around Lopali's sun. Kayleen stood close to me, not touching. She whispered, "I miss the moons. They used to tell us how the time would go. Three moons for luck and all of that. Most of the roamer wagons had three moons painted on them. Do you remember that?"

"Yes."

"Without any moon at all, how are we supposed to know what the night will be like?"

"We're standing on a moon. Maybe that's a sign we have to decide."

She nodded. "If this were one of our moons, it would have to be Faith."

"Or Destiny."

A rustling in the bushes told me Sasha had caught her dinner.

"No. This is a stop for us. But we just saw our destiny. I'm scared of it, Joseph. You'll be strong enough, but I won't be. I might have got lost tonight without you. But it is still where we are going. I feel it in my heart, in my bones."

I agreed with her. I didn't want to say how much all of those warships called to me. It made me feel dirty. I didn't want war or killing. I'd seen enough of those up close and personal already, seen friends die. But the moment I saw those ships, I knew I had been designed to fly them. Which gave a new urgency to my need to help the fliers, so Marcus would let us go on.

I hadn't quite figured out how to answer Kayleen, who often didn't expect answers anyway. We sat quietly for a long while.

Sasha bounded back toward us with a long stick in her mouth, and taking it away and convincing her we weren't going to throw it in the dead of night got us both laughing and the dog barking playfully. It felt good to have a moment with no moons above me, and no Marcus and no fliers with their wide-set hopeful eyes.

CHELO: THE HEART OF MOHAMI

Kala and her constant companion, Samuel, brought us to a simple, rectangular room for dinner, and served us steaming hot cups of tea, juice, and sweet breads for the children. Then they left. Liam and I sat on the wooden floor and played space ship with the children. Alicia sat still, staring off into space, her eyes narrowed and her chin angry, resting on her folded hands. Bryan paced, his feet making an irritating *slap slap slap slap* on the floor.

"Bryan!" I declared. "Stop. What is bothering you so?"

He turned to me, his deep brown eyes anguished. "Don't you know? I haven't heard from Ming."

Well, we weren't supposed to, not for a few days. And then, through Seeyan, who would travel more freely. "Have any of us heard from any of the others?" I asked.

Bryan shook his head. "Ming was supposed to contact me. We had our own agreement."

When Liam glanced at Bryan, he looked as worried as I felt, but he used his calm leader's voice. "Maybe she just decided to follow the original plan."

Bryan resumed his pacing, not looking at any of us. "She wouldn't do that."

"Give it time," I suggested, catching Caro as she careened across the small room spilling crumbs. Speaking to the child, I said, "Calm down."

Alicia's head came up from where she'd been contemplating the leaves of her tea. "Why calm down? He should be worried. I haven't heard from Joseph either."

"Were you expecting to?" Liam asked.

"Well, no. But that's not the point. We don't know how anyone else is doing. Maybe we've been kidnapped and they're storing us in this blissful place so we won't rebel. Beside, I'm bored."

Just as she said that, the door slid open, admitting Mohami, and the faint scent of the garden touched by early evening dew. He glanced at Alicia. "I am sorry that I overheard you. Being bored is"—he smiled, his voice and face full of warm humor—"boring. There is much work here for idle hands. We can keep you busy."

Alicia looked away and mumbled something about busywork.

To cover her rudeness, I quickly asked him, "What sort of work can we do? We would love to give back for the shelter you're providing."

A soft smile quirked across his face and he gave a bow in my direction. "Blessed Chelo. We are pleased to be able to house you. If you would like to assist us, we would be happy to provide you with work after tomorrow morning's ceremony. But there is no need. You may prefer to pass the time in contemplation."

Was he crazy? Pass time in contemplation with two toddlers? But then the glory of his offer sank in. Ever since leaving Fremont, the only work that had been mine alone was supporting Joseph, who actually needed Marcus more than me these days. And tracking the kids, of course. But I hadn't had any role in flying ships or plotting courses. Work would be wonderful. "If you stop calling me blessed, I'd love to help you." I glanced at the others. "I'm sure we'd all like to be useful."

Liam nodded, and Bryan. Alicia said nothing. "Alicia?" I queried directly.

She glanced up at me and then at Mohami. "I would prefer to pass my days in contemplation, if it's all the same to you."

Mohami didn't even flinch. Instead, he graciously bowed in her direction. "You may." He turned back to me. "I'll meet you an hour after the ceremony."

It sounded like a dismissal, but he actually sat down at the table with us, and Samuel and Kala reappeared as if they had heard some silent clue, bringing us each fresh tea. "Is there anything else you need?" Mohami asked.

Bryan leaned toward him. "Have you heard how any of the rest of our party is?"

The old man spoke easily and quietly. "You are my only concern." He held a plate that had been freshened with new nuts and fruits out to the children. Jherrel didn't hesitate, but took a great handful and plopped down in my lap to eat it. Caro ignored the treats and stood right in front of Mohami, watching his face, unblinking. She, of course, heard and saw things we did not. I cleared my throat, hoping it would dislodge her stare, but it didn't. "Mohami? Do you know what Wind Readers are?"

His gaze stayed on Caro, soft, accepting rather than penetrating. "Like your blessed brother."

Blessed. I was starting to hate that word. Maybe Alicia was right. Well, not exactly. But still . . . "Like Joseph. And Kayleen, Caro's mother. Yes."

He nodded toward Caro. "She is a Wind Reader?"

"Yes."

"I will find you a teacher for her tomorrow."

It unnerved me that everything we wanted showed up.

He smiled, eyes sparkling, as he took another sip of tea. It felt like Mohami and I were the only ones in the room, regardless of the fact that the others shifted and scraped chairs and Jherrel crunched noisily on his treats.

He wanted me to ask him something. "What did I see this morning?"

"What did you feel?" he countered.

I closed my eyes. I had cried. Caro and I had cried. Liam had been there, had watched over us, kept Jherrel quiet and focused. Alicia had been angry. Bryan had stood stoic, impossible to read and last in our family line, while I was first. So I hadn't really seen his face. But why did I cry? Without opening my eyes, I whispered the first word that came to me, "Acceptance."

Mohami's voice. "Of course. And?"

Nothing else wanted to be said. "Acceptance. That's it. That's the heart of it." I opened my eyes, searching his face. He had dark blue eyes that seemed to reflect us all in them, his pupils large and his eyes sunken from age. Wrinkles swept from his eyes to his temples, like the rays of a small sun. His head was bald. He wore a yellow-gold robe of thin material.

When he spoke, he sounded proud. "Yes. Acceptance. Almost everyone tries to add, but that is the goal of morning ceremony. To start the day here in center of Lopali as one being. All accepts all, even though we may disagree later in the day. This group is getting it now, they have all been here for some time."

"It made me happy."

He nodded. "I will send for a Wind Reader for Caro." Although there were no windows in the room, he said, "It is nearly dark. Time for you and the children to rest. I will have tasks for you in the morning."

I took his hand. "Please give me tasks that have meaning."

Mohami smiled and stood up. "All tasks have meaning." Kala and Samuel stood as he left, and then, in silence, they led us back to our room.

As soon as we closed the door behind us, Alicia blurted out. "That was really creepy. He's really creepy. This whole place is creepy." She folded herself down on the floor, leaned against the wall, and closed her eyes.

I stared down at her, exasperated. "These people are keeping us safe."

She opened one violet eye. "I don't want to be safe."

"No kidding."

Liam handed me Jherrel, and we became lost in the task of getting the children ready for bed. I took comfort, as always, in the routines of washing their faces and dressing them. If only Kayleen and Joseph were here, I might feel perfect. I took some extra time sitting by Caro's bed. She seemed so distant and lost, she reminded me of her mother.

Alicia and Bryan talked quietly in a corner, and occasionally one of them laughed. They climbed into their beds readily enough as the last of the light faded us all to dark silhouettes in a dark room, and the starlight began to rise outside. I fell asleep wondering if Joseph sat someplace in light and laughter, or if Marcus drove him endlessly.

I suspected he was exhausted and still working. At least he had a calling.

Maybe I was beginning to find one.

Caro woke us all over again. I half-expected to see Bryan and Alicia gone, but they were sound asleep, and smiled dutifully at Caro when she woke them. The morning ceremony seemed less alien, but somehow more beautiful, like a stream that you come to every spring to admire the first flowering of the redberry bushes. Tears streaked my face as the sun touched the fliers' wings for the first time.

The crowd had grown, and the unity of heart become bigger, too, rolling over the hills and out to cover the planet. I could feel Joseph and Kayleen and Jenna and Paloma and Ming and Marcus and Dianne and Seeyan all together, as if somehow they knew the secret depth of family I felt in that moment.

Like yesterday, breakfast was a cold buffet taken on a hill. The full warmth of the midmorning sun baked us as we ate. The softest breeze blew the scent of fresh grass across my nose, tickling so I sneezed from time to time.

Yesterday, Mohami had talked, but today it was a woman I had never seen before. Samuel and Kala listened to her as raptly as they had to Mohami. "Who is she?" I asked.

Kala smiled. "The Voice of the Fliers of Lopali."

Odd titles. Like calling Liam *The Understudy to the Leader of the Band* or something. Strange that wingless ones had titles that implied so much power. "The Voice?"

Kala put her fingers to her lips and, in fact, the entire hillside fell quiet, and faces all looked down at the Voice, expectant. Silence hadn't fallen so deeply yesterday. Even Caro and Jherrel stopped and stared, waiting. A single high note rose, and rose, and rose, so clear I shivered. The woman began to sing, a simple series of notes that rose from the ground below her and through her, as if Lopali itself sang. The other Keepers near her turned toward us and added a complementary melody. A few of the people close to us hummed. There were no clear words, but the song copied the rise and dip of winged fliers, and even seemed to change in pitch and cadence as real fliers went by overhead in apparently random groups that paid us no immediate attention.

Caro and Jherrel raced up and down the hill, gathering attention, but other than a few times when Caro loudly asked Jherrel to be quiet, they played silently, in rhythm with the Voice.

At the end of the meal and the song, we joined a line of people to clean our plates. I looked around for Mohami, sure this was the time he had promised to meet us. The other tourists—or seekers—seemed to be on their own, but Kala and Samuel stuck close to us. After the last of our plates had been dried and put away, they waited for us a little away from the crowd. Kala smiled at me. "Mohami asked me to see if you would like to work now, or you would like to go home for a time first."

I didn't hesitate. "Now."

Kala looked across us all. "Whoever would like to work, may follow me."

"Me!" Caro called out.

Jherrel called out his own "Me!" twice as loudly.

Liam gave them a fatherly glare, then looked to Kala. "Can we all come?"

Alicia didn't even let her answer. "You all go. We'll stay back."

In yet another demonstration of infinite patience, Kala didn't remark on Alicia's interruption at all. She just looked at me and said, "Let's go," and after a moment of child-pointing and gathering, I looked back. Alicia and Bryan were walking away, the slender miscreant and the strongman. And at their side, Samuel, just like a roamer dog accompanying its owner into town, close and watchful.

I could imagine the looks Alicia was favoring poor Samuel with.

We soon lost sight of them in the crowd as they went back toward our room.

We crested a hill, crossed a valley, and walked up to another low hill lined with greenhouses. At the closest greenhouse, Mohami leaned out of a thin flexible door so translucent it looked like nothing more than a faint reflection, and waved enthusiastically. He had chosen the perfect chore for us; planting. I grinned at the clean scent of soil and seedlings.

He handed Caro a plant the size of her pinky, with yellow flowers shaped like stars. She took the plant ever so seriously, holding it between her chubby palms and keeping her gaze fixed tight on Mo-hami. He pointed to a rather large pot, and grinned at Jherrel. "Will you dig a hole?"

Jherrel nodded, and he and Caro planted the tiny life carefully, as if it were spun glass. "Now offer it your best wishes," Mohami whis-pered, nearly reverent.

Caro muttered, "Grow well and be happy."

Jherrel followed her, "And live a long time."

Mohami smiled as if he were trying to break his face in two parts, and then got me and Liam started on a nearly identical task. The old man stayed for a half hour, primarily overseeing the children, but oc-casionally admonishing us, "Speak to the plants. They need to know you, that you see them." He brought us each cups of cold water poured from a spigot outside the greenhouse. I laughed to see the kids take the cups in their dirty hands and drink greedily, then hand them back carefully and ever so seriously. Mohami leaned down after he had the two muddy cups safely in hand and looked equally seriously at the children. "It's good to laugh, even when you work."

The kids broke out into high giggles.

"How long would you like before I return?" he asked me.

I tilted my chin toward Caro and Jherrel. "They're probably good for another hour."

He raised one eyebrow. "All right. By then the Wind Reader should be along for Caro."

The relentless pleasure of planting reminded me of home-building on Islandia. Maybe I wasn't trying to stop a war right then, but some-one has to plant if there are going to be gardens. It clearly wasn't my destiny, but I could live here and follow Mohami and keep the gar-dens and admire the fliers for a long time. It felt sweet to have time with just the kids and Liam, to laugh and talk together and not feel like anybody watched us, or could hear us, or wanted anything at all.

Kala and Mohami returned. Just as we were closing up the green-house, a woman jogged up and stopped in front of Mohami, panting audibly. "I . . . I guess I made it."

Mohami grinned and turned to me. "This is Jill. She's come to help Caro."

Jill, still panting, waved at us shyly. "Mohami . . . said . . . you . . . need a . . . Reader."

Liam smiled. "Yes." He introduced everyone around, and Jill nodded and repeated each name. She was slender and blond, with a slightly flat face and warm blue eyes almost the same color as Mohami's. Liam had saved Caro for last, and Jill knelt down to greet her, silently, and I grinned and pulled Liam close, pleased it was so easy to tell they were talking to each other like Joseph and Kayleen and Marcus did. We were left out, but Caro looked almost immediately more relaxed.

We walked back as a group, Jill and Caro talking, sometimes out loud, and other times between themselves. As we neared the hill our room nestled under, Jill asked, "Can I take her through the gardens?"

I glanced at Liam. We had agreed to always have two adults with the children, particularly Caro with her ebullience and unpredictability. But Liam and Jill or me and Jill would be two. "I'll go," he whispered to me. Louder, he spoke to Jill and Caro. "Can Jherrel and I go, too?"

Caro looked mildly disapproving at the idea of putting up with her slightly younger brother, but she knew better than to say no. Mohami turned to Kala. "I have an appointment. Will you take Chelo back to her rooms?"

Great. I'd rather go to the gardens. But someone should check on Miss Grump. But then again, maybe she was deep in contemplation. "There's no need. I can see our door from here."

Kala might as well have been deaf. "I'll go with you."

I gave Liam a peck on the cheek and looked at Jherrel and Caro. "Be good for Jill."

They both nodded. "We will."

A few moments later, I opened the door to our room, calling out, "Alicia? Bryan?"

Nothing. Maybe they'd talked their Keeper into a walk in some dangerous place. I went in, Kala following me. I turned to face her, still pretty serene after the morning. "I'll be all right. I'll just take a nap or something."

Kala's features had frozen mid-smile. He eyes grew wider, and then she let out a piercing scream.

I turned back around.

Samuel lay facedown on the floor with his arms tied behind his back.

24

JOSEPH: WE BEGIN

Marcus, Kayleen, and I sat together in the deep dark of a small room just on the far side of the war room. The smell of damp stone and earth seemed stronger for the lack of light. A thin ribbon of dull yellow limned the bottom of the door, barely enough to give form to Marcus's and Kayleen's bodies. Marcus had dragged one of the big black chairs from the war room into here, and he lay back in it. I leaned in close to him and whispered, "That's a Marcus Chair."

He laughed softly. "Shhhhh. Get ready."

Folded blankets formed lumpy cushions for Kayleen and I. We sat side by side near Marcus's head, leaning against the cool wall. My left hand found Kayleen's right hand, and we each touched one of Marcus's shoulders, forming a bridge to connect us all.

"Follow my breath," Marcus whispered, his voice so low we barely heard him even in the silence of the cave room. My hand on him rose and fell as he breathed.

In time our breathing matched, long and slow, the out breath the same as the in breath, the sound a faint metronome.

We slowed further, falling into the deep patterns Marcus had taught me long ago, and I had taught Kayleen.

The data here felt quick and lively, linked with the war room rather than Lopali; shields were built into the very walls of this room, the war room, and a few others. Shielding gave the information purity, and we fell quickly.

Marcus's skills awed me still . . . he knit a wall between us and everything, a place where no data leaked in or out. He had done this between he and I, on Silver's Home, but never between three of us. Even watching carefully, I wasn't sure I saw how to do it. After we were enclosed in a void of data, a place emptier than the dark of space, he allowed one great rope of data threads through; the fliers' patterns. Genetics and DNA, but also more, a linkage of nanotechnology and DNA, of machine and human.

Pure biology would not have been enough to keep the fliers human and let them fly, even here. Or to keep Marcus, me, and Kayleen more human than AI, more man than machine. This close, the complexity of creation awed.

Always teaching, Marcus fed us data bit by bit, streaming what he saw through his very being and into us. Kayleen and I gripped hands from time to time as some new insight came, the physical activity an anchor, something felt in our bodies as well as in the data streams we had nearly become, a ghost of who we were inside of who we were. Touch served to slow us as well. It kept us safe from the hyper-speed of taking in too much data too fast, of becoming overwhelmed the way I had been when I first encountered the richness of Silver's Home.

Touch had another purpose. As Marcus fed us the thin bones and supple skin of flier genetics, we gave him our strength, pouring steadiness and support into his energies, making a lattice of all three hearts: of blood and bone and family and common design. As he helped us see the machine cells that repaired the fine strength of fliers' bones and turned food to fuel fast enough for flight, we fed him back what we saw, the three of us deepening and correcting, three observers making what each one saw more true for us all.

We were inside the skins of one another, and I knew Kayleen and Marcus both more than I knew Alicia, more, perhaps, than I knew myself. To know another human so deeply is more than love.

Paula's facial features layered through the data, patient and trusting as always. This was not her, but a simulation, a place to adjust and change balances and fulcrums until we found a new design that would allow a flier woman to bear a child who would be ready to become a flier.

A living simulation made of the marriage between a moment in time of Paula and all the knowledge of the genetics databases from Silver's Home that Marcus had been able to squirrel away over time as a maker. Some bore Chance's signature; information he had brought from Silver's Home when he came here years ago.

A pause. A moment when we all hung in understanding, seeing Paula as she was when this full scan was taken, seeing the many moving parts that make life continue forward, the simulation so real she might have spoken and we might have replied. Rivers of blood ran smoothly, slowing and speeding up slightly with the thumping of her heart. Cells divided and grew, died and disappeared. Neurons fired. Tissue and bone flexed where they connected.

Life vibrated.

We had done this already with a simulation of a normal human, and now Marcus clarified the differences: finer, stronger bones; larger lungs; eyes that saw above and behind almost as well as in front; a longer, broader torso above slender hips. Even though she had no wings, Paula's back was designed to flex wings. It would be strong enough had she undergone the changes forced on flier children. The base structures for flight existed in front of us, longer and lighter muscles, more muscles, changes in the shoulders and the shoulder blades. Strengthening all along a spine more flexible than ours.

My focus felt both heightened and laser sharp, and split between Marcus, Kayleen, and the figment of Paula that we all held in common. There was nothing else in our consciousness except each other and this Paula. No stray data, no wind, just a single being as complex as a world in front of us. A miracle to see so much, and hard to hold it all even stripped to just essence. Yes, it was a simulation, but we would need to change it perfectly to do the next thing. Our actions here would form the foundation we needed to make them real. Marcus's garden grass and light-link butterflies, only a thousand thousand times more intricate.

Marcus began to work. He strengthened the walls of organs, shifted veins, built structures: a painter in data and simulated flesh.

All the time, cells divided, a heart beat, and Paula's simulated face held its patience.

He went forward and back—trying and undoing. Trying again.

Sometimes he gave me very simple things to do and steadied me with questions. *Will enough blood reach the ovary?*

How do I tell?

Check the organ itself, the new tissue. Are the cells growing stronger or weaker?

Weaker?

You tell me.

Yes. So more?

Only a little.

My touch felt hesitant. *I'm afraid.*

Let go.

More of the interrelationships of cells and machines, of blood and tissue, and breath and life flowed into me. It felt like a ghost of what had happened back on the High Road at the height of battle, when I could see all of the ships and all of the people and all of the data and it was joy and beauty and strength, and I had the strength to fling the ship into the sea.

I flinched, lost threads.

Don't back out!

Damn you.

Claim your power. It is only a simple thing.

Compared to what he did. But I made the blood flow stronger.

Relax now, and watch me.

Gladly. I had nearly thrown us all out. I couldn't worry about my past right now, maybe I never could.

Time passed. I didn't count my own heartbeats or the simulation's breath and heartbeat either, until I began to feel my energy lag, and the ragged edges of Kayleen's strength begin to ebb away from us. In her thinning, I felt my own weakness.

I couldn't leave Marcus. He was totally focused on forming a wider hinge on the hips in front of us, on thinning the bone even further, each move slow and careful. Who would have thought that manipulating data that you could never feel would be so physically hard?

Marcus pulled on me as he shaped and sculpted, needing my strength and my focus even as Kayleen drained back into her body, taking some of my power.

I clamped down on Kayleen's physical hand, sparing reserves to send her way.

She yelped softly, and her energy withdrew like a wave falling away from us, pulled out by some other tide.

I had to stay with Marcus, to get his attention.

Vibration. Kayleen's voice falling into me, speaking to someone. Not me! "We'll . . . just . . . be right there. Hold on."

Marcus noticed her absence, finally. I felt his regret as the simulation thinned to us and we rose up to feel our own breath and heart. We'd only started.

Marcus's voice next. "Who is it?"

"Induan," Kayleen whispered to Marcus. "Can you open the door?"

For he had to, or it had to be done from outside, and Induan knew not to disturb us. Being so deep and shielded from any other data left us vulnerable, and she and Sasha guarded the corridor.

The door lock made a soft sound and the door opened. I should not have been surprised—I had done such things on the *Dawnforce* when we freed the children from the mercenaries. I blinked, the sudden light so painful I came back fully, the simulated Paula fading like a dream after awakening. Sasha bounded into me, licking my face, nosing at me. One look at Induan's face made me bite my tongue and wait. Her lips were drawn tight and her face even paler than usual. A tear hung in the corner of one eye, the only bit of her that wasn't anger and anxiety. One hand gripped the edge of the door frame. Her voice quivered, the words spoken faster than I'd ever heard her. "Alicia and Bryan are missing. There's been no more word from the Gang of Girls."

Alicia had been with Chelo.

Kayleen drew in a sharp, pained breath.

"Chelo and Liam and the kids?" My voice sounded like a frog's. "Are they okay?"

Induan swallowed. "I think so. You need to hear the whole story. Seeyan is here to tell."

Marcus pushed himself up and stood to face Induan. I could see him struggle for the control that usually cloaked him, see the deep slow breath he forced low into his body, the tensing and releasing of muscles. After a second deep breath, he reached a hand out for me and Kayleen, helping us stand. "Let's go," he said.

Sasha stuck close by me, and Kayleen kept a grip on my hand as we followed Induan's pale form closer to the mouth of the cave. Daggers of early evening light pouring directly into the cave forced my hand up over my eyes and made a silhouette of Seeyan's tall, slightly misshapen form. We sat in a rough circle, with the back open so no one would have to stare at the sinking sun. A breeze blew in the scent of dust and flowers.

"What happened?" Marcus asked.

Seeyan shook her head. "No one knows. Chelo and Liam and the children were in the gardens, and when they returned, Alicia and Bryan were gone. Their Keeper said—" Seeyan choked and looked away. "Their Keeper said Alicia and Bryan tied up a Keeper."

How Alicia. "Did she say why?" I asked.

"Do they know where we are?" Kayleen's hands twisted knots into her hair. "It's always Alicia. It was her at home, too. She ran away from us on the Plains."

"Shhhh." I said. Maybe Seeyan didn't need to know Alicia was our risk-taker. "Let Seeyan tell her story."

"There isn't any more. The Keeper—Samuel—didn't know. But it's a grave choice to mess with a Keeper of the Morning. She's offered a deep insult to us all."

Marcus nodded, his face blanched so white his lips were nearly colorless. "And you brought her there. We are sorry."

"Where are the Keepers of the Morning?" Chelo was there. I could find her.

Seeyan shook her head and looked beseechingly at Marcus.

Anger showed in the set of his jaw. I watched him swallow it and waited him out, hoping for a clear answer. When he looked at me, sorrowful eyes peered from a determined and unhappy face. "I'm sorry. Maybe we will have to go there." He gestured at the open window of the cave mouth. "But not now. We'll see what other news comes by morning."

"But . . . but Chelo! I have to know she's safe. And Jenna. Jenna saved us. We have to save her."

Kayleen added her voice to mine. "What if Alicia does something stupid?"

A short barky laugh escaped Marcus's lips. "She already has." He turned to Seeyan. "I'm sure Chelo's safe. Still no word from Jenna or the others? Ming?"

Seeyan shook her head, her normal calm seeming to have fallen back on her now that she'd warned us we'd offended her, and maybe all of Lopali. She and Marcus. How did they do this? Did living a long time make you calm?

Kayleen seemed more like I felt; not exactly calm. "Tsawo is here." She gave me an almost apologetic glance. "Maybe he knows why she would leave. They've spent a lot of time together."

I immediately disliked the idea. "Not in the past few days, they haven't. He's been with us."

She looked hurt.

"All right." Maybe it was a good idea. I just didn't like it. "What else should we do? Marcus, do you promise we'll leave in the morning?"

"I didn't say that. I said we'd see what news the night brought. This may be the safest place for you on all of Lopali. I should have planned to bring you here in the first place."

That was as much of an apology as I'd get. How was he still thinking of work? With Jenna still missing and Alicia running amok?

Seeyan stood gracefully. "I'll go and look for them, or for news. I'll return in the morning."

Induan spoke up. "I'll go with you. I can use my mod."

Marcus didn't stop her. The two of them walked into the still-bright sun and disappeared down the trail. Kayleen glowered at the door. "Why does she get to go?"

Marcus spoke softly. "She doesn't matter as much as you do. Either of you."

"You know, I really, really hate that."

Kayleen took my hand. "It's true. You saved us."

"Don't you get that way on me," I said. "I need to be just like I always was. And I need to find my sister."

Marcus still looked at the place Induan and Seeyan had disappeared. "Your sister's safe. The people she's with wouldn't hurt her. But we three had better eat and get back to work."

"Is that all you think about?"

"Food or work?"

"Both." Work. But I didn't want him to think I didn't want to work. I did. I just wanted to work and find Chelo and sleep all at once. "I need a minute alone. I'm going to take Sasha out."

He sighed. "Don't leave."

"I wouldn't know where to go."

"Can I come with you?" Kayleen asked.

I didn't really want her. I wanted the dog and the coming sunset and a few moments of peace. But I'd already said hurtful things to her a few times today and she didn't deserve any of them. "How about if you two get food, enough for me, too, and we can watch the sunset together."

I got a reward; they both smiled.

Outside, the sun had slipped far enough down to lengthen shadows so I looked absurdly tall and slender. It softened the edges of the cave mouth and slightly dulled the flowers and vines hanging down from the rocks above and around the cave. Even here, where there was some raggedness, Lopali felt too ordered, too neat. Too safe, except we were missing and separated all over again. A place I didn't even need to worry about the safety of a dog. Still, I whistled Sasha close. I sat on a rock, her beside me with her nose on my shoulder and a bit of her weight leaning in while I stroked her soft fur.

The evening smelled of stone and releasing heat, and the rain that would wash across the land in a few hours. The first high clouds turned gold and red above me, the sunset a show repeated every night here, where the weather ran on clockwork schedules. "What are we going to do, Sash?" I whispered. "I want to be back on a ship and away from here. All planets are poison."

Sasha had no answer. She probably liked it better here. Room to run and ready game. I didn't. Here, I didn't really know who was friend and who wasn't. On Fremont, my friends and enemies had been easier to tell apart.

What did Alicia think she could accomplish? We didn't know this place or these people. Not yet. What did she want, except maybe just to be bad? She'd been bored; I'd left her out of so much that I was doing. But what choice did I have? I wanted to be more like her; I always had. I fell in love with her for her wildness. But the older I got, the more things I had to do that just weren't wild. We'd been made—me for flight and Reading the Wind, her for risks. I didn't want to lose her, not ever, even though I'd be willing to bet they didn't make us for each other. When she followed her core nature back on Fremont, Chelo had saved her. This time, I wanted to save her. But how could I abandon Marcus? And how would I find Alicia anyway?

"I hope she's safe," I whispered into Sasha's ear, and the dog leaned even harder against me for a moment. The two of us stared down the ravine path together, Sasha's nose questing the air and me taking in the shapes of stones and vegetation. We got to sit that way, alone together, watching the light change for so long I began to actually feel better. Then Sasha stirred and bounded off, smelling Kayleen's and Marcus's approach before I heard their feet scrape on the stones.

"No new word?" I asked.

"No." Marcus sat down beside me, in the spot Sasha had vacated, and the dog and Kayleen sat across from us both, the last soft rays of sun making an unnaturally light halo of Kayleen's dark hair. Marcus looked as outwardly calm as normal, but he was close enough that I could feel his anxiety. Deep work in data together always left a bit of something Kayleen called "glow" between us, as if we had more access to each other's emotions than before. It would slide away. But it hadn't yet. He squinted toward the sunset. "It's past time for flying, anyway. The rain will be in before we could get to Oshai."

Was he trying to convince himself or me? "Good thing it doesn't rain on space ships."

He laughed.

"What happens to the simulation since we got interrupted?"

He shrugged. "We'll see. I left it running with what we'd done. Mistakes should surface by the time we get back."

"So it wasn't that bad to stop?"

"First runs-through almost never get it right. Especially not in people."

I hoped we hadn't wasted all that effort. I wanted to be done with this and to go on, to leave here and be with the fleets. Or back home. Or anywhere else.

Kayleen fed Sasha bits of meat and root vegetables, and Marcus handed me a sandwich and a flask full of water. I savored a long drink and the three of us ate in silence. As soon as Kayleen and Sasha finished their shared meal, Kayleen said, "We should have all come here. I think we should swear we'll never be separated again. No matter what. The six of us, always."

"Just six?" Marcus asked.

Kayleen covered her mouth with her hand. "Well, I suppose we have to include Ming, the way Bryan is hanging around with her."

Marcus laughed. "First we need to get together again. There's no price on Alicia's or Bryan's head, or even Ming's. They should be all right."

"There's a reward for Jenna," Kayleen reminded him.

He swallowed, and looked a tiny bit vulnerable. For all the things he often looked—amused, tolerant, frustrated, intrigued—vulnerable was a strange sight. "You really love Jenna, don't you?" I asked.

"I love her fury and her independence. Those will keep her safe."

He loved more than that. He loved the soft heart it had taken years for me to see. "That's why I love Alicia." But Jenna wouldn't do anything stupid. "I can't imagine Jenna not being safe. She kept us all safe for years. It's Alicia I'm worried about."

"Yeah. Well, I'll keep an eye out for her, a little, even from here."

He had resources everywhere. But I didn't have access to his net or resources, and no matter how much I admired and trusted him, I needed to do more than worry. Besides, it was going to be too dark to walk back to the cave soon. "Ready to go find Tsawo?"

25

JOSEPH: SHADES OF GRAY

Early evening blurred the edges of the rocks outside the cave and faded the black of Sasha's coat into the landscape so her white feet and nose looked like ghost dog parts approaching the cave. Stepping through the barrier between the outside and the inside, the hum of conversation and machinery assaulted us. Any calm I'd gathered outside left quickly.

Tsawo and Angeline weren't immediately visible. Kayleen pointed. The two fliers sat on top of a storage building at the far side of the cave, off to the right. I started toward them. Kayleen walked beside me, her steps as determined as mine, and Marcus dragged a bit behind, maybe lost in data. Out here in the main cave that meant Lopali data, soft and seductive and full of lies and half-truths and deep truths.

We stood at the bottom of the storage building, a nearly two-story box with no windows, and rows of closed doors along the bottom. It was made of the same stuff that lined the cave walls, smooth light gray material that could be molded into almost any shape. From this close, it was easy to tell the building's roof had actually been set up for fliers with stones and perch-tree branches arranged pleasingly to make a sort of outdoor/indoor sitting room. The two fliers, black Tsawo and white Angeline, held their heads close together, talking. I called up, "Hello!"

Angeline looked down. "Come on up!"

We weren't going up the sheer walls in front of us. Marcus headed around the building. "Here."

Steep, shallow steps had been cut into the cave wall, more like a ladder than a staircase. We started up, Sasha struggling behind us. Kayleen, last in line, looked down over her shoulder. "Sasha. Wait. You don't like fliers anyway."

Sasha barked, clinging to the wall, and then gave up and fell the three steps down, landing on her feet and whining softly.

"You'll be all right," I told her.

At the top of the ladder, Marcus helped me and then Kayleen over to the top of the building. We sat opposite Tsawo and Angeline, climbing up on seats clearly meant for fliers; once again our feet didn't touch the ground. I sat in the middle, with Marcus on my right. From up here, the cave looked bigger and emptier than it did from below. The walls and turns were all rounds and angles, more like a space ship than a cave. Rock, but carved by people. The roof was still far above us, although our new height revealed a doorway behind us at the level of the top of the building. We hadn't figured out where people lived yet. Maybe here?

Now what? Angeline prompted me, her blue eyes bright in her pale face. "What can we help you with?"

I watched Tsawo's expression. "Alicia's gone missing."

He winced, but didn't look surprised. "From where?"

Kayleen was her usual subtle self. "Near Oshai. We're not supposed to know where the others are. But Seeyan said she and Bryan tied up a Keeper and got away. We need to find her."

Tsawo's features tightened and Angeline's eyes widened. "A Keeper!" she exclaimed. "Was the Keeper all right?"

Marcus's answer came quickly. "Yes."

"Good. They're valuable to us." She sounded like she thought of the Keepers as pets. Maybe she did; Seeyan acted like they were a club, but whatever they were in Lopali's overt social structure, it was less than fliers.

"Alicia won't hurt anyone," Kayleen said. "She's just wild."

Tsawo's face gave away nothing; smooth and pretty and controlled. "You think I can help?"

A small uncomfortable silence ensued. I spoke into it. "I thought . . . you'd spent so much time with her. I was hoping she told you something to help us?"

Kayleen added words I'd only been thinking. "Or maybe you told her something about Lopali that she wanted to go find. Alicia's curious."

Marcus remained quiet and watchful, his energy partly gone again as he double-dipped between the physical and the world of data. Hopefully he was looking for Alicia and Jenna his own way.

Angeline and Tsawo shared a glance. The dark flier looked back at me and took a deep breath. His words sounded soft, like a stream of peace, but were actually hard. "Alicia is willful. She has no calm, no access at all to her inner core. I tried to teach her to fly, and she couldn't get close enough to her own fears to even see them, much less overcome them." He paused, the look on his face almost exactly the one I'd seen on Alicia's face when I asked her about Tsawo. He seemed to be proud of her and mad at her all at once, about like me. He drew in a slow breath and calm touched his muscles one by one, until his face was again serene. "She's probably gone to find some poor soul from the warring worlds that will help her try to kill herself by attempting to change into a flier."

His words had gotten Kayleen all worked up. "Alicia's better than you're giving her credit for. She's undoubtedly trying to help us. She wouldn't just run away and she wouldn't tie someone up on a whim. She's smart. She'd know we might get in trouble, so it must have been worth the risk! She must know something we don't."

That might not be hard.

Angeline spoke up. "Lopali is a patient place." She looked at me, and then at Marcus and Kayleen. "You three have shown patience, and I'm grateful for the work you're doing. There are more forces at play than you realize. A saying we have for visitors is, 'Patience skins your soul.' "

Kayleen's soul hadn't been skinned yet. She just plowed ahead, pleading with the fliers. "She's got this invisibility mod. We're not going to be able to find her by looking for her. Don't you have any ideas about where she is?"

Tsawo shook his head. "Our eyes aren't any better than yours at seeing the invisible."

Kayleen blinked up at him, looking disappointed. "What about the other women who were with us? Have you seen them or heard anything about them? My mom's with them."

He leaned back away from her, looking slightly assaulted. Maybe he wasn't a guy who understood women's feelings. Maybe fliers didn't know what a mother meant to someone. I glanced at Angeline, who probably should know, but her face was as serene as Tsawo's. But then, she hadn't birthed, or really raised Paula. Mari had. I tried a different tack. "Chelo said that you're protectors. What does that mean?"

His feathers rustled softly against the stones he sat on. "It means we're protecting Lopali against the war." His gaze stayed steady on me, unblinking, and I refused to look away. Finally, he looked at Marcus. "I know your goal. You want to drag us into war, but we want peace."

Again, Kayleen said the first thing that popped into her head. "Chelo doesn't like war, either."

"I admire that," Angeline said. "I hate the idea of Tsawo dying in some strange place, or anyone else."

I glanced at Tsawo. "You can fly a space ship?" It would give us something in common.

His laughter sounded bitter. "Not me. Fliers are seldom Wind Readers like you; we don't command most of our own ships. We learn as children that ships are cages."

Marcus spoke up. "So then why is Angeline worried about you going to war?"

"Because if there is a war, I will go." He glanced at the other flier. "Angeline, too. But I far prefer flying here to flying through space."

And I preferred flying ships to flying myself any day.

Angeline interrupted. "But what about you two? Do you want to stop this war?"

Marcus answered her. "We need you. With Lopali at our side, Islas will back away."

"I didn't ask you," Tsawo said. Marcus's jaw tightened, but he didn't reply.

Kayleen answered him. "I hate fighting."

He looked at me.

I wanted to fly the ships I'd seen in the war room. More than that, I expected to; they called to me. But the end of the only real battle I'd been in made me want to puke for months. So that's what I talked about. "I killed some people in the battle on Fremont. I hated it. Especially afterward." When their screams stayed in my head for months and when they came back to haunt me, like they had when we were working on Angeline's daughter's simulation. Now, because I had made the mistake of thinking about them. My ghosts.

It wasn't enough answer for him. "This war. What do you think of this one?"

I didn't know. I shook my head, feeling stupid. Chelo had a stance; if it was war, it was wrong. Marcus's every breath went into stopping this war, but he would fight it if he had to. Alicia would like it. Bryan, too. But what about me? People were fighting about the freedom to do what Marcus was teaching me to do. The same stuff that Islas hated enough to go to war to stop. I took Kayleen's hand. "We'll do what's right."

Angeline's gaze was softer than Tsawo's. "Do you know what that is?"

"Helping you is right," I said. "Whatever happens with the war, I want to help you. You shouldn't be owned."

She nodded. "We agree." She paused, and her voice softened. "At least you're willing to tell us what you don't know."

Tsawo slid down from his perch and stretched his wings. "I can't help you easily. But if I see Alicia, or I hear about her, I'll let you know."

Angeline smiled wistfully. "Good luck." She, too, spread her wings.

"Wait," I said, but not before they fell off the edge of the building. A wing beat or two later they rose again, flying out the cave mouth, side by side, and so fine-looking I lost my breath for a moment.

"What are they to each other?" Kayleen asked Marcus.

"Brother and sister."

"Really?" I'd thought they might be lovers. "Genetically?"

He shook his head. "I don't know. Matriana and Daniel raised them both." We were still sitting on the slightly-too-tall-for-normal-humans perches, and he started to slide off. "I want to check on the simulation."

"I saw you in the nets. Did you find Alicia? Or the others?"

Disappointment crossed his face. "No. But I'll keep looking." He narrowed his eyes at us. "Don't you look. You're not subtle enough here, not yet. You leave trails everywhere you go."

I hated that he was probably right.

He started toward the ladder in the wall.

"Wait," I said. "I need to know something."

"What?"

"What are we doing? Sometimes I can't keep all this straight. You're a creator. You want to make things like fliers, and like your kitchen garden back home."

He nodded.

"That's what Silver's Home is fighting for, right?"

"Except they want to own the fliers. That's wrong. What we did to the fliers enslaved them."

Kayleen jumped down and started pacing. "Wait—the fliers . . ."

"Just a minute," Marcus said. "Go on Joseph."

I think he knew my question but wanted me to ask it. "And Islas wants to slow Silver's Home down, too?"

"Yes. But they want—different curbs. They want to control creation themselves. Centrally. That's not right, either. You and I wouldn't be able to choose, nor would any being that had been made."

Kayleen stopped and frowned at him. "But what you want sounds closer to what Islas wants than to what Silver's Home wants."

"No. Not really. Islas sees us as too strong, too dangerous to their own laws. They say we're eroding the careful way they've built their society. But it's our very freedom that attracts change. Some of their own people, like Dianne, come over as spies or diplomats, or both, and they leave and come here."

Kayleen cocked her head. "Was Dianne a spy or a diplomat?"

"Wait." I didn't want to let the focus drift. Marcus was still next to me on the perch, both of us above Kayleen. He looked out over the cave, as if he didn't want to meet my gaze. "Look at me," I asked him.

He did, his green-gold eyes bright in the artificial light.

"I know you want to stop the war. If Silver's Home wins, they'll have too much freedom. And if they lose, they won't have enough. That's what you're telling me, right?"

He nodded.

"And if the war doesn't happen, then what? What do you want instead?"

"What I've wanted all along. I want every being that gets made, and can think, to have their own rights to evolve, like we can. Rights for every kind of smart being. And more. If they can't make up their minds, like my light-link butterflies—who are about as bright as dust motes, if prettier—to have a right to live. Anything that's stable and can reproduce."

On Fremont, everything was a check and balance for everything else. Herds of grazers fed paw-cats and demon dogs. "But someone still has to make decisions. Who is that?"

"A group of us."

"You?"

"And you."

Me? Make rules? Be like the Town Council at home? I wasn't old enough. I searched his face to see if he really meant it. He was the closest thing to a real father I'd ever had. Steven had raised me well on Fremont, even though he'd adopted me and Chelo as spoils of war. But he'd died, and the man who took his place, Tom, was married to a woman who hated me. I'd finally found my physical father, only to find he had broken his moral compass when he'd abandoned us. He'd tried to kill a whole planet full of people in vengeance.

Marcus was better than any of them. He was passionate and smart and had taught me things I'd used, over and over.

But that didn't mean I was ready to trust him to run the world.

Or me either.

His one little comment had almost paralyzed me. When I didn't answer, he continued. "We have allies. Independent, unaffiliated. Almost an affinity group of people without economic ties to each other. They all want a world created and managed, but not by any central source. Not by just me or just you or just Silver's Home or just Islas. By a set of guidelines that say all self-aware beings need to own their own future. Machines and things can be made and sold, except true AI's. But not biology."

Kayleen came and stood between us, bidding for attention. I slid my arm around her waist. "So how does stopping the war make that happen?" she asked. "I don't get it. If Silver's Home wins, they'll keep doing what they're doing, right? And If Islas wins, they'll make you stop, or they'll kill you. Maybe you're better off letting Silver's Home win and going from there."

He looked down at her, his features softening. He liked her. More than he liked Alicia. "If we have to go to war, we want Silver's Home to win. But I want peace instead."

"And the fliers help how?" she asked.

"We use them to make Islas bargain."

I saw a problem with that. "But if you can win, why would Silver's Home bargain?"

He looked away. "There's a lot of us working on that."

"How many?"

Now he shook his head again. "I can't tell you. Not yet. There's a bounty on your head, and I can't risk a lifetime of work." He did look genuinely miserable.

"But what if something happens to you?" Kayleen asked.

"Then Dianne or Jenna will take care of you."

"Or Ming?" Kayleen pushed. "Should we trust Ming, too?"

He shook his head. "I can't answer your questions. I'm sorry. You have to trust me."

"I just want to understand," she said. "Who's right? I don't get it."

He shook his head. "This isn't an easy fight. There's right and wrong on both sides. That's the real world. Children think wars are fought over right and wrong, and that the word truth has a capital T and can always be seen. But the real world doesn't have absolute truths, and so you have to think."

She started to open her mouth again and I pulled her closer. "I trust him." Even if he did want to take over Silver's Home.

Marcus asked, "Are you ready to go check on our work?"

I glanced behind us, curious. "Where does that door go?"

He shook his head. "I don't know."

"Can we look?" Kayleen asked.

I shook my head at her. "Sasha's waiting down below."

Sure enough, she sat at the bottom of the steps, looking up and wagging her tail as soon as we started down. If only I had the patience of dogs. I wanted to find Alicia, not head back to secure rooms and play with genetics. And find Paloma for Kayleen, who must be worried sick, and Jenna for Marcus. We should be finding our family instead of trying to save the world.

Maybe I didn't have the same drives Marcus did.

I wanted to stop and check on the war room, but Marcus passed it by quickly and led us into the small room beyond. It took an extra few minutes to wipe the dregs of the conversation with Tsawo and Angeline from my head and get down into the simulation.

Like before, Marcus built walls of safety around us. "Ready?" he asked.

"Yes."

"Yes."

There was nothing there. Marcus's disappointment touched all three of us. "What happened?" I asked, still deep, the question as much a feeling as words.

"She died."

Kayleen gripped my hand. Silence, and then he said, "Get ready. We're going to watch her die, and see how to start again."

Great. Just what I wanted. "Do sims die often?" I asked.

He sounded bitter. "Every time we make a mistake."

26

ALICIA: AT THE FESTIVAL OF HIGH SUMMER

I kept expecting a shadow to swoop down from behind us and take us back to the Garden of Deadly Morning Routines. To make it worse, we really couldn't look up all the time just in case we needed to duck, or run, or fight. So I felt like I was walking around with the short hairs permanently climbing up my neck.

It felt good to spot the painted wooden sign that proclaimed, *The Festival of High Summer*. I leaned into Bryan and whispered, "At least we know what season it is, now."

He looked puzzled for a breath before he got it, then he held his arms out as if accepting the warm late-morning heat into his body. "The land of always summer."

"Yeah, isn't that sweet."

He frowned. "Like your mood."

"I bet Chelo's truly mad."

"I had to go."

"We did." This was the second time I'd run out on her. We'd still be slaves on Fremont if I hadn't done it the first time, and once, Chelo had even agreed with me after we'd both had some wine on one of the ships. But I never really felt forgiven, and this might even be worse. Well, maybe not. I could see her face though, the way her eyes would look betrayed and her mouth would be a sharp little disapproving line.

We hadn't planned. We'd left because Samuel had politely refused to leave us alone to talk. I just couldn't take him anymore, or being without Joseph, or hiding while bad guys were theoretically chasing us down. Bryan swore he needed to find Ming, but I think he'd finally realized Chelo and Liam and the kids were wrapped in about five layers of sanctimonious safety and no one would dare kidnap them. It wasn't as if they were ever alone.

Besides, we should have heard from the others.

We wore blue. We might need to find this Juss, and Seeyan had said to wear blue. We'd also stolen some food, although we'd eaten it all last night and this morning. I wasn't really hungry yet, but I would be.

All morning, waiting, while we hid by walking purposefully through town and back, and then sitting quietly for a while under a tree, Bryan had been listening inside himself. Hoping for a call from Ming. Instead of looking angry or tense, which fit the Bryan I knew better, he just looked lost. As if missing Ming was missing half of him.

I missed Joseph fiercely, but I wasn't missing myself over him.

At least now there were other people walking alongside us. For the first time, I saw a real flier child, maybe fifteen. The child had black wings with deep purple highlights, and black hair that hung over her face, almost obscuring black eyes. She was thinner than an adult, and even less steady on her feet. But what really gave her away was the protective looks of the three fliers who flanked her. Bryan reached for my hand. "Don't stare."

Well, there was plenty more to look at. Sculptures had been scattered across the grass like windblown petals. We passed a tall thin rendering of three raindrops playing with a cloud. Nearby, as if the cloud fed them water, grand yellow flowers swung in the wind and tinkled softly against each other, the fake flowers giving off a real, sweet scent. Another sculpture consisted of fifteen or so perches all jumbled so close together it would be hard for fliers to occupy even a few of them. Its rounded base let it rock lightly in the wind. "If a flier did land on it, they'd get a ride," Bryan said.

"Or fall down. I wonder what the artist meant? Do they want the fliers to sit closer together?"

He stopped and stared at it, too. "I don't think so. It looks pretty hostile."

We neared the open gates. About ten other parties also converged on the path in a steady stream. Most were human, a few in formal robes like the ones Kala and Mohami wore, others dressed more like Seeyan. Maybe half looked like offworlders; either in the simple tan pants and mono-colored tunics of Islas, or the foamy silk dress of Joy Heaven. For allies, the two couldn't have looked more different. To a person, the wild Islans looked more severe than our own pet Islan. At least Dianne had let her hair grow out from its just-above-the-shoulders blunt cut. People from the pleasure planet dressed with a hedonistic flare that was meant to look abandoned. Once, when I'd asked Marcus about the odd alliance, he'd said they were the light and dark of each other, and I figured he meant the Islans for the dark.

Paradisers, our allies, dressed like us, but had more muscle. Not Bryan's brawn; more like a subtle strength that showed in the fine lines of their limbs and the graceful strength of their movements.

The fair smelled like sugar and fruit and wood shavings. Booths lined both sides of wide paths. Some drew the eye with bright colors and ornate shapes, or flapping flags. Others were understated enough that my eye wanted to pass right over them. Here and there, a booth-sized space held fountains or chairs or benches or both, some meant for water and talk stops, some perhaps as ways to admire the sculptures. In every direction, movement: people, flags, colors, fliers coming or going. Even standing here at the gate it seemed bigger than all of Artistos or Li Spaceport or Pilo Island. The immensity made even finding a man named Juss look tough, not to mention five people who were hiding.

Crowded places were tough to be invisible in. Even if you were watching in front of you, people could walk into you from the back. If I ever got to pick another mod for fun, it was going to be a second set of eyes in the back of my head.

Right inside the gate, two sculptors worked. An ebony-skinned man with bright yellow eyes and long yellow hair touched up the fine ridges of feathers on a twice life-sized wooden flier with spread wings. The flier imitated the sculpture I'd seen on Silver's Home, except that the face had tears streaming down its cheeks, falling periodically down to water a garden in a pot at the flier's feet.

The second sculptor was a thin brown man, shorter than me. He painted silver fins on a ship headed toward a gas giant planet, the whole thing swinging on nearly invisible wires and the yet-unpainted part made of an unfamiliar whitish material. Both artists were failed fliers, with visible nubs on their naked backs. A small crowd seemed to have split between watching each of them, rapt, and talking among themselves. It saddened me to see two men who'd lost the ability to fly making art that detailed flight.

Bryan dragged my attention back to our reason for being here. "Do you see any of them?"

"Not yet." The fair was laid out in a huge square, more than we could possibly cover in a full day. It looked busy in every direction. "Let's go right."

"Why?"

"We have to start somewhere."

I walked beside him, looking right while he looked left. "I haven't heard from Joseph yet, either."

"You didn't expect to."

"That doesn't mean he's safe. We have to be all right on our own."

He stopped and looked at me as if I'd shrunk a meter. "No. We don't. We need each other."

"I'm helping you look."

"You don't really want to be alone. I know you don't."

How did he know? "That's not it. But we shouldn't be dependent on each other. We should be okay no matter what happens."

"Well, I'm not. None of us is. We're family."

He'd saved me once, and I'd saved him once, which made us more than family. Out of the six of us on Fremont, we two had had it hardest, except for Jenna. We were the angriest, maybe also except for Jenna. She was harder to read now that her body and face had been fixed. I adored Kayleen, and wished I could Read the Wind and be a better match for Joseph, except she was half-crazy. The other three were good at everything.

Bryan's eyes had narrowed and his jaw tightened, his mouth a downturn of worry, showing how hard he bled inside for Ming. Wherever she was, she'd better be bleeding for him. I took his arm. "I'm glad we both came."

"Me, too."

After that we didn't talk for a few minutes. We passed jewelers and painters and three-dimensional holo painters who made us jump as alternate realities passed over our perception. Unlike Silver's Home, there were no genemod booths in easy evidence, although I'd heard mods could be bought here. One booth had a few simple pieces of jewelry designed to highlight small feathers, like the one Caro had gotten at the first party we attended here. The proprietor was a slender human woman, so not the mysterious Juss. I pretended to want one of the simpler pieces long enough to find out the price.

Marcus hadn't been kidding about the value.

We walked until after midday, wandering and looking, and looking, until my eyes hurt. I finally stopped. "We're never going to find them this way. If they're here, they're in a booth."

"So what do we do?"

We didn't dare use credit to buy food, or we'd be found for sure, if anyone was looking. "We find some people to talk to. And maybe we see if there are any traders here."

"Oh—like the roamers."

"That's right." All I had was my jewelry, which I didn't want to sell, but still, maybe we could trade work for information. "Look, let's not stop looking. But we should look faster."

We tried. My belly felt ever-emptier, and after a few hours, the balls of my feet and my heels hurt when I stepped on them, in spite of the soft path. We went up every other aisle. Sometimes we stopped and rested on arty benches and drank the water that ran out of fountains. Water gave me enough energy to keep going, but not enough to improve my mood. After a while, we stopped whenever something drew us: hand-carved string instruments, a small, thin man giving away samples of bread and honey, a booth of colorful shirts like the ones Liam had brought us when they came here earlier, even though he said he found them in a store.

I had no bearings.

After we went back twice for more bread and honey, I started to feel better, and more frantic. I didn't want it to get dark. If the festival closed, and we hadn't found Ming and Jenna and the others, where would we go? Last night, we'd hardly slept at all. Another night like that would keep me from thinking straight.

We passed a few large clear areas with stages along one side, and semicircles of perches and benches. One had a human storyteller and a thin crowd of children, all human as well. On another stage, two men strummed musical instruments and a third chanted, more sounds than words. We also passed two empty stages.

The closer we got to the back of the fair, the more we found useful items: kitchen and gardening tools, fine human wings, plain shoes for the wingless and shoes with strings and decorations for the winged. Here and there, personal services like massages or hair-braiding could be had. Fewer tourists seem to make it this far; most people were locals or fliers. Some of the booth owners were failed fliers, which made me think again of the two sculptors showing off for the crowd near the front. "Maybe this is where they were planning on coming," I mused.

"Probably. Doesn't help. I don't see them. Should we find this Juss person?"

I wanted to solve our problems ourselves. Besides, who could we trust? The sun sent long slanted rays through the booths, catching dust motes in gold light. We needed to do something, soon.

"Sit down," I whispered to Bryan. "You look more intimidating than I do." I waved him to a seat in one of the bench clusters, and walked slowly up and down the aisle, watching the thinning crowd. After a while I found two people who looked like they were from Silver's Home: a man and woman in bright clothes. Her multicolored eyes gazed out from under purple lashes as long as my thumb, and he had the telltale signs of perfection that screamed layered mods. "Excuse me."

She turned to me. "Yes? Can we help you?"

"I've only just gotten here, and I can't seem to find a list of all the vendors." I turned my eyes down so I wouldn't look like a threat. "I was wondering if you could help me access one."

Perfect Guy blinked at me, and Purple Lash Lady fingered a black stone hanging on a chain around her neck. "You don't have any interface devices?"

I shook my head. He looked slightly irritated and pointed back the way we'd come. "You can get them near the entrance. They're keyed to individuals, so you can't use ours."

It was almost refreshing to talk to someone who hadn't been washed out by the peace of Lopali. Maybe that was why we'd been wandering so aimlessly. I grinned at them and said, "Thanks," slightly pleased at the puzzled look on their faces.

Going back to the beginning wasn't as bad as it might have been. We walked fast. I wanted to see how the sculptures turned out anyway.

Except the sculptors were nowhere to be seen. At least those two. The ship and planet and the flier had all been moved out into the open grass in front of the fair, and two more pieces had been started, although barely.

Sure enough, we'd missed the rock necklace interfaces, and the wristband interfaces and, in fact, three booths of interfaces. They were boring compared to the booths next to them, and I shouldn't have let Marcus's prohibition on having local interface devices keep me from knowing we needed one now. At the guest house, we'd had to work with tightly controlled built-ins he'd tweaked the security on.

We still had the credit problem. Bryan frowned at the booths, looking stymied. I grinned at him. "We'll figure something out. Let's split up and see if someone will let us try one."

I went to the closest booth, which was staffed by a dark-skinned man wearing a simple shirt and shorts over sandals. He smiled broadly, the smile actually touching his bright blue eyes and reddening his cheeks. "Hello." He gave a small bow. "Guide to the festival for my lady with the violet eyes?"

"Please."

He waved his hands over his wares as if feeling for the right one from above. "And where, may I ask, are you from?"

I wanted his attention, and to get what we needed. Maybe I was just too tired to be cautious. "Fremont."

"Where the Maker came from?"

I blinked. Chelo had said they called Joseph that. "Yes." I pointed to a necklace like the tourist's, except with a lavender stone. "Can I try that?"

He shook his head. "It will get you caught. You have to give up your ID to access it, and there're people looking for you."

I shouldn't have given him the clue. I took a step back and cocked an eyebrow at him. "Who's looking for us?"

"A few wingless here, a few fliers there."

Great. My blood ran so much faster that I felt it in my neck and my palms. "Anyone else from Fremont looking for me?"

A quirky grin touched one side of his lips, and his eyes had a bit of a challenge in them, as well as a drop of warmth. "I don't know who you are. I know people are looking for folk from Fremont."

"Who's looking for people from Fremont?"

"Mostly people I don't like."

Well, that was a relief. Sort of. He looked earnest enough. "So why do you care?"

" 'Cause I like the Makers. That's why I have my booth here." He gestured toward the two sculptors. He did, in fact, have the best view of the platforms. He was equating the sculptors to Makers? Artists to Joseph and Marcus?

"I need to look someone up. Is there a way to do that?"

He looked around, maybe checking for potential customers. "Come sit in back with me. I'll close up for a few minutes."

Wow. "I need to get someone."

He didn't look happy about that. Bryan was two booths over, turned so his back was to me, and standing stiffly. I turned back to our maybe-benefactor. "I'll be right back." Without waiting for him to answer, I headed over to Bryan.

He was talking to a tall, heavyset man who had a look on his face that suggested he thought Bryan was thick in the head or something. "I have to have credit first." He glanced at me, giving me a dubious smile. "Maybe your lady will understand?"

I tugged on Bryan's arm. "Come on. I think I found something for us."

Bryan gave me a long look, then nodded, and without a backward glance at the man he'd been talking to, he let me lead him to the guy with the booth, catching him in the midst of covering up the interfaces on his table with black cloth. He frowned at Bryan, but led us into a blue tent with full sides, a door in front and in back, and a netted roof. The roof was interesting; designed to keep fliers out?

A neat row of boxes lined one wall, and three chairs sat in the middle of a large empty space.

I didn't introduce Bryan, or say my name, since I didn't know how much trouble we'd gotten into by leaving the Keeper tied up. Even standing inside the tent, I felt exposed. The interface merchant knew more about me than I did about him, we were surrounded by strangers while he probably had friends in nearby booths. The look he gave us felt like being stripped naked and then found to have a slightly bulgy belly or too much fat in the thighs.

But then, the interface merchant hadn't offered his name either. His gaze fell away from us and he got a lost look on his face, slacker even than Joseph and Kayleen got. A Wind Reader? Selling interfaces?

Then I noticed his hand turning and twisting on his wrist, touching a wristband that must have sensors in it. Not a Wind Reader, just someone with enough money for internals, like retina views, or a mod from Silver's Home. Just as I was getting worried about his silence (who was he calling? It was like my invisibility), he looked up and grinned. "Bryan. You've got to be Bryan."

Bryan nodded, his eyes wary.

"And so you're Alicia the Brave."

Wow. What was he reading?

"That's bad, though. Everyone's looking for you."

A voice sounded behind Bryan. "That's right." The man Bryan had been talking to at the booth next door stood in the doorway of the tent, looking directly at me with a satisfied grin bisecting his thick face. "But I found them." He stepped all the way into the tent and let the door fall shut behind him.

The interface merchant's eyes had grown wide, and they turned even brighter blue. Mods? Another interface? "Get lost, Jackson," he said. "I found them first."

27

CHELO: THE KEEPERS

Early morning light brightened our window frame for the second time since Alicia and Bryan had disappeared. I wrapped my blanket closer around Caro's slender shoulders and looked across at Liam, who had Jherrel tucked in with him. They refused to sleep on their own. As hard as we pretended it wasn't so, the kids knew something was wrong. Trapped in this room, Liam and I couldn't talk about it.

Across from me, Liam stirred gently, wiping the hair off Jherrel's face and looking over at us.

It would be time for the ceremony soon. I should look forward to it. I'd felt disconnected yesterday, had floated through the greeting of the day as if I were a wraith. Caro lifted her face, her eyes still closed, snuggling tighter against my chest. I had to keep a good face for her.

"It's time," Caro whispered.

As if she'd heard Caro, Kala's drum sounded three times outside the door, too loud.

"Be right there," I called. I kissed Caro on the top of her head, and wished for more quiet snuggle time with the kids. "Did you hear?" I asked Liam.

He grunted, but I could already hear him moving.

In a few moments we had both children up and both adults at least sitting up in bed. The kids headed for the bathroom together. Liam watched them go, then stared at the door.

Kala would stand outside patiently until we opened it.

I slid over next to Liam, taking his hand. I tried to pitch my voice below the kids' excellent hearing. "Surely we'll hear from someone today. Seeyan, at least."

"I hope so."

He looked so lost I kissed him thoroughly, something I didn't do nearly often enough anymore. It took a moment before he responded, and then he might have been starved. We broke up as the kids came out of the bathroom, and separated out to help each of them dress, him with Caro and me with Jherrel.

As I was tugging pants onto Jherrel, he asked, "Will we see Mommy Kayleen today?"

He smelled like sleep and a little like Liam. I helped him stand up. "I don't know."

He glanced at Caro. "What about Aunt Alicia?"

Caro stood behind Liam as he sat on the bed. She looked up from dragging a brush through his hair. "I can't find her."

She was looking? In the nets? Why hadn't I worried about that before? Liam squeezed my hand and knelt down by her, giving her his most serious look. "Caro, maybe you shouldn't look for her. Trust Alicia to find us when she needs to. Her and Bryan."

"I like looking."

I filed that away to talk to Mohami about. I wanted to talk to Joseph so bad I swallowed past a lump in my throat, and the effort to make myself smile almost cracked my cheeks.

As I pulled a blue shirt down over Jherrel's head, I noticed how being in real sunshine had lightened his hair and tinged it with soft red streaks. I'd stacked my own pants and shirt at the bottom of the bed; simple black leggings and a bright blue and sunshine-yellow shirt that screamed tourist. Kala had brought it yesterday, saying it was a hopeful shirt.

"Okay," I called to Kala. "We're ready."

When the door opened, it admitted Mohami. "Shouldn't you be getting ready?" I asked, blunter than usual. "I mean, the ceremony . . ."

The old Keeper had wrapped himself in his serenity even tighter than usual. He ignored my question, and smiled warmly. "Good morning, all of you. Please follow me."

The light in the windows suggested it must be close to time for the first flight. I didn't want to miss it. I needed the calm. I wanted the morning ceremony in every day of my life, forever.

Caro led us after him, her steps measured and swift.

He didn't take us out to the garden, but instead, he entered the room he'd first met us in, and stood to the side. I walked in right behind Caro, and saw her intake of breath before I drew in my own, nearly overwhelmed with the fullness of wings that met us. Tsawo and Angeline nearly filled the small space, even with their wings swept back. Nothing in here had been made for fliers, so they stood slightly bent forward to keep their wings off the ground. Tsawo's pale face seemed dark next to Angeline's wings, and his wings shone ebony, the light in here accentuating the black tones, barely drawing out the deep purple. His dark eyes caught mine, and for a moment he looked sorry for me.

"What happened?" I asked.

"Word surfaced yesterday that Jenna and her sister, Ming, Dianne, and Paloma are being offered in trade for you and Joseph."

I froze. It took a moment for my brain to figure it out. Five for two. Paloma, who was the weakest of any of us. At least they hadn't caught Alicia. My brother might be stupid enough to trade himself for her. Liam came close to me and curled his free arm around me, the other holding Jherrel.

"Who?" Liam said.

"The Port Authority."

"Not the Wingmakers?" I pressed.

"Assume they are the same. The powers on your home world are greedy."

I'd never been there. But Marcus, Jenna, Tiala, and Induan had come from there. "I don't think everyone on Silver's Home is bad."

"Nor is everyone here enlightened," Mohami said quietly.

No kidding. "Did they mention Caro or Jherrel?"

Tsawo shook his head. "But there's more. This morning, I heard that Bryan had been seen at the festival."

He didn't look surprised. So he knew they were gone. "And Alicia?"

He grimaced. "I've heard nothing. But she's probably invisible anyway."

Liam spoke up from behind me. "When did you hear about Bryan?"

"On our way over."

"How's Joseph?" I asked. "And Kayleen? Does she know about Paloma?"

Tsawo shrugged. "They told me about Alicia and Bryan."

So they were okay, wherever they were. Kayleen must be worried sick about Paloma. Small chance anything about this place except maybe the Keepers would value the old woman for herself. So all she had going was that she might be traded for one of us.

I was worth a world, had started a war, and now two women who had almost been mothers to me had been kidnapped to make me give myself up. Although I suspected whoever had done this would underestimate them both. Neither Jenna nor Paloma would want me or Joseph to give in.

I looked at Mohami. "They took our children for this same thing, once. We have to keep them safe."

He nodded. "Of course."

"And everyone else." I looked to Angeline and Tsawo. "Who knows we're here? How many of you? I thought it was just Seeyan." And we hadn't hidden. There were hundreds of people here, maybe thousands, who'd seen us.

Caro, who had been sitting quietly at Mohami's feet, must have finally figured out what Tsawo had said. "Why do they want to trade for you, Mommy? What do they want?"

I sat down on the floor and pulled her into my lap. "They want your uncle Joseph to stop helping the fliers."

Caro looked up at Tsawo, a very serious look on her face. "I can help you. I can do whatever Joseph can do. He told me so."

Mohami seemed to be lost for words. I had to struggle not to clutch her tight to me, and maybe scare her. "Someday, sweetie. But not yet. You have to grow up first. You can help by learning and by staying safe."

"No! I can do things now. You just don't believe me."

Actually I did. Not that she could redesign the fliers, but that she already had some of the eerie power of her uncle Joseph? Maybe so. But she was still a baby. The look on her face said she was scared.

We'd never given them any stability at all. What kind of parents were we?

Mohami pulled my attention back out of my navel. "You are fairly safe here. Most of the seekers have been on-planet for longer than you. But there will be new seekers coming in a few days. A bigger worry is that Bryan and Alicia know where you are."

"I know."

"We will work on a new place for you to go. In the meantime, go to the ceremony. It's just starting, and you won't draw too much attention there. We've also added a few eyes to watch over you."

I didn't want to go now. But I doubted we were safe anywhere. Liam and I had sworn not to raise the children in the dark of a cave long ago, and I still meant it. I glanced behind me to see a mask of worry on Liam's face. But he stood up and swung Jherrel onto his shoulders, nodding once at Tsawo and saying, "Thank you."

I turned to Angeline, who had said nothing, and I told her, "Please keep an eye out for Alicia. I won't be able to do it from here." Although I couldn't have explained a reason if asked, it felt more right to ask her than Tsawo, even though he had been Alicia's teacher.

The beautiful, pale flier blinked her wide blue eyes at me and nodded her head, keeping her silence for whatever reason. Joseph had told me about her daughter, the wingless young woman born of fliers, and so I added, "And I hope that Paula stays safe."

A small smile emerged from the pale pink line of her lips and she spoke softly. "May we all be safe."

Tsawo gave her a look that might have withered someone else, but she had an inner strength greater than his outward bravado, and I felt the steel in her even while Tsawo frowned. He turned back to me. "If my sister says so, we will watch for your sister."

At least I'd played that right. I bowed a little to him. "Thank you. If you see him, tell Joseph not to look for Alicia. Tell him to keep doing his work."

And then Mohami's hand was on my arm, and behind me, just through the doorway, I glimpsed Kala and stern Samuel. I needed to talk with him. How do you explain someone like Alicia to a holy young man?

We headed for the morning ceremony way too fast for the calm of the walk to descend upon us.

We didn't join the circle this time, but instead Kala led us to the top of the hill, looking down just as the first flight drew our eyes to the sun. Three other Keepers took seats nearby, watching behind and beside us. I kept my eyes on the ceremony, hoping for peace even close to the look on our watchers' faces. From up here, the fliers burst into the sunshine at our eye level, the wings and the ribbons and beads in their hair reflecting as points of light. Kala was next to me. I touched her arm. "How do they fly without being blinded?"

"They close their eyes."

That was impossible. They flew too close to each other. But Kala whispered, 'They understand the wind on their wings, and all the concepts of space between objects. The ones who fly here are our best, and they practice every day. It makes them almost one being."

I left my own eyes open and watched them, marveling. Perhaps we had created something better than the original humans. At home, where the people had struggled to stay pure and untainted by genetics, I had never seen such unity. "Is it engineered into them?" I asked.

Her voice sounded slightly disapproving of my question. "I believe it is training and engineering. Fliers with no sense of the air around them die."

"How—"

Caro put her index finger in front of her lip and frowned at me. She was right. I sat still and watched, the first flight, the second, the swooping, the moving off of the fliers. Even from this distance, I felt the raw need for the fliers' return, and the pull of the mandala gardens below me. I couldn't participate from here, but as the chant started, it buoyed me and I closed my eyes, imagining peace.

28

JOSEPH: MAKING AS WELL AS WE CAN

Kayleen's sobs woke me. She stretched out a foot away from me, Marcus on her far side, all of us on the hard floor with our heads pillowed on the edges of the black chair. Kayleen and I and even the very air smelled like sweat and exhaustion. The light glowed softly, making Kayleen appear part shadow, part girl. I touched her shoulder. "What's wrong?"

For answer, she curled tighter into a ball, drawing her knees up near her chin. Marcus moaned and flopped to his side, facing us, his eyes opening for just a second before nearly rolling back into his head, showing more white than green and gold before he went back down under. I'd let him exhaust himself. I should have been better help to him, but watching even a sim die had been hard. Strange growths had started on her organs, filled her belly, and she'd thinned around them. Her heart had been unable to take the strain of movement. The sim had stopped and lain still until she could no longer breathe.

After, we'd passed out.

It didn't matter that it had been only bits of information and not Paula. If we failed, it would be the real fliers we tried our magic on. There were ways and ways and ways to fail—in these steps, in the time when we made the nanotechnology and modified biological agents and put those things—too small to see, but real—into the living, breathing beings. Things we failed at, and didn't recognize as failures, might kill someone three or thirty years from now.

When Marcus drove us to start rebuilding right after the failure, the energy I'd fed him had been wild with hunger and fury and unfocused with exhaustion. Dirty energy, when he deserved better.

He wasn't going to be able to help me with Kayleen. I slid beside her, curling my slightly longer body around her so she was nearly folded inside, and stroking her back like Chelo used to do for me, running my fingers up along her spine and massaging the hard knotted muscles in the back of her neck. Her unruly hair had tangled even more than usual, and twice my hands caught in it so hard the pull must have hurt her, although she didn't react except to arch her head back to give me room to free my fingers.

Her cries shifted to little whimpers. My hands kept making circles on her back, as softly as possible, as if driven of their own accord. From here, with only her back and her dark hair, she could have been Alicia, except Alicia no longer cried near me. At least not visibly.

Kayleen's breathing calmed and became even. Just as I wondered if she had gone to sleep, she rolled over and whispered, "Thank you."

"What made you cry?"

She shook her head, and for a moment I thought she'd fallen truly asleep rather than answer. Her voice came out very soft. "I'm floaty. I don't know where I am all the time. Am I lost in the data watching a real girl die or am I in the real world watching an experiment fail? I mean, right now I know, but I didn't know when I woke up."

I whispered. "Well, you're here now. You're with me."

"I know it wasn't really Paula, but still it felt like she was here and we were making her. We killed her."

"I know. I felt it, too."

"I miss Paloma, and I'm too old to want my mom, but I do. It's cold here." She glanced briefly at Marcus and I hoped he was too far asleep to hear us, that he didn't understand like I did that she meant he was cold. She'd told me that before, that he drove her and drove her.

He had to, but she didn't have any way of knowing why, hadn't been exposed to much yet, not really. Besides, it was how he taught. No nonsense, no excuses. It was harder for her than for me, and I hadn't been able to convince her to love him. "Jenna used to teach us that way," I said. "She made us work for everything."

"She still does. They're wearing me out."

I couldn't argue with that. My own eyes would barely stay focused on her. She had turned onto her back and I reached over and stroked her cheek. "I want to go find them, too. I want everyone back together." I glanced at Marcus, noting how steady and still his breath remained. Hopefully he wasn't listening. "We have to get this done. Whether or not it has anything to do with the war, we have to help the fliers be free."

"What if we want to be free?"

A good question, but I was saved from trying to answer it when the sharp trill of Sasha's bark blasted through the door: a warning. Induan was no longer there to protect us, so we'd left the dog and a pail of water in the corridor.

I sat up. "Marcus," I hissed. "Get up. Someone's outside."

He blinked and pushed himself up, then collapsed again. It took him three tries to sit all the way up. When he did, he kept his hands on the ground, as if he needed them there to steady him. He'd never looked so weak. We hadn't eaten, even though our stomachs had been mewling with emptiness, because we had been even more tired than we were starved. A mistake.

I needed to take care of him. If I'd worked better with him, given him cleaner energy, he wouldn't be so weak.

Sasha barked again, a little calmer. Someone we knew, or someone who wasn't actually coming closer to the door. We needed to find out.

Marcus yawned and Kayleen sat up between us, and then I stood and stretched, looking down at them. "Ready?" Marcus had a hand to his head and looked like he might throw up, except he must be as empty as I was. "Are you okay?" I asked him.

The door opened.

Seeyan knelt outside, Sasha beside her with her nose on Seeyan's leg. The woman looked up, and her eyes gave away that something was wrong.

"Come in," Marcus whispered.

No. I had to take care of him. Whatever it was, none of us needed it on an empty stomach and shaking. "We need food. Now."

Marcus blinked at me. "Uh-huh. Okay." When he stood up, he

swayed. Before he could fall, Seeyan was beside him, supporting him. Good, because we probably couldn't. Everything seemed bright and hot except my strength as Kayleen and I helped each other down the corridor, following Marcus on Seeyan's arm. Seeyan didn't look a whole lot better than we did. In spite of her own drawn, pale face and the slump of her shoulders, she settled the three of us and brought four cups of col and a plate of crackers and herb spread from the common kitchen. Then she had the common sense to let us empty the plate and most of our cups before she sat back and looked at Marcus. "How is it going?"

He looked better for the food and drink and moved with more of his usual grace, although his eyes still looked colorless and flat. "Tough. We lost our first sim last night, and we couldn't finish the second one before we crashed."

"You've run the pure math parts of the models?"

Her sophistication surprised me, and then I flinched at my reaction. She may be socially less than a flier but that didn't make her dumber. Marcus seemed unfazed. "Of course. But what we put into the real sim always changes based on what feels right."

She nodded. Marcus had told me once that was what made us creators, and better than computers. Statistics showed we failed less than computers. Marcus said, "We should get back to work. What else did you come to tell us?"

"They have Jenna for sure."

He went still and silent. Kayleen clutched my thigh. Her fingernails dug into my skin. When we worked on the sim, we didn't have access to any other data: it was the only way to keep our own work pure. And then we'd slept for hours. "What happened?" Kayleen said. "What about Paloma and Ming and Tiala? Where's Induan? Has anyone seen Alicia?"

Marcus sat still.

Seeyan watched him, not responding directly to Kayleen, who kept talking. "They did this before. They took our kids."

I pried Kayleen's hand off my thigh and put my arm around her. "And we got them back. Besides, Jenna isn't helpless."

"But Paloma . . ." She trailed off and pulled away from me, standing and tugging at her hair, looking around as if a solution lay in the air.

I went for her and brought her back. "Sit down. We'll plan. We'll get the women back."

Seeyan blinked at me. "They want to trade for you two and Chelo."

She meant me and Marcus.

"No," Marcus said, the word coming out like it was dragged from him. "We won't get them back that way. They're fighters. Dianne and Jenna, at least, are fighters. We'd probably get in their way."

Kayleen glared at him. "You mean we aren't going to do anything?"

His voice softened. "Of course we are. We're going to keep working. They're not trying to hurt any of the people they have—they're trying to stop us. So we have to succeed."

Kayleen looked at him incredulously. "You want to just leave them?"

"They aren't helpless," he said.

"I'll try to free them," Seeyan said. "I'll get word to you if I can help. Even now, Induan is at the fair. Bryan has been reported there, and we expect Alicia's there, too, although no one has seen her."

Kayleen laughed. "No one will see her, either. She'll keep that damned mod on all the time."

"She has to charge it," I said. "But we should want her and Induan to be able to hide."

Marcus looked at Seeyan. "It's not Islas. It's the Wingmakers and someone else. I can't tell who, yet. But they're pretending to be Islas."

He must have gotten that from the nets.

Seeyan paled.

"Tell them—tell them we're thinking about it," he said. "Buy us time."

Her voice shook as she said, "I'll pass that along."

I looked at Kayleen. "You asked me a question back there. You asked, 'what if we wanted to be free?' We won't get free until people stop fighting over us. Which means we hide until we succeed."

She gave me a long, quiet look. A sane look. "We can't hide here."

"I know."

29

ALICIA: INVISIBILITY COUNTS

The interface merchant with the startling blue eyes took a step forward, staring at the man named Jackson. For a brief moment, his eyes seemed to soften, to become midsummer sky, and then they turned the blue of winter river ice.

Jackson nodded at me, sharp, and raised his arm. He stepped toward Bryan. Blue-eyes raised his arm to block, fast, and a red welt drew itself across his forearm, beading blood. He yelped a curse but held his ground, and didn't reach for his bleeding arm. Jackson feinted, trying to drive around and strike Bryan with the nearly invisible wire he'd just used to draw blood on the merchant's arm. Jackson's hand moved so fast I barely made out a slender handle in it. A flick of air across my cheek whistled danger, but missed. Jackson snarled at the interface merchant. "Amile! Help me!"

Good to have a name for our protector.

Amile shook his head.

"I'll share," Jackson growled.

Bryan stepped in so all three men were closing on each other, a knot of strength. He threw aside two of the chairs and I drew the other one away, making room. Going out the front door would get us attention, but I didn't know what the back door opened up to.

We hadn't learned anything useful yet, and Bryan was in fight mode, not looking at all like running.

Very well.

I turned on my invisibility mod and stepped away from where I had been standing.

All three men stared at each other, like camp dogs about to fight. Jackson kept most of his attention on Bryan. Even though Jackson was taller and might be as heavy, Bryan was compact and broad, everything about him strength. The veins in his neck stuck out in anger and subtle flicks of his wrist slicked his fingernails into sharp knives. The look in his dark eyes should have been enough to scare the older, fatter man away.

Amile's back was to me, but his dark skin rippled with energy.

I'd be willing to bet we were stronger than either Amile or Jackson. Bless Marcus for keeping us in high-g travel and making us work and run and fly.

Everyone moved at once.

Jackson raised his weapon.

Amile clutched his bleeding arm and put his head down to butt at Jackson.

Bryan grasped Jackson's free arm in his broad fist, his knives-for-nails digging into the man's skin, drawing second blood.

Amile bounced off Jackson's torso and looked up at him. He shook his head violently and grabbed for Jackson again, getting a grip on his wrist, the one that had the handle in it, for just a second.

Jackson stepped away from Bryan, ripping Bryan's nails through his arm so the blood welled faster, the slickness of it helping him jerk free. At the same moment, he slid out of Amile's grasp.

Momentarily free of the others, Jackson looked around for me, his eyes widening at my absence.

The surprise cost him a split second.

Bryan spun and closed on him from behind, his face more furious than I'd seen it since the last battle on Fremont.

Jackson flicked his invisible whip behind him and a small cut bloomed on the edge of Bryan's ear. He grunted in pain and took a step back.

We had to make sure the weapon didn't matter more than our strength. Bryan had stopped for a moment, close to Amile, both of them watching Jackson's full fist closely. Blood dripped down Amile's arm and Bryan's neck. Jackson brought his arm up, snarling.

Amile feinted left, Bryan right.

I yelled, "Here!"

Jackson turned toward my voice, letting Bryan slip behind him.

Bryan grabbed Jackson's head and jerked backward, making Jackson stumble back, almost falling, struggling not to have his neck snapped.

I saw my moment. Careful of my footing on the blood-slicked floor, I reached, plucking the handle from Jackson's hand.

It came free. The handle disappeared into my hand, my invisibility mod affecting it as soon as I'd grabbed it, analyzing and doing its nanomagic until the whole weapon became invisible. It was slick with Jackson's sweat and hard to hold.

Amile laughed, smiling at the place I had just been, looking far less surprised than Jackson, who went down in a heap on the floor as Bryan pushed him. I'd moved seven or eight steps to the side.

I raised the weapon above my head, careful to avoid the invisible stinging tail of the whip, ready to bring it down across Jackson's face.

Then Bryan's body was in the way, and I couldn't use the weapon. I dropped my hand and watched Bryan lean on Jackson's shoulder, pinning him. Bryan nodded at Amile, who took the big man's feet.

Jackson struggled, grunting.

The tent door was still closed, although I heard people just outside. I couldn't catch individual words, but curiosity laced their tones. They'd be in the door soon.

Amile heard them, too. He glanced up at Bryan. "Use the back door and go."

Bryan shook his head, although Amile was right. Still . . . we didn't know enough. I knelt down near Amile's ear and whispered, "Who is looking for us? Who is he?"

To his credit, Amile only jumped a little at the voice in his ear. He whispered back, "He's an opportunist. There's a reward out for you two."

"Us in particular?"

"Any of you. A lot, enough to live well on for a year or go somewhere else, get off this place. And more for the Makers and Chelo."

I looked at Jackson, who still couldn't see me. He watched the two of us, his whole body tense. I wondered if he was afraid I'd slice him with his own whip or if he was still looking for a way to win as one against three. Clearly he'd counted on Amile being on his side.

"Why are you helping us?" I asked.

Amile shrugged, then grinned. "I'm bored. You're more likely to get me away from here than your reward is."

All right. I could buy that more than altruism. "Do you have anything to tie him up with?"

Amile held out his hand. "Leave the weapon. So I can hold him long enough for you two to get away. Go now. There'll be a hundred people here any minute."

Bryan gave a quick nod.

Jackson tensed.

Bryan slammed his fist into the big man's cheek. "Stay here," he hissed. "And don't hurt our friend." He glanced at Amile. "We'll be back."

"I'll find you." Amile nodded at the door. "Go."

Good. I hated letting go of the fine-handled steel weapon with its own near-invisibility. Besides, I had a lot to ask Amile. But not in front of Jackson. The back of the tent had a flap door like the front, and in just a moment, Bryan and I were through it.

I liked Amile. Hopefully I would see him again.

Outside, we saw the back of another tent, a set of wooden chairs behind a booth, and then one of the sitting areas, luckily empty. We crossed through there. I wanted to avoid crowds, so I tugged on Bryan's sleeve to signal him to go right, where there were fewer people. We needed to hide Bryan so I could go back, invisible, to find out what Amile knew, or to find Juss the jewelry man.

It had grown late enough so the booths cast shadows taller than real life on the ground. If anything, more people now hung around the festival than before, and some booths that had sold cold drinks in the heat of day were heating grills and setting out cooking supplies.

We passed a huge metal sculpture of six fliers rising up out of a glittery and realistic fire, their faces beatified to the point of silliness and their wings burning with the same flames that scorched their feet. A stone wall had been built around the base of the sculpture. Even though I still wanted real wings, this was garish. Fliers as martyrs of the world, or something. The fake fire emitted heat. "Sit down," I whispered. "Watch the pretty art."

He laughed, tension draining from his cheeks and neck. I ripped the hem of my shirt, trying to do it artfully enough to pass if I turned myself back into view. The rip in Bryan's ear was clean, and deep into the fleshy part. "Good thing your ear was in the way of your throat." I pressed the fabric against it, watching it soak quickly with blood, careful to stand in such a way my hand couldn't be easily seen. Strange effects happened when I touched others in this mode. "Does it hurt?"

"Only a little. It didn't hurt at all, at first."

"I wish I'd kept it."

"Me, too."

I went silent for a moment while a couple holding hands walked around the sculpture, commenting on how realistic and painful the fire-singed pinion feathers looked. It took a few long moments for them to leave.

"You need to find a bathroom and wash your hands. There's blood under your fingernails."

"I need to find Ming. What if someone like Jackson found them? What if she's hurt?"

"You can't just wander around. You'll get found."

He didn't say anything, a sign he was preparing to be stubborn.

"I'll look. Maybe you can stay here."

He glanced up at the fliers above us, the closest one a woman with black hair streaming out behind her, nearly touching the artsy flames licking up her wings. "I don't think so."

As if to illustrate his point, two fliers came and stood silently gazing at the sculpture.

Where would he be safe? I hated the idea of splitting off from him, but if two people had recognized us already, he couldn't just walk around openly. Especially now that we'd been spotted. It wasn't going to be easy to hide a strongman here, either. Bryan's mods were plentiful on Silver's Home, but a planet designed for flight didn't attract many people with Bryan's body type. "Maybe we should leave," I whispered, "and then I'll come back."

He shook his head. "I'm not leaving without Ming."

Stubborn man. I glanced around to be sure no one paid attention to Bryan talking to thin air. But then, for all anybody knew, he could be using his built-ins. "We don't even know Ming's here."

He frowned. "It's getting dark soon. It will be harder for people to see me."

He was going to be stubborn. "It won't help if you get caught."

"It might, if they take me to her."

What kind of spell had she stuck on him? I guessed I didn't have to ask that. He needed love more than any of us. I reached over and up, getting my arm almost around his broad shoulders, and squeezed. "We'll find her. Don't go getting captured. It won't help."

"It might," he muttered under his breath.

"Not." His tendency to get darkly angry got under my skin. Well, if he wasn't going to leave, the best place to hide was always in a busy spot. Not far off, the deep sound of drumming and the high whistle of flutes or something like them rose over the booths. I pulled him to his feet and led him toward the music, finding a bathroom to clean up in along the way.

We hit the edges of the crowd long before we could actually see the singers. "There're too many people. I have to get visible, or go and meet you back here."

"Maybe Ming is dancing up there."

"Maybe she is. I still have to go find out if we have any friends." Although Amile had said he would find us. Well, when you don't know what to do, do something. "If Amile finds you, ask him more. See if he can help us find the others."

Bryan nodded.

I stood on tiptoe and kissed his cheek. He just kept moving for a breath, taking another step, intent on seeing through the varied assortment of bodies and wings between us and the music. I did it again, and this time he stopped and looked at me, his eyes sad and angry. He bent down and returned the kiss, cheek for cheek, his lips dry against my warm skin. "Be careful," he whispered. "Don't do anything . . . anything you shouldn't."

I grinned. "I won't take too many risks. Stay in this general area. I'll be back in an hour. No more."

"I hope I find Ming."

"I hope the music's good." Someone behind us bumped into me, exclaiming. I slid away before they could grab what they couldn't see, then stood at the edge for a moment, watching Bryan's back. He looked strong from this angle, all muscle and brawn, his movements exact as always. But ever since we'd left the Gardens of Earthly Delight and Morning Ceremonies, he'd seemed to get smaller and more lost.

But then, he'd done a pretty adult job on Jackson. Maybe I was underestimating him. After he partly disappeared behind a flier with pale gold and blue wings, I faded farther back, then jogged toward Amile's booth, careful not to step where I'd leave footprints.

I managed not to run into anyone before I made it back to the entrance. The sculptors had stopped, the crowds watching them all dispersed. The work in progress had been covered for the night, and so had the tables in Jackson's booth. Almost half the nearby booths had been closed down, so it didn't look unusual.

I ghosted into the tent where we'd fought. Blood still stained the grass, but there was no sign of Amile, or anyone else. Now what?

When I first came here, I wanted an interface. I knelt down and opened the top of one of the merchandise boxes that lined the tent.

"I wouldn't do that if I were you."

I leapt sideways and ran into the hard edges of two invisible palms. "Induan!"

"Shhhhh . . ." and lower, so low I could barely hear it, "Follow me." Her hand grabbed mine, and we went out the front door and out of the gates of the festival. I followed Induan's lead and did my best to walk soundlessly. Even invisible, it was possible to see us if you knew how to look. Most people would never manage it, but heat could give us away, or a blur as we passed in front of something colorful, or a faint flicker as the mod adjusted to a complex set of inputs. She was better at finding me than I was at finding her.

Her goal seemed to be to get us as far away from people as she could. We turned east out of the gate and crossed the road we'd come in on, and climbed a low hill. From here, the huge festival was laid out below us, too far away for fine detail, but now that I'd been there I could pick out a few locations; the gates, the burning-fliers sculpture, etc.

She let go of my hand. Since she kept her mod on, I kept mine going, too. We'd moved enough to stay charged. Her words came out soft, even though she'd clearly picked this place because no one was near or would be near. "Stay away from the webs here. Marcus is right. I don't want you caught, too."

She'd been in the group that left with my sweetheart. "Is Joseph okay? And Kayleen, and Marcus?"

"I saw them yesterday. They were okay then."

Good enough. "Bryan's down at the fair. Will he be safe?"

"Maybe not."

Her answer didn't surprise me. "What about the others? Do you know where they are?"

"I know who has them. It's people from Silver's Home pretending to be from Islas. But there's more than that looking for you. Some of the Star Mercenaries."

Who really were from Islas. "We're that important?"

"You're wild cards for both sides. There're also people of Marcus's trying to find you all, and Seeyan, and the other Keepers. All for better things, I think. I hope. I'm not sure they're all talking to each other."

The night was warm, but the idea of so many people hunting me gave me goose bumps that were half fear and half excitement. "Who do you trust?" I asked her.

"I think I trust us. Marcus and Jenna and us. Maybe not even Dianne and Ming."

"Me, too. Except Marcus. I don't know if I trust him. He's part of all this craziness about telling stories on us, making Chelo and Joseph bigger and brighter than they are."

She was quiet for a moment. The lights below us grew stronger, the shadows blending onto the darkness of the ground, the sky still streaked with color even though the last radiant edge of the sun had gone below the horizon even from up here on our hill.

Induan must have stood up, because her voice came from above me. "The stories are a strategy. Life on Silver's Home is so busy it's hard to catch attention. So Marcus uses stories. They're remembered. For example, he's used stories to make people aware of the fliers. There were already stories about their beauty, and the pain they have, but all the stories the fliers tell say that's okay—that the pain is needed for the beauty. But that's not true. So Marcus spread stories about how it didn't have to be that way. I think that's how the fliers decided they might be free."

"But you didn't know Marcus before we left for Fremont." I knew that—I was the one who'd asked Induan to go, and I'd picked my mod to match hers on purpose.

"I knew of him. Everyone knows of him. Just like they all know about Joseph and Chelo now."

"Why us?"

"Because people are more interested in stories about someplace and someone different. I couldn't be the subject of these stories. Joseph has Marcus's strength or more, and so he can be a hero, too. See, if Marcus wasn't one of the best Wind Readers ever, it wouldn't matter what he thinks. But that alone makes him powerful, and rich, and scary, all at once. Only people see him as a good guy, as a hero."

I stretched, watching fliers spiral out of the sky and into the fair, thinking we needed to get back down there. Soon. "Is Marcus a hero?"

"As close as it gets. He's trying to change things that matter. The problems in the Five Worlds are bigger than any of us. Sometimes people who think they're doing good are really doing harm. Either the war will kill us, or greed and stupidity will do it. Marcus used stories to make himself a legend before he did it to you all. He lived up to it. He was a hero when I was a little girl."

A long time ago. Induan was older than Paloma, even though she looked younger than me. "How was he a hero?"

"He changed the mod for swimming so it doesn't kill so many people, he made the Port Authority apologize for burning up a ship out of fear, he helped make us accept people like Dianne from Islas." Her voice sounded nearly reverent, and I recalled that tone from when I'd first asked her to join us. The recollection made me frown slightly as she continued. "There's more—he's been a maker and a rebel and a fighter. He used stories to get greedy people unelected and he challenged an appointment to the Five Worlds Court that would have been bad. When he taught at the university, fewer of the Wind Readers went crazy."

There was clearly more. I interrupted her. "All right, I get it. Marcus is a good guy. He acts like a hero." Kind of like Mohami the perfect.

"So far, you have, too. Joseph saved Chelo, and maybe he'll save the fliers."

I hadn't been a hero yet, except me and Induan saving the babies. That was in some of the stories, and nicely expanded on, too. But of course, Marcus had had a lot more years to be a hero in. And Joseph saw him as a father, or maybe more. What was more than a father? "I hope he doesn't die trying, and that Kayleen doesn't go stark-raving mad."

She'd moved around; her voice now on my other side. Spooky. "Maybe Marcus will find a way to get through this war so we come out a better people on the other side. That's what he wants. And humans all need heroes and stories. You're just it, right now. And Marcus."

"Just us?"

"Well, since the Port Authority and the Wingmakers are stupid enough to feed the stories, yeah. At least you still have steady attention. We're competing against stories about families being torn apart and brave young fighters and newly made tech. All wars breed stories. It's our job to make sure your story doesn't get lost in the noise."

Our job? "How close are you working with Dianne and them on this?"

"I'm helping. It's a strength of mine."

Ugh. "Well, if I'm going to give you any heroic stories to tell, we'd better go find Bryan. I told him I'd meet him in an hour; I've got to go."

"He's being looked after. Seeyan asked me to keep you safe for a few hours."

I hadn't left Bryan alone just to spend the night sitting on top of a hill. "What about Juss? Seeyan asked me to find Juss, only I never did."

"He's one of the people looking for Bryan. To take care of him."

If he'd been looking very hard, surely he could have found us. "How do you know that?"

"Seeyan told me."

Seeyan wasn't on our list of who we trusted. "What about Amile? I told him I'd find him, only he wasn't there." I stood up, pacing the top of the hill. It had grown completely dark now, so dark we'd have to be careful getting back to the fair. "I want to find him."

"How do you know he wasn't going to kidnap you?"

"He saved us from the other guy."

"Why?" she asked. "The reward for Joseph and Chelo is pretty big. What if he was trying to be your friend so you'd lead him to them?"

He'd said he wanted away from here. I believed him. Besides, I had a good feeling about him. I knew things, I really did. Just no one believed me much. Joseph, sometimes. "I don't know, I just trust him."

"It's risky."

So? "Well, when they made me a risk-taker, they must have built in some way to tell which risks are safer than others."

"My brain is wired to be a strategist, but I still had to learn the difference between a good strategy and a bad strategy."

I made sure I was a few feet in front of her, partly down the hill. Just in case I needed to get away. "I can't sit here anymore. I'm going to find Bryan, or Amile, or Juss, or someone. Are you coming?"

"Be patient. We need a plan. You need to think bigger than yourself."

"I am. I'm thinking about how to save my friends." I started down the hill. She'd be able to tell from my voice. "Coming?"

"I promised Seeyan I'd get you out of danger."

"You kept your promise. I bet I've been out of danger twenty whole minutes."

"Alicia. You're acting like a child. Let us help you. Seeyan went to talk to Joseph—she'll be along soon."

My heart hoped. "Is she bringing him?" She'd come closer to me. I stepped a few feet away, still unsure of her.

"I don't know," she said from too near. She was keeping up. I looked down. Maybe she could see my footsteps even in the dark.

I didn't care about her. I needed Joseph. I needed us. "I'm going. I can't stand still. I'm not made that way. But I'll be stronger with you. A strategist and a risk-taker belong together."

She grabbed my arm, bringing me close. "Promise not to talk unless I do? Promise to be still and quiet?"

"I'll try."

"That's not good enough."

"I'll do the best I can. And that's going to have to be good enough." I'd learned long ago never to make an absolute promise. It bound you, and I hated to be tied up in promises. I'd been tied up that way almost all my life, all the time in Ruth's band.

She must have heard that I meant it. "I'm coming."

I wondered what I should make her promise, but I couldn't think of anything. She was still holding my arm. I took her hand off, and held it, so we could travel together, and started down the dark hill toward the lights of the festival.

30

JOSEPH: LETTING GO

The small room beside the room of war felt colder than it had been, or we were all sleepier. Kayleen was on her back, in the middle between us, closer to me than Marcus. Even in the half-light, I could see the mess of her dark hair, now so tangled it might be hopeless.

"We have to keep going," Marcus said, his voice dragging tired but determined. "The sooner we finish our work, the sooner no one will want you."

People had been chasing me ever since I got to Silver's Home. "Do you really believe that? That there will ever be a day when no one wants to find me for the wrong reason?"

"All right. The sooner we can be free to find the others."

"That's better. Did people chase you your whole life?"

He shifted position, pushing up on his elbow so he looked down on us. "Most of it. That's the price of ability."

"So why wasn't I born more of an idiot?"

Kayleen stirred. "Would you really give up your skills?"

"No." *Although I'd take some of yours away if it made your life easier.* Except I couldn't say that. One look at Marcus reminded me of his impatience. "Are we ready?"

Kayleen rubbed her hands over her face. "Can't we sleep first? And shower? Wouldn't we have a better chance if we'd had enough sleep?"

"No." Marcus shifted in his portion of the paired black chairs the three of us shared uncomfortably. We'd had one, and then a few hours ago, we'd dragged a second one in—all that would fit. Surely this was meant to be a closet and not a shielded data room. The extra chair kept me and Kayleen off the floor, but left Marcus less comfortable, too. My hip ground into a bit of the support for the chair, and I couldn't find an easy way to shift that wasn't disrespectful of Kayleen. I missed Alicia's body tucked into mine, close, the way I'd be with Kayleen if we had a few inches less space. I missed Chelo, and Kayleen must miss her, too. And her babies. I took every chance I had to make Kayleen comfortable, but in this strange place I had to be careful lest we both fall into an unreal world we'd regret.

That didn't make it easy. We could both use comfort.

Our third try for a successful sim had just started deteriorating, but we'd pulled up just the same. Why watch it die?

Marcus had fallen silent, but then he said, "Sleep won't help. In fact, not having sleep might be better. There's art in creating." Even though it was Kayleen's question he was answering, he looked at me. "It's all our knowledge of biology and machine nano and biomachines and art. You've got to have all that. And the ability to dive deep in data streams while you work. I do, and you've learned, you've been learning every day. Between us, we know more than enough to do this. But if data was all it took, a computer as dumb as a ship's AI could do this—put it all together into a simulation and run scenarios until something happens."

"Good idea," Kayleen murmured. "Then we could sleep." She shifted a little, giving me enough room to slide my hip off the hard lump it had been hugging.

I sent her a grateful thought, more a feeling, and she returned warmth.

Marcus sounded far away, as if he were in a conversation with someone else. "It doesn't work. If it did work, we'd have machine-made organics everywhere. We have machine-designed machines, machine-monitored climates, little machines to weed and clean and organize our world, machine sensors everywhere."

He'd talked about this before, lifetimes ago, during my first few weeks on Silver's Home. "But machines can't make life," I finished for him, remembering.

He smiled. "Life speaks to life. And it's not your head that does it, not the part of you that's done all the studying. You need that part, too, but Making—Making is more, and less, than that. It's something that comes through you but is more than you. That's where you and I need to get to." He touched Kayleen's shoulder gently. "And you, too, if you can."

She gave him a faint smile, but I could see the whites around her eyes, and I was sure that if I held her hand, it would be trembling. Maybe mine would, too. I knew what he wanted. And the last time I'd done it, the last time I'd let myself go and become all the world that I could sense, I'd used the power to kill. "I'll do my best."

He whispered, "That'll do."

And so we went down again. This time, more than exhaustion licked at me. Memory. A memory I couldn't see without fear. It had been . . . so beautiful . . . to be so far outside myself. The strongest moment ever, a moment when my soul was the soul of the world and the soul of Fremont, and it felt like the entire universe was in me. The nano in my blood and the blood in my heart and the data in all of it had resonated as one note, one beat, then another, synchronous, a dance so deep and full it showed the way everyone linked, enemy and friend, predator and prey, sun and moons, machine and man.

I hadn't gotten close to that moment ever again.

I couldn't even remember how I'd done it. Why. It had come up on me unawares, and had made all the difference in our last battle. I'd had to find that place to win, even though I hadn't been looking for it. Chelo had been next to me, always my strongest help. And the others had been in danger. I'd had more net—Fremont's own, a net I'd built myself, and the Islan net put up by the Star Mercenaries. Different. But not so different as this one.

The day I threw the ship into the sea had started as a tiny tunnel on the net, as sensor data flowing innocuously into a starship. Only all the data in our world had been added, bit by bit, letting me expand into forever.

Marcus, show me. You do it here, you let go. I want to feel how you let go and stay safe. You've kept me out of their nets, but give me more. Give me the extra capacity in the war room next door.

Hesitation. Kayleen answered with feeling, showing me she saw the right of my need. She'd been there. She'd glimpsed where I'd gone, even though she hadn't followed.

I still needed to get past the fear, but I'd need power to do it.

I need more, I repeated. *If you don't want me in the winged net, you have to let me in your other feed. The war feed. There's capacity there.*

It will be . . . distracting. If you lose control, I may not be able to shield you well enough.

If you think I'm strong enough to save the fliers, to save the Five Worlds from war, then you have to trust me now.

Still, there was silence. Did he believe in me as much as he said? He had to. He'd practically created me.

There hasn't been enough time. The first sign of the wind that burns is disorientation. Promise me you'll stop if you no longer know yourself?

Right. How do you know when you don't know yourself? The drop from sanity off the wall of the wind into the fires of the burned was sharp and fast. I knew that much.

Kayleen spoke up. *I know what it feels like. I'll watch for him.*

She had not fallen off. She'd been there, at the edge, tipping toward insanity, and love had brought her back. My sister and Liam. They'd loved her in spite of the bloom of craziness in her, helped her tame it. Bless them.

I'd be okay.

If he didn't make me wait much longer. Waiting for him to decide might burn me all by itself.

Marcus's silence seemed to go on forever, and so I picked up data threads one by one, absorbing the state of the sim, preparing. Anything was easier than waiting.

Maybe that is what we all need. Ready?

Good! But who would watch out for Kayleen? I'd have to do that, too. Somehow. I reached for her. *You ready?*

Yes.

Okay.

I braced, but there was no flood, just all of us breathing together far away from my consciousness, but still in tune one with another. The simulation in front of us. The same, but richer, every detail more distinct. Paula, who wanted a baby she could grow wings on.

Paula, who was more than us and less than us, a complexity of machine and human, of biology and engineering.

I followed Marcus, Kayleen following me, all side by side and linked, together, but led one by the other by the other, there was simply more to accept. Enough, finally. I hadn't fed on so much data, so rich and sweet, since we left *Creator*. Paula became huge inside me.

And then I was inside her.

We'd been the surgeons, the ones outside wielding the knives of change. Badly. Now we were . . . something else.

Marcus kept his word, showing me what he felt, what he did. No wonder we'd failed and failed and failed. I had been skimming the surface of her before, and I hadn't even known it. Maybe he had been this deep in her, and I hadn't seen it, but now she was open entirely to me. To all of us. I took a deep breath of the data, synchronizing my breath to Paula's simulated breath, trusting Marcus and Kayleen to follow.

Kayleen felt strong, if distant. Marcus, strong and supportive, nearby, with me. He and I were outdistancing Kayleen.

No help for it. I sent to her: *Stay as close as you can. Watch me and I'll watch you.*

Of course.

Enough dataspace existed for me to use, more than enough. I expanded, breathing in more with every breath, my self-in-data linked to my physical body. With every out-breath, I simply held what I had. The biological rhythm served to ground and contain me, to keep me distinct as myself. If I forgot to notice my breath, I might become lost.

Unused room for data existed between the parts I needed and the flow of warship statistics and locations and chatter; a buffer. I left it there, remembering Marcus's warning, appeasing myself by saying I would come back and taste it later. For now, I didn't have any trouble keeping my focus on breath and heart and bone and blood vessels and ovaries.

We began to work.

Kayleen, as always, bolstered and commented and added strength. Yes, she watched me more closely. I watched her back. Maybe staying aware of each other would keep us safe, and grounded.

Marcus felt more sure, more confident. Perhaps he had needed this, too. We couldn't be timid or afraid. If we were, it would take months to accomplish this, and we didn't have months. The safety of our family depended on doing this right and now. Someone had Paloma. Jenna. That thought formed another bridge between this moment and the moment of Fremont. It goaded me.

So I focused and let go at once. There are no words that really tell how to let go. It's being loose and tight, heavy and light as air.

Paula's history and her being and her needs filled me even while the pulse of blood in a vein or the flash of a neuron attracted my attention. A universe inside a woman's body. No wonder Marcus had thought a plant too much not long ago. Life was big and chaotic. Intricate magic.

Flier children were born from normal mothers and then changed. Paula had the right parts for sex, canted at slightly different angles since no flier could ever lie on their back without crushing wings, except in special harnesses. But sex didn't need the parts for reproduction. Paula's uterus and ova had been shriveled to nothing. Thankfully, not removed entirely. We built and strengthened, reminded the organs what they had been meant to become. This building and rebuilding was completely separate from any part of my sexual or love life, not relatable in my head to Alicia or Kayleen or my own parents or sex or birth.

Even though we had done this part before, it was different. It came more easily, almost a dance; still exhausting. It had taken hours before, but now it went fast, maybe just minutes. Hard to tell. I could feel it all working, feel us as part of a change that made her better and stronger. Beyond that, too: heart, blood, breath, nerves firing, and even hope. Feeling hope in a sim gave me hope, and better, looped it among the three of us.

Intuition: the emotion of the Maker at the point of his creation matters. It affects the outcome.

Once the structural changes took in proteins and cells (new instructions placed in the building blocks of her), her glands needed balancing.

This was the point where the last two sims had begun to die on us. Runaway hormones made weak bones and unbalanced growth, and affected the delicate bodies of fliers more than normal humans. Emotions had become unrecognizable, had eaten the health of the sims.

But this, too, came more easily. We worked through glands and endocrine systems together, adjusting and testing and redoing. This part felt even harder; something a woman should do. My own internal balances weren't the same. Trying to pull Kayleen into the work failed; she was too insubstantial at these speeds and depths, a wraith with us but not with us. Faint.

Trust yourself.

Easy for him to say. Even if he was right, how?

Just keep working.

Oh. Oh! I did. Then we were past that, expanding into Paula's nerves and muscles, testing organs to be sure nothing we'd done would cause too much stress. I could be her. Her heart beat louder than mine, drawing my own physical cadences to match hers.

Marcus, beside me, covering me, putting himself all around me, his energy firm and unyielding as ship-skin. *We're done for now.*

I'm not ready. There's more I can fix. I could. I could strengthen her shoulders more, build it into her DNA so her children would have the change.

His reply was full of laughter and accomplishment. *They did not ask to be remade!*

So I was getting carried away. *Okay. See you at the surface.* I reached for Kayleen. *Ready?*

Kayleen-in-the-data sounded thin and foggy. *Did we do it? Will she work?*

Marcus answered her. *We did well. It's bad luck to bet before time passes. Let the sim run.*

Good. I'm taking a shower.

Leave as carefully as you came in.

Marcus was always warning. Almost always right. As we neared the surface layer of data, it felt like squeezing down and becoming small in order to fit into our bodies.

I'd done it! Not so big a space as all the webs on Fremont, but open enough to let go. As I came fully into it, I found my body had let a tear run down its cheek. A second one hung like rain on my lashes, and then dropped.

Kayleen touched it. "Why?" she whispered.

I didn't really have an answer. I felt . . . elated and completely drained. I felt like the first time I gave all of myself to Alicia, for her instead of for me, the first time I passed the blushing-boy stage and made love to her like a man. I had floated then. "I guess . . . I guess I'm just tired."

She gave a soft nod. "I've never been so tired." She wrinkled her nose at me. "And dirty. How about we clean up and go eat?"

A half hour later, all three of us sat in the cafeteria, smelling less of sweat and salt and more of berries and bread and tea. Sasha curled under the table, making sure some part of her touched each of us.

I'd avoided col, wanting sleep. Needing sleep.

The fact that my eyes would only stay half open explained why I didn't see Marcus's friend Stark, from the war room, until he was sitting across from me. And even then I might not have noticed him except that Sasha had sat harder on my feet and was giving a low warning growl. I grabbed her by the collar.

His countenance looked serious and his eyes were dark in his dark brown skin. He ignored me and Kayleen. His being here did give me a spark of energy. "They're coming. Islas."

"When?" Marcus asked.

"They're five days out. They're already slowing, and they have an obvious trajectory. Looks like Oshai spaceport." He frowned and looked down at his big hands on the table for a moment before looking back at us. "I should've seen it sooner. It's not the military proper, but the Star Mercenaries."

Of course it was. I should have a visceral reaction, but I just didn't have the energy.

Kayleen grabbed for my hand. I gave it to her, watching Marcus's face. Surely now we should go to the others.

Marcus nodded and pursed his lips, not looking at any of us. He must be lost in thought or data or both. Or as tired as we were. Who knew what? And I'd been more worried about the Port Authority. "Why would they follow us here?" I asked.

"Someone's paying them," Marcus said. "Maybe Islas. Or maybe not." He sipped his col, and took a bite of bread, looking far less worried than I felt. "I wish we had Dianne," Marcus mused. "She'd have a good guess." He looked back at Stark. "Can we be ready in two days?"

Ready for what?

"Two days is longer than I recommend."

Marcus glanced at us. He looked as drained as I felt. "I bet we need two. Sim's got to run forward ten or twelve hours before we know if we're done here."

"Could it have been that easy?" Stark mused. "A few days of work? And the fliers never got it done before?"

Marcus's eyes narrowed. "A few days of work for us. Chance and others have spent years. It's partly what they did that made it possible for us to do what we did. If we did it." He glanced at me and Kayleen. "We don't know yet."

I nodded and squeezed Kayleen's hand. We weren't going to try anything again until we rested. It better have worked. It had felt like it worked.

Stark looked at us. "I'm sorry. Like I said, I wanted to spend some time with you all. I'm pleased to have you here."

Kayleen's face had gone white and her hand shook in mine. I wanted to hold her, to calm her, but I didn't have the strength to move. I managed half a nod. There was no adrenaline left. I'd burned it all on the sim. My body didn't care if the Port Authority and the Star Mercenaries and the bounty hunters were after me. Hell, it didn't care if it took its next breath.

The table came up to meet my face.

31

ALICIA: FRIENDS AND ENEMIES

Darkness had transformed the Festival of High Summer to a sensory feast. As we slipped invisibly though the entrance, I stopped for a moment in a clear spot. Every tree branch or high protrusion of any kind had its hard edges dotted with multicolored lights. A soft yellow glow came from under the paths, as if they'd been built on light. Music rose and fell from multiple directions, drums and flutes and stringed instruments. The air was scented with wine and tomatoes and other fruits, and frying breads. I tugged Induan close to me, and whispered quietly, "It's magical."

All I got in return was sharp shushing sound.

Too bad she didn't have a sense of wonder. But she was the trained strategist, so I shut up and walked fast and quiet toward where I'd promised Bryan I'd meet him. We passed Amile's booth, still closed up. No sign of Jackson either, although his booth was open. A tiny blond woman chatted with customers across the table, a big smile on her face.

In another few minutes, we were near where I'd left Bryan. We couldn't get close; impossible to stay invisible in a standing-room-only crowd. I climbed up on a tall rock, pulling Induan up behind me. From this vantage, we could see the performers, although they were still too far away to make out their features. A mixed band: human and fliers, two of each. The sight made me smile involuntarily.

In front, humans crowded near the stage, some swaying and stomping their feet to the music. In general, the fliers stood farther back, needing room. All of the perches were full. Other fliers gathered in small groups. Rocks, like the one we stood on, often had fliers on them.

Pale light bathed the whole crowd, punctuated with the individual lights of features like chairs and a fountain, and with the bobbing moving lights of decorated hair and wings. Bryan's blocky body should be easy enough to spot.

Nowhere.

Induan squeezed my hand and leaned in to me. "I'm going to look around. Stay here."

So she could whisper and I couldn't? "All right," I answered quietly. There was probably no one looking for her. She left my side, and a few moments later I saw her emerge, visible, from a booth close to my rock perch. At first I tried to track her through the crowd, then I lost her behind a cloud of fliers and settled down to watch and listen.

The music sounded pretty good. I slid off my shoes and let them fall on the ground below, visible but not noticed. I stood on my rock and danced, liking the idea of dancing invisible. It felt good to stop worrying for a few moments and feel the wind in my hair and the stone under my feet, still warm from the day. The drums washed over me, rhythm, the flute adding melody. Even though the music was as bright and light as the music of the morning ceremony, it sounded better in the dark under the lights. I could never live with the Keepers under the hill, but I could run a booth here. It would be kind of like being a roamer on Fremont, only safer.

"Who's there?" a voice asked from behind me.

I stilled.

"I hear you breathing."

I turned and found a human woman I didn't recognize looking quizzically in my direction. I leapt lightly from the stone to land near my shoes, not answering. Good thing, since a green-winged man landed right where I'd been. I used the noise of his landing to slip my shoes on and slide a few feet sideways, far from the woman. She stared at the top of the rock and the flier, until he said, "Excuse me?" and she blushed and stepped away.

I should be more careful. I spent the next few moments dodging people walking by. Induan didn't reappear and I didn't see Bryan.

Another two songs played before I jumped, startled by Induan's hand on my arm. She'd become invisible again. She led me away from the crowd and whispered, "No sign of him."

"Or Ming? Or anyone?"

"No."

"Seeyan told me to find Juss."

"I know where his booth is."

"Take me."

She didn't answer but just went, her hand in mine slick with sweat even though it wasn't very hot anymore.

Juss's booth was near the center, just like I'd thought. It was a big square with bright purple and blue walls and silver display cases. Juss—if it was Juss in the booth—was a tall man with blue hair, a blue shirt, and a blue belt over black pants. I still wore my blue shirt, but of course he wouldn't see.

He had customers; three Islan humans looking at clever metal pendants with small feathers. Most of the cases held similar items. One was all feathers, none the size of pinions, but some clearly from the bigger feathers that lined the wings rather than the small fluff that filled the other jewelry, or like Caro had gotten the first day we got here. He dickered with the customers a while, smiling the whole time. His face looked kindly, and his voice sounded gentle.

I didn't trust looks.

I watched while two more sets of customers came and went. A Paradiser bought a long, slender mauve feather, which Juss set carefully into a wooden box that he wrapped in a red-and-gold ribbon. A failed flier with wing-bumps like Seeyan's took a small trinket and leaned in a few times to talk to Juss in a tone too low for me to hear.

I crept in closer, waiting for the Keeper to go, ready to pop into sight and see how Juss took it. Induan would probably have a fit, but dancing on rocks aside, it was high time we made some progress. I looked around, checking to be sure no one besides Juss would see me. After all, I didn't want to give Induan a reason to have a fit.

A tall slender woman came up the walkway to the booth with long, anxious strides, her face set in a worried look.

Seeyan.

I stepped back, bumping into Induan, who goosed me with a sharp finger.

Seeyan stepped up to him, glancing around just like I had been, as if making sure no one could overhear her. I tried to remember if she even knew we had the invisibility mods. Maybe not. Whatever. She leaned in. "Any sign of Alicia or Bryan?"

Induan slid an arm around my torso, pulling me in close.

Juss nodded. "They got in a fight down by the main gate—some idiot interface merchant down there heard about the bounty and was watching for them."

Jackson and Amile were both interface merchants.

Seeyan picked up a small round pendant with a yellow feather in it. "Did they get caught?"

"I don't know. Not then. I have four or five people out looking for them, but no one's reported any sign."

Juss still looked kind. I was beginning to doubt it. "Are Marcus and Joseph coming to save the day?" he asked.

"No." Seeyan put the pendant down and picked up another one, this one a knotted string with beads and no feathers, although it had the suggestion of a feather's shape in the way the knots fell. She held it up to her neck, looking in a mirror, a distracted look on her face. "Marcus is so focused on saving us that even Jenna being gone isn't distracting him."

Disappointment flickered across Juss's face. "Joseph?"

"Does what Marcus says."

Which I was fiercely glad of for the first time in my life, since it looked like Seeyan had been trying to trick them into something. But what? Chelo was the one who'd spent time with her. I knew Seeyan's story—abused flier kid that no one wanted once she couldn't fly. A lot of their stories were that one. But you'd think that would make her want the flier/baby situation fixed.

Seeyan put the pendant down and leaned into Juss, pecking him on the cheek. "Anything else for me to report?"

He shook his head. "I'll let you know if we catch them. General Loni called asking, and she sounded unhappy."

"Yeah, well, I am, too."

I couldn't ask who that was, but I filed the name away. General Loni. A woman.

Juss's booth seemed to appeal to Islans since two more came up. Seeyan turned away, and he spoke to her back. "Be careful, little one."

Whatever was going on, he cared about her. The tone of his voice made that clear. He turned to the Islans, and I noticed he seemed to know one of them. But Seeyan was getting away. She might lead us right to Jenna and Paloma and the others. I pulled Induan after me, following Seeyan.

Induan didn't complain.

I expected Seeyan to leave the festival. She didn't. She went on through the middle, along the back of the concert where we'd failed to find Bryan (and where I still didn't see him when I spared glances into the crowd), and through the crowd, carefully, until we came to a series of long, low buildings that looked like small warehouses. A few open doors supported that theory; boxes of goods stood stacked inside one, and another one had huge blocks of wood that would probably become fodder for another day's sculpture.

Seeyan's palm unlocked a gate in a tallish wooden wall and she slipped through a door. Before the door closed, I slid a finger in the last bit of opening, biting my tongue to keep from crying out as it tried to shut on me using some automatic mechanism. There must have been a safety built into it since it stopped, my finger trapped neatly and me swallowing hard with tears bunching in my eyes.

The door swung back open—undoubtedly helped by Induan, and we slid inside and let it close. Seeyen, steps away, looked back quizzically, but then shrugged and kept going.

Only then did I breathe out. Good thing my finger was invisible. Surely it was swelling and bruised.

Inside the big fence was a small compound of four or five buildings, a few tables and chairs and, here and there, perches. Dim lights set the buildings' shadows and the perches' shadows into each other at odd angles, and gave a few of the perches multiple shadows. Seeyan slid through a door into the nearest building. We didn't make it inside before the door closed behind her.

Induan and I stood still, watching. The dark shape of a dark-winged flier took off from one of the buildings farther away from us, soon lost to view. That explained all the lighting around the festival; a way for fliers to avoid running into obstacles. From this distance I couldn't tell if it was Tsawo. I wouldn't think so, but I wouldn't have expected Seeyan to be selling us short either.

Two people walked around the grounds together, talking in low tones. They were dressed in dark clothes and wore soft shoes. Guards?

A flier passed close enough over our own heads that I ducked when I felt the wind in my hair.

We needed to move. The windows in the building Seeyan had gone into were covered; I didn't hold out much hope of seeing anything of interest. I tugged on Induan, angling us toward the building the flier had emerged from.

We made it two thirds of the way to the building before the guards, on another round, seemed too close to us for safety. I stopped, keeping my breathing down. Induan's breath was barely audible, but her hand on my arm was warm and reassuring. Two other people walked by, too close for comfort, and I was glad we'd stopped. After the way seemed clear again, and the building we were headed for was between us and the guards, I started us forward again.

As we got closer, building details resolved. The outside was a dark color, blue or blue-gray, and it had small windows that looked like they might also be covered. Light leaked from the bottom of the windows, and from under a plain door. It was shaped slightly more like a house than a warehouse, but still one story and low-slung. The thickness of the roof on the side toward us indicated it was probably still wide open to the stars, and fliers. Flower beds butted up to the walls, most of the plants low and controlled, except along one side, where wide-leafed plants with tall-stemmed slender bells of flowers crept up trellises, scenting the air with something too-sweet that threatened to make me sneeze.

A rush of wings behind us made me turn and look around. The guards stepped around the side of the building and the two people who had passed us earlier now flanked us, too. We were inside a circle.

Uh-oh.

Our would-be captors stared at each other, except for one of the fliers, who looked right at me and Induan. He had gray eyes that clearly saw us. Or since they didn't meet my gaze, saw where we were. How?

He pointed at us, and the wingless walked slowly nearer, surrounding us, their eyes wary.

Induan's hand slid off my arm.

She didn't need to tell me. Go in different directions.

But where? The four were close enough to leave little opening. I'd been trapped before. It wasn't going to happen again.

The other flier had bloodred wings trimmed in gold. She was short for a flier, with cropped red hair to match her wings and gold pupils in her eyes. The gold in her wings sparkled even in the artificial light, and probably reflected sunshine almost blindingly when she flew. She watched the gray flier, admiration clear on her face. The guards and the others all looked at us, at where he pointed, and even though their slightly off gazes told me they couldn't see me, I felt naked under their eyes. Prey. But she wasn't even looking for us. So I charged her.

She didn't move, didn't feel me coming.

Head down, I rammed into her chest. She felt lighter than I expected, but not brittle. She gave with my rush, nearly falling. I reached for a wing and tugged, trying to pull her sideways so I could pass her and run for the wall.

Her hands came around me, clutching for balance. We danced a moment, holding each other.

I had been caught after all.

Our feet tangled and she tipped back, the center of her weight higher than mine because of her wings. I pulled away, backward, wanting to help her fall forward so she wouldn't break a wing. I whispered, "Sorry, so sorry."

She reached toward me, her face twisting, surprise and a cry for help clear in her features. She raked fingernails along the top of my right forearm. I pulled away, gently but still fast, not minding that she hurt me, but desperate to get free.

She landed on her hands and knees, with a cry of pain. I'd hurt her. I didn't want to hurt a flier. I didn't want to ever hurt a flier.

I'd hit a flier.

What was wrong with me? I backed carefully away from her, looking for another opening. A long red feather, from midwing, lay between my feet. I must have damaged her wing in the struggle. Without really thinking, I reached for it, scooping it with my left hand, and turning immediately right, ducking to do what I should have done—knock the wind out of a wingless.

The gray-eyed flier called out. "Alicia! Stop. You can't get out anyway."

32

JOSEPH: A FRIEND IN NEED

A long damp tongue scraped against my cheeks and nose, and I put my hand up over my face, pushing Sasha gently away. Too bad the artificial light of the cave never really turned off. It would be so nice to open my eyes to darkness, pet the dog, and then roll back over and sleep. My eyes were crusty, and my mouth tasted like sand. I remembered falling onto and then off the table, and then crawling over to the side of the cave against the wall, Marcus's voice egging me on, and someone else—Stark?

Something soft pillowed my head. I turned, feeling a shoulder bone. Kayleen? I couldn't quite brave the cruel brightness yet to tell for sure, but it must be her. My pillow gave a soft little snore, and I smiled. Yep. Kayleen. I was still so tired. Surely we'd only slept a few minutes. Maybe an hour?

Something must be wrong.

I sat up, wiping at my eyes with one hand and pulling Sasha to me with the other. Once I could actually see, I found Stark next to me with a glass of water. I took it, and it tasted as good as the first water after being frozen on one of the ships. Like every cell had a deep thirst, and the water saved them, one by one, from death.

I reached my hand out for more, but Stark said, "Slow down. Let your body take that much. I've got col here, too. Wake the others, first."

I wanted more water. I looked back and found Kayleen had rolled away from me. Her long hair, which she'd combed meticulously after her shower, had already started to tangle again. It obscured most of her face. She moaned and put a hand up to her cheek, scratching at her ear. Beyond her, Marcus slept unmoving, looking as unperturbed as usual, except he still had less color than he should. Sasha looked at them, too, as if contemplating whether or not she should lick their faces. I knew it drove Kayleen nuts, so I put a hand on Sasha's head and said, "No." I turned back to Stark. "They look like they should sleep more." I put my hand out for more water.

He filled it, narrowing his eyes. "You've slept through a whole night."

Really?

"Marcus'll want to check on the sim, and you've only got a day or a day and a half until you've got to go."

That's right. Star Mercenaries. Lushia again? Someone else? I was still too tired to get amped about it. Or anything else. But he was right about the Paula sim. I wanted to know. I glanced back at Marcus to check and see if he was still asleep. "Where are we going?"

He shook his head. "If Marcus didn't tell you, I won't."

"He was just tired."

Stark's laugh was gentle but firm. "So wake him up."

A loyal soul. I drank the water, buying the others each a few more breaths of sleep.

Kayleen rolled again, to me this time, wrapping an arm around my calf. I shook her gently, whispering, "Wake up."

She mumbled something. I leaned down to hear her. It sounded like "Liam." Well, she must miss him. Her arm tightened around my calf, and I picked it up and moved it carefully. "Kayleen—wake up."

It took three more tries before she looked like herself when she opened her eyes. As Stark handed her water, I woke Marcus, which took one easy nudge. Once we were all sitting up with col in our hands, Marcus closed his eyes. I knew he was building a secure tunnel and diving through it to check on our work.

And when he opened his eyes, I knew we'd failed. Whatever energy the water and col had given me faded in disappointment. Kayleen was watching him, too. "What happened?" she asked.

He looked crushed. "She lived almost all night. The sim managed the pregnancy all right, but she died delivering."

"So we got a lot further than we had before."

He nodded. "We almost did it. We have to go back."

Stark grunted. "You've got about thirty hours. And you might need to sleep some more."

"We'll sleep on the ship."

Ship? Not without Chelo.

Kayleen had a deep frown. "Did the baby die?"

Marcus nodded.

I needed to keep my head clear enough to think. "So we really didn't get as far as Chance did just using what he had? I mean, Angeline had Paula, right?"

Marcus stood up and stretched. "But Angeline didn't bear her. Mari did."

Kayleen said, "But Paula was okay, and this baby wasn't. This one died. Doesn't that mean we failed worse? It makes us as bad as Silver's Home. Maybe."

"The baby was okay until the birth process strangled him."

I stood up next to Marcus. "We can analyze all this later. We need to get Chelo." Kayleen rewarded my words with a smile and held out her hand. I helped her up. "Now. We need to get her now."

"No." Marcus sipped his col and looked many times calmer than I felt. "Chelo's safe. We know where she is." He looked at me. "Alicia's the only one of yours that's missing."

"And Bryan." Why did people always forget Bryan? "Has anyone heard anything?"

"And Bryan," Marcus acknowledged.

"And my mom," Kayleen added.

Marcus closed his eyes for a moment, and I wished we were already on a ship, where I'd always had all the data access I wanted, any time I wanted it. I knew better than to dip in here—it wasn't Marcus not trusting me, it was that we were hunted. Besides, it was all too sweet for my taste.

When he opened his eyes again, Marcus said, "Nothing, except Alicia was in a fight, she and Bryan. They got away, and no one has seen either of them since."

That only meant there was nothing I could do. I didn't wait for him to tell me what came next. "How much work do we have to do to get one more try on the sim?"

He gave a pleased, surprised smile. "Same as last time. Why don't you two freshen up and take the dog out, and then meet me back here in half an hour?"

When we finished with this one last try, I was going to go find Alicia and Bryan and Chelo and Liam and the babies and everyone else, and I wasn't going to get on a ship until I did. And if Marcus didn't already know that, he should. So I didn't bother to tell him.

Ten minutes later, Kayleen and I were outside with Sasha. As soon as we found a quiet place to sit, she started talking in her old Kayleen-babble. "What could be happening? Why do they want you so bad? And Chelo—is that just to get to you? I bet we haven't heard from Alicia because she's invisible, but I haven't seen Induan or Seeyan, and they should have come back, unless they came back already and we didn't wake up. And I had bad dreams. I dreamed about the sim, and in some of my dreams she was Paula and she was sweet like Paula, but in some of them she wasn't, she was like the mercenaries, all mean and full of technology. . . ." She put her head in her hands. "And I wanted Liam, and Chelo, and they were going farther and farther away from me in my dreams, they were getting small. . . ."

So much for me being worried. I took her in my arms and held her. She started crying. Sasha came up, curious, and laid her black-and-white nose on Kayleen's thigh and didn't whine or bark, or even move. The flower-sweetened outside air gave me strength, and I willed my skin and my body to drink of it, to drink in the sun. I might not have another fifteen minutes of sunshine for a long time.

Kayleen's hair felt soft under my hand and I watched the curve of her cheek against my shoulder. Back on Fremont, she'd always been one of the happiest of us, but she'd also always been more fragile than Chelo—who never broke—or Alicia, who broke violently, but had been strong enough to survive being beaten and locked up. Even though she'd been loved, Kayleen had always reminded me of excited fog rising from a morning river, fast and pretty, yet insubstantial. I leaned down and kissed her gently on the top of her head. She nuzzled her head into my lips, but didn't turn her face to me. I lifted my head back up.

Surely that was a friend's kiss. My body wanted to offer her more, but she wasn't mine to offer myself to. I wasn't free, and I didn't want to be free. So I let her cry, and managed not to kiss her again. Instead, I drew pictures of Alicia's face in my head, and remembered her hot, hungry kisses and the feel of her body. Hopefully she was okay. Surely she was okay. Alicia could survive anything.

Only Sasha was simple. If not for her, I would have felt incredibly alone out there soaking in the sun and my friend's tears.

Kayleen cried so long we were late getting back.

We found Marcus pacing where we were supposed to meet him. He had one of his intense thinking looks on, the one where he drew his eyebrows in and picked at the thin line of his lips. To his credit, he didn't ask what kept us. He had three plates of fruit and cheese and bread and nuts piled up for us, and a bowl of bread soaked in milk for Sasha. I would have far preferred a big slab of djuri steak, but the bird people didn't eat much meat. I was sure Sasha would have preferred to hunt, but she had known I needed her. I gave her a pet and whispered, "Thanks," in her ear.

We went back to the small dark room and lay back down, uncomfortably, on the big dark chairs, and fell away from our bodies into the same larger river of data we'd had before. And like we'd seen on multiple tries now, Paula dangled in the air exactly like she'd been when scanned up into the computer, a canvas waiting for us to paint health and fecundity across. I pictured her alive and walking around, fat with a baby, laughing. She was pretty anyway—more than pretty. But pregnant? I made her glow. I wanted to go in with the final picture in mind. Ah. I added her with a baby. Better.

It might have been the sleep, or the col, or the knowledge that this was the last time we'd see her in this state in this place. Maybe it was sheer desperation. But we fell deeper and further, and I pulled Kayleen after me, the two of us feeling more connected after her long cry on my shoulder.

Marcus pointed out what he thought we'd missed, and we changed it, and we changed more. The sim felt . . . even more right than last time. Maybe the process of creation went on infinitely, but for now, she felt just right. Strong enough. Healthy enough.

In that moment, we three were together, nearly blended with each other and with the Paula sim, breathing aligned. Kayleen had followed us almost all the way, holding more data than I'd ever seen her hold, expanding with me into the numenous silver light feeling of being full with data, completely sated, and yet still knowing there was more if we needed it. More data, more information, more places to grow and expand. More becoming.

We were all we could be. Makers. The three of us—for a golden moment—as one, with our creation perfect.

Marcus called us out.

Leaving all that power meant shedding it, letting things that had been parts of me blow into the wind of data, losing layer on layer until I came closer to my essence. Success happened when my heart beat in my ears and my blood flowed through the tips of my fingers. When I felt my own breath.

The pronoun inside me had changed to I.

It felt like falling off a cliff.

I couldn't feel Kayleen.

At least the lights in here were dim, so I could open my eyes and turn to her. She was still. Scary still.

I put a hand on her chest.

She breathed. Barely. I couldn't *feel* her essence at all. Even in the dim light she looked pale, and her eyes danced under closed lids.

I went back under, diving fast and deep.

She wasn't there, either. Not in the data. Not close. I was sure she'd been with me. Right? She had been up until we turned, but after? Had she known we were leaving or had we stranded her with too little of herself to follow back?

I had years of training on her.

I'd trained her myself.

Had I failed?

I came back up, snapping my eyes open, momentarily disoriented by the speed of returning to my body.

She still lay there, not moving, not changing.

"Marcus!"

"Huh?"

"Is she okay? What happened?"

33

CHELO: CARO'S LINK

Blue butterflies landed on gold flowers, and Jherrel laughed and clasped his hands together in a cup, trying to catch one. He was nearly fast enough. The butterfly headed up into the sun, then dived down again a safe distance away. The mandala garden was open every afternoon, and since Caro was off with Jill, Liam and I had decided to keep our exercise discipline and take Jherrel out into the garden.

The little imp rewarded us by leading us on a long chase through spiral paths, finally settling on a small lawn surrounded by butterfly flowers and benches. Ever watchful and silent, Samuel followed us around the garden.

A whole day and a night and part of another day had passed with no word from anyone. Even Seeyan didn't come. Tsawo didn't fly down like a dark tide of feathers. The morning ceremony had gone well. At breakfast, three women poets started and finished each other's works while the crowd hummed softly.

Even now the movements of others who were nameless seemed linked to mine as they went about their service for the day: planting, culling, cooking, laundry. All the myriad chores and ways of being busy felt like a connected dance. The evidence was slight, just a way of feeling, but I liked to imagine it similar to how Joseph and Marcus and Kayleen felt being able to talk amongst each other through thin air. It helped keep my worries down.

Between one breath and another, something felt slightly wrong. A ripple in all the connections. I stood up and looked out over the garden. The sun beat down, warm enough to draw beads of sweat on my forehead. Nanobees buzzed through the flowers, the gold dust of pollen on their little metal feet barely visible. Keepers kept: trimming and feeding flowers, raking dirt. As peaceful as it looked, something was wrong.

Then I heard my name. "Chelo!" Kala's voice, too loud for this place, too loud for any time. Edged.

The last time Kala screamed, we'd found Samuel tied up.

I raced toward her, worries crowded in my head. Joseph. Kayleen. Alicia. Seeyan. Marcus. Paloma!

I heard Kala's labored breath from a distance. Her face had reddened with exertion, and her immaculate robe had dirt streaks along the bottom of it. "Come. Caro." She was gasping for breath. "Jill says come."

Oh. No. It took a moment to sink in. Caro should be safe with Jill, learning elementary skills about Reading the Wind. "Caro? Did someone hurt her?"

Liam had come up beside me, Jherrel clutched tightly to his chest. "What happened?" he demanded.

Kala had caught enough breath to speak in full sentences. "Caro is screaming about Kayleen. She says her mommy Kayleen is lost. Jill told me to get you."

The peace of the mandala garden shattered. We hurried after Kala, Samuel trailing us. Kala, the quiet and serene, looked frantic. If Kayleen was hurt, where was Joseph?

We found Caro in Jill's arms in a small garden I hadn't even known about. The two of them sat on the lawn, Caro staring toward us, but seeing something else. Her face had gone sea-sand white and her eyes were red from crying. Liam called her name and ran toward her. She lifted her hands, fastening her eyes on him. "Daddy!"

He put Jherrel down and folded Caro in his arms. She burst out into such deep sobs that she couldn't tell us what she felt for a few moments. I knelt down and held Jherrel, who trembled as he watched his big sister bury her face in her dad's shirt. Liam stroked her hair, his eyes so worried I thought for a moment he might cry himself.

Jill's face had lost almost as much color as Caro's. She explained.

"We were working on shielding—teaching her to block out data she doesn't want to be bothered with. I've never tried to teach anyone so young . . . usually kids are six or seven before it becomes a problem, but Caro's not even four yet." Jill's voice shook. She must feel guilty. I glanced at Caro, still sobbing, and waited for her to go on.

Mohami came in the door and sat down silently on the floor, watching us all. It felt like he brought a tiny bit of serenity with him, enough for Jill to continue. "She started screaming for her mommy. I thought she meant you, Chelo, but then she started calling for Kayleen. She said Kayleen's lost, and she needs to be found.

"She called for her uncle and for her mom and she almost passed out—her eyes rolled up in her head. Then she started screaming. I tried to follow her into the nets, but I couldn't." Sweat beaded Jill's brow and her eyes looked worried and faintly guilty. "That's not how I teach. Not me following. Me leading."

She paused again. Mohami smiled at her.

"Shhhh," I said. "It's not your fault."

Jill swallowed and licked her lips. "I couldn't follow her. She's stronger than me."

I wasn't surprised. One look at Liam told me he wasn't surprised either. He clutched Caro even closer to him, and stroked her spine, his hands big enough to cover half of her small back.

Mohami signaled Samuel, who brought water.

We drank, and waited.

Caro quieted. Jherrel left his snuggle with me and walked over to Caro, very solemnly handing her his own glass of water. She drank, her eyes still wide and the glass shaking in her hand. Jherrel took it from her and offered it to Samuel, and my heart went out for him. So like his dad, to be there and take care of whatever needed to be done.

Liam whispered to her. "What happened?"

"Mommy Kayleen is gone in the nets. Uncle Joseph is looking for her. She's lost, and she needs me. But I can't find her either."

"How do you know she's lost?" Liam asked.

" 'Cause she told me." Caro's lip quivered. "She told me she loves me and if she doesn't come back she'll always love me."

What was Kayleen thinking? Poor Caro. Poor Kayleen. Why would she say such a thing? "How do you know the message was really from Kayleen?"

"Because I know what she feels like in the data."

Well, I didn't have any way to argue with that.

Caro curled her little hands into fists and looked up at Liam. "We need to go find her, Daddy."

Jherrel said, "I'll help."

Mohami put his hand on Caro's arm. "We'll send someone out to look."

Caro contemplated him for a moment, her eyes narrowing so she looked older than she was by years. "If Uncle Joseph can't find her, no one can."

Smart kid. "She's right." I watched how Liam held his daughter, and remembered how I'd held Joseph when he was only a little older, and Kayleen later, in the cave during the war. Even a Wind Reader needed touch. Maybe touch could help bring her back. I'd done that before, over and over. I'd have to go. "Have you seen Seeyan?" I asked Mohami.

He shook his head.

"Should you have seen Seeyan?"

His voice was quiet. "The Keepers network is often interrupted. She may have had a task to do. We are Keepers first, and only then we are what we strive to become."

I didn't understand that, except that it meant Seeyan was late. It was time to test whether we were captives or guests. I glanced at Liam. "Will you stay here?"

His eyes widened. "We should all stay here."

"But Kayleen!"

"I know," he said. "Joseph is surely looking."

"I abandoned her once before. Remember?"

"We both did."

Mohami interrupted. "You should stay here, Chelo. We will send someone."

Maybe I liked it here too much. No matter that the morning ceremonies connected me with everyone, Kayleen lived deeper in my heart than any stranger. "I'm going."

Liam shook his head. "They want you. Maybe this is a trick to get you out in the open. We know people are hunting for you and Joseph. We don't know anyone is hunting for me."

"But I'm more likely to know what to do with lost Wind Readers."

Mohami stared at me, his face unreadable. Samuel busied himself with the water glasses. Kala sat on the floor with her legs crossed, her face serene, her eyes fastened on some point on the wall visible only to her.

I looked at Caro, who still clung to Liam. "She needs you. And I need to do this. Neither of us is a Wind Reader, but I could often find Joseph at home just by knowing where he is." And all of my meditations here had made me more open. "I'll find him. And that means I'll find her." I addressed Mohami directly. "I must go."

I was used to seeing joy on his face. Or serenity. Or even love, in a sort of universal fashion. A few times, puzzlement. What I saw then was sadness. "We all must meet our destiny."

I clutched Jherrel to me, smelling his hair, absorbing his warmth. I would do this. Mohami's words had made it real.

Liam wanted to argue. Dear sweet Liam who wanted to lead everyone. Every muscle is his face had tensed with worry, but to his credit he just met my gaze and nodded almost imperceptibly. This was mine to do. Not only would Caro be happier with her dad here, but I owed it to Kayleen from a long time ago. Plus, I knew Seeyan better. "I'll start at the festival and see if this Juss Seeyan told me about knows where she is. She knows where Joseph and Kayleen are."

34

ALICIA: CAPTURED

When the gray flier called my name, I froze. He had looked at me. He'd *seen* me. One glance his way suggested he still saw me.

The red-winged flier was still on her knees, an awkward pose for a winged woman. I so wished I hadn't caused her lost and pained look. It stripped her some of her flashy, ethereal beauty. She raised a hand and called out to the gray flier. "Amalo. Help me."

"In a moment." He hadn't stopped looking at me. "Even if you get away from us, you cannot leave the compound."

"How do you see me?"

He sounded impatient. "There are mods available to fliers. I can see in the dark, which means I can see heat."

Oh. Well then, we were well and truly caught. At least for now.

He stood still and regarded me, letting me think about this new wrinkle.

Well, I needed someone to ask about this place, and about Paloma and Ming and the others. I flicked my mod off. The wingless in the circle showed relief and, maybe, a bit of wonder as I blinked into full existence right in front of them. Usually, it entertained me when I surprised people, but right now I felt vulnerable, and guilty. For being caught. For hurting a flier, even though I'd made sure she wasn't hurt badly. And for picking up the feather, which was now visible in my left hand, like an advertisement about how stupid I was. I walked over to her and extended my right hand, helping her stand.

Her gold eyes watched me. She looked puzzled, but kept her silence.

I held the red feather toward her. "I'm sorry. This . . . this is yours. I should not have kept it."

She took a step back and shook her head. "I can't use it now."

Amalo spoke, slowly, as if addressing a child. "Alicia. I know you will have heard that fliers' feathers bring luck." He paused, clearly for effect. "But taken in anger, they bring a different sort of luck. You will have to live with whatever Marti's feather brings you."

Great. I felt the importance of this moment, but I didn't know what to say. Induan was nowhere to be seen, so perhaps my mistake had helped her get away. She could be standing right next to me, but I didn't think so. If Amalo could see me, he could see her.

Hopefully she'd escaped.

If so, I was on my own, and this wasn't anything like what I'd hoped, which was just to rescue everyone and get out.

There was more than one way to take a risk. "I need to know what happened to my friends. I believe they're here. Can you help me?"

He didn't seem surprised by my question, although he offered a very different one. "Would you have a cup of tea with us?"

Surprised, I said, "Sure," before even thinking about it.

He nodded at the guards and the other two people. "Thank you. Please return to your duties."

They melted away as fast as they had come, clearly used to moving quietly and used to taking orders. Amalo turned to me. "Keep the feather, but know you owe another flier a good turn some day to make up for what you did to Marti."

If that was all, it was a light sentence. "I will."

"Come on, then."

If I didn't know better, I'd assume he'd been watching for me. But that didn't make sense; how could he have known to look in this compound?

Amalo didn't lead me and Marti into the same building the black flier had risen from, or the one that Induan and I had been stalking. Instead, we crossed the compound to a low-slung building with soft light pouring out of wide windows.

Simple perches and benches lined a deck outside the building, all empty. Amalo and Marti perched near each other, and I clambered up onto a perch so I could look them in the eyes. Marti sat still and examined the heels of her hands, which looked scraped and red. Amalo watched me. I looked back and forth between them as I struggled to find a comfortable way to balance on the perch and hold the feather all at once. There was, of course, no back support, so I had to find a way to hook my feet together for stability.

A tall wingless woman in a long dress came out, and Amalo asked her to bring tea. After she left, I asked, "Do you know where my friends are?"

He sat back in his chair. "Of course I do." He waved a hand out at the other buildings. "I'll take you to them after this. But I have been looking for you, and I'm pleased to find you so easily."

I made sure I didn't sound cowed. "Why do you want me?"

"I know you want to be a flier."

Wow. Tsawo must have told him. But why would Amalo care about that? And what did it have to do with Amalo or Seeyan or Juss or whoever was running this show wanting to capture Chelo and Joseph? One part of me wanted to be silent, and another wanted to lie, and I also wondered if Amalo could help me.

And more than anything, he was right. I wanted to be a flier. I wanted to be a flier so hard I could barely answer him. The words got stuck in my chest and then my throat. But finally they came out. "Yes. I want to fly, with real wings. But what does that have to do with my friends? I need to know they're okay."

"They're fine." He looked like he was trying to suppress a laugh.

I decided not to be mad at him for laughing at me.

The wingless woman came back with real tea, rather than col. I sniffed it, delighted with the heady, herbal aroma. I looked up to thank the woman but she had already turned away.

I sipped. The tea tasted like Paloma's lace-leaf and dried ponga-berry tea, except a tiny bit sweeter. Marti and Amalo drank, too, and for a while no one spoke. It felt surreal to sit outside with two beautiful and silent fliers who had captured me and now fed me tea. Quite strange. From beyond the wall, the faint sounds of music, and sometimes laughter, reminded me of the festival, and Bryan.

I studied my companions. Amalo, whose gray eyes matched his

gray wings and gray clothing. His wings had black barring on them near the tips, but were otherwise a single color designed to drink light rather than reflect it. His face was long, his eyes even wider than most fliers, and his hair caught back in a long braid. All things about him spoke of quiet, composed power, and it dawned on me he reminded me of Marcus. He didn't look like Marcus, but he felt like him—calm, and sure of himself. In clear contrast, Marti's showy colors didn't quite match her diffidence. She met my eyes but looked away quickly, glancing at Amalo as if he would have the answer she wanted.

He broke the calm. "What does it mean to you to be a flier?"

I didn't know how to answer. It was something I'd wanted since I first saw a statue of a flier.

"Just say whatever comes to mind," he prompted.

"It's freedom. You're so beautiful and so free. So calm." When I paused, the other two remained silent until I spoke again. "When I was young, we lived on another planet, not one of the Five Worlds, and I was very different. People wanted me to be like them. They didn't want me to run as fast as I could, or climb as high, or even be as strong. I got in trouble when I didn't pretend to be the same as everybody else. They even tried to kill me for it." I paused, sipping my tea, thinking. "But you don't have to be the same as anyone. You are just . . . yourselves."

Amalo's mouth quirked into an ironic half-smile. "You can't fly away from who you are. If you didn't like people telling you to slow down, why would you like people telling you to fly?"

"No one is telling me to fly. In fact, most people are telling me not to. They say the risk is too big. But I want to fly. I've wanted to ever since I saw my first flier, and even more since I got here."

"So pretend you have wings," he said. "What would you do with them?"

"Fly." I sipped the bottom dregs of the tea, which were more bitter than the top of the cup had been. I wasn't convincing them. The looks on their faces told me that. I paused a moment, thinking. "When we first got here, I watched the fliers out of my window in the morning, as long as I could. Humans need flight, or at least I do. It's the most beautiful state ever. As if all our evolution has been striving to become free of the ground."

Marti spoke. "You can already fly."

"It's awkward and heavy, and I can't even do it well."

She gave a little half-smile at that, making me wonder if she knew how truly badly I did fly. "But you think you can transform with wings?"

I couldn't let them see any doubt. "Of course I can."

Amalo looked at Marti, and they shared something between them—unspoken. She nodded, briefly, and he spoke to her. "Marti. Can you share why you chose to become a flier?"

Oh. Wow. So she was a successful mod? From wingless human adult to flier? I looked more closely, but didn't see anything to suggest she was less a true flier than Amalo or Tsawo or any of them. I couldn't even see signs of the change in her face—her eyes were closer to the sides of her head, like other fliers, maybe a little less, but she had a flier face. Her bones seemed as fine as Amalo's, and her chest large, like his.

For the first time, it dawned on me how much change I wanted. Everything would change. I might not know myself in a mirror.

But I wanted wings. I wanted blue wings in a hundred shades of blue, sky and river and summer-flower and near-violet. Marti looked directly at me, her gold eyes another change. I would keep my violet ones. She was waiting for me to say something. "Please, tell me why you changed."

Her voice was very soft. "To fly is to be the soul of humanity."

Huh? "That seems like something Mohami would say."

Amalo's eyes narrowed. "Don't discount Mohami, who is the soul of human giving."

Marti held up a hand. "There is balance in the world. The Keepers are necessary so that we can fly, and their equivalent exists in all humanity. We respect Mohami, who keeps our traditions alive. Our job is to display the beauty and the pain of all that humans strive for. The pain is in how we are made, and the beauty is in how we fly."

"And that," Amalo said, "is why it is so sacred when regular humans become one of us."

Meaning it was more special to go from human to flier than to be born flier?

"Why?"

"Because if you succeed, the pain will mark you for life."

No one had told me that. It made me want it more. My throat was so dry I could barely ask, "What do I have to do to become one of you? How do I ask?"

"Are you asking?" he asked me.

"Yes."

"And someday we will answer."

No. I wanted to know now. He was hard to read, but still felt like Marcus. He wouldn't give me anything for free. He'd make me earn it. "How do you choose?"

His eyes and his facial features softened. "We will know." He stood up. "But you aren't my captive. I was merely called to find you and since I have, I have other business for now. Come with me, and I'll take you to your friends."

35

JOSEPH: DOWN IN THE CAVE

Marcus hurried up steep stairs behind a door I'd never noticed and along a cold hallway that opened to rooms and offices. I suspected it was the area we'd glimpsed when we sat on the roof talking to Tsawo and Angeline. Kayleen hung limp in my arms, as much a rag doll as a human. Her face was completely white, her eyes closed, her head lolling so I held her the way one holds a baby, supporting her neck. Her feet banged against my thighs. Sasha trailed behind, whining softly.

Marcus took us to a well-lit room with bright overhanging lights and chairs on each side of a soft bed. I lay Kayleen on the blue coverlet, which would match her bright eyes if she opened them. When she opened them. I picked up her hand to lay it over the coverlet, her fingers limp and almost cold. Marcus brought me a lightweight tan blanket from a closet and helped me tuck it around her. Worry lines surrounded his eyes. His every movement seemed so controlled he must have been seething.

We'd spent an hour or more trying to revive her in the room, retracing paths of data, holding her, talking to her. Nothing had changed her condition at all. Here, she simply had more room and looked more comfortable in the bed but, in a way, sicker. I sat beside her and ran my fingers across her fragile face. "Stay with her," Marcus said. "I have to go find Stark. I'll also look for other things to try. She may just—wake up."

He didn't sound hopeful.

"We can't leave with her like this, can we? She's lost in the data here. If we take her away from her *self*, the part of her that's lost, then how can she ever return? Should we even have moved her away from your shielded network?"

He put a hand on my shoulder, squeezing gently. "I'm sorry Joseph." His voice had none of its usual confidence or humor. "It was a hard thing we three did. It may have had a cost."

I needed to hear it. "Meaning?"

"She may never find her way back. She was never as strong as you."

"Then I'll find her."

"You've already tried. We both tried. It's not safe here—you'll be like a candle in the Lopali data."

I'd be a fire. I was going to try again. What more could go wrong, anyway? After all, people seemed to know where we were. Mercenaries were coming. Half our group had been captured. I wasn't going to be too afraid to save Kayleen. But I needed to start. Maybe for her, maybe for me, but I needed Marcus gone in the worst way. I nodded at him, hoping he'd interpret that as acquiescence. "Good luck."

He stood up and left, his shoulders slumped. A long time ago, he'd had a reputation for keeping his students from being wind-burned. He should have been looking out for her more. I should have, too. In our abandon and joy, in our power, we might have killed her. If so, this was the second time I'd killed in power.

It couldn't be. Not Kayleen.

As soon as he left, Sasha came over and licked my hand, clearly responding to my sad determination. I patted her head and then kissed her wet, cold nose. "Go on, girl, go lie down."

She went to the corner and curled up in it, nose on paws, giving a soft doggie sigh that suggested discontent. I curled up next to Kayleen, under the blanket, close enough for her to feel my body heat. Best to start with the physical and go back into the data if that didn't succeed. Kayleen and I were one family. I held her hand in mine, and with my free hand, I stroked her face. I whispered her name, talked to her. "Kayleen. Our best flier. Remember being in the air on the way here, doing loops and laughing, watching me struggle on below you. Remember your little girl, who needs you and me to keep her safe. Caro needs her mom. Chelo will need you, too. She is so serious, she needs your silly questions and she needs to be needed, the way you need her. Come back to us. You are part of Liam's band. Who will he lead if you don't come back? Paloma loves you, came all the way here and left her home to keep being your mom." Who else? "Bryan loves watching you climb, you and your big feet. Jenna will have lost a daughter—you know we're like her family, too. She saved us on Fremont, more than we ever knew. Over and over. I learned some of that when we flew all the way home from Fremont the first time, when she was still one-eyed Jenna." I paused. I was rambling. Like Kayleen rambled. "I love you. Come back for me."

There was no change.

I repeated it all, twice over, using different words but saying the same thing—we loved her and we needed her and she needed us. She couldn't die, couldn't stay lost.

If she heard it, she showed no physical signs at all.

The opposite.

Her fingers grew colder, even the ones I cupped in my own hand. They should have warmed to my touch. Her breathing stayed even but slowed. It felt like I cuddled close around a ghost, as if all that made Kayleen herself had fled.

I kissed Kayleen's cheek, another chaste kiss, and then I closed my eyes and matched my breathing to her thin, slow breaths. A hard choice, my body didn't want to slow that much, but I craved resonance with her.

I released myself into the data, starting by picking it up thread by thread, feed by feed. Unshielded, the fliers and Keeper's raw data still threatened to carry me off in bells and calm. To resist, I kept Kayleen's face in my memory, and the feel of her energy signature. Everyone felt like themselves in data; since the first time I met Kayleen here, deep in the Fremont data, I'd been able to find her, in all of the sources and flavors of data we'd shared at home and on the ships between here and there.

But now I couldn't feel her.

Maybe I needed to find sim-Paula, except she grew inside Marcus's shielding. She would be hidden. So deeper, wider. Maybe I needed to hold the Lopali data and let it make and be space for me the way I'd held so much data inside of Marcus's shield.

Marcus would warn me away from that. His voice was an echo in my head, something that might as well be real, edged with caution.

Kayleen's sweet energy was stronger.

I opened more, and more.

And more.

I held all of the myriad data coming in and out of the cave. I held the data from the vineyard; planting times and wines and varieties, sales figures. I held the data from the weather control systems, cruder than ours on Silver's Home, but they could be; Lopali had been made for control. The mandala of peaceful data about the rivers and streams and wild things that Kayleen had found. The transportation grid. The fair in Oshai. The Keepers, all connected one to another to keep the planet.

I tried to stay careful, to sift the world of data in a way that set off no alarms.

I tasted a few other people I didn't know as I went. I'd known there were other Wind Readers here, but it was not like Silver's Home and built by us, not changed by the minute by varying classes of Wind Readers from student to master. Except for me and Marcus and Kayleen and Caro, there were probably no more than twenty or thirty who lived here. More at the spaceports, of course. A few hundred on the whole planet.

And then, I felt a Wind Reader I recognized. Slow. Thrashing. It felt like Kayleen but not; too different to be her. Since she was strong and wild and unshielded and lost, it took time for me to be sure.

Caro.

Looking for her mom.

You don't come near someone in data the way you do it physically, it's a sharing of the signature ways we process and think, and a recognition of the thoughts we have. Only Kayleen thinks in the randomly bubbly way she does. Marcus was always sure of himself. And Caro had a baby stubbornness she was showing right now, bulling her way through information by accepting and rejecting stream after stream of data. She didn't have the capacity or the control to do much more, but seeing her strength I wished harder than ever I'd had time to spend with her.

I felt immensely proud of her.

Perhaps, if I couldn't find Kayleen, her daughter could.

I inched near Caro, going slow until I felt her recognize me.

She wanted reassurance. I did my best, but the only real comfort either of us needed required finding Kayleen. It took a while to settle Caro, to find a rhythm we could use together. She was still so unformed I had to fold her in myself, guide her, but hold her loose enough that she was following her own senses in the data. Concepts and questions she had no words for came and went through her mind, unformed but amazing. Either she was a special child, or all children were more special than I had ever known.

My niece was a marvelous little person.

How had she gotten here?

It didn't matter. The search—our search now—mattered. My physical link to Kayleen's body, our matched breath, told me how thin and insubstantial she had become. We were running out of time.

What if we stopped moving and tried to bring Kayleen to us?

Caro. Think about your mommy.

Okay.

Feel her. Talk to her in the data.

How?

Like you're talking to me. Send her your love.

I am.

There was nothing coming back. I couldn't tell Caro to try harder—she was trying as hard as she could. If we lost her mom, I couldn't let it be her fault. I joined her in calling, doing the triple duty of watching over Caro, calling for Kayleen, and looking for anything new in the data that said we had been discovered. It felt more like we were an ember in the data than that we were fire, but even an ember warmed. And Caro had none of the shielding I did, none of mine and Marcus's and Kayleen's skill at looking like the data we were in, appearing to be a part of it instead of something foreign.

Her call for Kayleen echoed through the Lopali nets. A plaintive sweet voice that saddened and called to action at once. It couldn't be going unnoticed.

Still, I didn't feel Kayleen anywhere.

I felt something or someone, weaker than us, originating from Oshai.

Friend?

Yes. Someone boosting Caro's call.

I accepted it; we needed it. Caro's data voice reached further without weakening.

And then two more joined us. More strength. I had not been a fire, but an ember, and Caro the spark. Now we had a fire.

Marcus must have felt it. He slammed into my data signature, demanding attention. *What are you doing?*

Feel it? Feel the help?

Our enemies will find us.

They knew we were here anyway. Help us. Help us or leave.

A brief moment of surprise. For a breath, I thought he was going to shut us down. He withdrew.

And then Caro was gone ahead, surfing a wave, sending her mother before the rest of us. I dove after her, and the collective of what must be most of the Wind Readers on Lopali pushed us, like a wind.

Marcus surged back, helping. Security structures turned to air around us, data blending from the war machines of the two fleets and the peace machine of Lopali. He opened a hole in the world for us to go through.

When Marcus committed, he committed.

Bless him.

As we neared Kayleen's unique data signature, my heart fell. There was no babbling, no movement to find and take or even release bits of data. She hung like still water, wide and diffuse and full of holes where data blew through her.

I reached toward her, nudging her gently.

No response.

I tried harder.

No response.

The most wind-burned students on Lopali simply never came back; the universities fed their bodies for a year and a day and then disconnected them, and they died, every one.

Call her, Caro. Call harder even though she's here.

Mommy! Came back to us. A voice as pure as the heart of a young being in need, like a baby's first cry. Lusty and single-focused. *Mommy! Mommy, come to me!*

Nothing.

Mommy! Her stubborn nature amazed me. *I'm not leaving without you! Come back now.* If she could have stamped her feet here, she would. I almost laughed, except that it was so bittersweet.

We'd gone where the others who'd blown us here could be felt, but only barely. Kayleen could be felt, but only barely.

I joined my voice to Caro's, chose to follow her lead. *Kayleen! Come back now. If you leave your daughter to know she got this close and you wouldn't come, I will never forgive you!*

Me either, Caro called. *I need you. Come back now.*

And she did. At first it was slow, just a coming together of the bits of her that had been recognizable, but scattered.

Keep coming, I sent. *Breathe. Feel your body breathe.*

Oh my God. She wrapped Caro up inside of her. *Oh baby. How did you get here? Come back with me now. It's dangerous way out here!*

Fear made her energy draw into itself. If she became too afraid, we might lose her again. *She's okay. Get yourself back.*

And then Kayleen began to feel the others, still helping. *Oh! What happened? Why so many? I was gone; I thought I'd gone forever, floating. You wouldn't let me float.*

Never. We will protect each other always. I included Caro. *All of us.*

Caro echoed me. *All of us. Even them.*

Marcus: *Hurry. Reach for us.*

We did, going back up the path we'd come down, only faster and surer. The people who helped us knew this data, Lopali's data. They gathered us in, helping, encouraging.

I tracked them. Six pilots. A Keeper named Jill who knew Caro—and who had been the first voice. She'd gathered the others. Sweet Jill. Three other Keepers. Someone from Silver's Home who'd come here as a seeker. An ex-patriot from Islas, like Dianne, named Kyle.

Caro and Kayleen stayed close, with me herding them both, and still trying to do the double and triple duty of watching. And then they began to separate as they came into more and more contact with their own physical bodies. Kayleen was in the cave in the hill, and Caro in Oshai. Caro couldn't have much experience finding herself, and we'd gone deep. *Jill: watch Caro. Take her. The rest of you, too. Thank you, all of you. Thank you.*

Words and feelings came back.

I've got her.

You're welcome.

Call us again if you need to.

We'll listen.

We're our own affinity. Everywhere. Always.

And then a curtain built between us, Marcus creating more security, urging us into our bodies, where we were going anyway. Sasha's wet tongue scraped across my cheek and I pulled her down beside me, feeling her warmth and weight. I opened my eyes and looked at Kayleen's face, just inches from my own. Her breath had returned to normal speed and her eyes fluttered open. They did match the coverlet. "Thank you," she whispered, her voice thin and reedy.

I let out a long, slow breath to control my elation, to give Kayleen the calm support she needed. Still, my heart leapt with the joy of her return to us. "Without Caro, I would never have found you."

She gave a quick nod. "I'm afraid for her."

"We were more afraid for you. I'm sorry. It was my fault."

She pushed back the covers and I helped her sit up. She took my face in her two hands. "It's not your fault. Nothing is your fault. The world made us and it needs us, but you did not make the world."

I laughed, gently. "I can tell you were lost in Lopali data."

She dropped her hands, taking one of mine in one of hers. "There's beauty here. It didn't happen because of the people who created these poor fliers, or because of the world they made, but because the human heart and soul itself is so magnificent. Lopali has become the soul of the Five Worlds, and most of the people on the other worlds don't even know it."

If it was the soul of the Five Worlds, it included kidnapping and coercion. She wasn't even really babbling. She felt different. When I looked into her eyes, they were calm pools, unrecognizable as belonging to the Kayleen I knew.

"Do you promise to stay with us?" I asked her. "You won't go plunging back into the bliss of data for a while?"

Her smile was beatific. "Yes."

As gorgeous as she was in that moment, she was not the Kayleen I knew and loved, at least not exactly. Maybe this state was residue. Please. I wanted my Kayleen.

Marcus came in the door, moving fast. "We have to go. Every Wind Reader on Lopali knows where you are now. Not all of them are helpful." He leaned down a bit and looked at Kayleen. "Can you move?"

"If you'll take me to Caro."

Kayleen, telling Marcus what to do. Even he looked taken aback. "The sooner we leave, the sooner you'll see her."

One of his non-answers. But Kayleen had done the same thing. "Kayleen—can you travel?" I asked. "Are you strong enough?"

She smiled and stood up, reaching for the ceiling and then bending down and placing her hands flat on the floor beside her long feet. She stood back up, slowly, and smiled at me. "Let's go."

When she started for the door, she tripped, and I barely caught her before she fell. I slid my arm around her for support and whispered to her. "Are you truly all back?"

She turned her newly serene eyes on me. "Maybe not. Maybe I'll never be all the way back."

Marcus clapped his hands above her head hard, startling her so she nearly fell again, clutching my waist with both of her arms. The look he gave her was calm, but merciless. "You'd better be fully in the present. The next few days will demand even more than that. They'll demand twice what you've ever given."

She blinked up at him, then closed her eyes and shook her head. She pushed away from me and, this time, when she looked back, it was the Kayleen I knew, the more hesitant Kayleen, that gazed at me.

I wondered which one was stronger.

I offered my arm. She took it, and we made it to the door, where Stark waited, a worried look on his face. Even though he didn't say anything, I felt like I was being chastised. Instead of the wings I expected we'd need, he held three packs. I raised an eyebrow at Marcus, who said, "There is another way out."

Stark led us through the door into the war room. Marcus stopped a moment, contemplating the wall of fleets. They seemed far removed from us, as if we watched some entertainment video. But Marcus's eyes narrowed as he watched.

"What is it?" I asked him.

"Three ships from Silver's Home, all representing the Wingmakers, have declared neutrality. They claim we're trying to drag their property into a war."

"So our own side is still fighting us, and we're still the cause. What's new about that?"

Stark rewarded me with a nod of agreement. Kayleen asked, "What about the sim? Is it still alive?"

Marcus nodded, but then cautioned. "We still don't know if it's a good take. We may need to do more." He hadn't taken his eyes off the screen. He swallowed, and then turned to Stark. "I'll let you know where to get us from. Wish us luck."

"Of course."

Marcus walked up to a wall, and a door opened in it, just like that. I was sure it had been invisible before. Of course, everything in this cave had been made, and so I shouldn't have been so surprised.

Dim lights illuminated a long thin corridor behind the door. Marcus led us in, holding the door open to include Sasha before it swung shut behind us. I looked; there didn't seem to be any mechanism for opening the door from this side.

The tunnel angled down a few degrees, the floor a rough surface that our feet scraped on as we went. The air smelled stale, although every once in a while, fans blew fresher air in via round ducts in the ceiling. Sasha whined softly, and sniffed at the air and the floor.

Kayleen still wasn't walking as fast as usual, but she didn't need either of us for support. We kept her between us, Marcus in front and me behind, Sasha patrolling front to back.

From time to time the corridor branched. Marcus had been here before, since he seemed to know instinctively whether to turn left or right at any given intersection. We saw no one else in the underground hallways, and given how loud our footsteps were I'm pretty sure we would have heard anyone there.

"What is this place?" Kayleen whispered.

Marcus gave a soft, ironic laugh. "It's left over from when the Wingmakers made Lopali."

He was old, but not quite that old. "How did you know about it?"

"My father's father was a Wingmaker."

Oh. Wow. I hadn't know anything about his history. "What was your dad?"

"Short-lived. He left the Wingmakers because he didn't like the choices they were making. He's the one who taught me not to be part of any affinity group, but to just be myself. Free agents are both stronger and weaker than groups, but if you violate your own principles as a free agent, you can only blame yourself."

We turned again, right this time, and the downslope became steeper. Sasha's nails scraped on the surface as she struggled not to slide. Kayleen spoke up instead of whispering, like we had been. "But you need family. Family matters. I'd be . . . I'd be gone somewhere if it weren't for Caro and Joseph . . . and you."

I agreed. "How is a family different from an affinity group?"

"Sometimes it isn't. Some affinity groups are run by a family, or only admit family members. There's one in banking that manages to get cuts of half the credit flow on Silver's Home, and another family group in tourism that's been known for booking the best vacations for three hundred years. Mostly, they're built around an idea or a business. Say you're interested in making space ships? Well, there's at least seven or eight premier affinity groups that do that, and two or three of those have been doing it since we colonized Silver's Home. Others are trying to get a name in the business. You'd research them all and then choose."

"But you don't have to join an affinity group, right?" Kayleen asked.

"No. But you have to have something to sell if you don't. I sell my ability to fly and my ability to create."

"So Joseph never needs to join a group?"

Marcus laughed. "Not if he doesn't want to." And then he added, "But, technically, I'm pretty sure you are all still members of the Family of Exploration. You'll show on their rolls until you reject your rights."

"Huh?" Kayleen asked.

It would take too long to go there now, and I was too tired. "I'll fill you in later."

The slope changed again, and we were walking almost straight now, with just a little downhill. It seemed like a good time to ask about something I didn't understand. "But all those people in the war room, and the person that lends you the ship storage space on the Silver Eyes, and other people like that, aren't you all an affinity group?"

"We're not registered as one and we don't get taxed as one, and some of us are in others. We're just aligned."

Oh. I got it. "Like the Wind Readers that just helped us. They said they were something—in affinity?—but of course they work for other groups."

"Nicely deduced," he said.

Even though we were going downhill, Kayleen's breathing sounded louder. "Can we have a short break?"

"Not until we get off this planet."

"What I want to know," Kayleen wheezed out between steps, "is about your dad. It sounds like he died."

"He went crazy."

Oh. No wonder part of Marcus's life had been dedicated to keeping students from being wind-burned. "So it's not a coincidence you're here?"

"It's mostly one," he said. Then he stopped and turned to Kayleen. The light was dim enough I couldn't read Marcus's expression as closely as I wanted to, but his voice sounded grave. "But this is one important thing that needs to be done, and I was available to do it. And we needed Joseph, and maybe you, to do it."

"Is the sim okay?" she asked.

"Too early to tell. But she was when we left."

I felt relieved, especially since we were apparently leaving more than the cave behind. After we found the others. Surely we weren't going to walk all the way to Oshai. And surely we would find them.

36

CHELO: A FORTUNE

As I walked away from the Temple Hills, the orange and red rays of the setting sun lent urgency to my steps. I'd dressed comfortably, as plainly as I could, except that I wore Sasha's knotted belt around my waist. Mohami had drawn me a map, and I wanted to find the festival before dark; Lopali still seemed strange, if beautiful. I hadn't been alone like this since sometime back on Fremont. A few years on space ships had kept my alone time to walks and exercising, and of course, being part of a family of five didn't make it common to spend much time by myself, either.

I followed the road we'd driven in on, walking by the side, occasionally passed by people on cycles or running. Fliers made shadows over me from time to time, and I struggled to ignore them, to make sure I looked like I belonged. Kala had found me a blue wrap left behind by a seeker who had returned to Paradise, and she had also done up my hair in high braids that helped my face look so narrow I barely recognized myself. When the kids saw me just before I left, Caro had shrunk back in Liam's arms until he convinced her I was really me.

I needed Joseph. He and I could do this together—find the others and free them and go away. But he wasn't here.

It took almost an hour to walk to the festival, and by then the sky had faded to black, lit by stars and stations and ships. I would have preferred moons, but of course, everything orbiting here was as man-made as Lopali itself. Fliers had stopped going by overhead, but a few walked now, or moved on wheeled platforms, and the foot traffic of Keepers and ordinary humans had grown.

Approaching the entrance, I paused as shadows quivered around me. Statues loomed and shone and glittered and moved under bright lights, and small groups of humans and fliers walked, some in silent appreciation and other engaged in animated conversation. Between the art of bringing souls together in the morning ceremony and the art around us, the creativity of Lopali awed me.

I dragged myself through the sculptures as quickly as I could manage, actually relieved to get inside the festival itself and be surrounded by smaller art, booths, music, and people. I could feast on the scent of warm, spicy foods and the sounds of new instruments and conversation, except I had a mission. This had been a great place for Jenna and Paloma and the others to hide. So what had gone wrong?

I found directions to Juss's booth by keeping my eyes down like a penitent seeker and asking. The second person I asked had known the general area to look, and the third had given me exact directions.

The booth was empty, so I walked in, dressed in my blue just like Seeyan had said. A man all in blue with blue hair looked up as I came in. "Juss?"

He nodded, looking bored.

"A friend of mine, Seeyan, mentioned a Juss that sold feathers and fortunes. She said maybe I should find you if I needed anything. I don't really, except I need to find Seeyan." What I really needed was to stop babbling, so I shut up.

He looked a lot more interested than he had when I first walked in. He stared, and then his eyes widened, and he whispered my name, "Chelo."

"Do you know where Seeyan is?"

He chewed on his lower lip for a moment, and then shook his head. He smiled at me, but the intensity of his gaze made me feel a little bit like a specimen brought back from winter roaming to show Artistos. "She's supposed to come by here if you want to wait. And she's right, I sell both. But for you, I'll give you a fortune."

He didn't feel like a friend. Not like I expected him to. I wished I hadn't come. "Maybe later."

His grin lightened, even though it didn't touch his eyes. "You are the beautiful woman worth a world. A poor fortune-teller seldom gets such grand subjects. I would be honored if you would stay for five minutes."

I blew out a slow breath. What would I do if I left? Wander the fair looking for people in the dark? Juss's booth was eerily quiet even though the festival outside had been noisy. I took a step back from him. "Five minutes."

He smiled again, the smile avoiding his eyes as if they had a plague. His eyes—blue, of course, an unnatural blue that glowed, like the blue of ice in winter with the sun on it—made me shiver. But then he closed them, and took a single long breath, in and out quietly. When they opened again he looked calmer. He did that two more times, his hands turning a blue stone over and over. When he opened his eyes the third time, the pupils were small dark dots in a field of deep blue. "Chelo who is worth a world, Chelo who began the war, you have three things in your immediate future. One is what has been in your past. You have lost people you love in war, and you will lose people you love again. Your destiny is to be dogged by the evils of humanity, and to help them see the beauty in their hearts in spite of themselves. But the price will be high, as the price of freedom is always high. As the fliers suffer to learn and grow, so will you. Your tears will drive forward a fight already begun, and add heart to the fighters. Your tears will drown you for a time, and then they will give you strength and resolve."

Great. I should never have stayed. What he said had been some-thing almost surely true anyway, that we children of Fremont would have trouble surviving in this vast, complex world. I held my tongue, wishing more than one minute of the five had passed.

The stone in Juss's hand turned faster and his eyes nearly rolled back in his head. "A friend will appear to betray you, but she will be helping you. It will be hard for you to trust her, but you must. She has only your best interests at heart."

Alicia. Maybe Alicia had already been here. I should ask as soon as he finished.

"And that is not the only betrayal that waits for you. Another in your party wishes you well, but wants a success that is different than the one you want."

Two betrayals. Dinner and dessert. I didn't believe him for a minute. At least that was the three things. I opened my mouth to tell him I was leaving, but he stiffened and held up a hand.

"So you will cry and you will be betrayed, and your children will heal some of what you cannot. That is the last part, and it is not in the now but in the future. Take care of your children."

Fine. Like I wouldn't. At least something he said had a grain of hope in it. His five minutes were up. "If you haven't seen Seeyan, have you seen anyone else in our party?" I didn't want to name names—if he was reading the stories he knew them anyway, and if any of the Gang of Girls still hid here, I didn't want to give them away. I wanted him to tell me he'd seen Alicia, but he shook his head, violently, once, sending his blue hair flying about his face.

His eyes looked normal again, more normal than either time before. He looked over my shoulder. "You're in luck. Here comes Seeyan now."

Good thing. But why had she ever sent me to anyone so creepy, and what did she have to do with him anyway? I turned and smiled, and she smiled at me and held out her hand. "Chelo! I'm so glad we found you." Her voice sounded too high, and her own smile looked too enthusiastic.

I had to get her out of here and find a place where we could talk. "I was just leaving. Will you go with me?"

Two men stepped into the booth from outside, and stood in the door. They were both half of what Bryan was, different than normal humans, but not entirely turned to strongmen. Paradisers? Anyway, they could take me in a fight.

"Seeyan?" Was this Seeyan's doing? She wasn't looking at me anymore.

I glanced at Juss, who looked triumphant, and not at all regretful. I realized I didn't know what was happening, not yet, but I couldn't keep my mouth shut. "Some fortune-teller. Do you tell women they'll find true love and then seduce them yourself?"

He glared at me. "Many people can play the game of telling stories. Perhaps children like yourself shouldn't try."

I felt Seeyan's hand on my arm and brushed it off. Every instinct told me to run. But I'd be caught, here in this strange place with these guards, and perhaps even by Seeyan. Damn Juss, I did feel the betrayal. Seeyan had always felt like a friend, like part of the sacred circle that held Mohami and all the good things here on Lopali. I looked closely at her. Her face had none of the defiance or the triumph of Juss's, but something more like resignation and the acceptance of an unpleasant task.

"I presume you won't let me just walk out of here, right?"

Her voice was soft. "I will take you where you came here to go."

To the others. Trapped like them? "Very well." But my feet wouldn't move forward. Seeyan knew where Liam and the children were, she was my link to Mohami. She was my teacher and my friend, and she'd taught Paloma how to find herbs here. She'd lost her wings, and told us she wished us well. Believing anything else about her felt like a lie, but it must be true. The guards were prepared to follow her orders.

My stomach and knees felt weak and I wanted to fall down there, on the spot. Of course that was no option, so I stood, breathing hard for two breaths, and then forcing calm. I pulled the cowl of the seekers' robes up around my head, hiding my dark hair and, hopefully, my fear. I didn't hide my eyes; I wanted to see where we were going.

The two men took the lead, Seeyan and I following. A man and a woman fell in behind us. The men walked far enough ahead they probably didn't look like an escort, and Seeyan walked casually, looking around here and there at the booths. I looked around, too, hoping against hope for a glimpse of an ally.

Sounds assaulted me everywhere I went, strange accents in voices and music so different each from the other they must have come from all of the Five Worlds. The noise of a single place full of more people than had been on my whole world.

We passed a rest room, and I whispered to Seeyan, "I need to stop." She nodded, following me as far as the doorway. The other four all stopped, too, but too far away to hear us. Seeing Seeyan standing there made me sick to my stomach as well as in need of voiding my body's response to the bad fortune of finding my friend. After, I splashed water on my face and neck, blotting the sickly smelling sweat from my skin. I needed to be stronger. Braver.

As I approached the door, Seeyan put a hand on my arm again. This time I just stood, not swatting it away. She was still beautiful, tall and willowy and calm. She spoke softly. "It's not so bad as you think. So far, everyone is okay. You can all be okay as long as you cooperate. Joseph will come for you. And then he will fail, which is all we need."

"Why? I thought you of all people wanted the flier children to be made normally, wanted to stop being enslaved."

She gave me a measured stare. "You passed the sculptures on the way in?"

"Yes."

"They were beautiful, right? They spoke of pain and love and yearning."

"I'm sure they were. I didn't get much time to look at them." It was hard to keep from sounding bitter. "I was trying to find you."

"But you have seen the gardens now, and the morning ceremony, and you've spoken with Mohami at least once. You've seen how beautiful the fliers are. You know how much peace means to us. You want the same thing. You and I talked about it, and you told me how much you hate war."

I hated lies and betrayal, too. "Yes, I hate wars. I want them all to stop, everywhere."

"If we don't have our pain, our trials, if our hearts are not ripped in two and three and four parts again and again, and put back in a place of calm, we will no longer be ourselves."

I didn't understand. "And your brother, Will, wouldn't have died trying to learn to fly, and maybe your wings wouldn't have been cut off."

She winced, and then recovered. "But if they hadn't been, I wouldn't be who I am. I wouldn't understand the breath of the world or Keep the Beauty. I wouldn't be close to ready to move into the central gardens and manage some of the outlying fields that the seekers play in. All of our sufferings are the price we pay for our art, for our songs, for our ceremonies, and for the beauty of our home."

"I still don't understand."

"Go look at the sculptures sometime. Maybe then it will make sense to you. After all, you have suffered. Who would you be if you hadn't had your family and friends ripped from you on Fremont?"

Happier? But I didn't say that. I didn't want to talk to her anymore. I walked past her out the door, leaving her to catch up to me. When she did, she whispered, "Chelo, what I'm doing is for you. You just don't know it yet."

"Why? You're doing it to the kids as well as to me. They need me. They adore you." And she'd truly seemed to enjoy them. She'd always looked forward to seeing them, and we'd left them with her for whole days. They'd always come back happy and tired. "You've betrayed the deal we made with Lopali. Why?"

"Because now Joseph will come, and the changes won't be made, and we'll stay out of the war. It's only for peace, Chelo, you'll see."

37

ALICIA: EMPTY BEDS

Amalo led me down across the compound toward a long, low hard-surfaced building with small, high windows. None of the others came with us, but I didn't try to get away from him; I didn't really want to. Not that I trusted him, yet, but I wanted to know more about the fliers and maybe he and Marti would help me with that.

Before we got to the building, I asked him, "So whose captive am I?"

He didn't turn around, but spoke up enough for me to hear. "The Keepers."

"But don't the Keepers work for you?"

Now he turned around. "No relationship is that simple. I know you're young, but surely you've learned that much by now."

That stung. But I couldn't talk back to him; he could help me become a flier. "Thank you."

We'd reached the building. He opened the door, but then stood aside, holding it for me. "You'll find your friends in there. Don't forget that we're the key to what you truly want."

I went in. The door closed behind me. I stood inside a small, dimly lit room with an interface desk and a few books in it, and no art on the walls. Two doors led into different parts of the building. A wingless man sat in a chair by the door. He'd gone a bit to fat, which was unusual here. He'd braided black ribbons into his longish yellow hair, the braids falling across his ample stomach and meeting in his lap. He gave me a long look up and down. "Violet eyes. You must be Alicia."

So they were expecting Kayleen, too? Or just hoping? How many of us had they caught? "I heard my friends are here."

He nodded toward the door closest to me. "Through there."

I opened the door. The long, high-ceilinged warehouse was largely empty. The women were small in the big space. A few tables and some chairs sat in the middle of the room. Eight cots lined the wall. One open door led to a privy, and the only other way out was a big square door with no handle on this side.

Four people looked up as the door opened. Paloma had been drawing something on a battered infoslate in front of her. Tiala and Jenna were at the other table, and Dianne, who stood by the far wall, stretching, spoke first. "Alicia? I'm so sorry."

They all looked exhausted. Dianne's hair was messy. Tiala and Jenna looked like they hadn't slept in days. Paloma had a vacant look in her eyes. At least they hadn't been harmed, or tortured, or starved. Pitchers of water sat on the tables, and Paloma had a plate of the ubiquitous sweet grapes and some bread in front of her. But there weren't enough of them. "Where's Ming?"

Dianne flexed her arms and raised them above her head, still stretching. "Either she got away or she gave us up. Have you seen her, or heard from her?"

"Bryan is looking for her."

Jenna gave me a sharp look. "Don't assume you can have private conversations in here."

Gee, she could be happy to see me. But then I'd always thought Jenna wished they left me back on Fremont. Or that I'd never been born. "They're trying to trade you for Joseph or Chelo or Kayleen. Maybe Marcus. The goon at the door was hoping I was Kayleen."

Paloma, who was always nicer to me than Jenna, got up and gave me a hug. "Are they still safe? Do you know?"

"Chelo was safe when I left her. I haven't heard anything about the others." Maybe Jenna was right and I best not say anything more about Bryan. At least he and Induan appeared to still be free. "How did you get here?"

Paloma led me over to the table where she'd been sitting. I could see what she'd been drawing: a field of flowers from Fremont, full of thorns and lace, the beauty and the price of Fremont. So she was still homesick, and she just hadn't seen the way the same thing played out here—that Lopali had thorns that made flowers. I popped a grape in my mouth and waited for them to answer my question.

Tiala, usually quiet, started. "We got all the way here. We found the booth Seeyan had reserved for us, and we set up. For the first day, we thought everything was fine. People came to see Ming dance, and me and Jenna led two classes, and so many people signed up for the next day we had to make a list. The only thing we weren't having much luck with was Paloma as a healer."

Of course not. People here never looked sick. Although surely they bumped elbows and wings from time to time. "Then what?"

"We were still careful. We didn't all sleep at once. But the second morning, just at dawn, we were surrounded by people. They led us here. And they haven't told us anything."

"It was Ming's watch," Jenna added.

I remembered how we had gotten in here. "Have you seen Seeyan?"

Dianne narrowed her eyes at me. "No." She was the one who had introduced us all to the wingless Keeper, used her story to help make everyone want to save the fliers from themselves. "She was supposed to go back to her life after she got you all away."

"She's here, in this compound. I followed her in."

"They're keeping her somewhere else?"

Apparently Dianne didn't want to understand. "She had a key to the door in the wall, and to at least one of the buildings."

The door I'd come in opened, and I looked up, expecting the doorkeeper with dinner or something. Instead, Chelo came in, and the door swung shut behind her. She stood there, pale, and looked around the room. Her hair had been piled high in braids, so she appeared at least ten years older. When she saw me, she frowned. "You didn't need to tie Samuel up. It was a disservice. He never meant you harm."

She was so mad at me for that, it was the first thing she thought of after being captured? "He would have stopped us. If Bryan doesn't find Ming, his heart will break. And there was trouble brewing, even if you didn't want to see it. Seeyan was supposed to come by and she didn't, and Ming was supposed to send Bryan notes, and she didn't. What were we supposed to do? Sit on our hands and get blissed out?" I didn't mean to sound so sharp. I loved Chelo with all my heart, but she was just so naïve.

Paloma snapped, "Stop fighting, you two!"

Chelo ignored her. "You still didn't need to insult them. They've been providing us shelter and taking care of us."

"Maybe. Not much here seems to be what it looks like on the surface."

She gave me an exasperated look and asked, "Where's Bryan and Ming, anyway?"

Jenna answered. "We don't know."

"What happened?" I asked Chelo. "I thought you were safe. Part of why we left was to find out how to keep you safe."

She sat down next to Paloma. "I don't think I've ever been safe."

Paloma handed her water and pushed the plate of food toward her. "Take a minute and then, when you're ready, tell us how you got here."

We filled each other in, although I left out Induan's part, and my conversation with Amalo and Marti. It really wasn't any of their business. I didn't learn much from the others, except Caro's scare about Kayleen, which worried me, especially for Joseph's sake.

Eventually we were all talked out. But there was still a deep hole in the conversation. Jenna must have escape plans, but she wasn't sharing them with me. Maybe she didn't want me to know. But maybe I didn't want to escape.

Jenna had us all strip down to our underwear and put us through a grueling calisthenics routine, working us for what seemed like an hour, so sweat poured off my face. No wonder everyone had seemed so tired. Slave driver. But she was smart to keep our strength up, and maybe it would intimidate whoever was watching us. Surely someone watched us. Jenna gave Paloma a break, but even she'd had to keep up with us for the first half hour.

We showered, putting our dirty clothes back on. Afterward, Jenna counted beds and noses. There were still three extra beds. That could be for either set—Liam and the kids, or Joseph, Marcus, and Kayleen.

I didn't like the way I was thinking, like we were going to get caught no matter what. There was another threesome out there. Induan, Bryan, and Ming. Bryan and Induan were on our side, and Ming was a question mark.

Jenna stood in the center of the room, her eyes sweeping over us all, measuring. "I think we should have two people at a time on watch tonight." Funny how she and I agreed on so much and yet liked each other so little. She assigned herself and Dianne first watch. I hadn't noticed how tired I was until I realized how grateful I was that I could sleep. I'd not really slept since Bryan and I left the compound. Chelo took the bed farthest from me, a sign that she was still mad at me for tying up our keeper-boy. It wasn't like we'd hurt him.

I didn't go to sleep as fast as I thought. What if Amalo did choose me? Would I really do this thing? It might cost me Joseph, but then, he might be long gone already. Surely, if he'd really wanted to, he could have made Marcus keep me with him. I wanted Joseph, but what place was there for me beside him?

He surely didn't want me to become a flier.

Maybe I could become a Wind Reader, but then I'd be in danger of going crazy like Kayleen. Maybe I should just stay myself until I knew more. But the image in my head when I finally did drift to sleep was me carrying great violet-and-blue wings lined with black bars in my arms, getting ready to pin them on my back.

38

JOSEPH: INTO THE LIGHT

Kayleen's soft breath beside me warmed my neck. She'd fallen asleep leaning on my shoulder during a rest break. Marcus stood by the door, his toe tapping. Sasha sat beside him, head cocked, watching us solemnly. "We should go," I said. "How long did we sleep?"

"Too long. But Stark will meet us with col if we can finish getting through the mountain."

I nudged Kayleen, pushing her gently off of me. "Let's go. We need to find the others."

She mumbled. "Caro. Caro needs to tell me something."

"What?" The data flows down here were thin, nearly nonexistent. "Can it wait? We'll be out from under here soon."

She blinked. "Maybe I was dreaming." She sat straighter, forking her fingers through her hair. "Is there anything to eat?"

Marcus said, "In your pack."

We found little packets of nuts and flasks of water, and finished them off pretty quickly, giving Sasha a bowl of water and a few nuts. She needed better, but it was what we had. Then we were up and walking back down nearly dark corridors. Eventually, the air started smelling crisper, and then the scent of dirt mixed in. Marcus pulled a door open, and we stood on a platform made of the same material that formed the corridors we'd been walking. Beyond it, fields spread out in three directions, and above and behind us the mountain we'd been walking through bulked up in huge cliffs. A faint dampness

from the night's rains still hung in the air, and here and there inden-
tations in the platform were filled with shallow puddles. The thin
sunlight of dawn striped the top of the cliffs above us pale orange,
and a soft breeze blew the fertile smell of growing things our way.
Three different roads came into the platform, and beside us, hunched
so tightly against the cliff I hadn't seen it on first glance, a longish
four-wheeled vehicle blinked its lights at us.

Sasha growled, and Kayleen startled. Marcus put a hand on Kayleen's shoulder. "It's okay."

A door opened, and Stark emerged with a flask of col in one hand
and cups in the other. As he poured the drink, Marcus asked him,
"All clear?"

"It was when I left an hour ago."

We'd been in the tunnels at least three or four hours, maybe more.
Time of day inside the cave was a slippery thing. I sipped the col. It
must have been unusually strong; I felt braced immediately.

"Anything else on the Star Mercenaries?" Marcus asked.

Stark poured himself a drink. "We think they're landing where
you were—in the spaceport near SoBright. That means they'll be
close. We're staging you out of Charmed."

I wanted to laugh. Maybe we'd be charmed away before the Stars
found us after they landed at SoBright. Hadn't whoever designed Lopali heard of more normal place-names? But Marcus just nodded.
Then Stark added something that took all the laughter away. "Rumor
has it that Alicia and Chelo have both been captured. And it looks
like their captors aren't from Islas or even Silver's Home. It looks like
they're from here."

I felt like I'd been punched. "When? Do you know where they
are?"

"Last night, and I think so."

Kayleen asked the next question on my tongue. "But we're helping
the people here. Why would they be after us? I mean, we gave them
their freedom, if the last work we did was good."

Marcus asked her a question. "You were lost in the Lopali data for
a long time. Think hard. Does everyone here agree with everyone
else?"

"Oh." Her eyes widened. "Well, more than at home. But yeah,

you're right." She still looked angry. "But Matriana and Daniel should have kept us safe. They hired us. They gave you the feather." She pointed to his leg. The feather sheath was still strapped to it, thin and almost invisible, like a tiny sword belt.

He fingered it, his thumb stroking the quill where it protruded slightly from the sheath. He glanced at Stark. "How do you know? Are you sure it's Lopali natives?"

Stark nodded. "But not who. Doesn't matter, really. Whatever group it is, their targets were Chelo and Joseph and you, and maybe Kayleen. And now they have Chelo." He paused and grinned. "So it's time you taught them a lesson, right?"

Marcus smiled. "I believe so."

I didn't say anything. I just wanted to go get my sister, and all the others, and then I wanted to leave here. I didn't care if we went to the war or if we just spent the rest of our lives in ships. I was done with Lopali.

Stark said, "They're at the fair. Whoever it is. In the area out back where they store booths off-season. You know where it is?"

"Yes," Marcus said. "Thanks. We appreciate your help."

"Just be at Charmed when you promised, okay? That's what we need most of all."

"We'll do what we can," Marcus said patiently.

I wasn't so patient. "I'm not leaving without Chelo." Or anybody else. But I let that go.

We climbed into the four-wheeler. Stark disappeared the way we'd come. We rumbled off the platform and down between two newly planted fields, driving slowly. There were no other vehicles on the road this early, although Keepers and slave bots walked the rows on one side of us, weeding and watering. They paid us no attention.

The long vehicle was only wide enough for two across, so I sat beside Marcus, and Kayleen sat behind us. Behind her, a cargo area carried wings. More than three pairs. I pointed behind me and asked Marcus, "Are we flying away with those?"

"They're there if we need them."

Kayleen mumbled, "Caro," from the backseat.

I turned around. "Did you reach her?"

"She says Mohami has her and her brother and Liam all safe in a room in the dark. She sounds happy enough, except she's mad she missed a morning ceremony, whatever that is."

I frowned. "Do you think it's true? If it's people from here that have the others, could they be captured, too?"

One look at Kayleen's face, and I wished I could take my words back. Marcus, however, said, "Probably not. Mohami is Keeper of the Ways of the Fliers of Lopali, so he'll side with Matriana and Daniel."

"So who's not siding with them? Tsawo?" I'd mistrusted him, but then he was uncle to Paula, and seemed to accept what we were doing.

Marcus shook his head.

I remembered the blond flier from the first night we were here, at the feast, and how she'd looked angry at us just for existing. But I hadn't seen her since, and I didn't know her name. So instead of asking about her, I simply watched the fields bump by, and the sun hit them, one by one, brightening the greens and golds. This far from civilization, only a few fliers graced the skies, even in this prime early morning flight time. Yet again, I wished skimmers were allowed on this world and we could fly in machines between places. Traveling on the ground gave me a long time to worry about Chelo, and Alicia, and Paloma.

The sun was fully up, maybe ten degrees above the horizon, by the time we got to the edges of Oshai. Marcus parked our vehicle in a lot beside a big building labeled PROTECTORATE OF THE FLIERS OF LO-PALI, and I struggled again not to laugh. "Are they going to protect us?" I asked.

"Are you a flier of Lopali?"

"Well, no."

"There you have it. But we will have help. Seeyan is meeting us here. She's gathered some other Keepers to help."

Kayleen stirred. "Keepers? Isn't it the Keepers who are the problem?"

"Surely not," Marcus said. "Why would they want to stop us?"

Sure enough, shortly after we climbed out and stood, stretching, the chestnut-haired wingless walked up, as if from nowhere. Her voice had a sense of urgency. "I'm so glad to see you. I know where they're keeping them. I've gathered some people to help you. Come on!"

"Where?" Marcus's voice had a bit of distrust in it, and I hoped she couldn't hear it.

"Near the festival. In back." Seeyan bounced on her toes, a picture of urgency. "There's a bunch of warehouses or something."

Her information jived with Stark's. "What are we going to do? Just break them loose?"

She bit her lip, then shrugged. "We have to do something. We can plan after you see what's there. I have some friends meeting me; maybe they're there already."

Kayleen frowned. I wanted to talk to her alone, but this wasn't the safe data of the inner caves or some starship. I didn't want to give anyone hostile a thread to follow, especially after the noise we'd made saving Kayleen. I settled for taking her in my arms and whispering, "It will be okay."

"Let's go." Seeyan looked genuinely agitated.

We might as well. I started off after her, but Marcus caught up to me and whispered, "Take the rear. Watch."

Good idea. Kayleen should be in the middle. So I dropped back, and as soon as there were three or four meters between me and Kayleen, an invisible hand touched my forearm. "It's a trap," Induan whispered.

Well, we knew that. We were walking into it anyway. "What do you mean?"

"Slow them down," she whispered.

I trusted Induan more than Seeyan. "Wait!" I called. "I forgot something." I turned around, as if to head back to the vehicle, and a glance back across my shoulder told me the others had stopped. An expression of sheer frustration flickered across Seeyan's face, and I knew I had guessed right. I opened the door and rummaged, buying time. Induan must still be here. "So now what?"

"Stall. There's help coming. More than me."

"How long?"

"I don't know."

"How are Alicia and Chelo?"

She laughed. "Alicia is as headstrong as ever. She's still ship-shocked and thinks she wants real wings. You picked a silly girl to love." But she sounded affectionate when she said it. "Chelo's as serious as ever.

I think they're okay—I haven't been able to get near since they can see me in the compound—they know to look for heat."

That was too bad. It would keep Alicia from using her easiest asset. "Why is Seeyan turning on us?"

"Because more powerful people than her told her she had to. She'll turn back if she gets a chance."

"That means I can't trust her at all." I stood up and called over my shoulder to the others. "Just a minute."

Induan said, "You're all right now. Stand up and turn around."

Seeyan, Marcus, and Kayleen were all looking at me. Which meant they didn't see the flock approaching them from behind. The image made me smile, three wingless, completely ignorant that they were being swooped down on. Seeyan was the first to turn and look up. She bolted.

Marcus started after her, but I yelled, "Look up," and he stopped, waiting for the fliers. There were five of them. Matriana, Daniel, and three others we'd seen the first night. I didn't remember any of their names, but they were part of the Convening Council of Lopali. Two of them flew off after Seeyan, and the scrabble of feet on the road told me Induan had chosen that path, too.

I walked back to Marcus and Kayleen, and the three of us waited for Matriana, Daniel, and the third flier, a brown-winged woman with golden hair and green eyes. After they landed, Matriana gave Marcus a deep bow. "We owe you our deepest apologies."

Daniel picked up the conversation. "We have a delegation massing to fly down on the oathbreakers and free your people."

They stood in front of us, looking uncomfortable and awkward on their feet.

Marcus touched the feather on his leg again. "We trust you. We would like to go in with your people. We've finished the job we promised, and we apparently have other enemies. We'd like to get off-planet."

Matriana's wide eyes widened even more. "You've succeeded?"

"Maybe. We think so. Chance has the results to double-check. But the sim has run successfully through ten lifetimes and twenty children. It breeds true."

Wow. I hadn't known that. I pulled Kayleen in close to me, feeling briefly celebratory. Maybe we could leave now. As soon as I got Chelo back. And then I wasn't going to let her out of my sight for a year or two. Maybe a decade or two.

I wished there had been time to ask Induan more about Alicia.

39

CHELO: ESCAPE?

I pulled the thin blanket closer around my shoulders. I had drawn last watch, along with Alicia, who sat across the room from me playing with a bright red feather. The windows were too high up to see out of, but they were beginning to grudgingly admit the day's first light. Good. Maybe there would be some warmth added, too. The metal roof had amplified the night's rains, and the creaking sounds of the building adjusting itself to the outside temperature jerked my eyes open every time I soothed them shut.

Surely something would happen today—Joseph would come for me, or Seeyan would come by, or Alicia would do something stupid and get us in more trouble. I glanced over at her, pondering what that might be. She seemed completely absorbed in the feather.

I stood up and walked, trying to keep my blood moving and warm up.

Alicia let out a long sigh, and I asked, "Share your thoughts?"

She shook her head, but after a moment she spoke anyway. "I thought this was the prettiest place I'd ever seen. Remember the day we got here, and the fliers all flew up from the perch-trees around the spaceport? I thought we'd landed in heaven."

"So why didn't you like the morning ceremony? It was prettier."

She was quiet for a minute. "I think because it was supposed to have a specific outcome. I don't like being a sheep."

I almost bleated for her, but I held my tongue. Our relationship was fragile anyway, and so was she. If I laughed at her, we might never make up. "You're still family. We'll get out of here, and then we'll get away from Lopali. We'll be safe somewhere."

Her laugh sounded even more bitter than I felt. "There doesn't appear to be anyplace safe for us."

"There will be." If I ever stopped believing that, I might as well just lie down and die. "We'll find a home. But I don't think it's here."

She didn't answer that, and we both fell silent as the light brightened the colors. Before I could restart the conversation, the door opened and one of the tallest fliers I'd ever seen stepped into the room. He had gray wings and gray eyes.

Alicia looked hopefully at him. "Amalo. Good morning. Do you have any good news for me?"

I barely managed to keep my mouth from falling open.

The flier simply said, "Come with me."

Alicia turned to me, a guilty look in her eyes, but she didn't say anything. She walked out the open door, carrying her red feather, and the flier walked out after her, closing the door behind him.

As soon as the door lock snicked into place, Jenna sat up. "Damn that girl."

I sighed. "What do you think that was about?"

Jenna stood up and came over to the table. "Nothing good. Wake the others. Tell them to get ready."

"For?"

She gave me a hug and whispered in my ear, "Us to leave."

I woke Dianne first. She rose silently, heading immediately for the facilities. I reviewed the room in my head. Two doors, one locked, one with no handle. Windows way too small to climb through, and too tall to reach anyway. As I shook Tiala's shoulder, I glanced at the ceiling, which was smooth, silver metal. "Jenna says time to get up," I whispered.

Tiala nearly leapt out of bed, a sign she was in on whatever her sister's plans were. But then the room was so open, everyone but me had to know. I peeled the blanket gently away from Paloma. Her eyes opened, and she smiled. She put a hand up to my face and touched it. "Chelo the beautiful."

I shook my head. What was that about? A thin scrape of metal on metal drew my eye to Jenna, kneeling by the door Alicia had just left through. Her biceps bulged, reminding me for a moment of the old, wild Jenna. Something moved, and she gave a satisfied grunt. She stood up and repeated the procedure, standing on her toes for extra leverage.

Paloma looked puzzled. "Where's Alicia?"

Jenna answered her in between grunts as she worked. "A flier came and got her."

"Will she be back?"

"Do you care?"

I caught the look on Paloma's face, and said, "We'll find her later if we have to." Paloma looked doubtful, so I added, "We might not be able to save her from herself. I don't like it either, but that's how it might be."

Jenna gave a last grunt and stood down and grinned at us, her hand holding two long metal pins that had been part of the door. She walked over to me and whispered low in my ear. "Now we wait. Have everything with you. We'll only have moments."

I didn't know what we were waiting for, but hopefully breakfast would arrive first. I killed the time pacing, making up the bunks, and pacing some more. Full daylight came in.

Tiala muttered, "They're late. Something's wrong."

I poked around on the plates. We'd eaten everything the night before. Tiala noticed me, and said, "There're worse things than being hungry."

"Thanks."

"You're welcome."

The stress must be getting to us.

Tiala muttered some more. "I bet this is Alicia's fault."

Paloma drew on the old battered infoslate she'd been doodling on when I came in. I looked; a perfect imitation of Kayleen's dead hebra, Windy, when she was a foal. I sat by the old woman and murmured, "She was beautiful when she grew up, too."

"Of course she was."

Paloma looked up at the windows, and then back down at me. "I'm glad you were there to take care of Kayleen."

"Me, too. I love her dearly."

"You'll keep taking care of her?"

"We all will. And I'll keep taking care of you, too."

The look she returned to me was wise and sad, and I remembered Juss's prophecy, and said a short internal prayer: *Let it not be Paloma. Keep her safe. And Liam, and the children and Kayleen and Joseph . . .*"

Before I could finish naming everyone I wanted kept safe, the door Jenna had been playing with fell off, hitting the floor with a loud thunk and a scrape. I jumped and Paloma pushed herself up. Jenna went through the door, followed by Dianne. Something crashed to the floor outside, hard sounds of plates and cups followed by a tinny clunk of a tray and the soft thud of flesh against the floor. Tiala followed Jenna, and I grabbed Paloma's hand, leading her through.

Just outside the door was the small room we had entered through. We stepped over the body of the guard, who had been bringing us food. I spared a moment to check that he still breathed.

"Hurry!" Jenna stood in the doorway, gesturing us out. Tiala must already be through. "Hold the door."

I did, while Jenna stripped the guard's chrono. She smiled up at me quickly as she stood. "The key."

Oh. She was past me and leading, running all out, and this time Tiala helped me with Paloma. We each had one of her arms, pulling her along.

By the time we got there, Jenna had the door in the outer wall open. She pocketed the chrono as she slid through it, waiting on the other side until we were all through. "Now," she hissed. "Walk normally. Just like nothing's happened and you're not a fugitive from anything. Be a tourist."

My breath came too hard to pull that off completely, but I did manage to slow down. Paloma wheezed, and her cheeks were a bright red. I took some of her weight, helping her recover, and then leaned down and whispered in her ear. "Maybe you should consider a few mods."

She rewarded me with a shake of her head and a slightly straighter spine. Well, I'd work on her later. It wasn't that she was old. Well, she was, a little. But with no mods, she was frailer and slower than everyone around her.

Footsteps behind us drew our attention. Paloma breathed in sharply and gave a slight moan. Seeyan raced toward us, chestnut hair flying. "Stop!" she screamed at us.

Two fliers flanked her, powerful wing beats sending wind to throw our hair back. Seeyan the betrayer, her body afire with urgency, speeding toward us with her avenging flier angels.

I glanced around, looking for somewhere to run. Walls lined one side, the other was too open. Fliers would be hard to run from.

A voice came from behind me. "Chelo!" Bryan's voice, frantic. Sweet Bryan. I didn't dare turn. Bryan barreled past me, head down. His finger blades were fully out, his arms pumping to give him more speed.

Seeyan threw her arms up, a futile warding gesture. Her eyes flared in alarm, then fear.

Bryan was big, four times Seeyan's girth, his biceps bigger than her thighs. He tried to brake, shifting his weight backward, but he had too much momentum. He landed on her, hard.

Something cracked. Seeyan, I thought.

The wind of two fliers closing in brushed my hair back, and I looked up, scared for him. The two fliers were almost on him, and then they suddenly back-winged, spiraling higher. They circled ten meters up, watching him and Seeyan. They looked familiar, but I couldn't place them for sure or identify them as friend or enemy.

Regardless, for the moment, they simply watched.

Bryan pushed himself up off of Seeyan. I ran to his side in time to see that her neck had been broken. His nails had raked her arm bloody, and the look he gave me was full of horror. "I didn't mean to. I didn't mean to kill her. I just wanted to stop her. We'd been looking for you, and looking for you, and here we'd finally found you and she was trying to get you caught." He leaned down and tried to straighten her up. "See, we know she trapped you."

I closed her eyes, barely managing not to withdraw my hand before I touched her.

Beside me, Bryan sobbed, and I slid my arm across his great, wide shoulders. "It's okay. It couldn't be helped. Shhhh . . . Shhhh . . ." He needed to pull himself together; we needed to go. Seeyan wasn't our only enemy.

His voice came out low and controlled, but he was my Bryan, my friend from forever, and I heard the anger boiling in his heart and feeding his words. "She was smaller than me. She didn't deserve it."

"Of course not. But you didn't mean to kill her, did you? You were protecting me. And we stick together, right?"

He lifted his face to me. "She was your friend. She loved your children."

No. Not my friend. "She betrayed me."

He blinked, and another sob caught in his throat, but that was the last one. We held each other's eyes for a long time. In his, I saw old pain behind the new pain and, like I always had, I wished there was a way for me to erase it from his past.

I'd always wished him happiness most of all of us; he ate anger in place of it, and now the anger had bitten him again, laid down a fresh scar.

Not that I could look at what had been Seeyan, either. In some moments, everything sucked. I cursed Juss, and then cursed myself for a fool. He'd only told the truth, and I'd seen that even then. I leaned over and kissed Bryan on the cheek, and he startled a little, then pulled me closer to him, his bulk making a safe place, however momentary.

Someone pulled at my free arm, the one that wasn't around Bryan. And Ming stood on Bryan's far side, and when I looked up Jenna's face swam into view above me. She was talking, and maybe she'd been talking to me for a while. ". . . need to go. Now. The fliers are gone. They probably went to get reinforcements."

40

ALICIA: ANGELS AND DEVILS

I followed Amalo out. Really out. We left the compound and ventured into the fair. The booths were still closed, although a few vendors had stirred and were making col or talking amongst each other. Near the entrance, two nearly finished sculptures stood, waiting for the artist's final touches. I startled: one was Joseph, Chelo, and Kayleen standing hand in hand together in a circle, each holding a baby. They wore Keeper's clothes, with grand smiles on their faces.

Where were the rest of us?

Amalo stopped, letting me look at it from all sides. When it was done, it was going to be beautiful, perhaps as beautiful as the first statue I'd seen of a flier, on Silver's Home. Tears came to my eyes, completely unbidden. The artist had chosen to show Kayleen graceful and strong instead of half-crazy. Her hair had been rendered in the manner of fliers, with silver charms in the shape of hebras dangling from her wooden braids. Chelo, as always, had her own stark beauty, and she appeared to be looking far away, perhaps into the future. Joseph's face had been rendered true, except the artist had given him a few years by adding tiny lines around his mouth. His eyes were right, soft and full of the infinity of knowledge, and I wanted the statue to climb down and hold me.

What if I didn't see him again? Could I bear that?

And where were strong, angry Bryan, and steady, loving Liam? Where was I? They needed a risk-taker. Jenna had said so long ago. If it weren't for me, we'd have never left Fremont. A tear slid down my cheek, and I swiped it away, keeping my face averted from Amalo's until it had dried.

"Let's go," he said softly. "We don't want to get caught."

He'd taken me without permission. They wouldn't have taken me if they hadn't decided to tell me yes. If I agreed, Joseph and Kayleen and Chelo would fly away from me. I wanted to be part of the statue in front of me, captured forever as one of the children of Fremont. Trying for wings felt like too big a risk, too irreversible.

As we walked out of the gates, we passed other statues, but none of them were as beautiful as the unfinished one by the doorway. Our progress was slow because of Amalo's awkward gait. He kept our pace wandering, going from sculpture to sculpture, pointing out the pain and beauty in each one. A few showed only one emotion or the other, but the ones Amalo prized the most were full of both. It felt surreal to move so slowly.

Eventually, Amalo took me to a flier's house close to the fair, all big rooms with oversize chairs designed to work as perches, and sweeping spaces in the kitchens and bathrooms. Inside, Marti waited with a wingless woman who offered me col and bread and nuts. I had never seen fliers without at least one wingless waiting on them. Was it hard for them to be alone?

Marti cocked her head at me. "Do you have questions? Is there anything you'd like to know about the process?"

My throat closed, and I coughed the words out. "Does . . . does that mean you've decided?" I knew the answer, but I didn't know how I'd react when I heard it.

Amalo spoke from behind me. "It will be a great honor to have you attempt to join us."

I froze.

He came around and sat beside Marti, so I could see them both. "If you succeed, you will be honored for all your life as our first flier from Fremont, and as sister to Joseph and Chelo."

I wasn't Joseph's sister! I was his lover. Now what. What if I said no? Now I knew that was what I wanted to say.

No.

How much had Amalo risked taking me from the jail they'd been keeping me in? What would he do to me if I refused, especially after I'd almost begged?

Even a risk-taker knows when isn't a time for risk. Or maybe I was finally learning. I tried to buy time. "Thank you for the honor and trust," I said. "I do need to tell my family."

Amalo hesitated, and then said, "That may be difficult."

"I know where some of them are." Maybe if I found them they would keep me safe from myself. Why did I always make that so hard?

"For now, perhaps we should answer your questions."

Okay. I had questions, anyway. Asking a question wasn't a commitment. "How long does it take?"

Marti smiled shyly and mumbled. "It took me three months. And then two more to condition to fly. For others it takes longer. Rarely less. You are already strong, and it may take you less time to teach your body to love its wings. I came from Silver's Home."

"What if I succeed, and then I change my mind?"

Amalo answered. "We could cut your wings off, and you would become like Seeyan, a wingless flier. But you cannot go back to being who you are now. You will be transformed."

"If you can turn me one way, why not also the other?"

"There has never been a demand to go the other way. The processes have not been tried often."

Interesting, that they had been tried at all.

Marti added, "But you will not want to go back. Perhaps you are hesitating now, but to fly is to touch the skies and see the world all at once, to gain a perspective that no ground-born can ever have." She made sure I was looking at her, and then she spoke softly but firmly. "Don't let your fear keep you from this. It is the most beautiful state in the world, to be a flier. We turn away thousands of petitioners every year. You've suffered, and because of your suffering you have the soul of a flier."

She clearly believed it. What had I done?

The slow flap of wings told me to look up. Tsawo and Angeline flew in the top of the house, Tsawo's face dark. Before they had even landed, another flier came in behind them; the blonde from the first day. This morning she looked even angrier than she had at the welcoming feast. On a flier's face, anger was a strange expression, twisting her features, elongating her chin. Their faces were made for serenity, and joy, and pain, but less so for anger or desire. Right after she landed, she shook her wings hard, as if needing to get every feather into place.

Tsawo turned to her before even acknowledging any of us. His voice dripped a bad welcome. "Mille. What a surprise."

She let him have it. "Why thank you for keeping me in the loop. You know they think Joseph succeeded? They think your niece can have babies. You will change all of our world!"

Angeline looked dryly at her. "You mean Silver's Home won't need you to broker babies anymore?"

Of course, that wasn't the position Mille took. "I mean we will no longer be the beautiful martyrs we are. We will become like all the rest, only less. We will be animals."

Tsawo laughed in her face and she backed up two steps, but she didn't stop her rant. "They will never admit us to the Court of Worlds. The Islans will no longer care about us. Everything we know will change."

Angeline again spoke quietly. "Marcus has already arranged a place for us on the Courts. It is done. We are full humans."

Wow. Good for him. I mean, I didn't know what that meant, not really, but it sounded good.

Mille looked like she'd swallowed a bee. She sputtered and glanced back and forth between Amalo and Tsawo.

It was like watching three jeweled butterflies argue.

Amalo cleared his throat. I expected him to talk to Mille, but he spoke to Tsawo, his voice full of authority. "What about our promise to take sides in the war?"

He was on Mille's side?

Tsawo answered politely, as if he did, in fact, answer to Amalo. "I have a plan."

Amalo frowned. "A promise was made. Even though you and I did not make it, all of us will be held accountable if it is broken."

Angeline grabbed her brother's hand and held it up. "I trust Tsawo. He should have his chance."

Amalo gave them both a look that would have withered a paw-cat.

Apparently Tsawo was used to it. He just stood, waiting, and while he and Angeline stood quietly, some of the anger leaked from Amalo. The feather around Tsawo's neck rose and fell as he breathed, and his hair blew a tiny bit in a soft eddy of wind that came in from the open roof, kissing him and moving on. Otherwise he might as well have been part of a carved statue.

Amalo finally said, "I'm old, and I didn't expect to see this day."

I didn't quite understand the conversation. I glanced at Marti, who hadn't said a word since the other fliers came in. The color had drained from her face. No one seemed to be honoring her because she was a wingless human given flight. Rather, she seemed afraid, and shrank back a bit from Mille. The other fliers all ignored her.

Mille cleared her throat and said, "I don't care who leads us or who made what promises to whom. We shouldn't let these children of our masters lead us to war."

This time it was Tsawo who seemed to temporarily side with her. "Not to worry. I won't."

"Or fly." She glared at me, as good as Amalo at sending scorn without a word. Maybe getting old made people good at that. "Don't give them wings."

I wanted to stick my tongue out at her, but I followed Tsawo's lead and simply stared back. Unlike Amalo, she didn't wither at all, and I thought perhaps we'd stare each other down like dogs until one of us keeled over from hunger.

Amalo cleared his throat and announced, "I am the one who chooses, and I have chosen."

Mille stepped back, looking like she wanted to raise a hand to him but didn't dare. Tsawo's head snapped around and his dark eyes bored into me, taking the place of Mille's more malevolent gaze.

I did turn away from him.

He stepped close to me and put a hand on my cheek, turning my face toward his. "You will lose your ability to run like the wind."

His words drew a shiver from my core, and it was all I could do not to look away from him. He rewarded me with a soft kiss on the forehead. "If you live, I will be your flying teacher."

And then he kissed my lips. He tasted of sweat and nuts, and the sweet clear air of Lopali.

I still wanted out. I wanted both things, for Tsawo to teach me to fly the way he did, to kiss him again, to kiss him every day, and to leave this place and never come back. To stay with Joseph and cheer him on, and make him take risks when he needed to.

Mille glared even harder at me and gave a great leap and a hard flap of wings, so hard she gasped in pain as she cleared the roof, and then she was gone. I immediately wished to never see her again.

Amalo did not appear to like the kiss that Tsawo had given me a whole lot more than Mille did. He gave me a slightly disgusted look, and took Tsawo by the arm, and gestured up. Amalo and Tsawo took off, far more gently and with far more control than Mille had shown. Angeline looked more confused than angry or disgusted, but she followed the others into the sky. Apparently they needed to talk without me.

I glanced at Marti, who shrank a bit from me this time. I sighed, loudly, and said, "I didn't kiss him. He kissed me."

She shook her head, as if she'd run out of words.

"Excuse me," I said. "I need to freshen up." When I said it, I really did mean to go to the bathroom. But as soon as I was there, looking in the mirror, it was the most natural thing in the world to turn my mod on, and walk right past Marti and out the door.

JOSEPH: THE JOURNEY

Twenty pointless minutes passed while we waited for word about Seeyan. We'd moved to a scrap of grass by a perch so Matriana and Daniel would be more comfortable. Kayleen and I sat below them, too close to talk without being overheard. Marcus paced, walking circles around us all. Beside me, Sasha's head followed Marcus, so between the two of them, I felt dizzy.

Kayleen looked quizzical. "How come you're so tense?"

"I keep expecting Induan to poke me out of thin air and make me jump."

She grinned. "I'd think you'd be used to it with Alicia and all."

I reddened. We had played night games that took advantage of her invisibility. "I hope Alicia's with Chelo and the others. Your mom, too, of course."

Kayleen smiled, her face soft. "Me, too. I'm happy for the few minutes of rest."

Of course she was. She'd had no break since we almost lost her. I had a map in my memory: Charmed wasn't far; as close to Oshai as SoBright, but more of a tourist destination. We needed to start soon, or risk Lushia or whatever Star Mercenary was after us this time.

Finally, one of the two fliers who had chased Seeyan off landed right behind Matriana and Daniel, the look on her face drawing us to our feet. She had black feathers with a few orange highlights on the tips, and matching highlights in her short hair. She gasped for breath.

"What happened?" Matriana asked.

"Chelo . . . we saw her." Gasp. "She's with the bigman with the knives for nails." She stopped for a few breaths. "He . . . he killed her."

What? No!

"Killed Seeyan. Seeyan's dead." Her eyes closed slowly, and then opened again, still slowly. "Her neck broke. She has flier bones; she didn't stand a chance." She looked as if she were trying hard not to cry.

"Where are they now?" Daniel asked.

"Coming. Following Atoni."

That must be the other flier. "What direction? Can you take us there?"

"No." It was a command from Marcus. "Wait. Let them come to us. Let's get the wings out."

Wrong answer. "I want to go to her."

He just stared at me.

"Why fly anyway? It has to be more conspicuous."

"Most of the people trying to hurt us aren't fliers. We should be able to avoid them."

I wanted to knock him aside and race down the road to find Chelo. Of course, he was right. He was always right. The strategist as well as the Maker. I gritted my teeth and started pulling wings carefully out of the four-wheeler. What had the flier meant? Bryan—she had to have been referring to Bryan. How could he have killed Seeyan? I understood what the flier had said, had been deep in the sims and knew how fragile they were, but that didn't really help me understand.

I just couldn't see it. Her dead, or Bryan killing her.

We pulled a dozen pairs of wings out of the vehicle, one after another, so many it didn't look as if they could have fit inside. I smiled when I saw Stark had included a set of power-assisted wings for Bryan. The efficient assistant. Just as I rested the last pair on the ground, Sasha whined, nearly drowning out the footsteps and wing beats that announced the arrival of a storm of our people. Chelo came first, racing right into my arms. She smelled of sweat and tears and of herself, and I breathed against her skin and clutched her to me, happy to hear her heart beating.

Kayleen flew past me and Chelo, heading straight for Paloma, who was flanked by Jenna and Tiala. They ran one on each side of her, with Dianne close behind, so the three women had her cupped. As Paloma swung around in Kayleen's embrace, tears glistened as the sun touched her cheeks.

I ran my fingers down Chelo's cheeks. They were damp, too. She ran her hands through my short hair. "You cut it."

"Induan cut it. Part of a disguise."

The flier landed, a man with white wings spangled with small black spots, like a peppered egg. Atoni.

Bryan and Ming seemed stuck together, both of their faces hard to read but Bryan's eyes angry and shocked all at once. Marcus stopped them, firing questions I couldn't quite hear, and didn't really care about. "Where's Alicia?" I whispered. "Where is she?"

Chelo pushed back from me, and ran the backs of her hands along her cheeks to dry them. "She went with the fliers."

"Who? Tsawo?"

"A gray flier. Gray wings, gray eyes. And a bright red flier girl, might be young. She's small, anyway. I didn't get their names."

"We're leaving," I whispered. "We're leaving Lopali."

"What about the babies? Liam?"

"They're coming." They had to be. "With a man named Stark, maybe. Anyway, with someone."

Her features hardened for a moment. "They better be safe." She let go of me and went to Kayleen and Paloma, talking to them in low tones. I looked around for followers. Surely there would be some.

Nothing. Not yet, anyway.

Marcus must have had the same thought. "Come on. We have a lot of flying to do. We'll have to go around Oshai."

Dianne put a hand on his arm and whispered in his ear.

He leaned down to listen to her, and a frustrated look crossed his face. When he stood his message had changed. "Get them food and water. Ten minutes and we need to go."

Of course. They'd been captives.

Their stories unfolded as we fed them. As I learned about Seeyan betraying Chelo, and Juss being a bad guy, I had to work at it not to be glad Seeyan was dead. Except I'd liked her, and I guess sometimes the people you like aren't what they seem. Like this whole planet.

We each selected wings. One set lay out on the ground unclaimed. Alicia's wings.

No one knew where Alicia had been taken. The women who had been imprisoned with her mostly thought she'd gone of her own accord; not a prisoner at all. Enough seemed sure she wasn't still in the compound to keep me from wanting to stay here.

Would she have left me of her own accord? A hole seeped into my body, the one she filled when we were close, when her head rested against my chest and we talked.

I was angry with Alicia and the gray flier, and mad at her for the gray flier, and I missed her.

I strapped my wings onto my biceps. As I fastened the chest belt, Sasha gave out a forlorn whimper, and I remembered she couldn't fly.

I knelt down. With my wings serving as balance, I kissed her wet, dark nose and whispered, "Run along with us. I'll carry extra water for you. I can't fly fast anyway." I wasn't willing to leave her here, not after I'd brought her all the way from Fremont.

She was a normal dog from home, with no enhancement at all, but she understood me. She licked my face and sat, her head cocked to one side, so she appeared to be listening for something. She was so patient and steady, so true. "Sash," I said to her, "you're my role model."

She merely cocked her head to the other side.

Chelo came up beside me. She had been crying. "Help me look out for Bryan."

I couldn't hold her because we both wore wings. "Of course. Did he really kill Seeyan?"

She nodded miserably. "He didn't mean to, and he hates it. It's hurting him. I thought . . . maybe . . . maybe you had a similar . . . you could help him."

I could. "As soon as we get away safely. There's not time now."

"I know. Thanks."

"Let's go!" Marcus called out. "Matriana and Daniel will lead. Then Chelo and Joseph, then Kayleen and Paloma, Jenna and Tiala, Bryan and Ming, and then me."

We went, following his order. Matriana and Daniel stayed really low through town, flying straight back the way we'd driven in.

The other two fliers, Atoni and the woman with black-and-orange wings, flew high above us all, as if watching for unexpected threats.

Sasha flowed along the ground below us, running all out. It was harder for her—we could fly straight and she had to go up and down the hills, and sometimes, around obstacles. I'd have to fly slower if she was going to make it. I might have counted on Seeyan to help me before, like she'd brought Sasha to the cave, and the thought made me bobble and lose altitude so fast Chelo yelled at me. When I got straightened back out, flying at the right level and beside my sister again, my dog had fallen behind. I thought I saw her topping a rise of hill behind me, and below the last of our group, but I couldn't be sure. It was too hard to look backward and fly frontward all at once.

We left the city behind and flew over open fields, our path keeping us from roads. Here, Matriana and Daniel led us higher in the air, and more fliers came in to join us, one by one by two by one. Soon we had an escort of twenty or thirty, which wasn't exactly a way to avoid attention. *Maybe.* My thought felt bitter. *Maybe Marcus was making this into a story to spin for the world and he needed visuals.*

We flew over an hour before Marcus called a halt. The whole crowd of us landed by a copse of trees near an open field, and three Keepers jogged out of the trees and gave us water and nut-buttered bread and fruit, hand-feeding us so we didn't have to take off our wings. The man who fed me and Chelo kept his head down, and his hands shook. He had a huge smile the few times he let us see it, a clue the shaking was more from pleasure than from fear. As he left he said, "Bless you. Bless you all."

Chelo and I looked at each other, and her eyes looked like I felt—like she was caught up in some strange dream and that the dream itched. We didn't talk about it, but just checked the buckles and straps on our wings. I watched for Sasha, hoping to see her bound up over a rise, ears flapping.

She didn't show.

My shoulders felt the strain by the time we finally got close to Charmed, and I had fallen farther to the back. Chelo flew next to me. Kayleen looped back and forth between us and Paloma. Marcus had the rear, with at least four or five of our ever-growing escort. I couldn't really be sure how many were behind, but when I'd last counted the escort it had grown to over thirty, plus the eleven of us. Bryan and Ming were in the front, Bryan looking almost graceful in his power-assisted wings.

Charmed's spaceport looked a lot like the one at Oshai, complete with cargo vehicles and a ring of perch-trees. Sunshine gleamed on two of the most elegant deep-space ships I'd ever seen. They stole my own attention from my aching shoulders and lower back. Both were tall and slender, one twice the size of the other. Something about them spoke of the joy of flying, although I couldn't have identified what piece of the design gave it such elegance if I'd been asked directly. The smaller one was the same class of ship as *Creator*, and the bigger could have held our group ten times over. Its sleek exterior suggested it hadn't ever dirtied itself carrying much cargo. Probably we were going to take the bigger one.

To test, I let myself sip the spaceport's data. Flier ships. I couldn't wait to get in one and see the details.

The fliers at the front of our group pulled up, gaining height. Making room for us to go in and land by the ships? I glanced toward Marcus, hoping for a clue as to which ship, so I could make sure I had the right trajectory. He was too far away for me to see the expression on his face.

More fliers rose from the perch-trees. Ten, twenty, thirty.

They were beautiful, flying up into the late morning sun. They rose, and rose, and rose.

Our escort rose with them.

More fliers leapt off the perch-trees. Seven waves of ten or fifteen each.

Too many.

Marcus figured it out at the same time I did. *Joseph!* he screamed inside my mind. *Get down. Land. Protect yourself.*

Kayleen's voice, *No!*

The fliers from the spaceport were heading toward us all, mixing with our vanguard already.

Get down! Marcus repeated.

Fliers weren't supposed to use weapons.

Bryan and Ming were already surrounded. They still flew forward, and the other fliers hadn't struck them or anything, but they flew very close to each other, and close to Bryan and Ming, closer than any of us would dare fly to each other. Among them, I spotted the blond woman with the blue dots on her wings, which made me snarl.

I couldn't be sure, but it looked like a few of our fliers were circling outside the group that surrounded Bryan and Ming. It looked more like a ball of waving color in the sky, maybe a huge seething kite, than a bunch of winged ones surrounding a wingless.

What do they want? I needed to know.

To make you land, said Marcus.

So you want me to land?

If they make you fall, you'll die.

Kayleen? What should we do?

She felt unusually calm, like the girl we'd pulled back from the nearly dead. *I'm going to go tell Mom to land, then I'll go down.*

Smart. Luckily, Paloma was close ahead. Kayleen added length to her wing beats and left me behind. I looked for Chelo, found her on my right. I turned and flew toward her.

Stay separate! Marcus commanded. *Make them work harder.*

Groups of fliers converged on each other in front of me. Except for wings I recognized, like Daniel's orange and Matriana's silvery white and gold, I couldn't tell who was on our side and who wasn't. A large group headed toward me and Chelo. "Down!" I yelled.

She nodded and immediately began to slow and spiral toward the ground. Half the group of fliers heading toward us went down after her, the other kept chasing toward me.

None of us, not even Kayleen, could outfly a real flier.

I took another quick look around. Everyone else was too far ahead, already engulfed in the strange wings.

Marcus, loud, insistent, fear lacing his sending. *Down. Down before you die. They're trying to stop you. They won't use weapons. Hold onto your balance.*

Huh?

Then the wind of the other fliers surrounded me. A man with dark hair and angry brown eyes flew in my face, swooping past me, beating his wings hard; the wind lifted my right wing. Another blast of wind from an enemy I couldn't see drove my left wing down.

Two more fliers did the same thing, and then two more, and I bobbled seriously, tilting sideways to the ground.

I couldn't watch out for anyone anymore. I focused on my wings, on my posture, on swinging my feet down and starting the right downbeats to land, although I was way too high. Tsawo's voice played in my head from an early lesson. "If you have to fall, sacrifice your feet. You can get new feet, no one can make you a new head." Tsawo was like that, literal and dry.

Three fliers came so close to me I slowed lest I hit them. A near-stall. Fear gave me the power to go again, forward now, no ideas about landing yet, just getting away.

I didn't know where to go. Everywhere I saw wings. Blue wings and black wings and bruised purple wings. Even a pair of white wings, white as summer clouds, trying to knock me out of the sky.

Frantic fear gave me power. I kicked one of them in the wing and he fell away fast. I couldn't tell if he fell all the way down or caught himself. For a moment I gained space.

Data. That was my strength. Use it. Except from the air if I lost my sense of physical self at all I'd die. I was going to die anyway. I had to do something.

My breath burned.

Under me, I glimpsed the silver of ships wheeling. Pointed noses, hard sides, hot from the sun. Nothing to land on.

I opened, slowed down my thinking, accepted the data of the spaceport again, deeper than the first time. The mandala of the spaceport. The harmony that Kayleen had shown me.

The disharmony of the fight screamed across the data, like mismatched colors in a painting designed to shatter perception. Now I knew who was on what side. Not why, but I didn't care. We had to survive, and at least now I could see my attackers' movements from afar, tell who was flying in close to me next. I braced for a woman dive-bombing from above, for a pair of nearly matched male fliers with clay-red wings coming up from below. I flapped between two other men who'd been coming head-on, brushing one of their wings.

It became a dance. Me and the data against the quick, sharp movements of the attacking fliers. I drove them down, and down, and down, until I was near enough to the ground I had to back-wing into a landing. I slid on my knees, one wing breaking off above the handhold.

It would be nice to quit breaking wings.

Fliers fluttered over my head, so close I felt their wind, not near enough to touch. I hurled the broken bit of wing into them, grunting with satisfaction when it knocked a orange-winged flier ten feet backward and drew a nasty word from him.

I stripped my other wing off, and threw it, too. It didn't hit any of them.

Others had made it down. I spotted Chelo, Kayleen, and Paloma. The fliers seemed content to circle above us, feeling hostile. But then, why would they land? We'd beat them in a ground contest. I raced toward the others.

We stood together on the ground, searching the sky for the rest. Eight fliers surrounded Marcus, driving him away from us.

Jenna and Tiala were engaged in similar struggles. I watched Jenna kick a flier out of position, pinwheeling back over hindquarters, a full two somersaults. The kick disturbed her balance, and she started to fall, then adjusted wings and feet and forced herself stable. I cheered. Even Chelo cheered.

The flier plummeted to the ground, too far away for us to tell if he or she had died of the impact. It had been hard enough I was willing to bet they'd at least be wingless.

Why attack us? What did they get out of it?

"Look in the data," Kayleen said. "Come back."

I'd dropped the threads when I landed.

I kept my eyes open, watching, letting the most local data flows mix in with what I saw. They didn't want us near the spaceport.

So we should go there.

I took Kayleen's hand, and Paloma's. Chelo took Paloma's other side. I spoke out loud for Chelo and Paloma's sake. "There's nothing we can do for the ones still up, but hope. We need to keep going, get in among the ships. They'll have to spend more energy trying to stop us."

We jogged forward, watching above and behind.

The local data felt out of balance with the fight, disturbed so it almost whined. The sharpest danger was near Marcus. Daniel and Matriana fluttered around the group that had him.

He fell, wings clasped close together, plummeting toward the ground.

Kayleen saw it and screamed, even though the data signaled he meant the movement by feeling hopeful. It was like listening to the score for a fight.

Marcus snapped his wings down and out, arching his back, slowing himself. A powerful beat sent him straight, free of the others. Matriana and Daniel rode above him, shielding him.

Four fliers dived down toward them.

"Bryan!" Chelo screamed.

I followed her pointing finger. He was falling out of the sky. Fast.

Chelo took off, racing toward where he might fall. I followed her, and I heard the other two following me.

Data told me Marcus was still all right. I didn't send him anything, I didn't want to distract him.

Bryan slammed into the ground in front of us, a cloud of fliers hovering above him.

Ming's attackers had momentarily forgotten her as they watched Bryan fall. She positioned herself to land. The blonde with the blue dots dove and spread herself in Ming's way, and Ming kicked her in the chest, pushing her aside.

I gave Ming a thumbs-up.

Chelo reached Bryan's inert form.

Ming landed, racing toward Bryan, ungainly in her wings.

I came up behind them both.

One leg had crumpled under Bryan, bone shoved through the thigh, the knee shattered and bloody. The other seemed disconnected from the hip, bent sideways, like he was trying to do the splits. One arm had clearly pulled away from the socket. One wing had stabbed him in the back, and blood leaked out from under him, staining the grass.

He'd saved his head.

I couldn't stop the sudden, dizzy thought that it would have been kinder for him to land on it.

His face twisted with pain and his lips bled. Chelo stroked his cheek, moaning. She leaned down and kissed him on the forehead, murmuring something too soft for me to hear. Her voice cracked. Her tears splashed into the blood flowing down his chin.

Ming couldn't quite bend down to him, even with her dancer's grace. She stared down at him, croaking his name. I helped her get one wing off, and she knelt over her lover, the one wing she still wore shading his face so I couldn't see what passed between them.

Chelo had sat back on her heels, tears flowing down her face, scanning the sky to give Ming her last moment with Bryan.

More fliers came in from all directions, most landing, a few staying aloft. I recognized one, then another. They were on our side.

The data song here saw the balance change, and stabilize, turning into a more joyful set of tones. It wasn't really sound as much as balance, hard to describe, a sense unavailable to me anywhere else, but such a part of me I felt more all right, in spite of what was happening at my feet.

The fliers stayed, wings rustling, not one of them speaking even though they must have a million things to say to each other after the fight.

Chelo sobbed harder, and I knew Bryan had died. My brother. One of us six.

42

CHELO: THE SPACEPORT, CHARMED

When we were kids, Bryan was shorter than the rest of us, and more awkward. He used to follow us around, hopeful, waiting for an opportunity to use his extra strength to help us. My first kiss had been Bryan, when I was six and he was five. I had giggled, and a hurt look had crossed his face, so I'd kissed him again. Once, he held my hand so hard my fingers popped. He'd apologized for a week. I remembered his bruised face after other kids beat him up on Fremont, and later, in the bowels of *Migrator*, when all his physical hurts were healed, but he held my hand in his and looked as lost as a stray pup.

"I'm sorry, Chelo, we have to go." My brother's voice, coming from far away and just above my head all at once. His hand on my arm. "The fliers aren't our only enemies."

I blinked up at him. The fliers weren't our enemies. *Except the ones that killed Bryan.* The next thing I knew, Joseph had pulled me up and folded me in his arms, and his shirt was soaked with my tears. Then Marcus stood beside us, his green eyes snapping with anger and betrayal. Dianne clutched Ming in her arms. Paloma stood over Bryan, looking down at him sadly and shaking her head. She leaned over and closed his eyes.

"Let's go," Marcus urged. More hands. Fliers. Matriana and Daniel. Our fliers. The white one with black spots. Jenna with her arms around me, pulling me toward the spaceport.

"We can't just leave him here!" I protested.

"We'll take care of him," Daniel soothed.

Nobody would take care of him ever again. I would never take care of him again. He would never hold me in his arms again, never scratch me with his fingernails, never again lecture me to push myself to climb and run.

I shouldn't have stayed for Juss's fortune. Or I should have acted more on what I heard. I should have made this not happen. That was my job, to keep everyone safe. Damn the blue man. Damn Seeyan. Juss had said people would die. If I'd just stayed with Liam and the kids, maybe no one would have died.

I got my feet under me, and ran with them all. The fliers took off and flew just above us. Then we were swerving through the circle of perch-trees, ducking and weaving, the fliers flowing above. Out in the open again, we ran across the hard surface of the spaceport.

Joseph glanced longingly toward a ship that looked like the bigger, gleaming cousin of *New Making*, but Marcus drove us to a squat cargo ship instead. We streamed up a wide loading ramp similar to the one we'd streamed down when we first got here, the day I danced on the spaceport floor and thought the perch-trees were real and friendly.

Only now there was one less of us. I couldn't think about that.

Where were my babies? I needed Jherrel and Caro. I needed them now.

The metal ramp echoed under my feet, under all our feet. It sounded good, even to me.

I'd never wanted to get on a ship again.

I needed my babies. And Liam. Dear sweet Liam. I barreled up the top part of the ramp, head down. And then, I smelled him. Sweat and worry and fresh air, the children and the ship. As I looked up, Liam swept me into his arms, swinging me around, lifting my feet. "Oh honey. Chelo, Chelo. I saw. I'm sorry. I should never have let you go."

I looked up into his welcoming, wonderful, steady brown eyes. "You're here. How did you get here? Where are the children?"

He pointed. Paloma was buried in her grandchildren. Jherrel had one leg and Caro the other, and Paloma was mussing both their hair, a smile on her tear-streaked face.

"I brought them for you." The voice, familiar and soft, came from behind.

I turned to find Mohami, his head bowed. As always, he was flanked by Kala and Samuel. "It is the last part of my duty," he said. "I will always remember being able to serve you." He looked sadder than I had ever seen him, and conflicted. He had never looked conflicted in my presence.

I used a long breath to pull myself together enough to remember who Mohami was. The Keeper of the Ways of the Fliers of Lopali. "Thank you for bringing the children. Thank you for taking care of them, and us."

He nodded.

"I'm sorry for your troubles today. I'm sorry that our coming here caused a fight between your people." He was not part of the group that had killed Bryan. He couldn't be. I couldn't be angry with this small, old man. "You helped me understand the heart of the world."

He smiled softly. "It is not your fault you brought change. We needed change. But I am sorry for your loss."

Kala and Samuel moved closer to him, protective.

He stepped away from them, putting them a half-step behind him.

Maybe it was the pain of my loss that drove me, maybe instinct. I knelt down at his feet, and I looked up at him. "Come with us. Stay with us."

His eyes widened, his look the closest thing to startlement I'd ever seen on his placid face. He raised an eyebrow.

"Please? I need you." I looked at the children, at Paloma. "They need you."

Kala and Samuel blinked at me and looked at Mohami and then back at me. They said nothing, except Samuel chewed on his upper lip.

Silence fell. Liam stood behind me, supporting. I kept my eye on Mohami, willing him to say yes.

Mohami looked at me, and all the vastness of the morning ceremony seemed to float in his eyes. I could fly a space ship into his pupil and have as many planets to explore as I did here and now. As outside, so inside. He'd told me that once in a private meditation session and now I understood what it looked like. I shivered at the power I saw in him in that moment. Then his eyes softened, and his gaze became the same peaceful, warm one I was used to. He spoke softly, "Very well."

Kala and Samuel looked at him, faces slack and patient. I wondered what was going on behind their placid eyes.

Caro laughed and other conversations started back up, so I almost missed Mohami's words to them. "Kala, you must stay with me. Samuel, you will go back and help Niall, who will take my place."

Samuel nodded, looking proud.

Kala had turned white-faced. "Will we be coming back soon?"

All three of them looked to me, their patience heavy. So, did I want to come back? Not if I could help it. If this was the soul of the Five Worlds, I was going far away and finding a different soul. Maybe after the sting of Bryan's death went away. Maybe in ten or twenty or thirty years. In a world where people didn't age, I shouldn't say never. So I just said, "Perhaps."

Kala nodded, and leaned over to hug Samuel, the warmest touch I'd seen between them, in spite of the love that always seemed to be there. "I'll be back some day," she whispered to him.

Maybe after this war. But there would be another one after this one. Still, I was bred to be hopeful. I glanced at Tiala, who had come up to ask Paloma something. "Tiala? Will you find a place for Mohami and Kala?"

She didn't miss a beat. "Of course."

"Thank you."

The two Keepers turned away from me and followed her. I watched their back for a moment. It felt right. I didn't know why, but I had done the right thing.

I cried again, for Bryan but also because Mohami and Kala and Samuel were grace in a world that pretended to more grace than it really had. They were golden people, full of love and serenity.

Liam's hand was still on my shoulder. "Where's Kayleen?" I asked.

"She and Joseph and Marcus and Chance all disappeared. Probably in the control room."

"Did it work? Did they change the fliers?" Did Bryan die for something, at least?

He folded me deep in his arms and put his chin on my head. "I don't know."

"I hope so."

Jenna came through, murmuring at us to find acceleration couches and strap in. We still stood at the top of the ramp, and I realized almost everyone else had already gone deeper into the ship. A few fliers walked slowly down the ramp, their wings canted far forward so they looked like they could take off the moment no metal blocked the sky.

Something was still wrong. Alicia! "Where's Alicia? And Induan? Did they come in with you?"

Liam shook his head.

"Even invisible?"

"Well, maybe." I could tell by his tone of voice that he didn't think so. "You may have to let her go," he whispered against my cheek, his voice as soft as he could make it. "Perhaps one of the little deaths that she needs is to stay here and see if she can live her dream and become a flier."

"You sound like your father."

"So?"

"It was a compliment."

He wrapped his arms around me tighter and kissed the top of my head, still watching the ramp with me, as if we expected to see the invisible ones walk up it any moment.

I pulled his hands gently away from my sides, getting ready to go on in, when he whispered, "Wait."

Four feet padded, running, up the ramp. Sasha's nose appeared in the square of ground we could see from here, and then all of her, speeding up the ramp to leap up our waists, tongue out, nosing our hands into petting her. I laughed and laughed. The dog had never made me so happy before. I scratched behind her ears. "It may have been Alicia's destiny to be stuck here, but not yours, huh? Brave little one."

She bounded past us looking for more family to greet, and we headed in.

The ramp slid almost silently into the ship and the door closed with only a small click of the locks moving into place. I kissed Liam, hard, on the lips. "I need to go find my brother. Save me a seat."

He laughed. "Good luck."

The ship was bulky and over-big, as if outsized cargo had to be maneuvered around every padded corner. She was so heavy with her own oily metallic scent that I could already barely smell a world in her.

I didn't mind.

I found Joseph in a wide corridor, walking toward me, holding Kayleen's hand. Sasha trotted at their heels, looking happy with herself. Joseph looked different; more controlled and sadder. Older. I searched Kayleen's eyes. She brushed a stray hair back from my cheek and returned my gaze, also changed. I had seen the one side of her being lost, Caro's side, and now I was really seeing how Kayleen looked for the first time. I saw sanity, and oddly, a bit of wisdom in her blue eyes. I wanted to kiss her and hold her and take her away and chat, but we didn't have time. Yet. She mussed my hair and they both held me close for a moment, the three of us almost one being. When we separated, Joseph grinned at me and gave a little bow. "We have to go, my sister-worth-a-war. There're Star Mercenaries after us, and Paula's coming soon, and we don't want the fliers' spat to keep us grounded until the bounty hunters get here."

"Hey! That's not my fault."

He'd already pulled away from me, but he gave my hand a squeeze. "It never has been."

I knelt to pet the dog while they walked off, still hand in hand.

"Wait!" I called. "Alicia?"

He looked back. He shrugged, pretending he didn't care. His eyes gave away the lie. "Maybe she'll show up before we leave the system."

"I hope so." Or did I? He could share things with Kayleen that Liam and I never could. We had our history, and our babies. And for all that I hadn't been sure about taking her into our relationship, I didn't want to lose her. Just the two of us, just me and Liam, would be entirely too serious; we'd lose our sense of play.

I could worry about that later.

Now it was time to go find an uncomfortable couch and Liam and our son. I let Sasha go, watching her scramble after Joseph and Kayleen, tail wagging like a flag of truce.

I still hated acceleration couches. This time, I lay strapped between

Liam and Jherrel, looking back and forth between them, drinking in the familiar comfort of every breath they took. Caro was on her dad's far side, her eyes closed, looking disturbingly like her uncle Joseph when he reveled in things I could never see.

Every ship in the universe seemed to think passengers should see the planet they were leaving recede below them, and this one wasn't any different. I thought about closing my eyes, but that wouldn't bring Bryan back, or put Alicia next to me.

We took off slowly at first, the ground, then the spaceport, then the ring of perch-trees visible. Beyond those, small groups of people gathered in three places. One of those must be around Bryan's body. Crying with your forehead strapped to an acceleration couch and your hand strapped to your side really sucked, so I didn't do it. I just whispered, "I'm sorry, little brother. I'm so very sorry. I'm sorry, big brother." I closed my eyes, making it a mantra.

When I looked again, Lopali was the size of a pongaberry in the viewscreen.

ALICIA: A HOLE IN CHARMED

Induan and I held hands, helping each other balance as we swayed somewhat precariously in our seats on the top of a cargo vehicle on its way to Charmed. She'd been waiting for me outside the house Amalo had taken me to, and her first words had been, "About time. I'm starved."

She still hadn't eaten. Here we were, stuck on top of a moving vehicle, almost surely going too slow to get where we needed to go on time. Loyal Induan. At least somebody cared to find me in spite of all her other troubles.

She pointed up. I followed her finger to see fliers flocking over us, all going in the same direction. I spotted Amalo, Marti, and Tsawo; part of a group of seven.

At first I thought they were after me, but they didn't even look down. Surely they'd be looking down if they were looking for me. Amalo, at least, could have seen me if he wanted to. Besides, they were flying too fast.

They joined a flight of other fliers, far away, like colorful dots in the sky. A dusting of wings. It was impossible to tell what they were doing, but for a few moments it had seemed like most of the fliers from Oshai had made their way to Charmed to dance together.

"I wish this thing was faster," I said.

Induan sighed. "Or we had wings." Even with our ugly wings, we flew faster than the unstable vehicle below us drove.

I squinted. "I can't see what's happening."

"Me either."

We watched in silence as the large groups of fliers broke into smaller groups and then landed. It looked like two of them fell, but surely that was my imagination.

By the time we got near the spaceport, whatever ceremony the fliers performed was done, and only a few remained in the sky. A large group that had been on or near the ground broke up, the fliers going different directions.

More time passed, us holding on and watching the sky. Somewhere, actions were being taken, decisions made. And I wasn't part of it.

No ships had taken off. When we got close enough to see the individual branches of the perch-trees surrounding the spaceport, a squat silver cargo vessel rose slowly over the cityscape of ships' noses.

"That can't be them," Induan said. "Joseph would pick a fancier ship."

My stomach iced, cold and hard. She was wrong. "It's them. I know it. I don't know how I know it, but I do."

"They'll come back for you if you want them to."

Did I? "Maybe." I wasn't actually sure. Chelo would. And Joseph. But Marcus the Great would be happier if I didn't darken his mission with risk. I wasn't sure what Jenna would do. "Maybe I won't tell them I'm here."

The ship with my family on it was now only a trail of disturbance in the sky.

"Maybe they didn't notice you aren't there."

"Quit worrying about it." I wished I could see her face. So much of communication is body language. What did I know? Her hand felt slick in mine, and her voice had been tense since she caught me up on my way out of the house. "What do you want to do if we stay here?" I asked her.

"It's not as much fun to be invisible by myself."

That was no real answer. It was Induan still trying to keep my spirits up. "You're the strategist. I'm the risk-taker. What do you think we should do?"

"I saw your face when they were talking about giving you wings. You want them."

I glanced back up at the sky. All traces of my family had gone. I felt . . . freer. Lighter. Like no one would make my choices for me. And bereft. I wanted to be in Joseph's arms and giggle with Caro. I had never wanted to be two people at once so badly before. "I don't know."

"The strategist in me suggests you decide soon. We'll be at the spaceport in a few minutes."

Why bother? They were gone. So the only real reason we were still on the lurching transport was that it hadn't stopped to let us off.

We neared the fields where the fliers had performed. Only a few still wheeled in the sky; it was hot enough that they should be seeking shade and getting ready to nap.

It took a long time to get close enough to make out the details and find the group Tsawo and Amalo were part of. Marti, too. They were still pretty far away but they walked awkwardly, with their heads down. They were carrying something. Someone.

I didn't like it. As much as I knew Joseph had flown away from me, I knew I didn't like this. "We've got to go see," I said.

"We can't just jump off this thing."

I eyed the ground blurring under us. She was right. I let go of her hand and inched up toward the front and the wingless driver. I squatted near his driver's-side window, turned my mod off, and knocked on the window.

He slowed the machine, fast, so fast it slewed to the right.

I jumped down and gestured for Induan to follow, changing to become invisible again as soon as Induan grabbed my hand.

Behind us, the driver opened his door and called out, "Who's there?"

"Nobody," I whispered, then giggled, hoping he heard the laugh. Nerves. I needed to see what Tsawo was doing. As we raced back along the trail toward Tsawo and the others, I flushed red, remembering Tsawo's kiss.

We pulled near enough to see what they carried. A wingless. Broken. Big. Bryan. Oh! Oh! Not Bryan, not again. I shivered, the cold of being alone now far, far worse. I'd left him, way back at the festival, I'd left him. I'd just . . . thought he hooked up with the others and got home. Chelo might leave without me but she wouldn't leave without Bryan. She loved Bryan.

So they knew he was dead.

I was rambling like Kayleen. Just in my head. But still, I needed to focus.

What if it was my fault he was dead? I could have saved him. Should have saved him. I should have at least worried about him.

A scream filled my spine, and I fought it back, choking on it, my stomach twisting. Induan grabbed my hand, whispering, "I'm sorry. Be quiet. Don't give us away. I'm sorry."

I couldn't stop gasping for breath. When we got near enough to really see what had happened to him, it took all my strength not to let the scream out.

He'd fallen from the sky.

Just like Tsawo always warned us.

He'd fallen.

Amalo said, "Hello, Alicia and Induan." His voice was mild, a little shocky. I stopped, confused. He wasn't someone I imagined losing control like that. Marti and Tsawo and the fourth, fifth, and sixth fliers, two men and a woman I'd never met, looked over at him.

Induan and I turned our mods off simultaneously, and I could finally see her face. She was crying for Bryan.

"How did . . . how did he fall?" I asked.

Amalo shook his head as if whatever I'd missed was too horrible to talk about. I didn't want to look at Bryan anymore, so I looked at the others closely. Marti had broken three long feathers on her left wing and her cheek had a deep bruise on it. One of the strange fliers walked funny, too slow, like he'd hurt his leg.

My breath stuck in my throat, and I gagged and then choked. Induan slapped my back, and the words finally came out of me. "There was a fight. Over what?"

Amalo said a single word. "Change." He fell silent.

Change? It was more than that. It was this war Marcus was trying to stop, the one that had spilled across my life and dragged me away from Silver's Home and back to Fremont. It was all the things Chelo hated. Bryan had been killed by people, and people were miserable excuses for beings.

Induan and I joined the procession, as silent as the others, our feet dragged enough by grief that it wasn't too hard to travel as slowly as the grounded fliers.

The fliers led us to a garden in the center of Charmed. Concentric circles of flowers selected for close shades made a bright rainbow on the ground, a thick band that snaked through lawns and pretty benches.

Tsawo broke the eerie silence. "Where would you like him to be buried? Since you're here, you can choose."

Clearly he meant for me to pick a place. I left the group and walked the rainbow. I didn't want to bury him anywhere. He was too young, too strong. It couldn't be him, except it was him. I wandered in a big circle. Would he like to be under a tree? He'd always liked to climb them. We didn't bury our dead; we burned them.

So I didn't even know how to think about this.

Their eyes followed me, waiting, tired, honoring us before they took care of what they needed to.

I had to think.

"Where do you want to be?" I whispered to him.

"Alive." I could hear his voice, see him laugh in my head, the same angry but ironic laughter he had all the time. "Put me anywhere," the ghost of Bryan told me. "It doesn't matter." It was all in my head, but I knew it was exactly what he would have said.

I found a large lawn surrounded by perches and benches, a place for fliers and humans together. Maybe people would sit around and talk, and Bryan would have company from time to time. He'd probably like that.

I went to Tsawo and took his hand and led him. "Is this okay?"

He nodded, and wordlessly extended an arm to pull me in close to him, so his wing enfolded me, blocking the breeze and making me feel warm, like I'd been tucked inside a living blanket.

We only stayed that way for a long moment, but it helped. I could have stayed that way forever, but Tsawo pulled away to speak to a flier I didn't know, who flew off.

Tsawo led me and Induan and another flier to Bryan's body, and the four of us carried him. His body swung between us, heavy, not yet stiff with death. I couldn't look down at what we carried. I was in the right front, and I just looked ahead at the trees far in front of us, biting my lower lip and carefully tracing the lines the trees made against the sky. But at least *we* carried him. His family. And we'd be here for a while, so he didn't have to be alone on a strange planet.

Even though we were all strong, Bryan's body was heavy, and sweat poured down my forehead by the time we put him down.

Tsawo took a seat on a bench, and I slid next to him. Induan took my other side. The rest of the benches and perches filled, first with the fliers, and then with others, including wingless. I had no idea where so many people came from, but they came, some of them winded and breathing hard when they arrived.

Almost no one talked. A slight breeze blew, and birds chattered, and feet moved, and people adjusted how they sat, but there was no loud talk to scrape my raw nerves.

I didn't know what we waited for. I tried not to look at Bryan's body. It lay in the middle of us all, just to the side of the center of the lawn. His deadweight seemed to be pulling me down into the ground.

Six Keepers showed up with shovels. Tsawo got up and went to greet them, speaking softly. He must have told them what he wanted, since they set the shovels down and carefully cut a large square out of the grass and pulled it back, rolling the grass and topsoil.

As soon as the ground was exposed, I took one of the tools and started digging myself. Better than just sitting beside my dead. The shovel slid in easily, the soil loose and rich, the scent of it oddly clean. It felt good to strain my back lifting it up from the ground and tossing the dirt onto a pile.

Induan came and took another shovel.

Tsawo came up and put a hand on my back. "You should let the Keepers do that."

I stuck the shovel back into the ground. "I'm not a flier yet. Let me bury my dead." I lifted a load of dirt and piled it and went back for more. Again. Again. I didn't even notice when Tsawo withdrew, although when I looked for him later, he had returned to sitting on a bench, watching.

I remembered how we gathered in the band on Fremont when someone died, and built a platform, and a bonfire, and sent the ashes of our dead out on the winds to fertilize the world. Most of the band sat up all night at a funeral, laughing and joking with each other. I thought about that while I kept digging the hole.

I remembered Bryan making us run, about Bryan and Liam pulling me out of the wagon I had been locked in and carrying me to town, clutched close to Bryan's chest. He'd smelled like sawdust from the mill and rain that night.

When I could barely breathe anymore, and sweat stung my eyes, I handed the shovel off to one of the waiting Keepers and stood between Tsawo and Amalo. Three more Keepers showed up with a wooden box, and set Bryan's body carefully inside it. Luckily, they'd built it too big, almost square, and so he fit inside in spite of the awkward angles of his limbs. His claws were out, and absurdly, I wished they could be retracted.

Two fliers held the lid and watched me.

The moment felt heavy.

I leaned down and kissed his cold forehead, and then stepped aside for Induan. She did the same. I said, "We love you, Brother. Thank you for all you were."

The crowd still watched me, silent and reverent. They needed more. I raised my voice. "Thank you for helping us help the fliers."

I glanced at Induan. She shook her head. So she didn't have any more words, either. I looked closely at her, noticing how still her features were, how hollow her cheeks looked. I leaned over and took her briefly in my arms. The feel of her, solid and yet shaking ever so lightly, made me think I should worry about other people more often.

After I let her go, I gestured for the fliers to put the lid on, and I went to stand by Tsawo. "Why so much ceremony for him?" I mean, it wasn't like Joseph or Chelo or Kayleen had died.

Amalo answered. "Because he is one of you six, and a hero. We will build a statue to him over the grave, and it will be a solemn place, good for contemplation."

Bryan would probably prefer to be forgotten, but there was no point in saying that. "Is that why you want me to become a flier? Because I'm a child of Fremont?"

The gray flier looked at the box that held Bryan. "That's part of it." He smiled sadly. "Maybe you'll bring us good luck."

Fat chance. I hadn't brought Bryan any.

Other people—fliers and wingless, Keepers and seekers—began to gather, too many for me to count them all. Some carried flowers.

After the hole had been dug, checked, widened, and then pronounced done, the box was lowered into the ground and the Keepers efficiently covered it with dirt, and then with the grass square, which they unrolled very precisely. When they finished, it was hard to tell where we'd dug.

One by one, people who carried flowers set them on the grass above Bryan, until the air was sickly sweet with the scents of them.

A strange, eerie chant started up, and fliers from the back began to rise up into the air, and then more, and then more. Amalo and Tsawo and Marti rose up last, forming the center of a circle of wheeling fliers, all chanting. There were no words, just sounds. More complex than the uu chant at morning ceremony, more melodic.

It might have been the saddest thing I ever heard.

Even with all the fliers in the air, a crowd of wingless still surrounded me. Someone put an arm around me lightly, and I looked over to find the blue-eyed interface merchant, Amile, swaying beside me in time to the chant of the fliers.

"Thank you," I said.

"I'm sorry," he replied.

"I know."

He turned to face me. "Let me know when you need more help."

He hadn't said if. Wow. "I will."

And then he was gone. I looked for him later, but he had disappeared into the crowd.

Tsawo landed and came up to me. "I have to leave. I'll see you in a few days. Stay safe."

I nodded, pleased he'd thought to tell me that much, and curious about where he was going. I glanced up in the sky. Amalo was clearly my primary host, and his wings still spread over Bryan's resting place.

Induan and I found each other near the end, after the fliers had started landing, one by one, or had taken off back toward Oshai or Charmed or SoBright. "So why did you stay? I had time to think about it, and clearly you stayed on purpose. Why stay here with me, and not go with the others?"

I swear I saw real caring flash across her eyes, something genuine and unfettered. She grinned, impish like the Induan I met on Silver's Home years ago. "There're going to be a lot of people telling their stories. Somebody needs to tell yours."

JOSEPH: THE LAST WORK

As Marcus, Kayleen, Sasha, and I sat in the command room of the cargo transport *Water Girl*, I realized I'd been on so many space ships I could no longer count them on one hand. We'd reached orbit, one of tens of cargo ships circling Lopali, heading for space stations that also circled, or simply waited. From time to time, small silver ships streaked across one or another of the four screens surrounding us. Flier space skimmers.

The two beautiful ships from Charmed had gone up shortly after us, piloted by Keepers, manned by Keepers and fliers. They'd disgorged the fine, small ships that flew a protective net around us. Not only was I grateful for their presence, but they were so fast, so agile, that I wanted to try one.

"Is that fliers or Keepers in the little ships?" Kayleen asked.

Marcus grinned. "Probably both." He stopped for a moment, clearly listening to someone besides us. Marcus was working on finding another ship to transfer us to, and I'd become used to ignoring his side conversations.

He signaled for our attention. "She's coming. Paula is on the way up."

"How long?" I asked. I wasn't ready. It was all too fresh: leaving Alicia, losing Bryan. Leaving Lopali.

"An hour or two."

"Okay. I'm going to take a walk."

He looked closely at me. "Are you okay?"

I didn't know. But I didn't want to tell him that; he needed me to be strong. "I just want to walk around."

I apparently failed at brushing aside his worry. He frowned at me. "Can I come find you after I find us another ship?"

"Sure." I left as quickly as I could, leaving Kayleen with him. Unlike a space-going ship, the *Water Girl* didn't have much human- or flier-friendly space. She did have corridors long enough for a good pacing walk back and forth. So that's what I did. For a while I just listened to my steps echo in the empty space.

Worry kept me pacing, shivering in spite of the sweat on my forehead. From time to time I passed people, but I generally said nothing, and after one look at my face, they said the same thing. Sasha remained as quiet as I was, padding behind me, clearly aware of my mood.

I'd given up on finding Alicia or Induan aboard, and Bryan's loss had made a hole in my chest as well. The only unexpected brightness was Sasha appearing at the last moment. At least I hadn't lost her, too.

At one end of the corridor, there was a small video porthole meant to mimic a real window. Lopali floated right in the middle of it. It might have been an artist's rendering of a world, all the colors perfect even from here, land and water tamed and harmonious. Circles of land floating on a circle of water. A sweet poison of a planet.

I hated it for what it took from me.

Sasha whined, warning me Marcus had begun pacing us. He came up alongside, his expression impossible to read, but his steps smoother and less angry than mine. We walked a full circle, almost a half an hour, before he said anything. "They're waiting."

"Yes."

"Are you ready?"

"No."

We walked another full circle. I let the ship come into me. Its heartbeat was steady, steadier by far than anything biological. Steadier than the planet below me. "Why did they attack us?" I asked Marcus.

"Because we might succeed, and their lives will change."

Something the man beside me had fought for. "Did you know so many of them were so scared?"

"No."

We walked again. I could feel the time passing. It passed in the ship's instruments and in the blood coursing through my body and with each step I took. It passed through me, and through me, and finally I was empty enough of the anger and pain to say, "I'm ready."

"Good, because she's here." Even though there was enough gravity to walk, he used the wall-pulls to hurry himself along the corridors, and I slowly caught his energy and started to hurry.

Might as well do the real work, and finally know one way or the other if we'd succeeded, if we would stop the war.

Marcus took me to a room in the middle forward part of the ship. Entertainment screens lined the walls, and the floor was half couches and chairs, everything arranged artfully for conversation and games, and well-used for the same. Red chairs with the ends of the arms worn to the underlying silver of their bones. Couches with indents from spacers sitting in them for long hours and grease spots on the floor from spills. Even the ceiling was dented and scratched in a few places. Tickets from restaurants and bars on various space stations and from the spaceports of Lopali had been stuck to the wall willy-nilly. Clearly the crew's off-hours lounge.

In one corner, Kayleen, Chance, and Paula waited for me on a tattered brown sofa with no back.

The real test. Would we be able to make the change Bryan had died for in a real girl?

Kayleen stood and came over to me, taking my hand in hers. Her blue eyes looked deep and a little shell-shocked, and I leaned down and whispered, "Are you okay?"

"Are you?" she countered. The same question Marcus had asked.

"Yeah." I glanced at Paula, who sat quietly beside Chance, her face as pale as Kayleen's. I knew what my pacing walk had let me do. "I had to forgive the fliers before I could do this. They were just scared. They didn't mean to fight us, and they didn't mean to kill Bryan."

Marcus watched us. The whole room watched us, listening to the exchange. "And do you?" asked Paula, her voice soft. "Do you really forgive us?"

"Yeah." I swallowed, and looked at Kayleen. "I had to forgive Alicia, too." I hadn't expected those words. "She was never as much one of us as the rest of us. Never even as much as Bryan." Surely everyone heard the sadness in my voice, but I couldn't hide it. I felt sad when I thought of Alicia. "She never even wanted to be one of us as much. She just . . . wanted to be loved. That's all she ever wanted. And her freedom. But she went back for Chelo, and she stuck with me. She loved us back."

"I know," Kayleen said.

"Maybe she'll be happy here."

Kayleen smiled softly. "Maybe."

"We all need forgiveness." I was done talking about it. I looked at Paula. "Are you ready?"

She looked more scared than ready, but she said, "Yes," in a clear, steady voice. She had been born and trained for this.

So had I.

I took a few breaths, remembering how my attitude mattered, centering myself, preparing to let go. "I'm ready."

Chance smiled encouragingly. "The sim is beautiful. You're ready."

I glanced at Paula. Her eyes were closed and she sat so still it took me a moment to verify that she breathed. "The woman is even more beautiful. We're ready."

Kayleen squeezed my hand.

Marcus led us, starting with a tour of the ship's data. *You need to know what might surprise you.*

He meant how the ship might warn us if something like Star Mercenaries got too close. But I didn't think they would. Not now. We had time, we were fine. I could sense the bated breath of Lopali waiting to see what we made up here.

We checked the Paula sim again. It had lived and lived and lived. Its babies had had babies. In some ways, everything the real Paula needed existed there already, waiting for Chance to pluck directions from it. But still, we needed to touch the biology, the breath, the real heartbeat with all its uncertainties and fears. That was the proof, and it would save years and years of slower work.

It was what we'd promised.

In spite of our practice at Chance's and during the long flight to the cave, the physical Paula was more difficult to get into than the simulated Paula. She was awake, though calm. At first we synchronized our breaths to each other, and then Marcus added, *synchronize with her.*

His advice helped. I remembered how slowly Kayleen had breathed when we almost lost her; Paula's meditative breathing was just a bit slower. With that memory, my body knew it could manage.

Water Girl didn't have as much available bandwidth as the war room in the cave. Nor so much distraction. Still, I needed all I could get. All three of us filled *Water Girl*'s dataspace, slowly, finding every available unused channel and bit of bandwidth. Where possible, we shared.

We turned to Paula. Our work began to feel familiar. She had moved on from the moment the sim had been taken: lost half a pound, cut her fingernails, stubbed her toe. But the time slices of her life were close enough that we fell easily there, her own internal nano sending signals we were used to from the sim, only slower.

Someone watched us.

I startled. *What?*

Kayleen saw it, too, but she just watched, serene.

It's okay, Marcus soothed. *It's Paula herself. You had to see that before you could work.*

Okay, I can do this. Changing Paula became something we had done and succeeded at. Familiar. Doable.

This time, I did more of the work. Kayleen fed the two of us more support. Her energy stayed strong and sweet, steady. Marcus directed, keeping as much attention on Kayleen as he kept on me. Like the last time with the sim, we expanded and grew and shrank all at once in way I have no words for, becoming Paula and yet being ourselves, becoming the dream we were building inside of this brave young woman.

It took a long time, and we forgot we were in the *Water Girl*, forgot we were far above Lopali, protected by fliers in little silver ships. We forgot everything but blood, and bone, and brain. Vein and organ and skin. Breath and heartbeat.

Paula.

When we finished and floated back up to the surface, Kayleen collected in with the two of us, sweat drenched my forehead. I could barely lift my head. But I did, and the three of us shared a smile, everyone as sweaty as me. Chance, watching us, smiled, too.

Paula blinked. She was still somewhere far away, carried on the waves of her training and her deep focus. It struck me that she knew at least as much as Seeyan had, that Paula's purpose ran deep and clear.

She blinked again, and then her eyes focused, alert and aware. Aware of everything. She smiled.

Before we left her with Chance, we each gave her a deep hug. When it was my turn, I marveled at how touch enhanced my connection to her, even though being in our physical bodies made far more separation than reading and programming the nanomeds and cellular structures that controlled her very being. I looked into her eyes, and the whole of her was so much more than all of the tiny parts. I whispered in her ear. "Good luck."

Her smile dazzled. "Thank you."

Marcus's hand on my arm pulled me into the corridor, and Kayleen took my hand, and we went to a room with couches and blankets. Tiala and Jenna offered water. I drank and lay down, and Marcus himself came and covered me. He knelt down beside me. "You are truly a powerful creator now. If you were my own true son, I could not be more proud of you."

His words played in my head at least three times over before I passed out, exhausted and strangely happy.

M arcus shook my shoulder. I blinked and yawned, trying to assess how long I might have slept. Not enough. A week wouldn't be enough. Maybe a month. But my belly and bladder and dry mouth demanded movement, so I moved. Still, I grumbled, "Why'd you wake me up?"

"There's a delegation from Lopali docking with us. We have about twenty minutes to get ready."

Great. Or not so great. "Who?"

"I don't know."

But then I surged with hope. "Did they bring Alicia?"

He looked as tired as I felt, even though surely we'd slept at least a few hours. "I don't think so. Meet me in the command room in ten minutes. I'll get the others."

Even though we were the only ones on the ship, the command room was way too small to hold all of us and any other kind of delegation. About half of it was table, and the rest was sink and art and video screens and open space. One of the myriad symbols for the Five Worlds took up the one wall that wasn't screens, a single elliptical orbit with all five planets strung across it as if they were the same size, all represented in three-dimensional relief with color. I noticed that Islas and Silver's Home were completely across the circle from each other.

Marcus, Chelo, Jenna, Kayleen, and I took chairs around the table, leaving room for three or four fliers to perch on stools Tiala had found in a storeroom. We piped camera feed to the others in the crew room we'd used to work on Paula.

We finished in time to wait.

I examined Marcus's face across the table from me. He looked positive, and more rested. It turned out we had slept six hours. Not enough. But now that I'd moved around I felt at least slightly alert. "We did it, right? We fixed the fliers and they'll join us and the war won't have to happen. Right?"

Marcus smiled, his face saying it was so, but his words were, "Don't count on anything until it's done." But he was excited; his eyes almost glowed.

Kayleen brushed at her glorious dark hair. "But Paula's okay, right? She's alive and well? She's . . . fixed."

He nodded. "Chance has already taken her home."

Surely we'd succeeded. It had all felt right and complete. Working on Paula herself had felt better than working on the successful sim. Paula had practically glowed when we were done, so much that I felt sure she was healthier. After all our work to prepare, after we finally settled in, it had almost been easy.

Almost. Not too easy.

And Kayleen had stayed with us. Not as strong as Marcus or I, but almost. And this time, finally, I had Chelo by my side again. In spite of Bryan and Alicia, it was going to be all right.

The ship docked with ours.

I expected Matriana or Daniel or both. A single flier came through the airlock, wearing a suit that looked more like a bubble than anything

I'd ever seen in space. Made of hard triangles with thin, flexible mate-rial between them, it slumped neatly down into a ring under the black-winged flier's feet.

Tsawo. Tsawo?

The only sign of surprise that Marcus gave was a narrowing of his eyes.

Our strategists didn't like this at all: Chelo drew her breath in. Jenna stiffened.

Kayleen piped up. "Hi Tsawo. How are you? How was the trip? Have you seen Alicia? Did you see Paula? Doesn't she look great?"

Maybe she hadn't changed that much. I had to suppress a smile as Tsawo reeled a bit under her fusillade of questions.

Jenna stood up and held out her hand. "We're pleased to host you. Will there be anyone else joining you?"

"No. I'm by myself." He did sit, across from Jenna and Marcus, shifting a bit until he found a comfortable way to place his wings. I watched him as Jenna brought him water. He was a rival; to all in-tents and purposes a rival who'd won.

I had to ask him. "Have you seen Alicia?"

Jenna shot me a disapproving glance.

He looked at the table and then over at me. It struck me again how beautiful fliers were, how pretty he was for a man. On the ground, they had a brittle strength, but nothing like the strength they'd shown in the air when they threw Bryan down. It had taken at least ten of them to do that, because Bryan had the bigger wings, the machine that helped him fly. I shut my eyes for a moment, dizzy with memory. I had not seen Tsawo in the fight, or I would have had trouble sitting there.

When he did speak, he said, "We buried your friend, the strong-man. I apologize for our people. It was . . . not me. Not the people I represent. But it was an act of my kind, and I'm deeply sorry."

He sounded like he meant it. It took as much strength as I had to stay calm as I asked, "So Alicia is all right?"

"She's choosing to stay with us."

I had thought so. Still, a lump rose in my throat. "Please . . . tell her . . . tell her I said good luck." I got up and busied myself at the sink, washing a glass that didn't need to be washed and refilling it with water just like the water I'd thrown out.

He sounded sure and calm as he said, "I'll tell her."

He could at least sound regretful. Surely he knew his words were knives. An awkward silence fell. Marcus was the only one with the presence of mind to fill it well. "Chance thinks your niece will have babies."

Tsawo's reaction was to simply nod and chew a bit on his upper lip.

I sat back down with my clean glass of water and watched. Even I knew Tsawo wasn't giving us the reaction we expected. He shifted on his seat. "I'm sorry. I mean, I'm glad. It will help us greatly."

Chelo pressed him. "What about the war. You will come with us, now, right? We'll go together?"

He shook his head, mute.

Marcus leaned in toward him, his voice strained. "We have an agreement."

Tsawo met Marcus's eyes, and spit out what he'd clearly come for. "And we have new leadership. We will not go to war."

Marcus's eyes narrowed further, and his shoulders sank. He blew out a long, slow breath, never taking his gaze from Tsawo's face. As if simply staring him down would change his message.

After an uncomfortable silence, Jenna spoke. "And you are the new leader." It wasn't a question.

He nodded, sitting up straighter. "And we will not go to war. Why be given this wonderful chance at life, and then throw it away? We will stay neutral."

Only three days had passed since Tsawo's announcement, but I still felt betrayed. We'd done the work! We'd given them what we promised.

Marcus had found us a new ship, purchased outright so that we were the only passengers and Marcus and I and Kayleen the only pilots.

Marcus had taken the extra day to have her renamed. So we flew away from Lopali in *Bryan's Hope*. I didn't actually like the name much, but Chelo seemed very happy with it.

The best thing about *Bryan's Hope* was a single large room big enough for all of us to gather in. It already had a wall of simulated sun for the kids and Chelo and Liam, so we would have daylight and night as we flew off to meet the fleet. It had enough workout equipment to please Jenna, and to make me groan. I knew what she'd put us through as soon as we were well and truly between worlds.

And it had a big entertainment corner with enough room for us all. We'd lost three: Bryan, Alicia, and Induan; and gained two: Mohami and Kala.

And, right now, I was as happy as I could be, given our losses. Everyone was in one place. The wall of simulated sun made it morning on *Bryan's Hope*, and the children played, each of them with a keeper bot by their side. Sasha sat at my feet, her tail thumping on the floor.